Ellen

Happy reading love Coral x

Coral McCallum

Copyright © 2018 Coral McCallum

All rights reserved.

ISBN: 978-1724219022
ISBN-13: 1724219022

Also by Coral McCallum

Stronger Within
Impossible Depths
Bonded Souls

The characters, names, places, brands, media and events are either the product of the author's imagination or are used fictitiously. Any similarity to real persons, living or deceased is coincidental and not intended by the author.

The author acknowledges the trademarked status and trademark owners of the various products referenced within this work of fiction, which have been used without permission. The publication/use of these trademarks is not authorised, associated with or sponsored by these trademark owners.

Thank you for respecting the hard work of this author.

Cover Design
Coral McCallum

Cover Image
ID 23302545 © Anikasalsera | Dreamstime.com

Ellen

There were a few moments earlier this year when I wondered if I would ever get this book into print.

As one of my favourite quotes says, "Dreams get you started. Discipline keeps you going". That quote, coupled with the love and support of loyal friends, family and readers, ensured I reached the conclusion of the tale, albeit several months later than originally planned.

Ellen was first introduced in the Silver Lake series and, as I finished writing Book Baby3 aka Bonded Souls, I began to imagine what her story would read like. Now, over a year later, it reads like this- Ellen.

For those of you who now class yourselves as "Silver Lakers", don't fret. There are a few "old friends" to be found in the pages of Ellen and, all going to plan, Jake and Lori will back next year in book 4 of the Silver Lake series.

I may be an indie author but I couldn't possibly do this alone. I am forever in the debt of my "Infamous Five", who again have each kept me going with their love, words of encouragement and unwavering support. (It was one of them who introduced me to the quote I mentioned earlier, a long time ago.) Huge hugs and much love to each and every one of you. I really don't know why you put up with me!

And huge thanks to my "cavalry", my two beta readers, who give the final draft their seal of approval. Love and hugs to each of you.

Thanks also to my family for their patience and understanding.

And, finally, to YOU for picking up this copy of Book Baby 4. Happy reading!

Hugs and much love to each and every one of you.

Coral McCallum
14 July 2018

He looked down at the phone in his hands and read the text message again. The words were still the same.

"Found her. Get your arse back here by Monday. Rocky."

With a sigh, he stuffed the phone back into his pocket and set off down the steep cliff path to the beach. Over the years, he must have slithered his way down the narrow, stepped path thousands of times. As a kid, he'd come here to play; as a teenager, he'd come here to surf and party in the cave. Now, as an adult, he came to the beach to think.

The coarse sand scrunched under his feet as he made his way towards the water's edge. He paused to pick up a few carefully selected stones as he went, then, when he reached the water's edge, he skimmed them across the calm water. His mum had taught him how to skim stones on this very beach. The memory tugged at his heart.

As the last stone skipped the surface four times, he watched it sink without a trace.

He continued his walk along the short length of sand, heading towards the cave. This part of the Cornish coastline was dotted with small, secluded, sandy coves, all much the same as this one and several of them had huge caves in the surrounding cliffs. As a boy, he'd believed if you dug the sand out from the back of one cave it would lead to a tunnel into the next, dreaming it was a network of secret passages used by smugglers in days gone by.

It had been four years since he'd last partied in the cave. That party had been a double celebration – his 21st birthday and his departure for his new life in London. The air temperature dipped as he entered the cavernous space. He wondered if the current generation of village teenagers partied in here as he had with his friends. The ashes in the stone circle that served as a fireplace looked fresh, suggesting that someone was using it. On the ledge up at the back left, there was a pile of driftwood, drying out ready to be burned. He turned to search for the larger ledge to the right. In the dim light, he could just make out the shape of the surfboard. After all these years, it was still there. Running his hand over it, he noted that it felt freshly waxed. Someone was still using it and caring for it just as he had before them. Behind the board, he found what he was looking for – an acoustic guitar. Lifting it down, he smiled to himself then strummed the strings gently. Not too far out of tune. Someone was playing it too.

He carried the beaten-up instrument to the mouth of the cave, sat on a rock and expertly teased the strings back into tune then he began to play.

"Taylor!"

The voice startled him back to reality.

"Taylor! Where are you?"

He was tempted to remain quiet but he figured she had heard the music. Without calling out, he stood up, set the guitar down and stepped back out into the sunlight.

"Oh, there you are!"

A young woman, the mirror image of himself, came striding towards him, her long dark hair blowing free in the gentle breeze.

"Here I am," he said simply. "Sorry. I had to get out of that house. Away from them all. All the fake displays of giving a shit."

"Nana was worried about you," commented his twin sister. "Matt wanted to come and find you but I said I would. I guessed you'd be here."

"I feel closer to her here," said Taylor, scuffing his feet in the sand. "I skimmed some stones just like she taught us."

"Want to skim some together for old time's sake? Bet I can still beat you."

Taylor nodded as he wrestled with his emotions. "You find some and I'll put this back."

By the time he'd returned the guitar to its hiding place and joined his sister, Jen, she had picked up a pile of skimmers. Handing him half, the twins stood silently, lost in their memories of their mother as they skimmed the flat stones over the calm water.

"Beat you!" declared Jen as her last stone skipped six times before sinking.

"I'm leaving tomorrow," said Taylor suddenly.

"Leaving?" echoed Jen. "But we've the lawyer to see and the house to clear out and the car to sell."

"I need to go back to London. I've been summoned," her twin explained. "I got a message just as we came out of the church on Friday. Maybe it's a sign. An omen that mum's watching out for me."

"But what about....." began Jen, her eyes filling with fresh tears of grief.

"Matt'll help you. Time our baby brother did something useful. And Nana can help. I need to do this. I have to give the band one last chance. Rocky's found us a new voice. I've a good feeling about it this time."

"Take the car then. Mum would want you to," offered Jen, understanding that her twin needed to chase his dream.

He shook his head. "Nowhere to park it. Can't afford to run it either."

Jen nodded. "Need a lift to the station tomorrow?"

"Please," said Taylor with a smile.

On the bed, the large wheeled suitcase sat half packed. It was surrounded by piles of neatly folded clothes waiting to go in, plus several small first aid boxes, clearly labelled with their contents. Her sapphire blue hobo bag lay open on the chair with a pile of travel documents beside it. Glancing round the bedroom that had been hers since childhood, Ellen smiled. In a few short hours she would close the door on the room and finally leave home.

"Ellen," called her mum sharply from the hallway. "Don't forget to pack those new pressure sleeves. I left them on your chest of drawers."

"In the bag, mother," she replied as she stared at them still lying where her mother had left them. With a sigh, Ellen picked them up and laid them in the suitcase, promptly covering them with a pile of t-shirts.

Eventually, she had the bag packed and the bed cleared.

Carefully, she pulled the zip closed and lifted the case down onto the floor. Scanning the room for anything she may have forgotten, Ellen sighed.

This was it.

Quickly, she checked her phone for messages. There was one new one.

"Won't be at the station to meet you. Get a taxi out to my house. I'll see you there about six. Rocky."

Her "big chance" was within her grasp. She could feel it.

"Ellen!" called her mum from the foot of the stairs. "Are you ready to go? You don't want to miss your train."

"Coming, mother."

Bump! Bump! Bump! Her suitcase thudded down the thickly carpeted stairs.

"Watch the paintwork!" cautioned her mother bluntly. "Your father only finished that last month."

"It's fine," muttered Ellen as she reached the bottom step.

"Are you alright? Have you remembered everything on the list?"

"Mum, I'm fine. A little anxious about travelling but I'll be at Rocky's for six. He'll look after me. Lizzy too. You've met him. He's a good person."

"I know. I know," sighed her mother. "Are you sure you are ready to do this? Ready to put yourself through it?"

"Mum, not now," began Ellen softly. "I'm going to London. Two hours away on the train not halfway round the world. I'll call and message you."

"Your dad worries about you. So do I."

"I know and I appreciate it," said Ellen, hugging her mother awkwardly. "This is my big chance though. My best chance. I'm ready to get back on stage and focus on picking up my career. This band is a great opportunity for me. My dream opportunity."

"And I hope all those dreams come true, darling."

Three hours later, as Ellen was trying to pull her large suitcase through a crowded station, her mother's words echoed in her head. Trying to thread her way through the throngs of commuters was a nightmare. Silently, she cursed her own limitations. For the first time she regretted being so stubborn about being able to cope with travelling into the city by rail on her own.

"Get a grip, Ellen," she muttered to herself.

She paused to check the signage to determine where she was to exit the unfamiliar station. The next moment, she was knocked off balance by a tall, dark haired guy carrying two guitars and a huge backpack. With a squeal, she felt herself start to fall then felt an arm grab her to stop her. She could feel his strong hand on her upper arm, feel the pressure of his fingers burn into her tender skin.

"Sorry," he apologized hurriedly. "I was too busy looking for the exit. I never saw you stop."

"No harm done," replied Ellen shyly.

His hand was still on her arm and part of her was desperate for him to remove it.

"You sure you're ok?" he checked.

Adjusting her tinted glasses, Ellen forced a smile. "I'm fine. Thank you."

"Well, sorry again," he mumbled. "My mum always did say I should watch where I was going. Guess that's another thing she was right about."

"Mums are like that," she agreed.

"Sorry again," he apologised. "See you around."

Without a backwards glance, he disappeared into the crowd. Spotting the sign, she had been searching for, Ellen set off again, heading for the exit.

Music was blaring out of the speakers in the lounge, filling the entire apartment with sound. Debris from the weekend of partying littered the room. The ashtrays were overflowing onto the polished oak floor. Someone had stubbed a joint out on the edge of the Persian rug, leaving an irreparable scorch mark. An empty champagne bottle was lodged in a vase beside a dozen wilting roses.

"Luke!"

Reaching for the remote for the sound system, Jack killed the music.

"Luke!" he yelled again, his voice echoing through the now silent apartment. "Cal!"

From down the hallway, he could hear muttering and

shuffling footsteps. Moments later, a half-dressed, hungover Luke Court appeared.

"Who turned off the fucking music?" he muttered almost incoherently.

"I did. We're late," stated Jack bluntly. "Band meeting. Dinner at Rocky's. Remember?"

"Yeah on Monday."

"This is Monday!"

"Fuck!" stated Luke, running his hand through his bleached blonde spiky hair. "Now?"

Jack nodded, "And we're late!"

"Five minutes," promised Luke. "I just need five minutes."

He turned to head back down the hallway.

"Where's Cal?" called out Jack, realizing the band's guitarist was MIA.

"Fuck knows," came the reply.

"Great," muttered Jack to himself. Gazing round the room, he shook his head and sighed. "Luke, I'll be down in the van. You've got five minutes then I'm leaving. Rocky's waiting. We're already late."

"Five minutes!"

When Taylor finally found his way out of the railway station, he glanced up and down the street for his bandmate. The pavement was as crowded as the station had been, making spotting his friend nigh on impossible.

"Tailz!"

He spun round, almost knocking his friend out with his backpack.

"Hey! Easy!" cautioned Cal as he grabbed Taylor's backpack. "You got a license for that thing?"

"Sorry."

"You back for good?" asked Cal, nodding at the size of the rucksack.

Taylor nodded, "Carrying everything I own. Well, apart from two boxes of books and shit that I left with Jen and Nana."

"How did the funeral go? Sorry I couldn't get down there," asked Cal awkwardly as they started to walk away from the station.

"It was tough," replied Taylor quietly. "Nana's devastated. Jen's staying with her."

A few moments of silence hung between the two friends.

Eventually, Taylor spoke, just as they arrived at the bus stop.

"What's Rocky said about this singer he's found us?"

"Not a lot. Says she's something a bit special. He hinted there's been something in her past that damaged her career but then said she's only twenty-three. Knowing Rocky, there's a story there."

"No doubt," agreed Taylor. "Here's the bus."

As the taxi pulled up outside a smart terraced house, Ellen felt her stomach lurch. There were butterflies the size of pterodactyls fluttering in her stomach. This was it!

Her hand trembled as she passed the fare through to the driver. Trying not to get herself tangled up in her bags, Ellen carefully climbed out of the car. She stood on the pavement and watched the taxi drive off before turning to walk up the path behind her.

The smartly painted green door with its oversized brass knocker reminded her of Bilbo Baggins' house in The Hobbit. With a nervous smile, Ellen lifted the ring of the door knocker and let it fall heavily back into place.

Her heart was pounding as she listened for footsteps approaching from the inside. The door finally opened with a creak and a petite grey-haired woman with bright brown eyes poked her head round.

"Hello," she said in a soft Welsh accent. "You must be Ellen. Come in. Come in. Rocky's been held up. He'll be here in a bit."

"Hi," greeted Ellen shyly as she stepped into the narrow hallway. "Am I the first to arrive?"

"Yes, dear," replied the older woman warmly. "The boys are never on time. If we see Luke before eight o'clock it'll be a miracle!" She paused then added, "I'm Lizzy, by the way. Rocky's wife."

"Please to meet you," said Ellen politely as she followed her hostess into a cosy family living room on the left.

"Leave your bags over there," instructed Lizzy, pointing to a space behind the settee. "One of the boys will take them upstairs for you later. Would you like a cuppa? Kettle's just boiled. Or would you like something stronger?"

"Tea would be lovely. Thank you."

"Sit yourself down and I'll be back in a minute. Milk and sugar?"

"Just a little sugar, please," replied Ellen.

"Won't be long."

Once alone in the room, Ellen gazed round. It was like any other family living room. Couch and two armchairs, coffee table, TV in the corner, stereo in the opposite corner and a display cabinet along the back wall. The mantelpiece and hearth were cluttered with knick knacks. Dozens of framed photos filled the wall behind the settee. Instead of taking a seat, Ellen stood gazing at the familiar faces smiling out from the various frames. There were photos of bands with gold and silver records. There was one obviously taken back stage somewhere of Rocky with the legendary Garrett Court of Royal Court fame. She guessed that one of the other two men in the photo was his band mate, Andrew Royal but she didn't recognize the fourth figure, an extremely tall, thin, dark haired man. Many of the photos were black and white but along one edge there were three or four more recent ones of a young band that Ellen guessed were the band she was here to join.

"Ah, you found the Rogue's Gallery," laughed Lizzy as she returned carrying a tray with two mugs and a plate of chocolate biscuits balanced on it. "Those are the boys from After Life."

"I thought so," said Ellen, still gazing at the photos. "Lots of famous names up there."

"All Rocky's boys and girls," said Lizzy with more than a hint of pride. "We never had kids of our own. Those are his family."

"Big family," giggled Ellen as she spotted an old photo of rock legends When The Chips Are Down. "And Rocky's managed them all?"

Lizzy nodded as she set the tray down. "At one time or another. Sometimes he'd have three bands on the go at once. He'd be gone for months on end. One tour after the next."

Taking a seat on the couch, Ellen accepted the hot mug of tea from the older woman with a quiet thank you.

"What are After Life like?" asked Ellen, curious to learn more about the four guys.

"They're good boys," began Lizzy as she unwrapped a chocolate biscuit. "There's Cal. He's from Glasgow originally. He went to school, boarding school, with Luke. Luke's the party animal. They both share a flat in Kensington. It belongs to Luke's uncle. Jack's the oldest and the most sensible. He's a bit of a deep soul. A thinker. And last but not least, there's Tailz. Taylor. He's had a rough time recently. Just lost his mum to cancer a week or two back. Funeral was last Friday. I've a soft spot for him but don't you tell him I said that."

"I hope I fit in," whispered Ellen almost to herself.

"You'll fit in, my dear," promised Lizzy warmly. "Rocky told me what happened. I loved that audition you sent to him. He's got high hopes for this. The last two singers just didn't have a voice that fitted with the boys' sound. There were a few ego issues too. They need a woman, a strong woman, to keep them in line."

"It's been a while since I was out there with a band behind me," confessed Ellen. "Over five years."

"You'll soon be back in the swing of things," assured Lizzy. "Rocky says it's like riding a bike. You never forget how once you've learned."

"I hope he's right," giggled Ellen nervously.

Their conversation was interrupted by a fresh knock at the door.

"I bet this is Cal with Tailz," said Lizzy as she got to her feet. "I swear that boy can smell a cup of tea a mile off."

Sipping her tea, Ellen listened as the older woman opened the door to the latest arrivals. She heard the thunder of feet on the stairs as someone ran up them. A few seconds later, the living room door opened and a young man with waist length auburn hair walked into the room.

"Hi," he said with a cheeky smile. "You must be Ellen. I'm Cal."

He extended his hand to her. Setting her mug down before getting up from her seat, Ellen reached out with her left hand to shake his.

"Pleased to meet you," she said with what she hoped was a welcoming smile.

"Love the shades," commented Cal as he took a seat in the chair to the left of the couch. "Real rock chick look."

"Necessity," countered Ellen quietly. "Long story."

Footsteps clattering down the stairs filled the awkward silence that had descended on the room. Seconds later, the door opened and a slender, dark haired, familiar face rushed in.

"Sorry. Went to dump my gear upstairs and to freshen up. I'm Tailz," he gushed. "Hey! Didn't we meet at the station earlier?"

Recognising him from the collision on the concourse, Ellen said, "I believe we did. I guess you found the exit."

"Eventually," admitted Taylor as he sat down beside her. "I get lost trying to find my way out of there every time."

"I was a bit lost myself," Ellen confessed as Lizzy returned with two more mugs of tea.

"Don't you eat all my Kit Kats, Cal," she cautioned as she handed him a Winnie the Pooh mug. "Dinner's almost ready. Should I wait for Jack and Luke?"

"I wouldn't," replied Cal bluntly. "Luke still hadn't surfaced when I left at three."

"Party last night?" quizzed Taylor.

"And Saturday night. And Friday night."

"Shit," muttered Taylor. "Heavy weekend."

"I bailed out last night," confessed Cal, taking a second Kit Kat from the plate. "Place was empty when I came back this morning. Looks like a wild one from the state of the flat though."

"Jack'll talk sense into him," said Lizzy. "He always does."

"Where's Rocky?" asked Taylor, changing the subject.

"On his way," promised Lizzy. "Play nicely, children. I'm going to check on dinner."

As Cal reached for a third biscuit, he said, "Loved that audition tape you sent Rocky. Great voice. Where've you been hiding it?"

"I've been between bands," began Ellen, shuffling her feet and feeling awkward at being the centre of attention. "I've done some session stuff over the last year or so. Couple of auditions but nothing's worked out up till now. I used to front a band about five years ago. We had signed a record deal then it all went to shit."

"What happened?" asked Tailz innocently.

"A bad trip to Thailand," replied Ellen softly. "We kind of went our separate ways after that."

"We've not had a female singer before," commented Cal.

"Think you can cope with the four of us out there every night?"

"Well, I've only met two of you...."

"Cal, leave her alone," scolded Taylor, sensing that there was something that their new singer was holding back. Turning to face her, he added, "He's messing with you. Ignore him."

Ellen smiled but remained silent while the two boys started to discuss rehearsal plans for the coming week. Gradually, their conversation turned to what songs they could add into the mix with a female vocalist until they wrote more of their own.

"Do you write any of your own material?" asked Taylor, curious to learn more about the girl who was joining them.

"Lyrics mainly," answered Ellen, setting her empty mug on the table.

"What about instruments?" checked Cal, sharing his band mate's curiosity.

Before Ellen could answer him, they all heard Lizzy call them through for dinner. The question hung unanswered in the air.

Taylor led the way down the hall to the large family kitchen, commenting on how good dinner smelled. Chivalrously, he pulled out a chair for Ellen at the table, making sure she was seated next to him. There was something about the girl that was intriguing him. Just as Lizzy was spooning generous portions of her chorizo pasta dish into bowls for them, the door opened and Rocky came striding in.

"Perfect timing," declared Lizzy as she lifted another bowl from the stack beside her. "Any sign of Jack and Luke out there?"

"Jack called. They're on their way," replied Rocky, taking his seat at the head of the table. "So, have you guys been getting to know one another?"

"A bit," said Cal with a grin. "In between biscuits."

"Cal McDermid, have you eaten all my biscuits again?" chided Lizzy, trying and failing to sound cross.

"I left you one," he replied.

Shaking her head, Lizzy took her seat at the other end of the table, telling them all to eat before it got cold.

Politely, Taylor passed Ellen the bowl of parmesan. She smiled shyly at him, thanking him quietly. Again, he got the sense that she was hiding something.

While Rocky quizzed her about her journey, Taylor

surreptitiously watched her. There was an air of fragility about her and he began to have doubts about her suitability as a vocalist. After Life couldn't afford to have a delicate princess fronting them.

"Tailz," began Rocky, interrupting his daydream. "How did everything go last week? Sorry I couldn't get down there on Friday."

"Don't worry about it. It was mainly family," replied Taylor, staring down into his bowl. "Jen is there to help Nana sort the rest of mum's things out. Matt's still about too. Not sure how much use he'll be to them though."

Silently, Rocky nodded. "If there's anything Lizzy and I can do to help, just ask, son."

"Thanks. Appreciate it."

Dinner was interrupted by another knock at the door. Excusing herself, Lizzy went to answer it and the others listened as she scolded the latest arrivals for being late. Still berating them, Lizzy ushered them into the kitchen, firmly instructing them both to sit down.

"Ellen, allow me to introduce the always late Luke Court and the overly tolerant Jack Smart," said Rocky as the two new arrivals made themselves comfortable at the table. "Boys, you're late...again!"

"Sorry," apologized Jack humbly. "Lord Party Animal has been holding Court all weekend. Blame him."

"Luke?" quizzed Rocky sternly. "Care to explain? I thought we had agreed on a few party rules after last time?"

"Yeah, yeah, whatever," muttered Luke from behind a pair of dark sunglasses. "Lizzy, any wine to wash down your delicious pasta?"

"No," replied the older woman firmly. "There's water in the jug on the table."

Pouring himself a glass of iced water, Luke noticed Ellen for the first time. From behind his dark glasses, he looked her up and down.

"Is this the new voice you've hired?" he asked bluntly.

"Manners, Luke!" stated Lizzy sharply. "This is Ellen and, yes, she is your new vocalist."

"Hi," he said plainly with a nod towards her.

"Hi," replied Ellen, feeling herself flush scarlet. "Pleasure to meet you."

"Hi, Ellen. I'm Jack," said the band's drummer. "Don't mind my hungover friend here. Manners never were his strong suit."

Ellen smiled, instantly warming to Jack.

A short while later, once the pasta dish and bowls had been cleared away and as Lizzy poured them all a coffee, Rocky suggested, "Ellen, why don't you tell the boys your story. Tell them a bit about yourself."

With an anxious glance towards the band's manager, Ellen nodded. She paused to collect her thoughts before she began, "Not sure where to start, Rocky. I fronted a band called Good Times about five years ago. Not sure you'd remember them now. We had just been signed to a small label when a bad trip to Thailand broke up the band. I took some time out after that. For the past year, I've been doing session work and auditioning."

Gently, Rocky prompted her, "Just tell them about that bad trip to Thailand, honey. Get it over and done with for your sake."

With all eyes on her, Ellen bowed her head and stared down into her lap. Silence hung in the air for a minute or so before she took a deep breath. Quietly, her voice barely above a whisper, she began, "I went to Thailand to celebrate my eighteenth birthday with two members of Good Times and my boyfriend. The second week of our trip we decided to splash out and have a big night out in a night club near our resort. Someone petrol bombed the club while we were in it. Destroyed the place. Killed thirty-four people. My boyfriend and my friend John from Good Times were among those killed instantly. My other friend, Alex, got out safely. Me? Well, I was badly burned and injured by falling debris. It cost me the sight in my right eye, my right arm and some skin down the right-hand side of my body."

"Shit," breathed Taylor as Ellen paused her tale.

"Yeah," she said with a wistful smile. "Things were pretty shit for a while. A long while. However, life goes on. If you're happy to have me along, scars and all, I'm happy to give this band all I've got."

"Rocky," interrupted Luke loudly. "Have you really fucking

lost it this time? We're a fucking rock band not a charity case!"

"Luke," growled Jack coldly. "Shut the fuck up."

"She's a fucking cripple!" yelled the bass player. "What on earth can she bring to the party that will put After Life on the map?"

"Maybe," began Taylor, instinctively eager to defend Ellen. "Maybe if you'd actually listened to the audition Rocky sent us, you'd understand."

"If you don't feel I'll fit in then I'll go now," said Ellen, trying hard to hide the emotion in her voice. "I'd prefer though if you gave me a chance. Let's rehearse. Jam a few numbers. If you don't like what you hear then I'll go."

"Can't say fairer than that, Luke," challenged Cal, also keen to defend her.

"Luke," stated Rocky coldly. "Let me put it to you this way. Ellen here passed the audition. The band unanimously voted to give her a shot. I don't believe you cast your vote. Right now, I don't believe you even opened the damn email I sent you. If anyone's position in After Life is in jeopardy right now, it's yours. You're out of line, son. Take this as a final warning."

"My uncle won't...." began Luke, looking flustered behind his dark glasses.

"Don't try to play the Garrett card with me. We all know he doesn't fund the band. He's already cast you adrift on your own there. Why he still lets you live in his house I'll never fathom."

"Fine. One rehearsal!" snapped Luke, getting to his feet, almost toppling the chair in the process. "Tomorrow. If she's shit, she goes."

As he marched out of the kitchen, Luke slammed the door behind him, rattling the display plates on the wall.

"I'm sorry," whispered Ellen quietly.

"Hey, you've nothing to apologise for," said Taylor quickly. "Luke's an asshole at times. He's the one who should be apologising."

"I didn't mean to start an argument though."

"Sh," said Lizzy, getting up and coming to put an arm around the fragile songbird. "Let's show you up to your room while these boys clear up in here."

Alone in the kitchen, the three members of After Life played "Rock, Paper Scissors" to decide who would wash, dry and put away. Rocky had muttered something about having calls to make and had followed his wife and Ellen out of the room. As he filled the sink with hot soapy water, Taylor asked the others what they thought of their new vocalist.

"I fucking loved her audition," declared Jack as he lifted the tea towel from the radiator. "Her voice really has something special. Something ethereal. An other worldly magic to it. I think we're onto a winner here."

Cal nodded, "And it takes some guts to tell a room full of strangers that story. She's not as fragile as she looks. That girl's got balls on her."

"I could kill Luke for acting like that," muttered Taylor as he scrubbed at the dish in his hands with a green scourer. "Maybe we should be looking for a bass player. I've about had it with his ego."

"Once he hears our little songbird, he'll change his tune," said Jack with a smile. "Trust me on that one."

Upstairs in the guest room, Lizzy sat on the bed beside Ellen and held her while she sobbed. Her fragile control over her emotions had cracked as they had climbed the stairs. Tears had flowed freely down her cheeks as she entered the room. The older woman sat silently beside her, smoothing her long, platinum blonde hair soothingly.

"I'm sorry," whispered Ellen eventually. "My mother warned me I wasn't ready for this. Said I wasn't strong enough. The stubborn side of me wanted to prove her wrong."

"Sh," said Lizzy softly. "What you told those boys down there took guts and a lot of strength. Rocky already told me all about what happened. You're an inspiration, young lady. Those boys could learn a lot from you, especially Luke."

"Luke already hates me."

"No, he doesn't," soothed Lizzy. "He's just your typical spoiled little rich kid. I probably shouldn't say but his folks died when he was about fourteen. Car crash. Garrett Court is his uncle. He's a lovely man but he knew nothing about raising a teenage boy. He sent Luke to the best schools then just showered cash on him. Hasn't done Luke any favours."

"What if they all hate me after this rehearsal tomorrow?"

"They won't," promised the older woman wisely. "Trust an old woman for a moment. I've seen more rock stars round my kitchen table than most folk see family. You've already got Jack and Taylor on side. Cal's not far behind. He's obviously a bit divided here. He lives with Luke. They went to school together. Got expelled together too, if truth be known. His loyalties are torn. I can see he wants to side with Taylor but he can't afford to alienate Luke."

"I understand," nodded Ellen with a sniff. "Guess I just need to put my big girl panties on in the morning and sing my ass off at that rehearsal."

"That's my girl!" said Lizzy, giving her a hug. "Now, make yourself at home. I'll send Taylor up with your case. He stays here more or less permanently. His room is across the hall. Bathroom's next to it."

"Thank you," replied Ellen with a smile. "Think I'll have an early night. I'll call home then call it a day."

"It'll all look better in the morning," promised Lizzy warmly.

Half an hour later, Ellen heard a soft knock at the bedroom door.

"Can I come in?" asked Taylor softly. "I've brought your case up."

"Sure," called back Ellen.

She had been standing at the narrow window, gazing out over the surrounding rooftops. As the door opened, she turned round.

"Where do you want it?" asked Taylor a little awkwardly.

"On that chair would be good," suggested Ellen. "Don't think there's any great rush to unpack."

"Hey, don't let Luke get to you," said the young guitarist. "He gets like that sometimes after a wild weekend. When the fog lifts, he'll see sense. We'll make him see sense."

"Thanks," replied Ellen as she crossed the room, turning her back on the window. "Can I ask you something?"

"Sure."

"Tell me about your normal rehearsals. What's the favourites on the set? I'm trying to work out how to approach tomorrow."

"Trying to impress Luke?"

"Not especially," said Ellen. "But I want to make a good first impression all round. I've not exactly got off to the best of starts."

"Want to know a secret?" teased Taylor with a wink. "A sure-fire way to get Luke back on side?"

"Please."

"He loves Led Zeppelin. Can you channel your inner Robert Plant by tomorrow?"

"Easily," confirmed Ellen with a relieved smile. "Any particular favourites?"

"Kashmir."

"Love that song," confessed Ellen.

"Well, it's Luke's favourite. First song his uncle taught him to play. Don't tell him I told you though."

"Band secrets already?" teased Ellen softly.

"Think of it more as the ace up your sleeve," commented Taylor, instantly regretting his arm reference. He flushed scarlet and stared down at his feet in an attempt to hide his embarrassment.

"I'd better nail it then," said Ellen quietly. "Seeing as I only have one ace to play."

An awkward silence hung in the air for a moment.

Looking up, Taylor said, "That was a really brave thing you did downstairs, telling us your story. I couldn't have done it."

"Thank you," replied Ellen. "I didn't feel brave. I felt like an idiot but I knew Rocky was right. Knew I needed to tell you guys the truth early on. Let's face it. I can't hide it."

"Sorry."

"You've nothing to be sorry about," she said. "I am sorry to hear you lost your mum though. It's hard to lose someone you love."

"Yeah," sighed Taylor, sitting down on the bed. "I've been pretty lost for the past couple of weeks. It's been tough. I miss her."

"If you need to talk, I'm a good listener," offered Ellen, sitting down beside him.

"Thanks. Still struggling with the talking about it bit," he confessed with a sad smile. "Now, if you're not too tired, do you fancy a quick rehearsal before tomorrow? We could run through

Kashmir a couple of times?"

"That would be good. Thanks."

"Let me go and grab my guitar," said Taylor. "I'll just be a minute."

Down in the kitchen an hour or so later, Lizzy was tidying up when Rocky came in at her back, carrying two glasses and a bottle of single malt.

"Night cap?" he suggested.

"A small one."

As he poured two generous measures of the amber liquid, Rocky commented, "Sounds like our house guests are playing nicely up there."

"Yes," agreed Lizzy warmly. "They've been playing for about an hour. I think Taylor's just trying to calm her nerves about tomorrow."

"He's a good boy," commented Rocky. "I just hope he's ready to be back in the band after all he's been through these past few weeks."

"My guess is that those two will get each other through the next few weeks," observed his wife wisely.

"Well, let's drink to getting through tomorrow's rehearsal first."

Ellen

After Life's usual rehearsal hall was in the basement of a former church. The church above it had closed its doors a few years before. When Ellen and Taylor arrived with Rocky next day, they found that they weren't the first to arrive, despite being deliberately early. Cal and Luke were already there.

"Morning, boys," called out Rocky loudly. "No Jack?"

"He's gone over to the music shop to pick up some drum heads," answered Cal. "He split two earlier. None left in the trunk."

"Two?" echoed Rocky, shaking his head. "That boy'll bankrupt us all at the rate he goes through them."

Casually, Ellen slipped off her leather jacket and laid it over the back of a nearby chair. She had dressed carefully but had chosen her outfit so that it didn't disguise her arm. It had taken the last remaining shreds of her self-confidence but, with the nude coloured pressure sleeve over the stump, she felt secure enough to risk a short-sleeved top.

As she crossed the room to join the band on the low makeshift stage, she was aware that all eyes were on her. Taking a deep breath to steady her nerves, she asked, "What's the plan?"

"To rehearse," stated Luke tersely. "And to see if you can deliver the fucking goods, princess."

"Luke," growled Taylor as he lifted his guitar from its case. "Cut it out."

With a sneer, Luke bowed his head slightly, "Humble apologies, Ellen. Ladies choice."

Before she could reply, the door creaked open and Jack came in carrying a bag with his new drum heads in it.

"Sorry, people," he apologized. "Are you all waiting for me?"

"Yeah," drawled Luke sourly. "And on Little Miss here deciding what we're playing."

"Kashmir," stated Ellen with a calm confidence.

"Kashmir?" echoed Luke unable to mask his surprise. "You mess this up and you're fucking history. Hear me?"

"Luke!" snapped Rocky. "Enough, young man! Give her a fair

chance."

"It's fine, Rocky," said Ellen, praying she sounded calmer than she felt. "Luke, I'll make a deal with you. One error and I'm gone. One from you and the result's the same. You go."

Both Jack and Cal laughed before Cal said, "You asked for that, mate."

"Harrumph," muttered the bass player sulkily.

"Luke, that sounds fair enough to me," said Rocky. "Especially considering the way you spoke to this young lady last night."

"Fine," he growled, inwardly seething at having been backed into a corner.

A few minutes later, Ellen stood centre stage with her trembling hand wrapped round the microphone. Taking a deep breath, she heard Jack and Luke begin the thundering drum and bass intro then Cal and Taylor came in on guitar. Precisely on cue, she came in, keeping her voice low and even with a hint of menace.

"Oh, let the sun beat down upon my face."

Over the next eight minutes, she poured her heart and soul into the vocal. Channelling every last ounce of her inner strength, Ellen shut out all thoughts of Luke and the pressures on her, focusing instead on nailing every note however high or long. Beside her, Taylor was playing with a passion to rival her own, almost as if he were willing her through the iconic anthem with his own music. As she reached the final couple of lines, Ellen's heart was pounding and her palm was sweaty.

"Let me take you there!"

Her voice rang out across the hall as the band finished off the song with a flourish. It didn't escape her sharp attention that Luke fluffed a section just before the end. With a small smile, Ellen raised her eyebrows and stared at him through her tinted glasses.

"Fucking insane!" declared Cal enthusiastically. "Awesome voice, girl!"

"That was quite something," agreed Jack from behind the drumkit.

Without looking at Ellen, Luke unplugged his bass, laid it down and stepped off stage. As he walked towards the door, he called back over his shoulder, "The bitch is in."

Taylor moved to go after him but Ellen reached out to stop him. "I'll go."

"Are you crazy?" he asked, his tone sharper than he intended. "You saw the mood he is in!"

Nodding, Ellen said, "I did and I'll go. Where will he be?"

"Out the back having a smoke. Follow the path round the side. You'll find him," replied Cal, sharing Taylor's concern in the wisdom of Ellen going after their irate friend.

Without another word, Ellen stepped down from the stage and followed Luke out of the door.

Once outside, she paused to take a few calming, deep breaths before she slowly followed the path round to the rear of the church and into a small graveyard. As she turned the corner, she caught a whiff of weed on the breeze. The band's bass player was standing with his back to her.

"Luke," began Ellen, her voice soft and a still a little husky from singing. "Can we talk?"

"Fuck off."

"No," she stated firmly. "We need to sort this out. You and me. No influence from the others. Now, what's your problem with me?"

The bass player shrugged his shoulders but kept his back to her.

"If we can't at least be civil to each other I may as well leave now," commented Ellen. "If we can't communicate off stage then we will never make it work on stage."

"You know I blew that last section," said Luke, turning to stare at her.

Ellen nodded, "But do the others?"

"Doubt it," muttered Luke almost under his breath. "Tailz might."

"Then we won't mention it."

"You nailed it back there," said the bass player, a hint of appreciation in his tone. "That's some voice you're hiding in that fucked up body."

"Thank you."

A tense silence hung in the air as Luke finished his joint. He kept his gaze firmly fixed on Ellen all the while, almost as if he was trying to fathom her out. Grinding the butt out with the heel of his boot, he eventually said, "Let's try Kashmir again and see if we can both nail it this time."

Satisfied that they had agreed a tentative truce, Ellen led the way back indoors.

It was late afternoon before Rocky suggested that they call it a day. Gradually, the four members of After Life had guided Ellen through their standard set. None of the songs they covered posed a challenge to her talents, although she confessed to being a little rusty on some of the lyrics.

"Right, boys and girl," called out their manager. "Same time back here tomorrow. Work up that set. Polish it. I've made a few calls and pulled in a few favours. Your first gig is a week on Friday."

"You've got to be fucking joking, old man!" yelled Luke angrily. "We need more time to work together here."

"I disagree, Luke," stated Rocky calmly. "You've a week. Plenty of time to sort out a forty-minute set. Do the rest of you agree?"

The others nodded, not daring to contradict their manager.

"What's the gig?" asked Taylor, finally daring to ask the question that was hanging in the air.

"Support slot for Time March at The Garage in Highbury," revealed Rocky. "Solid show to launch the new look After Life on the world. Ticket sales are looking good. Original support band have a scheduling conflict so the slot came up."

"We'll be ready," assured Ellen calmly.

"Glad to hear it," replied Rocky with a fatherly smile towards her. "Are you and Taylor OK to make your own way back to the house? I've an appointment."

"We'll be fine," promised Taylor.

It was raining when the band left the old church. Hauling his jacket collar up around his neck, Cal suggested they go for a quick drink. Surprisingly, Luke declined, muttering something incoherent about meeting someone to pick up a package. Looking slightly sheepish, Jack too offered his apologies, saying he needed to get home to walk the dog.

"Guess, it's us three then," said Cal. "Tailz, I believe it's your round."

"Isn't it always?"

The Anchor pub was just around the corner and, considering the early hour, was busy when they entered. It was After Life's pub of choice post rehearsal and the barmaid greeted Cal by name.

"Not my round, Maggie," he declared with a wink. "Tailz is buying. Mine's a pint."

"Taylor," said the barmaid with a welcoming smile. "What are you having?"

"Make mine a pint of cider," replied the guitarist. "Ellen?"

"Red wine, please."

"Shiraz alright, sweetheart?" asked Maggie, checking the shelf behind her. "Or Cabernet Sauvignon?"

"Shiraz," confirmed Ellen shyly.

"Come on," said Cal, touching her elbow. "Our corner's free. Let's nab it quick. Tailz can bring the drinks over."

He led her across the room to a corner booth. The Anchor was a traditional Victorian era public house and either side of an ornate fireplace were two red leather lined booths. With a smile, Ellen noted that the high mantelpiece above the hearth had an array of framed photos of regulars on display. A photo of After Life was perched at the end nearest their usual seat.

"Who's the guy in the centre of that photo?" she asked as she sat down.

Glancing up, Cal said, "That was Joe, our first singer. He left the band about two years ago. No idea where he is. Jail most likely. Had a temper on him. That's what got him chucked out of the band. He assaulted one of the security guys after a gig. Got charged by the police. Rocky fired him on the spot."

Over at the bar, Taylor was watching Maggie pull their pints. He'd never developed a taste for beer, preferring to stick to cider. His fellow band members teased him relentlessly about it.

"Who's the girl?" asked Maggie as she set the glass down on the bar.

"Ellen," answered Taylor. "She's our new singer. We're celebrating our first rehearsal with her."

"Don't recognize her," mused the barmaid, staring over to where Ellen and Cal were sitting.

"She's not local," revealed Taylor. "Think she's from Surrey or somewhere south of London. You know what my geography's like!"

"Yeah," laughed Maggie. "It's a good job your guitar playing's better."

"Awh, come on," protested Taylor. "I made it home and back this time without getting lost."

"Lord, it's a miracle!" she teased him. "That's twelve fifty."

"Thanks, Maggie."

He lifted the small bottle of wine and the glass, stuffing the bottle into his jeans' pocket before picking up the pints. With the drinks balanced in his hands, he headed across to join the others. Barely spilling a drop en route, Taylor passed Cal his beer before setting the empty glass down in front of Ellen.

"Budge up!" he said to her, indicating she should move into the corner.

He sat his pint down, then removed the wine from his pocket. The worried look that flashed across Ellen's face didn't escape his attention. Theatrically, he declared, "Allow me, miss."

Swiftly, he removed the cap from the bottle and filled the wine glass. Sliding it across the table, he said, "Yeghes da."

"Pardon?"

"One of my Nana's sayings," he explained with a wink. "Translates into cheers."

"You and your yokel colloquialisms," laughed Cal, raising his glass. "Slainte."

Giggling, Ellen raised her glass with a shy, "Your good health, boys."

Casually, they chatted about the rehearsal, commenting on songs that needed more work.

"Do you perform much of your own material?" asked Ellen eventually.

"Sure," said Cal with a nod. "There's half a dozen or so songs floating about. Not sure we've time for you to learn them all before this show."

"We could add in two or three though," countered Taylor. "I can work on them with Ellen."

"I think we should give it a try," agreed Ellen. "After Life don't want to sound like a covers band. We've a real chance here. Let's make this show count."

"OK. We can work on them a bit tonight then see how they slot in tomorrow," proposed Taylor. "Do you write any of your own music?"

Ellen nodded, then lowered her gaze, "I used to write more. You know…before. It's harder now. I've a pile of lyrics in a few journals looking for some music."

"What did you used you play?" asked Taylor softly, sensing he was treading on delicate territory.

"Keyboards and a bit of guitar," revealed Ellen, keeping her gaze on her glass. "I reached Grade Six for piano before I left school."

"We have a talented lady in our midst," teased Cal in an effort to lighten the mood. "I never got past chopsticks."

"Me neither," confessed Taylor. "My sister, Jen, plays a bit. Mum made her take lessons till we were about fourteen. And my Nana plays a mean honky tonk piano."

"She sure does!" laughed Cal. "I love that old girl!"

"Well, if either of you fancy writing the music," began Ellen with a wistful smile, "I can sing the lyrics to you. The music's all in my head."

"Tailz, my man, that sounds like a job for you and Luke!"

"You might be right," acknowledged Taylor warmly, "I've a few pieces looking for some lyrics."

"Match made in heaven!" declared Cal, as he got to his feet. "My round. Same again?"

When Ellen and Taylor finally arrived back at the house, Lizzy was just putting dinner on the table. As the two giggling youngsters tumbled into the kitchen, Rocky, who was seated at the end of the table, looked up and raised an eyebrow.

Mumbling his apologies for keeping them late, Taylor sat down in his usual seat. With a giggle, Ellen sat beside him.

"How many have you two had?" quizzed Rocky sternly.

"Three," replied Taylor honestly. "Check with Maggie. One round each."

"Leave them be, Rocky," said Lizzy as she placed a plate of

shepherd's pie down in front of them. "You're only one drink behind them."

"Did Luke not join you?" asked Rocky casually.

Ellen shook her head. "He said something about picking up a parcel."

"Yeah and you can bet it wasn't from the post office," muttered Taylor as he picked up his fork.

"I'll speak to him in the morning," stated Rocky bluntly. "He's been warned time and again."

Changing the subject, Lizzy said, "I hear rehearsal went well, Ellen."

"Well, I passed the Luke test," replied the young singer with a proud smile.

"You nailed Kashmir!" complimented Taylor enthusiastically. "Lizzy, you should've heard her. It was awesome!"

"Make sure it is on the set list for next Friday and I will."

"Your wish is our command," replied Taylor with a wink.

After dinner, Ellen excused herself, saying she needed to call home, and disappeared upstairs. Shoving his chair back, Taylor made to follow her.

"Not so fast, Taylor," cautioned Lizzy. "It's bins night. Can you take them round the front for me, please?"

"Sure," he said, knowing in his heart he'd do anything to help out Lizzy.

Upstairs, Ellen flopped down onto the bed with a weary sigh. Her arm was aching from being in the pressure sleeve all day and she was a little concerned that she'd overdone things. Sitting up, Ellen reached under her top and unfastened the strap of the pressure garment. Slowly, she peeled it down from her shoulder, feeling the air cool on her bare skin. Free from the constraints of the sleeve, she circled her shoulder a few times both forwards and back, feeling the muscles pull and the scars tighten. Methodically, she checked the fragile skin for signs of damage, satisfying herself that all was well. It was a familiar but vital routine. She could still see the marks where Taylor had grabbed her when they'd bumped into each other at the station but they looked paler than they had that morning. Removing her tinted glasses, Ellen got up and went to look in the mirror. The snow-white orb of her damaged eye stared blindly at her. Gently, she applied some moisturizer to the burn damaged eyelid.

Leaving her arm bare and her glasses off, Ellen wandered over to the window to call home. For almost half an hour, she listened to her mother ramble on about her lunch club ladies, the school board meeting that she'd attended then to her rant about Ellen's father forgetting to book theatre tickets for them and that the show was now sold out.

"We've our first show booked," Ellen revealed when she could finally get a word in. "A week on Friday. Want to come?"

"Oh, I don't know, darling," began her mother. "I don't come into London at night and I don't know if your dad's in or out that night."

"It would be good if you could both be there," suggested Ellen hopefully.

"I'll ask your dad and let you know at the weekend. He's away for business for a couple of days. Paris."

"Ok," said Ellen resignedly. "We'll probably be working late this week so don't worry if I don't call. I'll call on Sunday afternoon if I can. Will dad be home then?"

"Make sure you're not working too hard," cautioned her mother, using the patronizing tone that got on Ellen's worst nerve. "You need to get plenty of rest. Don't push yourself too hard."

"Mum, I'm fine," assured Ellen calmly. "I know what I can and can't do. I'm not a child."

"I know, darling, but you're still so fragile."

"Mum!" interrupted Ellen, her tone sharp. "Don't fuss. I can take care of myself. I know the routine. Christ, I've followed it day in day out for five bloody years!"

"Ellen, don't swear," chastised her mother sharply.

"Mum, let it go. I'll talk to you on Sunday. I need to go."

Before her mother could reply, Ellen ended the call and stuffed the phone back into the pocket of her jeans. With a heavy heart, she stood gazing out of the window at the sun setting over the rooftops.

A knock at the door startled her back to the present a few minutes later. Before she could move, Taylor opened the door and stuck his head into the room.

"Can I come in?"

"No. I mean, yes, but," rambled Ellen, sounding completely flustered as she realized she was trapped by the window.

"If it's not a good time, I can come back later."

"It's ok," sighed Ellen quietly, keeping her back to him. "It's just my glasses are on the bed. It's not a pretty sight without them."

"Want me to pass them over?" suggested Taylor, stepping into the room.

"Are you squeamish?"

"Pardon?"

"Are you squeamish? If I turn round, are you going to run off to be sick?" asked Ellen, deciding that if they were going to perform together he would need to see her unmasked at some point.

"No, I'm not squeamish, as you put it."

Bowing her head slightly, Ellen turned round to face Taylor. Belatedly, she remembered her arm was uncovered but it was too late to turn back now. She was aware of him watching her and of the fact he hadn't moved nor flinched. When she looked up, he was smiling at her.

"Nothing to be squeamish about," said Taylor, taking a tentative step towards her. "Your eye kind of looks like it has a white contact lens in. And your arm's not so bad."

"Thank you," whispered Ellen shyly, feeling completely self-conscious. "I don't like people seeing me like this, I feel a bit like a freak."

"Well you shouldn't," he scolded warmly. "You're a pretty girl, Ellen. You shouldn't hide that."

"My eye's still sensitive to light so I need to cover it for most of the day otherwise I get headaches," she explained. "The glasses are a necessity but they annoy me too."

"Why not wear an eye patch?"

"And go for the pirate look?" laughed Ellen.

"Or a witch look?" countered Taylor with a grin. "A hooded cloak, an eye patch. Lots of dry ice or a smoke machine. We could make you look really cool on stage."

Ellen threw back her head and laughed, a deep belly laugh. "I love it!

"You do?"

"I had been worrying about what to wear for this show. I've not been on stage since before the accident," she confessed. "Your witch idea might just solve a few problems."

"Well, we can speak to Rocky about finding you a cloak and whatever else you need. I think the guys will like the idea."

"I hope so," said Ellen softly as she slipped her glasses back on. "Now, did you come in to talk music or spells?"

With a laugh, Taylor said, "Music. Thought we could work on a couple of the band's own compositions. See how you feel about them."

"Sounds like a smart plan. Let me grab a glass of water first."

"Ok. Bring it to my room, will you? My gear's all set up in there."

"Give me five minutes."

A trail of destruction met Cal in the hallway when he returned to the Knightsbridge apartment. Laying the bag containing a takeaway curry on the hall table, he walked slowly towards the lounge. Crashing and banging, interspersed with swearing, echoed from the room. Luke was on a rampage and the Scotsman could guess why. Taking a long, deep breath, he entered the lounge.

"Hey, Luke, what's going on?" he asked as casually as he could.

"Fucking bastard's been busted. No blow," growled the irate bass player. "There has to be some in this fucking dump."

"There's none," stated Cal calmly, knowing that both he and Jack had gutted the apartment the previous night.

"You're shitting me!"

"There's none, Luke," repeated Cal.

Spinning round to face his band mate, eyes blazing, Luke demanded, "Where the fuck has it gone?"

"We cleaned up."

"We?"

"Jack and I. Last night after you passed out. Rocky's orders," revealed Cal, inwardly dreading his friend's reaction. "It's all gone."

"Fuck you! Fuck Jack! Fuck Rocky!" roared Luke as he pushed his way past his friend. "Fuck you all!"

"Where are you going?" asked Cal as Luke grabbed his jacket and his phone from the couch.

"Out!"

"Where?" pressed Cal.

"Emily's!" spat Luke. "You got a problem with that?"

Cal shook his head.

"Glad to hear it!"

The bass player spun on his heel, colliding with a lamp and sending it crashing to the floor. Two small plastic bags of white powder lay in the midst of its shattered remains. Grabbing them quickly, Luke stuffed them into his jeans pocket.

"Hah! You missed some," he gloated, giving Cal the middle finger.

Blood was pouring from a cut on his hand.

"You might want to see to that," commented Cal, noting that a shard of broken china had sliced two of the bass player's fingers wide open.

"Emily'll sort it," muttered Luke as he left.

With a slam of the front door, he was gone; with a sigh, Cal began to tidy up, his curry long since forgotten.

Next morning, Ellen and Taylor were the first to arrive at the rehearsal room. Both of them were still tired, having been up until after three working on the After Life songs. Having dumped his guitars down in a corner, Taylor headed into the small kitchen to make them both a coffee. While he waited on the kettle boiling, he messaged Cal to bring in some bacon rolls for them all. As the kettle came to the boil, he could hear Ellen talking to someone out in the hall then heard Jack yelling through, "Milk and two in mine, Tailz!"

Carrying the three mugs through with them balanced precariously, Taylor commented, "No sign of Luke?"

"Not yet," replied Jack, taking one of the mugs from the band's guitarist. "Cal said he trashed the house last night then stomped off to Emily's. Don't know why that girl puts up with him."

"Don't know why Cal puts up with him," muttered Taylor as he handed Ellen her mug. "What set him off this time?"

"Cal and I had cleaned up the apartment, if you get my drift," said Jack, wary of saying too much in front of Ellen.

"Ah, seeking Charlie, was he?" mused Taylor with a frown. "He needs to get that under control."

"No need to tell me that," sighed Jack in exasperation. "Anyway, did you guys manage to work out any of the songs last night?"

"But of course," said Ellen with a shy smile. "And Taylor here came up with an idea for my on-stage look."

"He did?" commented Jack, looking surprised.

"He did. Rocky's gone to pick up a few bits and pieces for me just now," replied Ellen. "He's acting as my personal shopper."

"I'm intrigued," said Jack with a smile. "Now, which songs did you guys get to?"

"Cyclone and In Hell In My Mind," replied Taylor. "We made a start on Rats but never got far."

"That's tonight's homework assignment," joked Ellen with a wink. "Plus two others that we were talking about in the car."

"Sounds like you two have another late night planned."

Behind them, they heard the door creak open and turned to see Cal arriving with a bag of bacon rolls and his guitar slung over his shoulder.

"Mornin'," he called out. "No sign of Luke?"

"Not yet," said Taylor. "Did you remember the brown sauce on my roll?"

"Shit. Forgot. Sorry, Tailz."

After Life had been rehearsing for almost four hours before they heard the door creak open again and saw a rather dishevelled Luke shamble in. Cal noted the bass player was still wearing the same clothes as he'd had on the night before and that two of his fingers were wrapped in tape.

"Afternoon," said Jack curtly. "Nice of you to join us."

"Fuck off, Jack," growled Luke. "Where's Rocky?"

"Not here," replied Taylor, sniffing the air and smelling a mix of cannabis and alcohol. "And I suggest you get cleaned up before he gets here. If he sees you in that state, you're out."

"Fuck you," muttered the bass player, slurring his words.

Laying his guitar down, Cal said, "Come on, pal. Let's get you home."

Firmly, he put his arm around Luke's shoulders and guided him back outside.

"And then there were three," commented Jack sadly.

"Should one of us go and help Cal with him?" asked Taylor still gazing at the door.

"Cal's got this," said Jack. "Plenty of practice. Wonder what's set him off?"

Checking the date on his phone, Taylor said, "Anniversary of his parents' deaths."

"Shit. I forgot."

"So did I," sighed Taylor wearily. "So, now what?"

The three of them stared awkwardly at each other before Ellen said, "How about we try to get the music together for those two songs I mentioned?"

"Sure," agreed Taylor, keen to hear the songs that she had written.

With her heart hammering in her chest, Ellen stepped up to the microphone. Slowly, she began a slow Gregorian chant in Latin, her voice clear but deep in her register. In one breath, she switched to a husky, powerful rock voice and poured her heart into the tale of being lost in the mists of despair. As she sang the final chorus, she reverted back to Latin, closing the song with a reprise of the chant.

"Holy fuck!" exclaimed Jack. "That was awesome."

Blushing, Ellen lowered her gaze, suddenly uncomfortable at being the focus of their attention.

"Wow!" said Taylor, nodding his head in appreciation. "You wrote that?"

Ellen nodded, not trusting herself to speak.

"That is one powerful song, Ellen," complimented Taylor warmly. "Not sure what the Latin meant but I felt like the devil was coming for my soul."

With a nervous giggle, Ellen confessed that that had been her intention.

"Alright, so the intro section doesn't need any music. The chants are perfect as they are. Let's hear the first verse again."

Two hours later, when Rocky finally arrived, the three members of After Life were still focused on composing the music for the song. While they had worked, Ellen had commented that the song was tentatively called Swirling Mists. Together they had collaborated on the melody line and guitar parts, leaving the drum track to Jack's expertise. He played around with a few variations before settling for a slow, snare based, almost "hissing" rhythm that echoed the Gregorian chant.

"Needs some tubular bells," he commented as Rocky entered the hall.

"What does?" called out the band's manager.

"Ellen's masterpiece. Our new song," called back Jack.

"Where's Cal and Luke or do I not want to ask?" enquired Rocky glancing round.

"You don't want to ask," replied Taylor. "I'll fill you in later. Want to hear Ellen's song?"

"Make it quick. Lizzy called to say dinner will be on the table at seven and its gone half six. Its curry night."

The band's manager sat spellbound as Ellen began to chant the intro to Swirling Mists. His toe was soon tapping and his head nodding as Jack and Taylor joined in. By the closing section, they could all see the approval on his face and the sparkle to his bright eyes.

"That, people, was incredible!" enthused Rocky when the last noted faded away. "And I agree, Jack. You need some tubular bells. Leave that thought with me for a day or two."

"I might be able to borrow some off a mate who's a music teacher," offered Jack as they began to pack up.

"I think I have some in storage," said Rocky, trying to visualize the contents of the storage unit he leased. "Let me check first. Ellen, you are one talented young lady."

"Thank you," she said softly as her cheeks flushed scarlet.

"And I got your robes. They're in the car. You can check them out later," added Rocky. "Right, hurry it along. Lizzy's waiting. Jack, you joining us?"

"Not tonight. I've plans," replied the drummer with a wink. "Ask Lizzy to keep me some curry and I'll drop by tomorrow for it."

An amazing aroma of warm spices filled the hallway as Rocky opened the door for the two young musicians. All of them could hear voices coming from the kitchen, instantly recognizing Cal's Glasgow accent.

"Sorry," apologised Rocky as they entered the kitchen. "Traffic's at a standstill out there."

"You've still a minute or two to spare," replied Lizzy, checking the time. "I'm just waiting on the naans."

Pulling out his usual chair, Rocky asked, "Cal, where's Luke?"

"At home. Sleeping it off," answered Cal awkwardly.

"Did you do as I told you to?" quizzed Rocky cryptically.

The red headed guitarist nodded, "I called him. Said he'd speak to him."

The band's manager nodded approvingly, "You did the right thing, son. Garrett'll straighten him out."

"Christ, I hope so," sighed Cal as Lizzy set a huge dish of chicken curry down in the centre of the table.

"Taylor, you dish up," she instructed firmly. "Cal, come and grab the rice till I get the bread out of the oven."

Soon the five of them were silently enjoying the best curry that Ellen had ever tasted. The discretion exercised by Taylor and Lizzy wasn't lost on her. Her fellow band member had displayed some theatrical chivalry as he'd dished up her meal for her while Lizzy had quietly slipped a torn off piece of bread onto her plate. Eating in front of people had been one of the hardest obstacles to overcome after the accident. Sitting in Lizzy's welcoming kitchen, Ellen felt the most relaxed about eating a meal that she had felt for years.

"Penny for them," said Taylor nudging her. "You looked miles away."

"Sorry," apologized Ellen quietly. "Lizzy, this is fantastic!"

"Glad you're enjoying it, dear," replied the older woman warmly. "Taylor, can you put another helping in my bowl, please?"

As he passed the plate back, the guitarist asked, "Anyone else for anymore?"

"Me, please," said Ellen shyly, offering him her empty bowl.

Once the meal was over, Cal and Taylor cleared the table without being prompted and began to debate who was going to wash and who was going to dry. Leaving the two guitarists to their chores, Rocky suggested that Ellen go and try on the new stage outfit that he'd sourced for her.

"Want some help?" offered Lizzy softly.

"Please," said Ellen. "I'm not sure how everything fastens."

"Let's take a look, shall we?" suggested the older woman. "Rocky, where's the bag?"

"In the hall. By the stairs."

Upstairs in the bedroom, Ellen opened the black holdall, curious to see what the band's manager had found for her. Inside, on top of piles of black and purple fabric, were two different eye patches. One was black with a gold Eye of Horus painted on it; the other was blue and gold with a red Eye of Ra."

"Wow!" exclaimed Ellen as she lifted them out. "I love these!"

"They're certainly dramatic," laughed Lizzy. "Here, let me lift that cloak out for you."

"Thanks," said Ellen, stepping aside. "Let me fetch a hanger for it."

"Fetch two, dear. There's two cloaks here. Maybe three."

Soon Lizzy had three different full-length cloaks hanging on the outside of the wardrobe door. The first was a rich black velvet cloak with a full hood and an imperial purple satin lining. The second was black cotton with a gold satin lining and the third one was a dark forest green colour with a bronze satin lining.

"Oh, I don't know where to start," giggled Ellen.

"How about with that Eye of Horus patch and the black and gold cloak."

With a little help from Lizzy to secure the eye patch in place, Ellen surveyed her stage look in the full-length mirror. It was a powerful look, especially with the hood of the cloak draped over her pale blonde hair.

"I love it!" declared Ellen with a huge smile. "Disguises everything."

"Looks perfect," agreed Lizzy, relieved to see her looking so happy and relaxed. "Let's go down and see what the others think."

When they reached the closed kitchen door, Lizzy motioned for Ellen to stay quiet for a moment. The older woman opened the door and, as she had hoped, her husband and the two musicians were sitting round the table with a drink. Casually, she switched off the overhead light, leaving the small spotlights under the cabinets illuminating the room. As she poured herself a shot of whisky, Lizzy said, "Ellen'll be down in a few minutes."

The boys were so engrossed in their conversation about the new song Ellen had brought to rehearsal that neither of them noticed her slip into the kitchen. Trying to ignore Ellen standing by the door, Lizzy asked about the Latin opening to the song that Taylor was attempting to recall.

"Oh, I can't do it justice," he said with a grin. "But Ellen was amazing."

Subtly, Lizzy nodded.

It was the cue that Ellen had been waiting for. Keeping her head bowed under her hood, she began the Latin chant.

"Jesus Christ!" yelped Taylor, almost leaping out of his seat. "How long have you been standing there for, girl?"

Giggling helplessly, Ellen said, "Long enough."

"That witch look is brilliant!" declared Cal with a broad grin. "You'd never know about..." His voice petered out as he failed to find the appropriate words to express what he meant.

"Never know I've half an arm and genuinely only sight in one eye," finished off Ellen with a mischievous grin. "Fabulous, isn't it?"

"You look fantastic," said Rocky warmly. "But, will you be able to perform wearing it?"

"We'll find out next week," replied Ellen. "As long as I wear light clothes underneath, I should be alright to keep the cloak on for an hour on stage."

"You could always take it off after a couple of songs," suggested Cal in an effort to be helpful.

"Perhaps," mused Ellen. "I'll see how it feels in rehearsals."

Rehearsals over the next few days saw After Life go through some highs and lows. For the first two days Luke never showed. When he finally strolled in on Monday afternoon both Taylor and Jack gave him a cold reception. Reluctantly, Taylor agreed to play the new songs that they had been working on for the unpredictable bass player. Over the weekend, Ellen had delivered two more of her own compositions that the band had immediately agreed to add to the set. This left Luke with three bass tracks to work out and learn in less than a week.

Having heard the new songs, Luke nodded approvingly towards Ellen, "You wrote those, princess?"

"Yes," she replied curtly. "Unfortunately, I wasn't able to write the music fully. I'm still working out a way to do that now that I can't play piano."

The wry remark caused Luke to smile and then to laugh. It was the first time in months that the band had heard their troubled bass player really laugh.

"Not much call for left handed piano players, eh?" he joked.

"Maybe I should advertise for a right-hand man," quipped Ellen.

"I think our Tailz would happily fill that position," observed Luke, staring at his fellow band member. "Right, play these through again, people. I'll record them on my phone and see what I can do about some bass tracks. My neighbours don't need sleep tonight anyway."

Next morning, when Ellen and Taylor arrived at the church, they found Luke already there, plugged in and working on the bass tracks. Judging by the dark circles under his pale blue eyes, he hadn't had much sleep. When he heard the others arrive, he glanced up.

"I hope one of you brought coffee in," he said with a yawn.

"There's some in the cupboard in the kitchen. The one above the kettle," replied Taylor.

"Wrong," stated the bass player. "I finished it a couple of hours ago."

"Have you been here all night?" quizzed Ellen as she slipped off her jacket.

"Not quite," confessed Luke. "I came back around midnight.

My neighbour called the police. Lodged a complaint about noise pollution."

Shaking his head, Taylor said, "I'll go across to the coffee shop. Usual latte, Luke?"

The weary bass player nodded.

"Ellen?"

"Americano. No milk. No sugar."

"Anything else?" checked Taylor as he headed for the door.

"Bring me a bagel. Blueberry if they have it," said Luke through another yawn.

As the door closed behind Taylor, Luke returned to the piece he'd been working on. Immediately, Ellen recognized that he was working on the last track.

"How far did you get overnight?" she asked curiously when he paused to note down the section he had just played.

"This is the last one."

"Fast work," Ellen observed.

"No distractions. Nothing better to do last night. Took my mind off things. Let me forget my shit for a while," replied Luke, staring down at his bass. "Felt I owed it to you guys too. I've been a bit of a dick lately. Someone made me see that."

"Your uncle?" The question was out before Ellen realized what she'd said.

Luke stared intently at her for a moment or two, as if judging whether to trust her or not, then he nodded, "Garrett called a few times over the weekend. Ripped me a new arsehole. Told me a few home truths. Threatened to come over here. He won't though. He won't leave his partner to fly over here. He yelled a bit. I hung up," Luke paused then continued, "He called back next day. I ate some humble pie. We talked. Really talked. Made me see things a bit clearer."

"And did it help?"

Luke nodded, "For now. Till next time. There's always a next time. I like to party, princess, and I party hard if you get my meaning."

"I'm not much of a party animal," confessed Ellen quietly. "But I get it. I hear you."

"We all need to let our hair down, princess," he said with a wink. "Now, do you want to help me here? I need your input."

As he crossed the street on his way back to the church, Taylor spotted Cal and Jack walking towards him.

"Hope one of them's mine," shouted Cal.

"Sorry," called back Taylor. "Didn't know when you guys would get here."

"I'll make one when we get in," said Jack as they reached the rusty wrought iron gate.

"No coffee. Luke finished it. He's been here all night working up those bass tracks."

"Luke? Working all night?" quizzed Jack. "You sure?"

Taylor nodded, "And he's come up with the goods on all three songs by the sounds of it."

"Ok," began Cal as they entered the church. "Who stole our Luke?"

Gentle strains of piano music greeted them as they entered the rehearsal room. None of them recognised the song; all of them were astonished to see Ellen and Luke sitting side by side at the piano playing together.

"Sounding sweet," commented Jack with a nod of approval. "New ballad?"

"Might be," replied Ellen getting to her feet. "A bit early to tell."

"Found yourself a right-hand man then?" quipped Cal as he handed her a coffee.

"For now," said the shy songstress with a giggle.

"Right, boys and girl," stated Jack firmly. "We need to draw up a final set for Friday night. Nine songs, maybe ten, depending on length."

"The three new ones for definite," said Taylor. "Kashmir, the three older songs and two more covers."

Taking notes on his phone, Jack typed up the seven song titles, numbering each of them.

"If we leave Kashmir in, we might only need one more. We'll need to check the running time of this," commented the drummer trying to figure out if the eight songs took them over their time limit.

"How about Smoke On The Water?" suggested Taylor. "Or Paint It Black?"

"If we can get enough smoke going for Smoke On The Water, I could disappear into it," mused Ellen. "I kind of like the idea of the "witch" vanishing. Adds an air of mystique."

"Like that," approved Jack with a slow nod of his head. "Right, let's run through this and time it."

With several strategic meetings under his belt, Rocky finally arrived at the rehearsal hall after four. He paused in the tiny hallway to listen, unseen, to After Life practice. Despite only having been together with Ellen for a week, the band were already sounding stronger and tighter as a unit. There was a new edge to their sound that was coming from all of them, not just Ellen. His gut instinct was still telling him that the gamble he'd taken on her was going to pay off. Despite the effects of her injuries, Rocky recognised the vocal talent that she had. Taking a deep breath and deciding to stay quiet about his day's progress, the band's manager opened the door and marched into the rehearsal space.

"Afternoon, boys and girl," he greeted loudly. "Do we have a set ready for me?"

"Yes, sir, we do," called back Luke with a grin. "We have a fucking awesome set for you."

Ellen

As eight o'clock approached, The Garage was filling up nicely. Backstage, After Life were all crammed into one sparse dressing room. A few minutes earlier, Lizzy had escorted Ellen through to the small ladies' room and helped her into her witch garb. The young vocalist was quiet and, despite the older woman's best efforts to engage her in conversation, withdrawn. Once back in the dressing room, she had sat quietly in a corner playing with her phone. Both Taylor and Cal were sitting on a beaten-up old couch playing their guitars softly. With a mutter, Jack had dashed out, saying he was going to check on his kit, convinced that he hadn't set it up right. Like Ellen, Luke sat playing with his phone, playing a game with a bottle of Jack Daniels at his side.

"Time to make a move," declared Rocky shortly before eight. "Show time."

Taking one long chug on the bourbon bottle, Luke was first to the door, "Come on, Princess, let's show these fuckers."

"Luke," growled Rocky, his eyes blazing with anger. "By the book tonight. You don't know who's out there."

"Yes, boss," said Luke with a cocky salute to the band's manager.

As the band stood in the wings, the house lights dimmed, the PA tape was silenced and the enthusiastic crowd cheered. Keeping the lights low and red, Jack led the band out onto the stage, leaving Ellen biding her time just out of sight. The smoke machine swathed the stage in a low mist. Clear as a bell, Ellen's Latin chant rang out over the room as she slowly emerged on stage, fully cloaked with her hood up, disguising her features. Her last, long note rang out, the lights pulsed, the band came in heavy on the bass and Ellen powered into the opening verse of Swirling Mists. As she had in rehearsal, she kept her voice low and husky but there was a newfound strength to her tone. In front of her, she could see she already had the Time March fans on side. Seeing their reaction settled her nerves. By the time the song returned to its Gregorian chant, her earlier nerves were long gone.

While the crowd cheered After Life's set opener, Ellen tossed back her hood to reveal her long platinum blonde hair and Eye of Horus eye patch. With barely a pause for breath, After Life threw themselves into their second song, Rats.

A few minutes later, at the end of the song, Ellen stepped forward to the edge of the stage. Crouching down and with an evil hiss to her voice, called out, "Welcome to the After Life, lovely people of London. This next song is City Of Bones And Heartache."

Over at the bar, Rocky was deep in conversation with a tall, cultured gentleman, who had his gaze permanently fixed on the stage. Beside him, Lizzy was keeping a watchful eye on Ellen, relieved to see the young chanteuse in control. Around them, the venue had almost reached capacity. As she glanced along the length of the bar, Lizzy spotted a man in his early fifties with platinum blonde hair. His features were vaguely familiar to her and she watched as he watched After Life out on stage. He never took his eyes off Ellen. Excusing herself, Lizzy made her way over to him.

"Hello," she greeted him with a smile. "Call it a hunch but are you Ellen's dad?"

"Eh.....yes," replied the man, looking startled.

"I thought so. I'm Lizzy. Rocky's wife. She's staying with us," explained Lizzy, shouting to be heard over the band. "She didn't think you were coming tonight."

"I know," he replied. "My wife refused to come. She was scared to be here in case it didn't go so well. I couldn't not be here."

"I understand."

"She's incredible, isn't she?" he said proudly. "After all she's been through."

"She certainly is," agreed Lizzy with a smile. "Come over and stand with us. Meet my husband. He'll be glad to see you're here."

Together, they made their way back along the bar to where Rocky and the mystery gentleman were still deep in conversation.

Out on stage, After Life had the audience fully on side. Using the voluminous fabric of her cloak to dramatic effect, Ellen was reigning supreme. With each song her confidence soared. It was beginning to get hot in the cloak but Ellen knew there were only two songs to go. Pausing to grab a mouthful of water, she turned back to the crowd.

"Thank you," she said humbly. "We've two songs left before the awesome Time March take over."

A deafening cheer interrupted her and Ellen paused until the noise died down a little.

"London, we'll leave you with two classic rock songs," she said with a smile. "Lizzy, this is for you. Kashmir!"

Pulling her cloak round her, Ellen listened for her cue. Backstage she'd playfully teased Luke about not fluffing it. Now, she was worried she'd let them all down.

"Oh, let the sun beat down upon my face."

Her voice rang clear and true across the room.

Over at the bar, Lizzy nudged Ellen's father, "She's fabulous! You must be so proud."

With unshed tears in his eyes, he said, "I am. I wish her mother was here to see this. My little girl...."

"Next time," replied Lizzy softly, laying a hand on his arm.

As planned, After Life ended their set with a cover of Deep Purple's Smoke On The Water. While the band played, two smoke machines billowed out from either side of the stage. Positioned either side of Ellen, Taylor and Cal were helping out with backing vocals on the chorus.

"No matter what we get out of this, I know, I know we'll never forget," sang Ellen as the smoke swirled around her.

Immediately before the boys led the final chorus, there was a flash of white light and Ellen disappeared from view.

The crowd went wild as After Life's set ended, loving Ellen's disappearing trick. Simple but effective.

With waves to the audience, the boys from After Life left the stage.

Time March were three songs into their headlining set before After Life joined their manager at the bar. As they threaded their way through the crowd, Ellen was deep in conversation with Cal and Taylor. The two guitarists were sub-consciously shielding her from being bumped by the crowd, protecting her vulnerable side. She had her leather jacket draped over her shoulder to disguise her arm from prying eyes and had replaced the eye patch with her usual round tinted glasses. When they finally reached the bar, Rocky shouted the band over to join him.

"Boys and girl, meet Jason Russell from JR Management," introduced Rocky loudly, shouting to be heard over Time March. "Mr Russell here has just agreed to add After Life to the books of JR Management."

"Wow!" gasped Taylor, lost for words.

"For real?" quizzed Cal, staring at Rocky.

"For real," said Jason in a crisp, public school boy accent. "We can discuss things over lunch on Monday. I have big plans for you."

"Recording plans?" pressed Luke, inwardly praying that they would finally get the chance to record their debut album.

"Most definitely, Mr Court," replied Jason formally. "Stunning performance, Miss Lloyd. Love the image. Clever."

"Thank you," said Ellen, feeling her cheeks flush at the compliment.

"Ellen," called Lizzy from behind her. "You've a visitor."

Immediately, Ellen whirled round and found herself face to face with her father.

"Dad!" she cried as he reached out to hug her. "I didn't know you were coming!"

"I wanted to surprise you, honey," he replied as he held her in his arms.

"Where's mum?"

"I'm sorry, Ellen. She wouldn't come. I think she was scared to," confessed her father.

"Scared I'd freeze?"

"Something like that, honey," he said softly. "You were incredible out there."

"Thanks, Dad," she said, inwardly disappointed that her mother hadn't made the effort to come along too. "Are you going to buy me a drink then I'll introduce you to the boys?"

Before her father could reach for his wallet, Taylor passed her a glass of red wine.

"Dad, this is Taylor," she said as she accepted the glass. "Tailz stays with Rocky and Lizzy too."

"Nice to meet you," greeted Taylor, shaking her dad's hand. "Can I buy you a drink, Mr Lloyd?"

"Just a coke, please. I'm driving," replied Ellen's father. "And it's Tim."

While Taylor fetched the drinks, Ellen introduced her dad to the other members of After Life. When he realized that Luke was related to Garrett Court, he started to quiz him about his famous uncle. Spying that the bass player was uncomfortable with the whole conversation, Ellen suggested that she and her dad move closer to the front of the venue to watch the remaining portion of Time March's set.

Midnight had come and gone before After Life were all packed up and ready to head home. Their roadie cum guitar tech, Michael, had loaded all the gear into the back of the van with help from Jack and Ellen's father. She smiled as her dad laboured beside the band, obviously enjoying feeling involved.

"Will you come back to the house with us?" invited Ellen as Michael slammed the doors closed behind them.

"Sorry, honey," apologized her dad. "I need to head home. It's a long drive and I have work tomorrow. Next time."

Nodding, Ellen smiled, "I'm glad you came."

"Me too," he said, kissing her on the forehead. "Stay safe and I'll see you soon."

"Night, Dad."

Around her the house was quiet and dark. From further down the hallway, Ellen could hear Rocky snoring loudly. As she strained her ears, she thought she could hear music, gentle guitar music. Sleep was eluding her, despite the fact that she'd been exhausted by the time they had arrived back at the house. In her mind, she replayed the show, going over each song with a fine-toothed comb. Considering it was her first stage performance for five years, Ellen was pleased with herself. The cloaked disguise had proved to be an inspired way to mask her true body image and it had also served as a comforting layer.

Smiling in the dark, Ellen was pleased that her dad had been able to witness her return. He'd always been her number one fan. It had hurt her feelings that her mother hadn't made the effort to be there too. Thinking back to past gigs, her mother had missed more than she'd attended.

The strains of guitar music coming from across the hall shattered her daydream.

It sounded like she wasn't the only member of After Life struggling to sleep.

On impulse, Ellen slipped out of bed, pulled on her discarded hoodie and tip toed across the hall to Taylor's room. A tell-tale strip of light shone out from below his closed door. Gently, she knocked the door. She listened as she heard him moving about and muttering. Her housemate opened the door, stripped to the waist with his jeans undone.

"Hi," she said, her voice still husky after the show. "I heard you playing. Can't you sleep either?"

"No," confessed Tailz with a smile. "I'm still buzzing after the show and the whole JR Management deal."

"Fancy some cocoa?" suggested Ellen, hoping he'd say yes.

"My mum's answer to everything," mused Taylor wistfully. "Why not."

Quietly, they made their way down to the kitchen and while Ellen found some mugs and the jar of cocoa, Taylor filled the kettle. When it boiled, he watched as she carefully filled both mugs then stirred them vigorously.

"Thanks," said the band's guitarist as she passed him his mug.

"You're welcome," replied Ellen, taking a seat at the end of the table. "It's a sad day when even I can't make a mug of cocoa."

"Was it hard adjusting?" The question was out before he'd really thought it through and Taylor felt himself flush with embarrassment.

"It took a long time," admitted Ellen sadly, staring down into her mug. "Accepting my limitations was harder. Learning or re-learning to do simple tasks was a challenge. Accepting that I can't do some things was harder. Not being able to play piano or guitar maybe the hardest of all."

Deciding to risk another question, Taylor asked, "Did the doctors not provide you with a prosthetic?"

Ellen nodded, "Several and I hated them all." She paused then added, "They told me it would be difficult to adjust to wearing one because of the burn damage to the rest of my arm. The scarred skin is hyper-sensitive, especially to pressure. That day you bumped into me at the station and grabbed my arm to stop me from falling, your fingers hurt like hell. I felt them burning into me through my jacket. Later, there were bruises almost on my skin. I could see exactly where you'd touched me."

"I'm sorry. I never knew," apologized Taylor awkwardly.

"No need to apologise, Tailz. You weren't to know. I'm just saying to explain how sensitive the skin is. The suction style prosthetics I tried made wearing them agony. They aggravated the skin. It got really nasty for a while. After about two years, I gave up. There's quite a collection of them in my parent's attic."

In an attempt to move their conversation onto safer ground, Taylor said, "Your dad seems like a nice guy."

Smiling, Ellen said, "He is. I'm glad he was there. Glad he got to meet everyone."

"Looked like he enjoyed seeing Time March too."

"Dad loves his music," she revealed. "We went to a lot of gigs together when I was younger. It was our time together. He still goes when he can but my mum isn't really into it. She was always more of a pop fan than a rock fan. More Radio Two than the rock radio stations."

"Pity she couldn't be there for you too."

"Her choice," muttered Ellen into her mug. "After Thailand, she wanted me to give up on music. Wanted me to go to college then get a "nice" job. I refused. She's very controlling. Tries to dominate people."

"Whereas, your dad lets you be you?"

"Exactly."

"My mum was the one who believed in me," revealed Taylor sadly. "Wish she was here to see us now. I can just picture her with your dad on the rail watching us."

With a giggle, Ellen added, "Both wearing After Life t-shirts."

Life for the band became a whirlwind of meetings and business lunches over the next two weeks. At their initial meeting with Jason Russell, he set a packed schedule for them to ensure that they met all the right people and established reliable key contacts. Within a week, they had new lawyers and accountants and, most importantly to them, had been booked into a recording studio to record their debut album. In the background, Rocky had been networking and had booked After Life three more shows in and around London and, at the end of the two weeks, secured them a support slot on a ten date UK tour with the Australian band Bodimead. Now that the wheels were in motion, the After Life machine was gathering momentum.

On the eve of their next show, Rocky called a band summit at the house. The band were under strict orders to be there at four o'clock sharp. After a brief morning rehearsal at the church hall, they'd all gone their separate ways, promising Rocky that they wouldn't be late.

For once, all of them were true to their word and by four o'clock were all seated round Lizzy's kitchen table with a coffee and a copy of the After Life itinerary for the month of April in front of them.

"Right, boys and girl," began their manager formally. "How's everyone feeling about tomorrow night? First headline show."

"We're ready," said Ellen calmly as she read over the itinerary in front of her.

"We sure are," agreed Cal with a grin. "Best set we've ever pulled together."

"Ninety minutes of magic," added Taylor with a wink.

"Glad to hear it," stated Rocky. "And you get to do it all again next week. Two nights in a row. 12th is the upstairs room back at The Garage and 13th is The Half Moon in Putney."

"Bring it on," challenged Luke bluntly. "When do we head out with Bodimead?"

"Monday 22nd," replied Rocky. "Still a few logistics to work out there. That run ends in Wales on the Bank Holiday weekend. Your last show with Bodimead is on the Saturday then we've booked you a slot at the Wales Open Air Festival for the Sunday. It's not the main stage. You're in one of the marquees. Jason's done a deal with the sponsors to get you on the bill around six thirty for ninety minutes."

"Is that the marquee for newcomers?" asked Ellen. "Isn't it sponsored by a magazine?"

"That's correct."

"I played it a long time ago with Good Times," she revealed softly.

"Is it any good as a venue?" quizzed Luke sharply.

"It's a big tent or at least it was six years ago. Holds about a thousand, maybe more. It used to attract a high-profile audience," explained Ellen, trying to recall the details of her previous visit to Wales.

"Still does. A lot of the bigger acts scout there for their support acts," added Rocky. "You get a few days off after Wales but you're expected back in London on 13th May. That's when the real work starts. Jason's booked you into the studio from then until 15th June. Five weeks to get that debut album in the can."

"Easy," said Jack calmly. "We can get it recorded in five weeks no sweat."

"Jason wants fourteen songs, all originals," revealed Rocky. "At the last count, I think you guys had about eight. You've a few more to come up with."

"We've plenty of time," said Taylor calmly. "I've a few ideas lurking about."

"Same here," said Luke. "And what about you, princess? Any more gems up your sleeve?"

"A few possibilities."

"Fine. As long as between you there are fourteen songs ready to go on that board when you get in the studio," stated Rocky firmly. "I'm still working with Jason to get shows booked for the second half of the year. He's got a few bands heading into Europe so there's a chance of some more support slots if this tour goes well."

"It's looking good, isn't it?" mused Jack, reading over the schedule in front of him.

"We've definitely turned a corner. Get the next few weeks right and, yes, I'd say things will be looking pretty good," agreed Rocky.

Sleep refused to come as Taylor lay staring up at the ceiling. A quick glance at his phone informed him it was 2:37am. With a sigh, he rolled over onto his side, hoping a change of position would encourage sleep. Drawing his knees up towards his chest, he listened to the sounds of the house around him. From outside, he heard a cat yowling; from across the hallway, he could hear singing. Sitting up, he listened again. He wasn't imagining it. He could definitely hear someone singing. Quietly, he crept out of bed and into the hall. A strip of light shone from under Ellen's door.

Avoiding the creaking floorboard just outside his door, Taylor tip toed across the hall and listened outside her closed door. For the next few minutes, he stood there listening to Ellen working at the new lyrics. Her voice was soft, almost husky and, even through the closed door, sounded soothing. The song sounded like a lullaby. As he listened, Taylor could visualize the music in his mind and found his hands forming the chords and picking out the melody line on an invisible set of strings.

Taking a deep breath, he knocked on the door.

"Yes?" called Ellen softly, a panicky edge to her voice.

"Ellen, it's me," said Taylor quietly. "Can I come in?"

There was silence for a few moments and the guitarist thought she was about to refuse but then Ellen called back, "Of course."

Trying not to make a noise and disturb Rocky and Lizzy, who slept at the end of the hallway, Taylor opened the door and slipped into the room. Only the small bedside lamp was lit and Ellen was sitting cross-legged on the bed, wearing just a baggy Led Zeppelin t-shirt. In front of her was a well-thumbed leather-bound journal and a chewed pen.

"Feeling creative?" quizzed Taylor, closing the door behind him, suddenly conscious that he was only wearing his lounge pants.

"I couldn't sleep. Kept over-thinking a few things. Was reflecting on stuff then the lyrics started to come through," she explained, her voice barely above a whisper.

"Confession," said Taylor, coming over to sit on the bed beside her. "I was listening out in the hall. I think I might have some music to go with that. A melody line too. Want to hear it?"

"It's a bit late to play it through, is it not?"

"Not if we're quiet," said Taylor smiling at her. "Give me a minute and I'll be back with Lou Lou."

"Who?" asked Ellen curiously.

Blushing, Taylor confessed, "My acoustic guitar. Lou Lou."

A few moments later, Taylor returned with his guitar and sat down, cross legged at the end of the bed.

"How does this sound?" he said with a smile as he began to play the music that had been playing in his mind.

Chewing on the end of the pen, Ellen sat and listened as her bandmate played a beautifully soft melody. He had captured the essence of the song that she had heard in her head. With a smile, she read over her newly penned lyrics as he played. She made a few tweaks as Taylor finished the piece.

"Well?" he asked, looking all too like a little boy seeking approval.

"Perfection," replied Ellen softly. "I just need to change a couple of the words around."

"Want to run through it together?" suggested Taylor as he brought the guitar back into tune.

"Please," said Ellen, shuffling further down the bed to be closer to him.

Both of them were sitting cross legged on the narrow bed facing each other, their knees almost touching. In the dim light, Taylor barely noticed that Ellen wasn't wearing her glasses, didn't notice her un-seeing eye. All he saw was a fragile songbird.

Keeping his playing muted, he began the song again from the top. The young guitarist had to really concentrate on his playing as he felt himself being drawn into Ellen's lyrics. It was a song about betrayal, about being let down. A tale of someone's lack of belief in the person. The pain and hurt in her vocal tore at his heart. He could feel his own emotions slipping as his mind wandered to thoughts of his mum.

When the song was finished, Ellen sat staring down into her lap.

On impulse, Taylor reached forward and brushed a kiss on her pale cheek.

"That was beautiful. Magical," he whispered as he kissed her cheek again.

"Tailz," began Ellen, her voice warm and husky.

The rest of her words were lost as the guitarist's lips met hers. With great tenderness, he began to kiss her. He felt her hesitate for a second before she responded.

Laying his guitar aside, Taylor drew her towards him as he delivered feathery kisses along her jawline and down her neck.

Almost with relief, he felt her put her arm around him and pull him closer to her.

Gently, Taylor nibbled her earlobe before kissing the sensitive area just behind her ear. His hand strayed towards her t-shirt. Instantly, he felt her flinch and go tense.

"No," she whispered as their lips met once more.

Taylor withdrew his hand and felt her relax once more.

"Is this a good idea?" asked Ellen as she leant against his bare chest a short while later.

"I've no idea," confessed Taylor as he twisted a strand of her long blonde hair round his fingers.

"Let's take it slowly," she suggested softly. "There's certain things I don't think I'm ready for."

"Like what?" asked Taylor, immediately regretting the question.

"Like you touching or seeing what's under this t-shirt," replied Ellen. "No one's touched me since…. well…..you know. This is going to take time." She paused. "And patience. I don't know how to do this anymore. It's a long time since I've allowed myself to feel anything for anyone."

"I hear you," said Taylor, kissing the top of her head. "Now, we both need to get some sleep. I'm going back to my room before I say or do something we both regret in the morning."

With a final tender kiss, he slipped off the bed, lifted his guitar and left the room, closing the door carefully behind him.

Alone in the dark, Ellen lay staring up at the ceiling. A quick check of her phone informed her it was 4:07am. Sleep was refusing to come. With a sigh, she rolled onto her side and drew her knees up towards her chest. She could still detect the faint aroma of Taylor's deodorant in the air. Running her tongue over her lips, she smiled. Kissing Taylor had felt good. Deep inside her, Ellen could feel a tiny spark of warmth beginning to glow. After all she'd been through, could she allow herself to get close to anyone? To Taylor? The first light of dawn was streaking the sky before she finally fell asleep.

Ellen

Sound check in the small room at the O2 Academy Islington ran smoothly. As they debated the final set list, Taylor sat on top of a transport case playing the melody he had worked out overnight with Ellen. Both of them had acted normally all day, taking care not to draw attention to themselves, but Jack had noted the way his bandmate was watching Ellen, allowing his gaze to linger a little longer than was necessary.

"Hey, what's that?" quizzed Luke, picking up on the new song.

"Just something Ellen and I were playing around with last night," replied Taylor as he continued to play.

"Is it finished?" pressed Luke.

"More or less," said Ellen with a glance towards Taylor. "We kind of planned it as an acoustic number. Maybe a duet. Could be a mid-set interlude."

"Let's hear it," suggested Cal, curious to hear the new song in its entirety.

Sitting side by side on the large transport case, Ellen and Taylor debuted the new ballad for the rest of After Life. Deliberately, Ellen kept her voice soft, adding a warmth to the song that only served to heighten the emotions she was trying to convey. To her left, Taylor was playing with a depth of passion that his bandmates had rarely seen.

"Wow," said Luke as the last lingering notes faded out. "Speechless. That's……"

"It's stunning!" interrupted Jack, feeling a lump forming in his throat. "A masterpiece."

"Genius," declared Cal. "Can you two play it tonight?"

"I don't know," began Taylor, glancing at Ellen. "We only worked on it last night. Well, early this morning."

"Does it have a title?" quizzed Luke bluntly.

"Eh….not yet," confessed Taylor. "Unless Ellen's named it."

"Well, I scribbled Lou Lou At 3am on the page in my lyrics book," admitted Ellen with a shy giggle.

"Works for me," agreed Taylor, thinking back to 3am that

morning.

"Who's Lou Lou?" asked Luke, looking confused.

"His guitar!" laughed Cal. "Love it!

"Guess we'd better work Lou Lou into the set," acknowledged Taylor.

"Opening encore song," suggested Jack. "Just the two of you."

"I'm not sure," began Ellen, sounding nervous.

"No arguments, princess," stated Luke. "Lou Lou At 3am opens the encore tonight."

"If you insist," she relented with a sigh. "Taylor, we need to work on this."

After Life were due out on stage at nine and, by five minutes to, were all gathered at the side of the stage, just out of sight of the crowd. Two local bands had opened for them as the venue had filled up. The room wasn't full but Jack judged that there had to be close to two hundred music fans out there.

With the hood of her cloak pulled up so that it hid most of her face, Ellen stood off to the side lost in her own thoughts.

"Penny for them?" said Taylor as he appeared beside her.

From under her hood, she smiled up at him before saying, "My dad just messaged me. My mother's out there."

"Is that good or bad?"

"Honestly," sighed Ellen, looking nervous. "I don't know."

"Just go out there and be yourself. Give it your all. When did she last hear you sing?"

"Over five years ago and she wasn't exactly a fan then."

Before they could continue their conversation, Rocky called them together with his standard, "Show time, boys and girl."

Discretely, Taylor brushed a kiss on Ellen's cheek as he turned to head out onto the stage.

With the houselights dimmed down low and the stage in darkness, from the safety of the wings, Ellen began her Gregorian Latin chant. As the green lights lit up the stage and the smoke machine created a layer of mist, Ellen glided out smoothly, still chanting. She held the last note just a fraction longer than usual then there was a flash of white light and the rest of the band launched into the powerful, heavy rhythm of Swirling Mists. Still hidden in her hood, Ellen commanded the stage as she morphed into After Life's rock queen. As she sang to the crowd down at the corner of the stage, she spotted her parents standing at the rail, Lizzy right beside them. With a small nod to acknowledge she'd seen them, she returned to the centre of the stage to finish the final verse. As the song returned to a reprise of the Latin chant, Ellen walked back towards Jack on drums. A single spotlight was trained on her as the rest of the stage was plunged into darkness.

The fans in the room loved the dramatic opening and showed their appreciation by cheering wildly as the last Latin notes rang out clear and long.

Despite extending their set to headline this show, After Life stuck with what was becoming their standard opening trio. Rats followed Swirling Mists then they began City Of Bones And Heartache. In a change to the norm, Ellen kept her hood up for all three songs.

Eventually, at the end of City Of Bones, she threw the hood off and laughed loudly.

"Beautiful people of Islington, welcome to the After Life," she hissed as she crouched down at the front of the stage. "This next song is Cyclone."

An hour later, After Life brought the main body of their set to a close with a spectacular rendition of Kashmir. Allowing Luke a moment in the spotlight, Ellen stood close to him as she sang the final chorus then crouched down in the folds of her cloak at his feet while he, along with the others, brought the song home to its conclusion.

"Thank you," called out Ellen, getting to her feet. "Islington, you've been fucking fantastic tonight!"

In the wings, Rocky had an open bottle of water ready for her. He could see the heat was starting to take its toll on her. The effort to perform a longer set fully cloaked hadn't been factored into the equation and he was worried that it would prove to be too much for Ellen.

"You ok?" he asked warmly. "It's hot as hell in here."

"I'm good," she said as she drank deeply from the bottle. "Hot. Sweaty but fine. Three songs to go. I've got this, Rocky."

"You sure?"

"I'm sure," she promised him. "Plus, I get to sit down for the first one."

A transport case had been wheeled on stage in readiness for the encore. Acoustic guitar in hand, Taylor led Ellen back out onto the stage to a huge cheer from the crowd. Carefully, picking up her microphone first, Ellen took a seat on the case.

"Folks, are you ready for something brand new?" she asked with an anxious glance at Taylor.

A loud roar of "Yeah!" came straight back at her.

"This one is so new that the ink's still wet on the lyrics," joked Ellen. "This is Lou Lou At 3am."

Just as she had in sound check, Ellen kept her voice soft and husky, the warmth of it adding emotion to the ballad. Together, both members of After Life poured everything they had into the song. Through the tone of her vocal, Ellen portrayed the pain of betrayal to perfection. Taylor's subtle guitar complimented it beautifully. When the song ended, the audience went wild, instantly falling in love with the newest addition to the set.

"Thank you," said Ellen, standing up to allow Taylor to push the transport case off to the side. "Are we ok to play two more for you?"

The responding cheer said that the crowd were ready for at least two more.

"Phoenix In The Mirror!" announced Ellen as the rest of the band returned to the stage.

All too soon, After Life found themselves playing the closing section of Smoke On The Water. As was becoming the norm, Taylor and Cal flanked Ellen as she sang the final verse. Smoke was billowing round them from all sides. Just before the two guitarists led the final chorus, there was a flash of light and Ellen vanished.

As soon as she was safely off stage, Ellen felt the effects of the intense heat wash through her. She staggered slightly before flopping down onto the discarded transport case that they'd used for Lou Lou At 3am. The heat of the stage lights and the exertions of her first full length set since her accident had taken their toll on her. After Life's fragile songbird was physically exhausted.

She was sitting slumped against the wall, relishing in the chill from the brickwork when the rest of the band came off stage.

"Ellen!" gasped Taylor when he saw her. "You ok, my lovely?"

The guitarist was on his knees in front of her before she could reply.

Wearily, she opened her eyes and nodded, "Just worn out. And hot."

"Let's get this cloak off you," suggested Taylor, unfastening the catch at her throat.

"Not here," she protested feebly. "Please."

"Someone fetch her a juice," ordered Taylor sharply.

In a few moments, Rocky was beside him with a bottle of Lucozade. When he saw how fragile Ellen looked, the band's manager shooed the rest of After Life back to the dressing room to give her more space.

"Ellen, you alright?" asked Rocky warmly. "Do you need me to fetch the first aid guy?"

Taking a drink of the cold, sweet juice, Ellen shook her head. "I just need a few minutes. Let me sit here with this. I'll be fine."

"You sure?" asked Taylor softly. "You're shaking."

"Tailz, I'm exhausted," she confessed quietly. "That set took it out of me. All of it. Plus, this cloak is so hot."

"There's no one else here now. Slip it off for a few minutes. You'll cool down quicker," suggested the guitarist, reaching to slide if off her left shoulder. As he leaned in towards her, he whispered, "Don't worry. I'll be discrete."

"Thank you," whispered Ellen with a smile.

"Taylor, you ok to sit here with her?" checked Rocky. "I need to see to the gear with Michael."

Taylor nodded as he watched Ellen slowly sipping the juice.

While Michael and Jack, under the supervision of Rocky, packed up the band's gear, Taylor sat beside Ellen. Gradually, she began to recover and, as she drained the last of the juice from the bottle, she smiled at him.

"Thanks for staying with me."

"No need to thank me. You feeling better?"

Ellen nodded. "That's the longest I've played since before Thailand. I just over did it."

"Call it a hunch, but it's more than your arm that's scarred isn't it?" quizzed Taylor, his concern evident in his voice.

With a tear in her eye, Ellen nodded, "My lungs were pretty scorched. I've also a lot of scarring to my ribcage. It restricts my breathing a bit. The doctors warned me when I got back to England that I might have issues singing. I vowed to prove them wrong."

"You've certainly done that," acknowledged Taylor, grinning at her. "Now, do you feel up to going through to get changed? Your folks will be wondering where you are."

By the time Ellen had changed out of her stage clothes and downed another bottle of juice, she was feeling more human again. When she wandered through to the small dressing room, the rest of the band were nowhere to be seen. In her pocket, her phone buzzed. It was a message from Taylor, "Enjoying a pint with your dad. There's a wine waiting for you. Tailz."

Most of the fans had left the venue, but a few were still milling about, hoping to meet the band. As she crossed the room to the bar, Ellen was approached by a few of them for photos and autographs. Calmly, she spent a few moments with each person before politely excusing herself, saying she had family waiting. Her dad was the first to greet her, embracing her warmly and holding her tight.

"That was more amazing than last time, princess," he said proudly. "Everyone's been talking about that new ballad too."

"Thanks, Dad. We literally wrote it last night."

Her mother stepped forward, interrupting them.

"Well?" asked Ellen as she hugged her mother awkwardly. "Still think I can't do it?"

"Oh, Ellen, you were incredible out there!" exclaimed her mother. "But do you need to hide under that horrible cloak? It makes you look like a crazed witch. And your language!"

"All part of the act," replied Ellen. "Plus, it hides a multitude of sins."

"Yes, I suppose it does," acknowledged her mother. "You don't want to scare off your audience before they've heard you. It's not a freak show after all."

"Mother!" exclaimed Ellen sharply. "Subtle as ever!"

Choosing this as the perfect moment to pass her the waiting wine, Taylor said, "We love the hooded priestess look. It adds to the mystique on stage, Mrs Lloyd. Plus, personally, I'd hate to see Ellen feeling self-conscious out there."

"I didn't mean...." began Ellen's mother.

"Oh, you did!" snapped Ellen bitterly. "Voice overs and session work you said. Something in a chorus line. Something out of sight!"

"Ellen!" shrieked her mother.

"Save it, mother," hissed Ellen angrily. She downed her glass of wine in one then turned to her dad. "I'm sorry, Dad. I'll talk to you later."

Before anyone could say anything else, the songstress stormed across the room, heading straight for the exit. Her hurt and anger clear for all to see.

When they arrived back at the house, Ellen fled upstairs, declining Lizzy's offer of a late supper.

As he opened his bedroom door an hour later, Taylor was surprised to find the light on and even more surprised to find Ellen sitting on his bed.

"I thought you'd be fast asleep," he said, secretly pleased that she wasn't. "This is a pleasant surprise."

"I wanted to apologise for my outburst earlier," explained Ellen quietly, her voice still a little husky after the show.

"You've nothing to apologise for. I get it."

"Do you?" she asked, looking up at him.

"I think so," answered Taylor, sitting down beside her. "When you sang Lou Lou to me last night, I thought it was about an ex-boyfriend that had betrayed you. Someone who had dumped you. I'm guessing now the song's about your mum. Am I right?"

Ellen nodded as a single tear rolled down her pale cheek, "Sometimes I think she wishes I had died in Thailand."

"That's a tad harsh."

"It's the truth," sighed Ellen with a heavy heart. "Having a burned freak for a daughter is bad for her social image."

"You're not a freak," stated Taylor, putting his arm around her. "You're one of the most incredible people I've met. You're an inspiration."

"You're either biased or drunk," accused Ellen with a wistful smile. "I was never that close to her. She was always so disapproving of my taste in clothes, music, boys. My taste in everything. After Thailand, she could barely look at me for months. My dad was the one who cared for me. Dressed my burns. Encouraged me. She tries and I know she loves me but she wasn't there when I needed her most. It was dad who flew out to Thailand the day after the explosion. He came on his own. She didn't join him for two weeks and, even then, only stayed for a few days."

"Everyone copes differently with things like that," defended Taylor quietly. "I didn't react well at first when my mum was diagnosed. I blamed her for getting cancer. Blamed her as though she'd done it deliberately. My sister and my Nana talked me round. I'm happy I made my peace with her before the end. Got to spend some quality time with her before it was too late."

He paused for a moment, as if lost in a memory, then continued, "I went home not long before Christmas for a few days. She wasn't too sick then. The weather was great. Sunny, cold, crisp, winter days. When she felt strong enough, we'd go for a walk on the beach. There's a special cove near the house. I'll show you it one day. We'd go there. Skim stones. Light a fire and watch the waves. We'd talk. She'd listen. I'll never get that back."

"I'm sorry," whispered Ellen. "You must miss her."

"Every day," confessed the guitarist as Ellen laid her weary head on his chest. "She'd have loved you. I wish you could've met her."

"I bet she'd have been so proud of you if she could see where the band's heading."

"You're not wrong there," agreed Taylor with a yawn. "We played a show in Exeter about eighteen months ago. As close to home as I've ever played with After Life. She was centre front all night, dancing away. My sister was right beside her. You'll like Jen. She's like my mum was. A free spirit."

"Maybe we should ask Rocky to look for opportunities for us down that direction," suggested Ellen, snuggling into his warmth.

"Maybe."

They sat in silence for a few minutes, each lost in their own thoughts. As Taylor felt Ellen relax against him, he realized that she had fallen asleep. Gently, he ran her long, silky, blonde hair through his fingers and sighed. Asleep, she looked pale and fragile in his arms. He deliberated whether to waken her and guide her back to her own room then decided against it. Carefully, he moved to allow her to lie down on top of the duvet. There was a spare duvet in the eaves cupboard so Taylor fetched it and spread it over her to keep her warm. His sleeping bag lay in a corner. Quickly, he hauled it from its tight-fitting bag and slipped inside, curling up on the floor between the bed and the radiator.

When Taylor awoke in the morning, the bed was empty.

Rain was pelting down as hard as it was able to as After Life arrived at the O2 Academy in Oxford for the first night of the Bodimead tour. Scheduling conflicts meant that they hadn't actually met the headliners, with all the arrangements having been made by phone and email. As Ellen walked into the empty venue, the Australian band were just finalizing their set up ahead of their soundcheck. Over the past few weeks, she had familiarized herself with the band's music. Their sound was loud and raw, in your face, hard rock. From the You Tube videos she had studied with the rest of After Life, Ellen had noted the energetic stage presence of front man, Flynn, and the flamboyant style of Blake, the drummer.

"G'day!" called out Flynn when he spied After Life approaching the stage. "After Life I assume?"

"Yup," called back Jack. "At your service, sir."

"Even the sheila?"

"Only if you want her to sing," cautioned Rocky bluntly as he clambered up onto the stage. "Ellen's off limits, Flynn."

"Yes, sir," answered the tall muscular Australian. "If you're looking for the boss, he's in the shit house. Ate something bad last night."

"Sure it wasn't too much beer?" quizzed Rocky, recalling how much this band and their manager had drunk each night the last time he had toured with them.

"He might have washed that curry down with one or two," laughed Flynn loudly. "We're just about to kick off up here. Give us about an hour then your boys should be good to set up."

"Fine," agreed Rocky with a nod. "We'll start bringing the gear in so we can get the van parked up."

While the boys worked together to bring the gear in from the van, Ellen stood over at the side watching Bodimead sound check. She swiftly deduced that, while they tried to create almost a caricature Australian loutish image, the five members of the band took their music very seriously. Keeping her focus on Flynn, their vocalist, Ellen studied his routine closely, hoping to learn from him.

"You seen enough, sweetheart?" he called down from the stage towards the end of soundcheck.

"Sorry," replied Ellen shyly. "Was watching and learning."

"You can watch and learn from me any day, beautiful," teased Flynn with a wink.

Blushing, Ellen turned her back on the stage.

"Hey! Wait up!" called Flynn, jumping down to follow her. "I'm sorry. Me and my big mouth. Didn't mean any harm."

"No worries," replied Ellen, avoiding his gaze.

"Cool shades you're wearing," noted the Australian, searching ineptly for something more complimentary to say.

"Thanks," said Ellen softly. "I see the boys have all the gear in. I'd better go and get ready for our own soundcheck, I need to warm up a bit."

"I'll warm you up," offered Flynn as she walked away from him to join the rest of her band.

It was almost six thirty before Michael and the boys from After Life had their gear set up on the stage. As they had placed their cabinets and put Jack's drumkit together, the Bodimead crew had kept a watchful eye on them. Time was tight and they had just finished when the venue doors opened allowing the first rock fans to enter.

The Oxford venue was the smallest one of the tour but it was sold out, making it potentially the biggest crowd After Life had played in front of. In the cramped dressing room, the four guys jostled for space as they got changed into their stage clothes. Leaving them to it, Ellen disappeared to the ladies' room to get dressed. Knowing that Lizzy wouldn't be there to help her with her cloak every night, Ellen had asked the older woman to sew a different fastener to it for her so that she could fasten it herself. In the limited space in the bathroom, Ellen struggled at first but finally managed to secure the cloak. Once she had her eye patch in place, she took a deep breath to steady her nerves and headed back to the dressing room.

"You just missed Flynn," commented Cal as she entered the room.

"Pity," muttered Ellen almost under her breath.

"He left us a case of beer," added Jack, pointing to a slab of cans of a well-known Australian lager. "And a bottle of champagne for you."

Sensing her unease, Taylor whispered, "We can share it later."

With a small smile, Ellen brushed a kiss across his cheek, "Maybe."

A few minutes before eight, Rocky led After Life to the side of the stage. Already the venue was more than half full. There were a few After Life fans along the rail, proudly sporting their After Life t-shirts. Over at the far side, Ellen spotted her dad and smiled when she saw that he too was wearing a band t-shirt.

"It's time, boys and girl," said Rocky calmly. "See you on the other side."

Seconds later, the house lights dimmed and the four boys stepped out to take their positions. Green light swathed the stage as the smoke machines billowed to create a low atmospheric misty layer across the room. Just as she was about to start her Gregorian chant, Ellen spotted Flynn in the shadows watching her. Ignoring him, she let her first Latin phrase ring out into the mist loud and clear. With the hood of her cloak hiding her face, Ellen walked slowly but confidently out on stage. The audience were hanging on her every word, even if they didn't understand the meaning. As the last notes faded out, there was a flash of light, a thunder of drums and the band launched headlong into the main section of Swirling Mists. Keeping her hood up, Ellen prowled the stage menacingly as she stormed through the thunderous vocal. Along the rail, the small group of After Life fans were singing along enthusiastically. Appreciating their passion for the band, Ellen crouched down in front of them for the closing Latin chants, leaving them hanging on her every word.

As she got to her feet, her cloak caught on the edge of one of the wedge-shaped monitors. Before she could grab it, her damaged arm was revealed to the crowd. Pulling the cloak roughly around her, Ellen heard the gasps of revulsion from some of the audience to her right. Swallowing down her emotions, she assumed her position for City of Bones And Heartache, thankful that her hood was still up and shielding her face from prying eyes. In a change to her plan, Ellen kept her hood up at the end of the song and signalled they should move straight into Cyclone.

By the end of the third number, she had regained control of her emotions and dramatically threw back her hood with a blood curdling scream.

"Oxford, how the hell are you?" she shouted to the crowd. By now the venue was more than three quarters full.

A huge cheer echoed back at her.

"We'd like to thank Bodimead for inviting us out with them," continued Ellen sincerely.

Another enormous roar threatened to swallow her introduction to the next song on the set. All that was audible was "Rats."

Half an hour later, as she sat on the transport case beside Taylor for Lou Lou At 3am, Ellen spotted Flynn and the rest of Bodimead at the side of the stage. It briefly crossed her mind to wonder if he'd seen her arm earlier then dismissed the thought as Taylor began the intro to the acoustic ballad. This part of their set was rapidly becoming one of her favourite moments every night. Along the rail, the small group of After Life fans were singing along in harmony to the chorus. Knowing that the Australians were watching, Ellen poured every ounce of emotion that she could muster into her vocals.

When the song ended, she got to her feet and curtseyed to the fans, while Taylor kicked the transport case into the wings.

"Thank you," called out Ellen. "We have two more for you before Bodimead take over. Two rock classics. This is Kashmir!"

In what felt like a matter of seconds, Ellen was singing the final verse of Smoke On The Water, watching for her cue to "disappear". Right on cue, the flash of lights came and she vanished, leaving the fans screaming for more.

The moment she was safely off stage and out of sight of the audience, Rocky was beside her with a cold, glucose drink. After her collapse at the Islington show, he wasn't taking any chances with her and had ensured that a supply of energy drinks was on the rider for every show. As she drank thirstily from the bottle, Flynn sauntered over, "Beaut set."

"Thank you," she replied between mouthfuls.

"Fake stump was a nice touch of gore," he commented then added, "Almost looked real."

Staring straight into his soul, Ellen said coldly, "It is real."

Without another word, she pulled her cloak round her and headed for the dressing room, tears burning in her eyes.

When the rest of the band piled off stage, Taylor scanned the backstage area for Ellen. He was worried when he couldn't immediately see her.

Suddenly, he felt a hand on his shoulder. Whirling round, he found himself face to face with Flynn.

"She's gone back to the dressing room," he said, pointing down the corridor. "I fucked up. Think she's mad at me."

"What did you say to her?" asked Taylor, wholly aware that the muscular Australian in front of him wasn't Ellen's favourite person.

"I thought the arm thing was fake. Made a crass joke about it."

"Shit!"

"Hey, mate, how was I to know?" protested Flynn, actually looking and sounding guilty. "No one told me."

"I'd better find her," sighed Taylor, dreading to think how angry and upset Ellen was. "And to explain, she lost her arm and her eye in a night club explosion in Thailand. She doesn't talk about it much. Goes to great lengths to hide it on and off stage."

"Shit! The eye thing's real too?"

Taylor nodded, "You weren't to know. I'd better go and find her though."

"When you do, tell her she has a fucking awesome voice," said Flynn as Bodimead's manager was trying to attract his attention.

"That would sound better coming from you," replied Taylor before turning on his heel and hurrying away from the stage.

Half an hour later, he finally found Ellen at the band's merchandise table standing with her father. On the stage behind them, Bodimead had the sell-out crowd eating out of the palms of their hands. As he approached them, half a dozen After Life fans crowded round him begging for photos and autographs. Patiently, Taylor obliged then politely excused himself and made his way over to Ellen and her dad.

"Tailz," greeted Tim Lloyd. "Brilliant set. Loved it. Great start to the tour."

"Thanks," said Taylor, casually draping his arm around Ellen's shoulders. "You ok? Flynn spoke to me when we got off stage. Think he's feeling guilty."

"Guy's an arsehole," muttered Ellen before adding, "I'm fine. He would've found out sooner or later."

"Found out what?" interrupted her father, a concerned look on his face.

"You wouldn't have seen from where you were watching from," began Ellen. "My cloak caught on the monitor and peeled back as I stood up at the end of Swirling Mists. The fans at that side and Flynn out there saw my arm."

"Ah!" exclaimed her dad. "You can't hide in that cloak forever, sweetheart."

"I know," sighed Ellen wearily. "I just still struggle with it all at times."

"Maybe your dad's right," suggested Taylor warmly. "We've a radio show in a couple of days. An interview and an acoustic slot. Tell the world then."

"Maybe."

Two days later, Taylor, Luke and Ellen were sitting in the reception area of one of London's rock radio stations. Off to one side, Rocky was pacing up and down as he talked animatedly on the phone to Jason Russell. There had been a quick rethink on the interview and acoustic slot, meaning that, at the last minute, they decided to head along without Cal and Jack. A scheduling conflict meant that they were meeting some journalists at the venue instead.

"Hi, folks," greeted the DJ, who was to host them on her lunchtime show. "I'm Debbie. Great to see you."

"Great to be here," replied Luke, turning on the Court charm.

"Luke?" guessed Debbie, extending her hand to him.

"Yup. And this is Taylor and Ellen," introduced the band's bass player, shaking her hand.

"Pleasure to meet you," said Tailz.

"Ellen," said Debbie with a smile. "We've met before. Metal Mania Newcomers Awards about five or six years ago."

"Yes, we did," replied Ellen shyly. "You presented us with our award."

"Whatever happened to Good Times?"

"The band split a few months later," said Ellen evasively.

"Oh, that's right!" exclaimed the DJ, suddenly remembering the tragedy that had marked the end of the band. Changing the subject, she asked if they were ready to join her in the studio.

While the one o'clock news bulletin was being broadcast, Debbie chatted casually to the three members of After Life, putting then at their ease. She then played Bodimead's latest single before introducing her guests as the sole support act for the Australian rock giants' UK tour.

"Taylor, I've followed After Life's rise quite closely and, if I'm correct, Ellen is your third lead vocalist but the first female voice. Why the change of tactics?"

"Have you heard her sing?" countered Taylor with a smile over to Ellen. "Seriously though, we listened to dozens of audition tapes. We were looking for something fresh. Something different. Something a bit special. For me, I knew within the first few seconds of Ellen's audition that she was the one for us."

"Did you feel the same connection, Luke?"

"Not immediately," confessed the bass player a little sheepishly. "But this princess has one hell of a voice."

Turning her attention to Ellen, Debbie asked, "And how did you feel about trying to keep these guys in line?"

Giggling nervously, Ellen replied, "I think Jack keeps us all in line, not me. He's the sensible voice of After Life. The voice of reason."

"I commented to Ellen before the show that I remember her as the vocalist from Good Times. Anyone out there still remember them from a few years back? Great band!" continued Debbie. "So, Ellen, where have you been hiding that voice since the end of Good Times?"

With an anxious look at Tailz, she recalled his words from earlier in the week and took a deep breath. "Good Times split when we got caught up in an accident in Thailand five years ago.

John, our bass player, was killed in the explosion. I was badly injured and it's taken most of the last few years to get back to full fitness. I suffered damage to my lungs from the fire among other injuries. It was two years before I could begin to sing again and it took another two before I felt ready to step back out on a stage."

"Sorry," apologized Debbie looking shocked. "I never realized."

"No need to apologise," said Ellen warmly. "It was a long time ago."

"Has the accident changed your voice?"

"There's a huskiness there now," confessed Ellen honestly. "My range is still what it was but that took work. There's no easy way to explain this, Debbie, so I'll be straight with everyone listening. I was a mess after the accident. I lost the sight in my right eye, lost my right arm and suffered burns down the right side of my body. It took a long time and a lot of breathing work to free up the scars on my ribcage to allow me to sing with any power."

"Wow! I don't know what to say...." spluttered the DJ awkwardly.

"No one ever does," admitted Ellen candidly.

"Me included," interrupted Luke, stepping in to her rescue. "I acted like an insensitive arsehole when we first met. Lost my temper with our manager over it. Then I heard Ellen sing. I'm not too big to admit I was wrong. She's the best thing ever to happen to the band."

Beside him, Ellen flushed scarlet at the unexpected compliment.

"Now, you're going to play a few numbers for us, aren't you?"

"If you ask nicely," teased Luke, relishing being in the spotlight.

"What Luke meant to say was "Yes, Debbie." We've three numbers worked out for you," corrected Taylor, keeping the attention away from Ellen for a minute. "The first one we've prepared is an acoustic version of Rats."

The normally hard and fast paced Rats leant itself to a slower, blues based, acoustic version. It was an easy start for Ellen too as the vocal was in her mid-range with a few higher notes towards the climax. They'd chosen it carefully, agreeing that it was a good warm up number.

Behind the desk, Debbie sat watching in awe of the performance going on in the studio. As the last piercing notes faded out all she could say was, "Wow!"

"Our electric version is a little different," admitted Ellen, before taking a sip from her water bottle.

"Is it easy to translate After Life's music into an acoustic styling?"

"Not all of the tracks lend themselves to it," commented Taylor, adjusting the tuning on his guitar. "The next song we're going to play was written as an acoustic ballad."

"Who writes most of your material?"

"Recently," began Luke. "It's been Ellen and Tailz. Our songbird brought some musical magic with her to the After Life. The rest of the time, we all add our bit. It tends to be a collaboration of efforts."

"Is there a story behind the song you're about to perform?" asked Debbie, hoping for an insight into the lyrics.

"I guess it's a song about betrayal," explained Ellen. "About feeling let down by someone you care about."

"Lou Lou?" suggested Debbie, raising an eyebrow.

Laughing, Taylor confessed, "Lou Lou's the name I gave my acoustic guitar a long time ago. We finished writing the song late at night and were struggling for a title. Ellen named it Lou Lou At 3am and its stuck."

"I guess, in reality, Lou Lou could be anyone," added Ellen, with a glance at Taylor.

Singing the acoustic ballad in the confines of the small studio felt extremely intimate. Both Taylor and Ellen were thinking back to writing it in the bedroom of Rocky's house; both trying not to distract the other as they played. If he noticed the looks that his bandmates were exchanging, Luke stayed silent.

Keeping her vocal soft and muted, Ellen poured all of the emotion that she had into the song. Beside her, Tailz accompanied her with equal delicacy.

"Beautiful!" exclaimed Debbie as the song ended. "Stunningly beautiful."

"Thank you," acknowledged Ellen with a smile.

"Is that in your standard set?"

"Sure is," said Tailz. "And so far, everyone's loving it."

"Will it be on your debut album? I hear you're due in the studio in May."

"You hear correct," Luke confirmed. "And Lou Lou will most definitely be on the board to be recorded."

"Is the album written?"

"Mostly. We're a few songs light but we're still pulling ideas together," revealed Taylor.

"Before you play one last number for us, remind me of the tour dates?"

"We're playing tonight in London. The Shepherd's Bush Empire then we head off to Glasgow, Newcastle, Leeds, Manchester, Nottingham, Birmingham and Bristol. After that we say thank you and farewell to our Aussie hosts and head over to Wales for the Open Air festival weekend."

"Then I collapse in a heap," joked Ellen. "We've four shows in a row to end on! It's been a long time since I performed four nights straight."

"Well, I'll be there tonight," promised Debbie. "And I'm covering Wales Open Air too so I'll be sure to catch your set there. Now, what are you going to end on today for us?"

"Swirling Mists," revealed Ellen.

Several hours later, as she stood at the side of the stage waiting to go on, Ellen thought back to the acoustic version of Swirling Mists that they'd performed in the radio studio. She began to mull over whether it would work in a live setting or if they should stick to the arrangement they had. A hand on her shoulder brought her back to reality. Turning quickly, she came face to face with Flynn.

"Sorry. Didn't mean to startle you," he apologized. "Sorry for being such a dick before."

"No harm done," replied Ellen, her tone deliberately cool.

"I'd like to make it up to you," continued Flynn. "Will you duet with me on a song or two?"

"Tonight?"

"Yeah. We're adding in Highway To Hell. Want to join us?"

"If you're sure," said Ellen with a smile.

"Sure. We're going to add it in two from the end of the main set. Just after Fire And Ice In My Heart."

"I'll listen out for my cue," promised Ellen.

"Awesome. Have fun out there, mate. Looks like a good crowd in tonight."

Before she could reply, Flynn had disappeared backstage.

An hour later, as After Life began their standard set closer, Smoke On The Water, Ellen spotted that all of Bodimead were in the wings watching. Their set had gone smoothly and the capacity crowd had swiftly been on side. Along the rail, there were more die hard After Life fans than before and she was starting to recognise a few familiar faces among them.

Crouching down at the edge of the stage, Ellen hissed at the fans then began a more demonic sounding vocal than the one she had rehearsed, "We all came out to Montreux…"

Picking up on her menacing mood, the band adjusted their pace as she continued the song. When Ellen came to stand between Tailz and Cal, they could both see the mischief glinting in her eye. Grinning, Taylor blew her a kiss, causing her to laugh as she started the final verse.

With the usual puff of smoke and flash of lights, Ellen vanished, allowing the boys to finish the song.

When she reached the sanctuary of the wings, Rocky was at her side instantly with a bottle of juice. With fatherly concerns, he watched as she drank thirstily.

"You ok?"

"Never felt better," declared Ellen with a wide grin. "I'd better go and get changed. Don't want to miss my cue with our Aussie hosts."

"Cue?" quizzed Rocky, looking confused.

"Flynn's invited me to sing Highway To Hell with them tonight. Peace offering, I suspect."

"Interesting," commented After Life's manager. "Well, don't let me hold you up."

"Thanks, Rocky," she said, brushing a kiss on his cheek much to the older man's surprise.

Down in the small dressing room, Ellen began to fret about what she was going to wear. Her choices were limited, very limited. She had shed her cloak and was wearing black leggings and a vest top under it. The nude coloured pressure sleeve was concealing her arm but Ellen knew she couldn't go out on stage dressed as she was. The only other clothes she had with her were another black t-shirt and her skinny ripped jeans plus a jumper.

A knock at the door made her jump.

"It's me," came Taylor's voice from the far side of the door. "Can I come in?"

"Sure."

With a squeak, the door opened and her housemate stepped into the tiny room.

"Rocky says you're going on with Bodimead."

"That's the plan, if I can find something to wear," replied Ellen brightly. Spying her friend's battered leather jacket, she asked, "How would you feel about loaning me your jacket?"

"Fine, if you want it," agreed Taylor. "Probably smells a bit."

"Right now," joked Ellen. "So do I!"

"Hot out there again, wasn't it?"

"Very but I'm getting used to it," she replied. "The pressure sleeve doesn't help."

"Why not take it off before you go back out?" suggested Taylor. "My jacket will keep things covered."

"I think I might," began Ellen. "But I need a hand with it. Would you mind?"

"Of course not. What do I need to do?"

"Give me a second to get my vest off," said Ellen. She paused then added, "This isn't pretty, Tailz."

"Sh. Just tell me what to do."

Carefully, Ellen slipped out of the vest top and asked him to unfasten the sleeve under her left arm. It was a new garment that she had tried that supported her ribs more than her other sleeves did. Lizzy had helped her into it before they'd left home that morning and had promised to help her out of it when she got back to the house.

With trembling fingers, Tailz undid the fastening then gently peeled the skin coloured garment back. He was standing behind Ellen and realised as he slipped the strap across her back that she wasn't wearing a bra. The skin across her back was unmarked but as he reached her right shoulder it became purple and puckered. As the sleeve peeled away from her ribcage, he saw for the first time the extent of the scarring to her slender body. There were several thick white cord-like scars snaking across her ribs, the surrounding skin a puckered deep purple.

"You ok?" asked Ellen softly as she felt the sleeve slip from the end of her stump.

"Of course," said Taylor, tossing it onto the table. Tenderly, he ran his fingers over her ribs. "Does it hurt much?"

"Sometimes," confessed Ellen quietly. "The pain was worse when it was still healing. Now it only hurts when I overdo it or if I don't wear that sleeve for a few days."

His voice husky, Tailz said, "You're still beautiful, though."

Before she could stop him, he'd begun to kiss the nape of her neck, his hand still lightly resting on her ribs.

"Tailz," she whispered. "Delicious as that is...."

Instantly, the guitarist stopped and stepped back.

"Sorry," he gasped. "I don't know...."

"Shh" cautioned Ellen, turning to face him. One side of her bare right breast was purple and overly smooth, its shape still perfect. As he gazed at her voluptuous breasts, Taylor thought yet again how stunning she truly was. Putting a finger to his lips, Ellen said, "Hold that thought till later."

"Promise?"

"Promise," she said with a smile. "Now, I need to get dressed and get to the side of the stage. We need to hurry here."

The Australian headliners had just begun Fire And Ice In My Heart when Taylor and Ellen reached the side of the stage. Gone was her witch look. Instead, she looked like any other rock chick. Her eye patch had been replaced by her round, steampunk, purple, tinted glasses; her long hair tamed into a loose ponytail. Taylor's jacket was draped casually over her shoulder completing the look. Together, the bandmates stood watching Flynn command the capacity London crowd in his own inimitable Aussie way.

"That guy's insane," whispered Taylor as they watched Bodimead's front man jump down into the midst of the crowd.

"Crazy but the fans are loving it," commented Ellen, keen to learn from the more experienced singer. "Not sure I could risk that though."

"You could venture into the photography pit," mused Taylor thoughtfully.

"Maybe," Ellen acknowledged as they watched Flynn scramble back up onto the stage.

The song came to a crescendo of an ending.

"London!" screamed Flynn. "We have two more for you."

The fans roared back at him.

"We also have something fucking awesome for you," he continued with a glance towards Ellen. "I'd like to welcome out a very special sheila now. Give a huge London welcome to the queen of the After Life, Ellen Lloyd!"

Confidently, Ellen walked out on stage to a deafening reception from the crowd. With a wolf whistle, Flynn embraced her gently, whispering, "You take the first verse, Together on the chorus. I'll take second verse."

Ellen nodded, understanding immediately how the more experienced vocalist wanted to split the vocal chores.

One of the stage crew thrust a microphone into her hand as the band's guitarist began the distinctive intro.

"Living easy, living free, season ticket on a one-way ride," began Ellen, her vocal clear and powerful.

By the end of the verse, her ribs were in agony and she was silently wishing she'd kept the pressure garment on for support.

While Flynn led the second verse, Ellen regrouped her thoughts.

Together, they stood shoulder to shoulder as their combined voices rang out, "I'm on a highway to hell."

It took all of her remaining strength but Ellen matched the energetic Australian note for note right through to the final, "I'm on the highway to hell."

With a theatrical flourish, Flynn bowed to her then addressed the crowd, "Let's hear it for the queen of the After Life, London. Isn't she fucking awesome?"

The fans screamed and cheered, almost raising the roof off the venue.

"Folks, I give you Ellen Lloyd."

"Thank you," she called back with a bow to the fans. "Till next time."

As Rocky stopped the car in front of the house shortly before three, Ellen stirred in the back seat. She had fallen asleep almost as soon as the car left the venue, her head resting on Taylor's shoulder. With a yawn, she tried to sit up, screwing her tired face up as a sharp pain stabbed her.

"You ok" asked Taylor, concerned that she had overdone it.

Sleepily, Ellen nodded but her face told a different story.

"Tailz, carry her upstairs," said Rocky firmly. "She's dead on her feet."

"I can walk!" protested Ellen sharply. "I'm tired not an invalid."

"Sorry," apologised the band's manager, sensing he'd inadvertently hit a raw nerve. "Tailz, at least see her safely up the stairs."

"Yes, sir."

Putting a protective arm around her tiny waist, Taylor helped Ellen into the house and up to her room. She stumbled a couple of times as they made their way slowly up the stairs and along the hallway. Wearily, the tired songbird sat down on the edge of the bed.

"I'll fetch your bag," said Taylor quietly. "Back in a minute."

Silently, Ellen nodded.

It only took Taylor a couple of minutes to run back down to the car to fetch their bags but, by the time he returned to Ellen's room, she had curled up on her side and was asleep with her clothes on. Guessing that sleeping like that wasn't going to be good for her, he knelt down at the side of the bed and gently shook her awake.

"Ellen, let's get you into bed properly, my lovely," he said tenderly. "What do you need me to do to help?"

"Let me sleep," she mumbled into the duvet. "Tired."

"No," he said firmly. "You need to get into your pjs."

Still more asleep than awake, Ellen sat up and allowed Taylor to undress her. He found her pyjamas under the pillow and carefully began to help her into them.

"Stop," said Ellen suddenly as he pulled her pyjama top over her head. "I need to do something first."

"What?"

"Pass me the white tub that's on top of the drawers. I need to do it every night."

"At least let me help you," suggested Tailz. "Tell me where you need me to apply that gunk."

With a sleepy smile, Ellen relented, "Over all the scars. After tonight my ribs need it badly. There's a pain reliever in it."

"Ok. I'll do my best. Let me know if I hurt you."

Tenderly, the guitarist spread the thick while emollient over her scarred ribcage. Even in the dim light of the bedroom, he could see that some areas looked more livid than earlier on in the evening. Touching the scarred flesh on her arm felt strange but Taylor diligently massaged the cream into the fragile skin.

"Done," he whispered softly. "Now, into bed. Sleep."

"Stay with me."

"You sure?"

"Stay," repeated Ellen as he helped her under the duvet. "Just hold me. Please."

"Ok, if you're sure."

Taylor lay curled round her back as Ellen lay on her side, breathing evenly. Every now and then she snuffled in her sleep and twitched. Despite his own exhaustion, Taylor watched her as she slept, marvelling again at her fragile beauty. Carefully, he draped his arm over her, pulling her a little closer. An overwhelming urge to protect her was swelling inside him. Already, he knew he was in love with her but he doubted that Ellen felt the same way. There were emotional scars to be overcome too before she would allow him any closer.

As his eyes grew heavy and sleep began to consume him, Taylor smiled, content for now just to be allowed to hold her in his arms.

The drive north the next day was dull and seemingly endless as After Life counted down the miles to Glasgow, using the motorway signs as their measure. When, after almost seven hours, the minibus finally crossed the border into Scotland, the five members of the band cheered loudly.

"We'll be in Glasgow in time for a late dinner," promised Rocky from the driver's seat. He'd split the driving chores with Jack and the band's only crew member cum guitar tech, Michael. Every few miles, he checked that the box trailer they were towing was still hitched to the minibus. The last thing After Life needed was to lose their stage gear half way up the M6.

"Cal, where's good to eat and drink in Glasgow?" asked Taylor.

"No fucking clue, Tailz," laughed Cal. "I left Scotland when I was fourteen. Never really been back except to visit my gran in Ayr. Not been to Glasgow since I was wee. My mum took me to the museum to see the dinosaurs."

Giggling at the thought of Cal as a little boy trailing round a museum with his mum, Ellen said, "If I remember right, there's plenty of places in the city centre. Loads of choice."

"When were you last in Glasgow?" quizzed Luke curiously.

"A few years ago with my folks," she replied. "We came up to support my dad run a half marathon. He ran a load that year to raise money for charity. Glasgow was last on his list."

"Think you'll remember your way round town?" asked Luke hopefully.

"I'm sure I can find us a decent restaurant then a pub or two for you."

"That's all I need, princess," sighed Luke as he settled back in his seat.

Safely checked into their cheap and cheerful hotel, Ellen and the rest of After Life set off on foot in search of a restaurant. Having been stuck in the minibus all day, all of them were happy to walk down to the Merchant City area of town, enjoying stretching their legs. As they meandered along Sauchiehall Street, despite it being almost nine o'clock, there were several buskers playing in doorways. The street was busy with people out for a Thursday night drink and there were groups of students milling about outside the various bars they passed.

"We should've brought some flyers and handed them out for tomorrow's show," commented Jack casually, never wanting to willingly miss a promotional opportunity.

"Show's sold out," said Rocky with a smile. "Got a message earlier. Apart from Leeds and Nottingham, the tour's a sell-out. Only a few tickets left for those shows too. Should sell out by the time we get there."

"I don't fucking believe it!" laughed Luke. "A sell-out tour! Princess, you're our good luck charm."

"Aye, she might be once she finds us somewhere to eat," grumbled a hungry Cal. "You sure you know where you are going?"

"Yes, I do," called back Ellen, "As long as Italian is ok with everyone. It's just down the hill then in to the left as the hill flattens out. Through an arch into a big square with a museum in it."

"Guess she knows where we're going," laughed Taylor, casually putting his arm around her waist. "Lead the way! I can hear a lasagne calling me."

"I can hear a fucking beer," muttered Cal, stomping along behind them.

A few minutes later, Jack held the door open for them as Ellen led them into the restaurant.

"Table for seven, please," she said politely as a waiter approached them.

"Through this way, please," he replied, leading them into the long narrow dining room.

Soon they were seated at a long table. The waiter took their drinks order then left them to peruse the menu.

"Pizza for me," stared Cal, tossing the menu back on the table. "Ham and pineapple with mushrooms."

"What do you recommend?" Taylor asked Ellen quietly. He'd gone to great lengths to ensure he was seated beside her, sensing she might need some discrete help with her meal.

"The lasagne is great but I'm going for the tortellini," she replied. "Or maybe the penne."

"Big decision," he teased gently.

Laughter and the chink of glasses and cutlery surrounded the After Life table as the band relaxed over their late but delicious meal. As the beer and wine began to loosen their tongues, they began to tell stories and even Rocky was coaxed into some storytelling. Tears of laughter ran down Ellen's cheeks as she listened to one particular tale involving Luke's uncle, Garrett Court. Luke too was helpless with laughter as Rocky told the story.

"I'll need to remind him of that night," said the bass player. "He'll kill you for telling me that story, boss."

"Probably," conceded Rocky, glancing down at his watch. "Right, boys and girl, I'm heading back to the hotel. Curfew of 1am. Anyone out later than that gets a fifty quid fine. It's a school night. No shenanigans."

"Yes, boss," said Luke with a wink towards Cal.

"I mean it, Mr Court," stated the band's manager firmly.

"I'll stay with these two," Jack offered calmly. "They'll be tucked up in bed before one."

"Good luck with that," laughed Tailz.

"And what about you two lovebirds?" quizzed Luke in an effort to divert attention away from himself.

"We'll join you for one then see how we feel," replied Ellen with a glance at Taylor, pointedly ignoring the "lovebirds" reference.

It was almost midnight when Ellen and Taylor made their way back towards the hotel. Hand in hand, they retraced their steps back up Sauchiehall St. There were still a few folk about, mostly couples like themselves, but the buskers were long gone. As they trekked up Scott St, past the city's O2 ABC venue, Ellen joked that perhaps the next time they were in the city they would be headlining there. Putting his arm around her, Tailz agreed that that would be cool.

The hotel was quiet when they entered and they were the only ones in the lift as they headed up to the third floor. The hotel staff hadn't booked the band into adjacent rooms. Ellen's room was at one end of the corridor and the room Taylor was sharing with Jack was at the other. The rest of the band were on the floor above.

When they reached Ellen's room, Taylor opened the door for her, standing aside to allow her to enter.

"Are you coming in?"

"You want me to?"

Ellen smiled at him and nodded.

"You sure?" he checked nervously.

"Sure."

With only the two bedside lamps lit, there was already an intimate air to the room. Casually, Ellen dropped her jacket onto the chair then turned to face Taylor. He was standing a little awkwardly looking out of the window. Gently, Ellen placed her hand on his shoulder and, as he turned round, she drew him into an embrace. As he lowered his lips to kiss the nape of her neck, she let out a soft purr-like moan.

"I believe this is about where we got to before," whispered Tailz softly.

Slowly, Taylor ran his finger along her jawline then tipped her chin up slightly. His lips met Ellen's which were already slightly parted in anticipation. Kissing her hungrily, he pulled her towards him. With one hand on the small of her back and the other tangled in her thick, platinum, blonde hair at the back of her head, Taylor savoured each kiss. His hand massaged her head, her hair silky soft to the touch, as he felt her tongue reach in to tease his in tentative exploration.

"I need you," he said between kisses. "I want to make love to you."

"Me too," confessed Ellen a little nervously. "It's been a while....."

"Sh," he interrupted her. "Relax. Trust me. I won't hurt you. I'll be gentle."

Before she could protest, the guitarist scooped her up into his arms and carried her over to the large king-size bed.

Laying her down in the centre of the soft, thick, white duvet, he removed her boots and her socks, smiling at the love hearts on them. He gently massaged her slim feet. With a smile, he noted her immaculately purple painted toenails. The skin of her feet was smooth and supple under his hands as he slowly massaged her toes then the balls of her feet before running his thumbs along the arch of each foot. Sliding his hands up the outside of her legs until he reached her waist, Tailz deftly unfastened her jeans and slid them down her pale, slender legs, tossing them carelessly onto the floor. Her top didn't prove to be a challenge. Taking extra care not to hurt her, he slid the black t-shirt over her breasts, pausing to kiss her cleavage as he slid the top up and over her head. With her long hair spread out across the duvet, Ellen lay on bed smiling up at him, wearing only her turquoise bra and lacy panties.

Silently, she watched as Taylor roughly kicked off his battered boots. He wrestled with the button fly of his jeans then hauled them off, kicking them across the floor. Keeping his eyes on her, he removed his t-shirt, tossing it onto the floor behind him. Wearing only his tight black boxers, he lay down beside her. Laying a warm hand on her smooth flat stomach, the guitarist bent down to kiss her again. As his tongue met hers, he moved his hand down between her thighs, lightly caressing her soft skin.

"May I?" he asked, indicating that he wanted to remove her bra.

"You may," giggled Ellen, trying to quash the anxieties about her scars that were threatening to engulf her.

Soon both her bra and panties had been tossed onto the pile of clothing on the floor. A few moments later, the guitarist's boxers joined them. Subtly avoiding touching Ellen's scars, Taylor explored her body. His lips and tongue caressed her neck, nibbling on her earlobe before travelling lightly down to her collarbones then breasts. Unable to resist the temptation of her erect nipples, he suckled her breasts in turn. Oblivious to the purple discolouration of her right breast, he swept a circle round each of her nipples with his tongue then blew a long, cool breath across them, encouraging her nipples to harden once more. While his tongue explored her cleavage, his long, slender fingers explored a more intimate area. As he slipped his fingers inside her, Ellen moaned softly, tilting her pelvis up to meet him. Teasingly, he explored inside her, using his thumb to circle her clit. Ellen could feel his erection pressing against her but could also sense he was holding back.

"Make love to me," she whispered, licking his pierced ear.

Taylor needed no second invitation. Withdrawing his fingers, he smiled down at her as he sucked them clean, allowing himself to linger over the taste of her. He reached over the edge of the bed, fumbled for his jeans and retrieved a condom from his pocket. With a grin, he ripped the packet open with his teeth then rolled the condom down over his long, hard dick. With a wicked smile forming at her lips, Ellen watched his every move.

Without taking his eyes off her, Taylor entered her slowly, feeling her pulsating around him. He was struggling to maintain control and, despite wanting to linger over their lovemaking, his body and hers had other ideas. His initial strokes were long and slow as he wanted to ensure that he wasn't hurting her. Gradually, their rhythm quickened as he moved deeper and faster inside her. With his desire surging through him, Taylor began to thrust harder and faster, penetrating deep into Ellen's moist womanhood. Responding to his urgency, Ellen thrust her pelvis up towards him, encouraging him to explore deeper inside. Moving in perfect unison, they both reached an all-consuming climax within seconds of each other. As her orgasm exploded, Ellen rake her nails down his back and howled his name,

Spent, Taylor sank down on top of her, burying his face in her platinum blonde hair. Reluctantly, he slowly withdrew from her, wishing that their moment of intimacy could have lasted longer.

"Thank you," whispered Ellen, a hint of sadness to her voice.

"You alright, lovely?" he asked, concerned that he'd been too rough and had hurt her.

"Never felt better," she confessed softly. "You made me forget everything. Forget the past. Made me feel......."

Ellen paused.

"Shh," said Tailz, putting a finger to her lips. "I hear you."

Early next morning, they lingered over their lovemaking, savouring every last second with each other. Their passion was still simmering but, by slowing things down, they reached a new level of intimacy. As they had made love, Taylor had tenderly caressed Ellen's scarred body. When he'd gazed down at her, he'd discovered her cheeks wet with tears.

Holding her in his arms, Taylor risked asking, "Why the tears, my lovely?"

"It's complicated," whispered Ellen with a wistful smile. "Lots of emotions. Thank you for last night and this morning. It's been special."

"You don't need to thank me."

"I know you don't get it but I kind of do," she said, snuggling closer to his warm body. "You made me feel like I never thought I could feel again."

"Shh," stopped Taylor, feeling himself growing embarrassed. "I'm going to have some explaining to do with Jack."

With a giggle, Ellen said, "Think he'll fine you fifty quid for not being in your own bed by curfew?"

"He'll probably try," laughed Tailz. "But, Rocky never specified that I needed to be in my own bed, did he?"

"No," agreed Ellen. "He didn't." She paused then asked, "What do you think the others will say?"

"About what?"

"This. Us."

"None of their business," stated Taylor. "But, Luke will probably find something to say when he finds out. Jack and Cal will be cool with it….I hope!"

"I hope so," she sighed. "What time is it?"

"Almost eight," replied Taylor checking the time on his phone. "I'd better get back to my room. I need a shower and a change of clothes and stuff."

"I guess. What time are we meeting Rocky and the others?"

"Nine thirty downstairs."

"Ok. I'll see you down there."

The hotel room door creaked loudly as Taylor pushed it open. He could see Jack's feet at the end of one of the beds that dominated the room. As he stepped in, all he heard was, "And what time do you call this to be waltzing in at, Taylor Rowe?"

Laughing, Taylor replied, "About eight o'clock, give or take a few."

"And what would your……" Jack paused, realising he had been about to say "mother" and that may just have hit a raw nerve.

"My mum would've tanned my hide," finished Taylor with a

grin. "But my Nana would have been secretly proud of me."

Jack roared with laughter, "I love that old girl. She's one of life's characters."

"That she is," said Taylor, visualising his beloved grandmother. "Hope I get home to see her after Wales. Miss her and Jen."

"So, would it be safe to assume you had an all-night song writing session with our leading lady?"

"Something like that."

"Not what I expected of you. Luke, yes, but not you."

"Shut up!" laughed Taylor. "I need a shower and a change of clothes."

"Well, make it a cold one," suggested Jack with a wink.

It was late afternoon before After Life entered the venue for that night's show. Their day had been a flurry of press commitments, a guest appearance at a local music store then a quick interview for a local radio station. Both Jack and Cal helped Michael to set up their gear while Rocky whisked the other three members of the band off for their final press appearance of the day.

Soundcheck was a rushed affair but fortunately ran smoothly. As they stood on stage playing to the empty hall, all five members of the band marvelled at the fading art deco majesty of the venue. Glancing up at the small alcoves on either side of the balcony, Ellen commented that she'd love to start Swirling Mists from up there.

"That would be quite something," agreed Jack. "But, you'd never get back to the stage on time after the intro."

"True," she sighed. "It would be kind of neat to pull that off though. Next time maybe...."

"When we headline here?" laughed Cal. "I admire your optimism, missy. We'd struggle to fill The Cathouse on our own never mind here."

"All in good time," she commented with a grin. "Ye of little faith."

By seven thirty, the venue was more than three quarters full and all the little boxes were occupied by rock fans keen to get a close bird's eye view of the stage. From their position in the wings, After Life could see their hardcore fans lined up along the rail. Several of those fans had been at all their recent shows and Cal had revealed, after a brief visit to their merchandise stand, that most of them were coming to all the shows on the tour. This had prompted a debate about whether to do some kind of impromptu meet and greet at the final show in Bristol and to perhaps offer them guest passes to the Wales Open Air event. With his business head on, Rocky had vetoed that but did say a meet and greet was a good idea, adding that they could perhaps invite them in for soundcheck too.

"Princess," came an Australian voice from behind them. "You up for a trip down the Highway To Hell tonight?"

"Always," replied Ellen, from under the hood of her cloak.

"Alrighty," said Flynn, rubbing his hands together and with a mischievous grin on his face. "Same as in London?"

"Fine by me."

"If this crowd go for it then stays in the set every night."

Ellen nodded.

"Great. Have a good one."

And with that, Flynn turned on his heel and disappeared from view.

"I still don't like him," muttered Ellen under her breath.

"But it's good for you and the rest of us if you get to sing your ass off with the jackass," drawled Luke.

"I know. I know."

At that, the houselights dimmed and the PA stopped. A huge roar rose from the crowd as the four boys from After Life crept out on stage to assume their marks in the dark. Spidery wisps of smoke began to spill off the front of the stage. The footlights gave off a low green glow as Ellen began the opening chanted section of Swirling Mists. An eerie hush fell over the audience as she stepped carefully out on stage. A green spotlight illuminated her in all her cloaked majesty as her last note rang out long and clear. Immediately, the main spotlights flashed almost like lightning and the rest of After Life powered into the song. Throwing her hood back, Ellen moved to position herself centre stage, right on the edge, singing with a new-found force and confidence.

For this show, After Life has opted to change the set around a little to mix things up. City Of Bones And Heartache followed with Cyclone completing the opening power trio. The energy coming from the passionate Scottish rock fans spurred the band on and encouraged them to interact a little more than usual with the crowd. Over at the corner of the stage, Luke was flirting with a group of girls, who were drooling over his every move. At the opposite side, Cal had his own fan club of former schoolfriends from his primary school days. Seeing the half dozen folk in his old school's uniform made him laugh. When they produced a handmade cardboard sign reading, "Miss Grieve's star pupil – Cal McDermid" he had to stop playing until he composed himself.

As the band prepared to play Rats, Ellen said to Tailz that she planned to venture down into the pit. Without missing his cue, the guitarist, nodded his approval.

Menacingly, Ellen prowled the stage as she sang the first verse and chorus, surreptitiously checking out the best way down. As Taylor played his solo, she slipped off stage going down the stairs at the side, re-emerging in time to sing the final verse as she roamed her way along the rail, pausing in front of the band's diehard fans to allow them a few brief seconds of opportunity to take photos with her. Expertly, the band improvised an extra, short solo to allow her time to scamper back up the stairs at the far side in time to sing the final chorus in her usual position between Tailz and Cal.

"Thank you, Glasgow!" she bellowed over the fans' cheering. "Time to slow it down a little for a minute or two."

Behind her, Michael had moved the transport case into position, the band had dispersed into the wings and Tailz was sitting on the box tweaking the tuning of his guitar.

"Ladies and gentlemen of Glasgow, this is Lou Lou At 3am," introduced Ellen as she took her seat beside Taylor.

The Scottish crowd hung on her every word as she poured her soul into the ballad. Beside her, Taylor's playing was filled with a renewed raw passion. Along the rail, the band's dedicated fans sang in harmony with the chorus, making both Ellen and Taylor smile. As the song came to an end, Ellen thanked the crowd, complimenting them on their harmonies.

While the transport case was removed Ellen seized the opportunity to grab a drink of water.

"Glasgow, we have two songs left," began Ellen when she stepped back up to her mic. "Then the mighty Bodimead with be with you!"

A deafening roar erupted around the room, indicating the fans total dedication to the Australian headliners.

"We were told you guys would be the best and the loudest crowd on the tour. Without a word of a lie, you have been. Thank you."

A second thunderous roar surged over the stage.

"We're going to leave you with two rock classics. The first one is Kashmir."

It was after midnight by the time the band sat down to a late dinner of fish and chips or, as Cal called it "a fish supper". He was seated across from Taylor and Ellen in the dressing room devouring a suspect looking meal.

"Cal, what in God's name is that?" asked Ellen, wrinkling her nose at the sight of his dinner.

"A puddin' supper wi' gravy," he declared with a grin. "Huvnae had one in years."

"Looks vile," stated Luke bluntly.

"Hark you and your steak pie supper," scoffed Cal.

"Well, this is the first time I've experienced a hamburger in batter," revealed Jack as he eyed his meal suspiciously. "Bizarre."

"Should've stuck to fish," said Ellen. "It's fabulous."

As soon as they were finished their meal, the venue staff were hurrying them along. All the stage gear had already been loaded into the van and their personal effects cleared from the dressing room.

"Right, boys and girl," called out Rocky. "Time to head back to the hotel. We've an early start tomorrow."

"What time do we leave at, boss?" checked Taylor.

"Nine o'clock sharp. You've an interview scheduled for one in Newcastle."

"Plenty of time," assured Cal. "It's only a couple of hours down the road to there."

"Nine o'clock," repeated Rocky firmly.

Over the next week, After Life settled into the routine of life on the road. No one specifically commented but it silently became accepted that Ellen and Taylor shared a room when they booked into a hotel. There was only once when their scheduling failed and they had to sleep in the minibus. Towards the end of the week, they had three shows in a row then faced the journey to Wales to appear at the annual Open Air Festival.

After the final show in Bristol with Bodimead, Ellen had been wiped out. As the tour had wound its way through England, Flynn had extended their duet to two songs. The three shows in a row took its toll on her and, as she came off stage in Bristol's Colston Hall, Ellen had half-collapsed into Taylor's arms. He'd scooped her up and carried her back to the dressing room, insisting that Rocky get her back to the hotel as soon as possible. A good night's sleep had gone a long way to restoring her energy but, as they had boarded the minibus for the drive to Swansea, they could all see how exhausted she was.

Sitting beside her, Taylor put his arm around her and asked softly, "You going to be ok to go out there tonight?"

"I have to be," she said quietly. "I can sleep tomorrow."

"Remember it's a full set tonight."

"I know. I'll be ok."

"We could extend the acoustic slot to two songs. Would that help?" suggested Taylor, desperately trying to think of ways to make it easier for her.

"It wouldn't do any harm," conceded Ellen. "What would the second song be?"

"Good question."

"We could do a cover of Every Rose Has Its Thorn?"

"Not one of my favourites. A few ghosts with that one," Tailz admitted. "Let's ask the others and see what they come up with."

"Fine by me," agreed Ellen as she snuggled into his shoulder. "Waken me when you've made a decision."

The band's singer was still sound asleep as Jack navigated the minibus across the festival site to their designated spot. While Ellen had slept, the band had debated which song to add into the mix to extend the acoustic slot. After much deliberation, they agreed to perform the acoustic version of Rats and to add in a cover of ACDC's Problem Child. They would run through it at soundcheck to confirm that Ellen was comfortable singing it.

While Jack and Rocky went to find the organisers and confirm their times for sound check and their set, Cal and Taylor set off to get lunch for everyone. As they trudged across the hillside towards the "food village", Cal asked his friend if Ellen was alright.

"She's just exhausted," replied Taylor, stuffing his hands into his pockets. "Think she's found touring tougher that she remembered. She explained to me that she's got some scarring on her lungs. Three shows in a row have taken their toll. I'm sure she'll be fine for tonight."

"She's a tough wee cookie," commented Cal with a smile. "Guess that stubbornness is what's got her so far. Must be tough on her."

"This past week's been tough on us all," laughed Taylor. "Want to know what's killing me the most?"

"What?" asked Cal. "Your fingers? Your wrists?"

Taylor shook his head, "My feet. They're fucked. I've blisters on the blisters. One toenail is black. Feels like I've run a marathon in my bare feet."

Cal burst out laughing, "You're just getting old, mate!"

"Hey, I'm younger than you!"

A few minutes later, the two musicians were heading back to the minibus weighed down with various burgers, portions of chips and bottles of juice. Music from the main stage was echoing out across the Welsh countryside. The festival was situated in a small valley in the midst of a natural amphitheatre. As Taylor gazed out across the site, he commented on how picturesque the location was.

"At sunset that crowd's going to look spectacular," he said almost to himself.

"Yea, gonna look great," agreed Cal. "Pity we won't see it though as we'll be on stage in that big fuck off tent over there."

"True. Hopefully I'll see tomorrow's from the beach at home."

"You heading back to Cornwall for a day or two?"

"Yeah," nodded Taylor. "I've hired a car. Plan to stay down there for the week. There's still stuff to be tidied up and I need to see Nana and Jen."

"Homesick?"

"A bit," confessed Taylor. "My young brother's bailed out and left Jen to cope with everything."

"You taking Ellen with you?"

"Haven't asked her yet but that's my plan."

"Your nana will love her."

"I hope so," sighed Taylor softly.

As they boarded the minibus, they discovered Ellen talking animatedly on her phone. From the look on her face, Taylor could guess she was talking to her mother and ,from her tone of voice, the call was not going smoothly.

"Fine, mother!" she snapped. "Maybe next time I've got a few days off you'll be home. Enjoy Italy!"

Trying to ignore Ellen's heated conversation, Cal and Taylor calmly went about sorting out the lunch order.

"Sorry, guys," apologised their lead singer. "That woman brings out the worst in me."

"Problems?" asked Cal casually.

"I called to say I'd be home tomorrow night for a few days. She's booked a last-minute break for them. They leave for a trip to the Italian Lakes first thing tomorrow morning," explained Ellen, flopping back down on her seat. "I just fancied a few days at home in my old bed."

Seizing the opportunity, Taylor sat beside her, "How about a few days at my home instead? You can even have my old bed."

"You serious?"

"Yup. I'd planned to ask you later on. I'm driving home in the morning. Nana and Jen are expecting me around lunchtime. I'd love you to meet them."

"Well, if you're sure," began Ellen, a slight hesitation to her voice.

"I'm sure," jumped in Taylor. "Say you'll come."

Ellen nodded, "I'd love to if you're sure I'm not intruding. A few days by the sea sound idyllic."

Their conversation was cut short by the arrival of Rocky and Jack. Chaos ensued for the next half an hour as they all sorted out who was eating what then clambered over one another to find a space to eat. With all seven of them on board, the minibus was somewhat crowded.

"Listen up, boys and girl," called out Rocky as they finished their meal. "There's been a slight change to the running order for tonight. After Life are now headlining in the Metal Mania tent. You've a full two hours at eight thirty. Curfew is eleven for the main stage but the organisers have brought it back to ten thirty for the side stages and marquees. Huge opportunity tonight, folks!"

"We've only worked up a ninety-minute slot," began Taylor with an anxious glance at Ellen.

"And?" quizzed Rocky sharply.

"It's fine," said Ellen calmly. "Let's take a look and see what we can add in. We can do two hours easy."

"What time's sound check?" asked Luke.

"There isn't a full soundcheck. You get twenty minutes to check the set up just before you go on. There's a practice tent out back but it's pretty crowded. You'd be better off back here."

"OK. Outdoor warm up it is, boys," said Ellen, hoping she sounded more confident than she felt.

Before any of them could comment further, a figure appeared in the bus's doorway.

"Can we join you?"

The band looked up to see Jason Russell from JR Management standing on the bottom step.

"Of course. Come in," invited Rocky, looking a little flustered. "I was just telling them about the change of running order for tonight."

"Ah, yes," acknowledged Jason. "Fantastic opportunity to shine. An extra thirty minutes to impress on stage."

"That's the bit we need to work out," muttered Luke sourly.

"Maybe I can help with that," suggested the person standing behind Jason.

The tall, music mogul climbed on board and was immediately followed by their mystery guest.

"Maybe you can," said Luke with a smile when he saw who the visitor was. "Dan Crow! How the hell are you?"

"Fine, son. How's that uncle of yours?"

"Closeted away in the music store with his pet vampire," joked Luke, getting up to hug the older man.

Around him, the rest of After Life had been stunned into silence. Dan Crow was the front man of legendary British rock giants, Weigh Station. The band's 25th anniversary show at Wembley Arena had just been announced and After Life had debated over dinner earlier in the week about who was going to it.

"Introduce me to your little songbird, Luke," prompted Dan warmly. "I caught your set in Oxford the other night."

"Dan, meet Ellen Lloyd," said Luke formally.

Wriggling her way out of her seat, Ellen rose to meet the older singer. Dan had been one of her idols for many years. Her dad was a huge Weigh Station fan and Ellen sorely wished he was here with them in Wales.

"Pleasure to meet you," she said, extending her left hand.

Dan raised an eyebrow then smiled knowingly. Tenderly, he drew her into a fatherly embrace and whispered, "Well disguised with the cloak, darling."

"You knew?"

"I saw in Oxford," he said softly. "I'm sorry."

"Ah!" sighed Ellen, flushing with embarrassment. "Now I know where you were watching from. You saw my cloak getting caught, right?"

Dan nodded. "And you coped beautifully."

"Thanks," she said, blushing again. "So, do you really want to join us tonight?"

"I'd love to," replied Dan warmly. "A duet with a beautiful girl? How could a man resist?"

"Cut the crap, Dan!" laughed Luke. "Allow me to introduce the rest of the band."

With the introductions made, Dan sat down among them and asked about the plans for the set. Excusing themselves, Rocky and Jason stepped outside to talk business, leaving the musicians to chat amongst themselves. Assuming a fatherly role, the Weigh Station front man asked to see the set list. Handing the scrawled list over, Taylor said that they'd planned to extend the acoustic slot to two songs to give Ellen a bit of breathing space.

"Is there room for a third bum on that transport case?" asked Dan with a smile. "We could do Long Travelled Roads or Miles From Home together?"

"I love Miles From Home," confessed Ellen and Taylor in unison.

"Miles From Home it is then."

"How about doing Wreckless too?" suggested Luke.

"You learned how to play it right yet?" teased Dan.

"Sure have," stated Luke proudly.

"Do you know the lyrics, Miss Lloyd?"

"Yes, sir," replied Ellen smiling.

"Looks like we just filled ten or fifteen minutes for you," said Dan casually. "Now, what else you got that you can add into the mix?"

"How about giving Jack the limelight for a bit?" proposed Cal. "Gives Ellen a breather."

"Good idea, son," agreed Dan swiftly, following his reasoning. "Don't overdo it though. You still need one more song in there. Lady's choice?"

"Communication Breakdown," replied Ellen without hesitation. "Use it as the song before Jack's solo. End it sharp and clean. Kill the lights then let Jack lead the way. Drum solo could lead nicely into Depths Of The Pit. It starts with drums anyway."

"Gets my vote," said Luke with a wink to the band's singer, acknowledging their mutual love for Led Zeppelin.

"And you have your two-hour set," proclaimed Dan, getting into his feet. "Miss Lloyd, Mr Rowe, I'll be back at six to run through Miles From Home."

After Dan left, the members of After Life sat staring at each other in stunned silence. All of them, except Luke, were totally star struck.

"Did that just fucking happen?" asked Cal eventually.

"Sure did," replied Ellen with a huge smile. "Gentlemen, we have work to do. Let's run through this."

The Metal Mania tent was full to capacity by the time After Life were due on stage. Rumours of a guest appearance by Dan Crow had flown round the festival site after he was spotted in the company of Rocky and Jason Russell and the thousand capacity marquee was crammed full. To prevent overcrowding, the organisers made a last-minute decision to open up one side of it, erect some barriers and thereby create extra capacity. The outside standing area swiftly filled up too.

Behind the black drapes that shielded the edges of the stage from prying eyes, After Life watched the crowd. As ever, their small group of diehard fans lined the rail. Ellen noted that there was a narrow photography pit between the crowd and the stage and judged that she should be able to make it safely along it during Rats. Off to one side, Dan was standing chatting casually to Jason Russell and Rocky. Beside them stood another man, who looked vaguely familiar.

"Shit," muttered Taylor, recognising him. "That's Mikey from Weigh Station!"

"High profile crowd tonight," joked Luke, pointing across to the far side of the stage. "The bass player from When The Chips Are Down just showed up too. And I think he's with Molton's bass player."

"Why are so many of these guys hanging around in a field in Wales?" asked Jack, looking puzzled.

"Metal Mania Award Ceremony is tomorrow night in Cardiff," replied Ellen calmly. "So, my guess is that they're all invited guests."

"Yeah," agreed Cal. "And When The Chips Are Down headlined on Friday night and Molton headlined last night. Tori's probably over at the main stage. I'll put money on her guesting out there later."

"I'd love to duet with her one day," confessed Ellen with a nervous giggle. "She's the Queen of Scream."

"Not your style, my lovely," said Taylor with a wink. "Must be time. Here's the boss coming."

As soon as he was within earshot, Rocky declared, "Showtime, boys and girl."

He gave a nod to one of the organisers, the PA tape stopped as the lights dimmed and a resounding roar echoed round the tent. Taking a deep breath, Ellen composed herself to begin the Latin chant to start Swirling Mists. Her hand trembled slightly with nerves as she saw Dan move towards her. Slowly, she began the song and silence descended on the crowd. Her powerful voice rang out clear and confident over the audience, leaving the last note almost hovering over them. With a flash of green light, the band powered headlong into the show opener.

When the lights settled on the stage, Ellen stood with her hood up in the centre between Taylor and Cal. Her raucous vocal soared alongside their guitars as After Life poured their energies into the set. There was no hint that this was their fourth show in four days. All of them were full of life, bursting with adrenaline pumped energy.

Two songs later, After Life began the intimidating eerie Rats. With her hood shadowing her face, Ellen prowled the width of the stage, keeping her vocal low and haunting. As Taylor stepped forward for his guitar solo, she slipped into the shadows, re-emerging a few moments later at the end of the pit. Keeping her hood up, Ellen worked her way along the rail as she sang the final verse. Slickly, Taylor played a reprise of the end section from his solo to allow her time to return to the stage for the final chorus.

"Wales!" screamed Ellen at the end of the song as she tossed back her hood, "How the hell are you tonight?"

The fans enthusiastic response made her nod approvingly.

"Sounding good. Looking great!" she complimented. "Are you ready for a trip into the After Life?"

A huge roar suggested to her that they were more than ready.

"Alright," she said with a smile. "We don't play this one too often. Not sure why but we're going to play it for you beautiful people tonight. This is Beyond The Edge Of Reality."

With a gentle snare rhythm, Jack eased them into the complex song. When they'd agreed to add it into the set, none of them could remember why they didn't play it more often. The lyrics alternated between a sickly sweet, feminine version of Ellen and an evil, hissing, demonic version. This split personality angle made it all the more fun for her to sing. In front of them, the fans were loving it and, if the reaction was anything to judge by, the song had found its niche in the set.

A couple of songs later, Ellen was somewhat relieved to see Michael bring the transport case out on stage. The lights dimmed, leaving two spotlights trained on the box. With a little intimate exchange of glances, Tailz and Ellen took their seats.

"Time to slow it down a little," said Ellen softly. "Quiet time. 3am time."

The crowd cheered.

"Lou Lou At 3am," introduced Ellen as Taylor began the delicate guitar intro.

As they started the song, it struck her that the band had made an error earlier in the set. They'd agreed to drop the electric version of Rats but had fallen into the trap of routine and already played it! Trying to remain calm, she poured her emotion into Lou Lou At 3am, reaching into the hearts and souls of the audience in front of her. Beside her, Taylor sat head bowed, lost in the acoustic melody, oblivious to their error.

When the song ended the fans erupted, their passion for the ballad clear for all to hear.

"We've screwed up," whispered Ellen to Taylor. "We've played Rats."

"Shit," he muttered. "Now what?"

"Trust me," she said calmly. "I'll confess our sins but I have a plan."

Gradually, the cheers died away. Off to the side, Ellen could see Dan Crow waiting for his cue to join them.

"Folks," began Ellen sincerely. "We've messed up a bit but I'm going to give you a choice."

The crowd looked on expectantly.

"We had planned to play the acoustic version of Rats," she explained honestly. "But we forgot and have already played it. So, you can choose the next song. Either we play the acoustic version as planned or we play a brand new After Life song."

She could feel Taylor staring her, a look of mild panic on his face.

"OK," continued Ellen. "If you want to hear Rats, scream now."

A huge screaming roar echoed round the tent.

"And if you want to hear a new song, shout now!"

A deafening roar thundered through the marquee.

"Alright, lovely people. New song it is," declared Ellen. "And trust me, this song is so new that Taylor here hasn't heard it."

"And she's not joking!" he added.

"Lovely people of Wales, I give you Broken Doll," announced Ellen, getting to her feet.

"What do I do?" asked Taylor softly.

"Nothing. Listen."

Casually, Ellen walked across the stage then sat down, cross legged, in the centre front, her cloak billowing about her. She took a few deep breaths to compose herself then began to sing with a pure crystal clarity that none of them had heard before. She sang of the pain and the loss of being broken, the heartache of being discarded, the fragility of being a "Broken Doll".

From his seat on the transport case, Taylor sat engrossed, lost in the pain of her heartfelt acapella performance. At first, he thought she was singing about a broken relationship then it struck him that she was singing about herself. She was the Broken Doll. She was singing about the tragedy of her trip to Thailand and the after effects.

Around them, the crowd was stunned into silence by her performance. By sitting down in front of them, Ellen had cleverly created a child-like scene and an air of fragility that perfectly matched the mood of the song. As she let the last note ring out over the audience, she bent forward, almost disappearing into the folds of the material of the cloak.

The fans went wild. Taylor, too, was on his feet applauding her. Laying his guitar down, he walked across the stage to help her back to her feet. Stealing a brief hug, he whispered, "Incredible song."

Tears were running down her cheeks but he was relieved to see she was smiling. Keeping a protective arm around her, Taylor addressed the fans, "Let's hear it for the incredibly beautiful and talented, Miss Ellen Lloyd!"

Beside him, he could tell that Ellen was blushing.

"Thank you," she said humbly as the applause died down. "Now, we have another treat for you. We'd like to welcome a very special guest on stage. Give it up for Dan Crow from Weigh Station!"

Right on cue, Dan loped out to join the two members of After Life. Having waved to the fans, he too hugged Ellen, congratulating her swiftly on her performance.

"We've not had much rehearsal time," explained Ellen as the three of them sat down on the large transport case.

"A mere twenty minutes," commented Dan with a wink.

"If that," laughed Ellen. "We worked fast though and re-worked a Weigh Station classic for you. Folks, as you've never heard it before, this is Miles From Home."

Instead of the better known hard and fast electric intro, Taylor picked out a gentler version of the melody. He kept his head bowed, focussing completely on the unfamiliar arrangement of the classic Weigh Station anthem. Exactly as in their brief rehearsal, Dan came in first, his voice lower and huskier than normal, and sang the opening verse, creating a bluesy feel to the song. Together in perfect harmony, he sang the chorus with Ellen then allowed her to lead the second verse. She too was ably demonstrating the versatility of her voice as she continued the blues tone in her own performance. Totally in sync with each other, they performed the second chorus before trading lines through the final verse and chorus.

When the song ended, Dan put his arm around After Life's leading lady, pulling her close, "Stunning, my darling girl. Stunning."

"Thank you," she whispered, feeling her cheeks flush at the compliment.

Together, hand in hand, they stood up and took a bow as the fans cheered and roared their appreciation. Behind them, the rest of After Life returned to the stage and the transport case was discretely removed.

"Ladies and gentlemen, let's hear it for the one and only Dan Crow!" roared Ellen to be heard over the enthusiastic fans. "Want him to stay for one more song?"

The resulting deafening roar clearly suggested they did.

"This is Wreckless!" screamed Ellen.

After Life commenced the fast, heavy, powerful intro to Wreckless, Luke's bass dominating the sound. Instantly, the vibe in the marquee shifted and the energy levels soared. When Dan came in on vocals, his voice was harsh and raw in comparison to a few moments before, the Welsh fans instantly joined in. All of them were word perfect. As Ellen led them into the second verse, she wondered if the fans would keep singing. They did! Hearing so many rock fans accompany her was a surreal experience. The rest of the Weigh Station anthem disappeared in a blur and, before she knew it, they were singing the last lines of the final chorus.

"Wales!" hollered Dan to be heard over the fans' cheers and screams. "Give it up for Ellen one more time for me!"

"And give it up for Dan Crow," added Ellen.

As the cheers began to die away, Dan took a bow and darted from the stage.

"Oh, how to follow that!" gasped Ellen with a glance round at her band mates. "Communication Breakdown!"

Singing the high fast Led Zeppelin classic so soon after Wreckless took its toll on Ellen and, by the closing section of the song, she could feel the fire of over exertion in her chest. Much as she loved singing that particular song, she was relieved when the lights went out as planned at the end, allowing her to step off stage during Jack's drum solo.

"You holding up ok, princess?" asked Rocky as he passed her a glucose drink.

"Starting to struggle," she confessed between mouthfuls.

"What can I get you to help?" asked the band's manager anxiously.

"Nothing," replied Ellen. "I'll deal with it later. I'll be fine. I won't let the band down. Or you."

While Jack wowed the crowd with his drumming, Ellen paced slowly back and forth, focussing on her breathing, working to slow it down. The sharp pain in her side began to recede a little and become more bearable. Slowly, she let out a long sigh.

"You ok?" asked Taylor, putting a hand on her shoulder.

With a weary smile, she nodded, "Just about."

"Only four more."

"Five," she corrected, visualising the set list. "You forgot we added Problem Child."

"We can drop it if you're struggling here."

Ellen shook her head. "I'll be fine."

All four of them stood at the side watching the closing sector of Jack's solo. Much to their amazement, he hadn't split any drum heads throughout the entire show. He nodded over to them, the agreed signal for the band to return to the stage as he began the long, slow drum intro to Depths Of The Pit. For once, Ellen was thankful for the slow demonic rhythm of the song. Despite being one of the lengthier songs in the set, it was easier on her vocally, its energy coming from the frenzied guitar duels rather than her vocals. Still on a high from her duets with Dan, Ellen was in a playful mood and added a few menacing hisses to the song as she roamed the stage restlessly among the band. Both Luke and Taylor played along and hissed back at her but Cal and Jack both just laughed.

After Life rounded off their main set with Kashmir. The crowd's energy remained at an all-time high and almost blew the marquee apart when unannounced Dan re-appeared for the final section of the song. The band were as surprised as the fans but after a few nods and some sign language, the last of the vocal chores were split and Ellen graciously allowed him to carry the song through to the end, thankful for a few extra moments rest.

By the time they began Smoke On The Water, she was running on empty. The sugar boost from her energy drinks was gone, the last of her reserves spent. Much as she loved the song and felt that she had just played the best show of her life, Ellen was relieved when it came time for her disappearing trick.

As soon as she was off stage, she stumbled into the arms of Rocky and Dan. Both of them took one look at her and, in unison, called for medical support.

"I'm fine," she mumbled. "I just need a minute or two."

"You need a doctor, darling," stated Dan firmly. "No arguments."

By the time the rest of After Life came off stage, Ellen had been whisked off to the festival's medical tent. Taylor was the first member of the band to reach there, having sprinted across the site. As he half fell into the tent, he glanced round anxiously searching for her.

"Over here," called Rocky from his right.

"Is she ok?" gasped Taylor as he made his way over.

"De-hydrated and generally exhausted," replied the band's manager. "Otherwise she's ok."

"Tailz," called Ellen softly from behind Rocky. "I'm fine. Really, I'm ok."

Coming to sit beside her, Taylor asked, "You sure? You gave us all a fright. I saw you faint and started to panic. When I got off stage, you were gone."

At that moment, the first aider came over, "Ellen, are you sure you won't let us call an ambulance? I'd feel happier if you got checked out at the local hospital."

"I'm sure," stated Ellen bluntly. "I just need something to eat and a good night's sleep."

"Ok but you're not going anywhere until you've finished that jug of juice. I'll pop back in a few minutes."

"Rocky," began Ellen. "Can you find me something to eat, please? I'm starving."

"Of course," replied the older man. "What do you want?"

"Anything. Food."

"I'll be back as soon as I can," he promised.

As soon as their manager was out of the tent, Taylor wrapped her in his arms and held her tight.

"You scared the crap out of me. You sure you're alright?"

"I'm exhausted. I just need a few days to recover," she said with a smile. "Someone mentioned a few days at the beach. That should do it."

"My nana will soon have you back on your feet. She'll be force feeding you her medicinal chicken broth. Jen'll smother you in kindness too," he replied, kissing her forehead tenderly. "We'll take care of you."

"Sounds good to me," sighed Ellen.

They were interrupted by a discrete cough from behind Taylor.

Both of them looked up to see Dan Crow standing there.

"Just wanted to check on our little songbird," he said warmly, reaching out to hug Ellen. "You gave Rocky and I a bit of a scare back there."

"I'm fine, Dan. And thank you for your help," replied Ellen as she tried to stifle a yawn.

"My pleasure," said the older musician warmly. "It's been a real treat playing with you kids tonight. Reminded me of the early days of Weigh Station. Long time ago. Roughing it through Europe in a clapped out old van. Do you have a hotel booked for tonight?"

"Yes, sir," answered Taylor. "Well, a guest house. We're taking off in the morning for a few days."

"You got transport sorted?"

Taylor nodded, "Band are dropping us at the guest house. I've a hire car getting delivered in the morning then we're off to Cornwall. I'm taking Ellen home to meet my family."

"Home cooking and sea air cures everything," said Dan with a wink before softly adding, "Well, almost everything."

"Thanks for today," said Ellen, sitting up a bit. "Wait till my dad hears that I sang three numbers with you. He's going to be so mad he missed this."

"It's me who should be thanking you. Now, you get some rest and I'll see you soon," said Dan as he prepared to leave. "Taylor, look after her. That's one hell of a singer you guys have there. A talented songbird with nerves of steel. Pulling off a brand-new song mid-set, unrehearsed. Impressive."

"I intend to," replied Taylor, shaking his hand. "And thanks for everything."

Not long after Dan left, Rocky reappeared accompanied by the remaining members of After Life and a box full of burgers, chips and beers. All of them sat around Ellen making sure she ate her fill and, under the watchful eye of the first aider, finished the jug of rehydration fluids. The band's relaxed banter about the success of their set helped to buoy her spirits and it wasn't long before Luke commented, "When were you planning on telling us about our latest song, Miss Lloyd?"

Blushing, Ellen confessed, "I had hoped to work on it some more and add it to the board when we hit the studio."

"It's fantastic," commented Jack honestly. "I can't see how you can improve on it."

"When I realised we'd messed up, I had to think on my feet," continued Ellen softly. "It was the first song that sprang to mind."

"Scared the hell out of me," laughed Taylor. "I hadn't a fucking clue what I was meant to do. I was shitting myself that I'd forgotten something or that I should be doing something to help you out."

"Sorry," apologised Ellen, squeezing his hand.

"It was an inspired moment of quick thinking," complimented Rocky, glancing at the time. "The fireworks to close the festival are due to go off in five minutes then we need to think about heading off."

"We'll meet you back at the van," said Taylor firmly. "You guys go on ahead. We'll catch up. Ellen needs to get signed out of here."

Taking the hint, the rest of the band plus Rocky departed. As soon as the members of After Life were safely out of the way, the first aider came back to check Ellen over. With a warning to keep her fluid intake up and to take things easy, accompanied by Taylor, she was allowed to leave the medical tent. Hand in hand, they headed slowly across the site as the colourful fireworks lit up the night sky above them.

"You ok?" asked Taylor as they paused to watch the finale.

"Tired but ok," assured Ellen, squeezing his hand. "Sorry for scaring you. Kind of scared myself too if I'm honest."

"As long as you're ok," said Taylor warmly. "Now, let's get this show on the road and find our bed for the night."

An hour later, their hostess for the night showed them both up the narrow staircase in the remote farmhouse to the attic guest suite. Having advised them that breakfast was served between eight and nine thirty, she wished them good night.

"There's a jacuzzi if you feel like unwinding," suggested Taylor, pointing towards the bathroom.

"Tailz, it's one in the morning," giggled Ellen.

"So?"

"I'm game if you are but just for a little while. Might help ease off the aches and pains."

"You get yourself sorted out then and I'll figure out how to fill it," suggested Taylor. "There should be a bottle of champagne in my rucksack. End of tour celebration."

"And glasses?"

"Eh......," stammered Taylor, looking sheepish. "No."

Spying two mugs sitting beside a kettle on top of the chest of drawers, Ellen said," "Problem solved. Mugs it is."

With the warm water of the jacuzzi bubbling around them, the two musicians sat back and let the warmth soothe away the stresses and strains of the last few days of tour. Taking a sip of her champagne, Ellen asked, "How long will it take to get to your Nana's house tomorrow?"

"About four hours or thereabouts. Longer if you want to take the coast road the whole way," replied Taylor with a yawn.

"What have you told them about...." she faltered, glancing down at her arm. "You know…"

"Not a lot. Just the basics," said Taylor. "Don't worry. They're understanding people. They won't pry. When they hear about tonight, both Jen and Nana will be smothering you in kindness. Just relax about it all, my lovely."

"I'm nervous," giggled Ellen beginning to feel the effects of the champagne.

"Nervous? You?" laughed Taylor. "Is this the same Ellen who stood on stage a few hours ago and sang a brand-new song acapella with no rehearsal? The same Ellen who duetted three times with one of England's biggest rock stars?"

"No," she giggled. "That was the After Life Ellen. The real Ellen is rather anxious about meeting your family. Terrified in fact."

"Why?"

"No one's ever taken me home to meet their family before," she confessed quietly.

"It'll be fine," promised Taylor with a yawn. "I just wish my mum could've met you."

After almost four hours in the car, Ellen finally got a sense that they were approaching Taylor's home. Once they'd left the motorway behind, he relaxed, navigating the smaller A class and B class roads with the ease of familiarity. As they passed a sign for Newquay's airport, he looked over at her and smiled.

"Not far now," he said with an impish grin. "I hope they're home. I left my keys at Rocky's."

"When do I get to see the sea and the beach?"

"You won't really," explained Taylor. "Not from here, unless I stop off in the village first. We can go for a walk later. I'll find you your beach."

"Did you grow up here?"

Taylor nodded, "Spent all my life in this area until I went to London to audition for After Life. Every chance I get though, I come home."

"You miss the sea when you're in London, don't you?"

"Every day," he confessed openly. "I grew up in it or on it. Boats. Fishing. Surfing. Swimming. There's worse places to grow up."

"You surf?" giggled Ellen, visualising him riding the waves.

"Yes, I do," he said with more than a hint of pride. "Quite well actually, even if I do say so myself. And I intend to tomorrow morning. Want to watch?"

"This I have to see," she declared as he turned the car into one of the narrowest roads she had ever been on.

A mile or so further on, Taylor turned right down a steep narrow hedge-lined lane. Gaps in the hedge indicated cottages hiding behind them.

"Home sweet home," he sighed turning into a narrow gap that opened onto a wide gravel driveway.

At the sound of the car crunching its way into a parking spot at the far side of the cottage, the front door opened and a young dark-haired woman rushed out.

"Nana, they're here!" she yelled as she ran towards the car.

"Jen," said Taylor to Ellen as he turned off the engine. Leaving the key in the ignition, he opened the door and had only just climbed out of the car when his twin sister flew into his arms.

"Hey," he said, hugging her close. "Miss me?"

"Every day," she said, squeezing him tight. "Where's Ellen? I'm dying to meet her."

Behind them, Ellen had stepped out of the car and was watching them looking on a little anxiously.

"She's in the car," replied Taylor with a smile. Turning round, he added, "Actually, she's beside the car."

"Hi," said Ellen.

"Hi!" squealed Jen, dashing round. "Great to finally meet you. Taylor's done nothing but talk about you for weeks!"

Blushing, Taylor growled, "Jen, be nice."

"Ignore him," giggled Jen with a wink to her twin. "How was your journey? Oh, and how did the Open Air show go last night?"

"The journey here was very twisty!" said Ellen, warming immediately to Taylor's sister. "Open Air was fantastic. Great crowd."

"We'll tell you all about it later," promised Taylor as he opened the boot to retrieve their bags. "It was a late night. We're both knackered. Hope you've got the kettle on."

"It's just on the boil, son," said a voice behind him.

"Nana!"

Dropping the bags, Taylor turned to hug the tiny white-haired lady behind him. He held her close for a few moments as he whispered something to her. With a smile, she patted his hand and nodded knowingly.

"And you must be Ellen. Oh, he's told us so much about you," said the old woman, her brown eyes twinkling with mischief. "Come round the back. We'll sit outside with our tea for a bit while it's warm."

While Taylor grabbed their luggage, Jen and Nana took Ellen round the side of the house. Smiling, he watched as she followed them hesitantly. He understood how anxious she got around strangers but he felt confident that she'd soon relax in the company of the other women in his life.

When he came out to join them in the garden a few minutes later, he was relieved to find Ellen smiling. Taking a seat on the bench beside her, he asked softly, "You ok?"

"Fine," she replied with a smile.

"Ellen was just saying that Dan Crow turned up to sing with you guys yesterday," commented Jen, looking impressed. "Hanging out with rock royalty, brother?"

"He just kind of showed up," replied Taylor, lifting his mug of tea. "Not sure if Jason invited him or if Luke had something to do with it. Luke's uncle's friends with all these big names."

"I think it might have been Rocky who invited him," countered Ellen.

"Maybe. He seems a really down to earth, regular guy. Hung about with us. Played two songs then sneaked out on stage for a third unplanned."

"Gate crashed by a rock legend!" teased Jen, clapping her hands. "Brilliant!"

"Surreal," added Ellen, her voice still a little husky after the four shows in a row.

"I don't know how you do it," laughed Jen. "Isn't it exhausting? All that travelling and performing? When do you sleep or eat?"

"Ten shows in fourteen days," mused Taylor. "It's been a busy couple of weeks."

"Well, Ellen looks exhausted," stated Nana bluntly. "Girlie, you're too pale. Too thin too. You need a few days of good, clean sea air and Nana's cooking."

With a quick glance towards Taylor, Ellen confessed, "I am exhausted. The last four days have wiped me out. Sea air and home cooking sounds like the perfect cure."

Before she could stop him, Taylor said, "Our little songbird here needs a lot of rest. She collapsed after the show last night."

"Tailz!" protested Ellen sharply. "I was dehydrated. I'm fine now."

"You were exhausted and dehydrated," stated Taylor bluntly. "Nana, this is one stubborn girl. You two should get along famously."

"I'm sure we will," said the old woman with a nod to Ellen.

Conversation soon turned to more family related matters and Ellen sat quietly listening to Nana and Jen filling Taylor in on the recent developments in the village and the progress with settling his mother's affairs.

"What about the house?" asked Taylor, draining the last of the tea in his mug.

"There's a tenant in it on a six-month lease," explained Jen. "An artist from London. He's looking for a property to retire to so he may make an offer on it if he falls in love with the area. Nice guy. Does lovely watercolours."

"And our baby brother?" quizzed Taylor, a hint of bitterness to his tone that Ellen had never heard before.

"He's still around. Drops by now and then. He's staying in Newquay with his friend from the surf school. I invited him over for dinner but we'll see if he bothers to put in an appearance."

"Speaking of surfing," said Tailz, moving conversation onto safer ground. "Is my wetsuit here? And my boards?"

"The wetsuits are in the hall cupboard," replied Nana. "And your boards are in the end shed over there."

"When are you planning to catch some waves?" asked Jen, understanding all too well her twin's passion for the sea.

"Every morning," answered her brother. "I checked the forecast. Surf's meant to be good this week till at least Friday. Wind's to change on Saturday. Might need to drive further afield for some decent waves."

"Still a surf bum!" joked Jen. "Do you surf, Ellen?"

"Never tried," she answered. "Don't think I've the balance for it now."

"Oh!" gasped Jen, flushing with embarrassment. "Sorry! I never thought. Christ, I'm an idiot."

"No, you're not," said Ellen warmly. "My balance is a bit off since the accident but I could maybe be persuaded to give surfing a try."

"Can you swim?" asked Taylor.

"Not as well as I used to but it's better than my piano playing," joked Ellen, deliberately poking fun at herself to lighten the atmosphere.

"Let's see how the waves are and you can maybe give it a go," proposed Taylor, relieved that she was already comfortable among them. "Nana, what time's dinner? I was going to take Ellen for a walk. Stretch our legs a bit after being stuck in the car half the day."

"Your sister's cooking tonight, not me."

"Six thirty," suggested Jen. "Gives you a couple of hours."

"Plenty of time," said Taylor, getting to his feet. "I put Ellen's bags in the front bedroom. Is that ok?"

"Both bedrooms are ready. Use what you need," commented Nana with a wink. "Just remember, I'm a light sleeper, Taylor."

Flushing scarlet, Taylor muttered, "Come on, Ellen. I'll show you where I put your stuff."

Inside, the cottage was more modern and spacious than Ellen had anticipated. A wooden staircase with a thick rope for a handrail led to the upper level where there were three bedrooms and a large bathroom. Another narrow spiral stair led up to the attic.

"That used to be my space," explained Taylor. "But Jen's moved in up there. We both spent more time here than at my mum's when we were young. Long story. One for another day."

The front bedroom was bright and furnished with pine furniture and gingham bedcovers and curtains. Ellen's bags sat on the floor beside the large pine framed bed.

"Are we sharing?" she asked softly. "Or…"

"I've put my gear in the back bedroom. We can work things out later. Feels a bit…you know… weird with family about."

Giggling, Ellen enquired, "Taylor Rowe, have you gone prudish on me?"

"Perhaps," he admitted. "Feel up to a walk?"

"Sure. Need some fresh air after being cooped up all week in that van."

"Put your trainers on rather than those sandals," he suggested. "You'll need them."

With promises to be back before six, Taylor led Ellen back out into the lane then turned right, heading further down the narrow hedge lined road. At the end, there was a small path that opened out after a few metres onto a well-worn cliff top trail. Taking her hand, Taylor walked slowly beside Ellen allowing her to set the pace. Overhead, gulls were circling then swooping down out to sea just out of their line of sight.

"Must be a fishing trip coming back in," mused Taylor, pointing to the flock of birds flying in frenzied circles. "They dump the fish guts out before they come back into the harbour for the birds."

They walked on in virtual silence for a few moments as they

both drank in the beauty and solitude around them.

"It's so peaceful," whispered Ellen with a sigh. "So beautiful but, I don't know, sad in a way."

"I know what you mean. It's an atmospheric coastline. Maybe it'll prove inspirational for your song writing."

"I'm on holiday," declared Ellen emphatically. "I'm just Ellen for now. Not singer Ellen. Not songwriter Ellen. Just Ellen."

"Hmm," said Taylor knowingly. "We'll see how long that lasts."

"What do you mean?"

"You'll see, my lovely," he laughed. "Come on. I want to show you somewhere. Want to introduce you to someone."

"Where are we going?"

"Church," he replied with a hint of sadness.

As they walked along, Taylor occasionally deviated from the path to pick some wildflowers and heather. With a smile, he tucked a large daisy-like flower into Ellen's hair then added two or three more into the growing posy in his hand. Before long, they reached a low crumbling stone wall and beyond it, Ellen could see the headstones in the graveyard.

"I'll wait here," she suggested. "I don't want to intrude."

"No," said Taylor almost instantly. "Come with me." He paused. "I've not been here since….you know."

"If you're sure."

He nodded. "This church is one of the oldest along the coast. It's rarely used for services but our family plot has been here for about two hundred years. Some ancient grandfather owned a tin mine and bought a large section of the graveyard. It'll take us another two hundred years to fill it!"

Smiling, Ellen allowed him to help her over the wall. Immediately, an air of calm descended over her. She could still hear the waves crashing against the cliffs behind them but, in the graveyard, all was still. Birds sang in the trees and bushes. Suddenly, it struck her that this small corner of the world was one of the most tranquil spots she had ever visited.

"This way," said Taylor, pointing to a well-kept gravel path.

A low fence with an ornate gate bordered the family's plot. As he lifted the latch, the gate squealed, disturbing the birds in the nearby trees. With a lump in his throat as fresh grief threatened to overwhelm him, Taylor led them to the spot where his mother had been laid to rest. Seeing the headstone for the first time tore at his heart. Almost forgetting that Ellen was with him, he walked forward to touch the stone, tracing the lettering with trembling fingers. Tears slid down his cheeks as he laid the flowers down on the grave. Kneeling beside them, he bowed his head, letting the tears flow.

Discretely, Ellen stood back a little, allowing him time to grieve in private. Late afternoon sun was shining on the gravestones and she couldn't help but be drawn to read the various names and dates. The one to the left of where Taylor knelt brought her up short. It was his father's grave. He'd never mentioned his father and she'd never asked, assuming wrongly that his parents had divorced. She read the dates on the weathered stone and realised that Taylor had only been three years old when his dad had passed away.

"Ellen."

The voice interrupted her thoughts.

"Ellen," repeated Taylor, his voice soft and husky.

Taking care not to stand on the graves themselves, Ellen moved over to join him.

"Mum," he began, his voice barely above a whisper. "This is Ellen. You'd love her. She's a lot like you. I wish you could've met each other. Wish you'd heard her sing."

He paused to roughly wipe away his tears.

"I miss you, mum. Miss your crazy text messages and silly Facebook posts. I miss your laugh and your smiles. I miss seeing your face in the crowd when we play."

Gently, Ellen rested her hand on his shoulder. Through a veil of tears, he looked up at her, "Sorry."

"What are you sorry for, Tailz? Being emotional? Missing your mum? Never be sorry for expressing how you really feel."

"Yeah and what would the others say if they could see me now?"

"They'd understand," she assured him. Kneeling beside him, she plucked the flower from her hair and laid it down beside his posy on the sunlit grass. "Mrs Rowe, you have a very talented, very kind son. He's been my rock since I joined the band. He's looked out for me. He's taken care of me. Loved me. You should be very proud of him."

Gracefully, she got to her feet, kissed the top of his head and said, "I'll wait over at the path. Take your time."

A few minutes later, Taylor came walking towards her, running his hand through his hair. When he reached her, he pulled her into his arms and held her.

"Thanks," he said, his voice thick and husky with emotion. "That was harder than I thought it would be. Kind of feels like I've lost her all over again."

"I understand," whispered Ellen. "Grief hits us when we least expect it. Just when you think you're alright, bam!"

Taylor nodded, "Don't tell the others….."

"Shh," interrupted Ellen softly. "This is your time. Nothing to do with them. I won't breathe a word. I'm kind of honoured you brought me here."

"Nana's suggestion," he confessed. "Said I was to introduce the two of you. Think it was her way of making sure I came here."

"She's a wise woman your nana."

"Yes, she is," he agreed with a smile. "Jen's very like her. Kind of an apprentice old woman."

Giggling, Ellen said, "Don't let her hear you saying that!"

It was enough to lift the sombre atmosphere and Taylor found himself laughing with her.

"Feel up to a walk along the beach before we head back?"

"A short walk."

"You ok?" concern echoed through the question.

"Just a bit tired," she confessed. "And my ribs are hurting a bit."

"Is that normal? I mean, after a show, is that the way they feel?" bumbled Taylor awkwardly.

"I'm fine, Tailz!" she said firmly. "Four nights in a row, especially when the last one was a full set had just strained me a bit. It'll settle down in a day or so."

"Maybe we should leave the beach till the morning," he suggested, worrying that the climb down the steep cliff face staircase might prove to be too much for her.

"Is it on the way back to the house?"

"Yes."

"Then let's go," she said with a smile.

Negotiating the cliff side stairs proved to be tricky for Ellen. Part way down, as she was forced to "bum" her way down, she confessed to not liking heights. Eventually, they both felt sand under their feet as they reached the bottom. Hearing Ellen breathe a sigh of relief, Taylor laughed, "You'll be running down that path by the end of the week."

"I doubt it," muttered Ellen. "That's scary!"

"Only the first couple of times."

With the coarse sand scrunching under their feet, he led Ellen down the beach to the water's edge.

"Is this the main beach?" she asked, looking round the small secluded cove.

"No," laughed Taylor. "This is just….well…it's just one bit of it. When the tide's really low you can reach the main beach from here. There's a couple of ways but the easiest is to swim round those rocks to your left. This is the beach I hung out at with my friends as a teenager. My mum brought us here as kids to play. It's more sheltered than the village beach and safer. Quieter."

"It's beautiful. Your own private beach," she declared, gazing round at the rugged cliffs. "Is that a cave?"

"Sure is. Party cave," replied Taylor with a wink. "Come on, let's take a look. Want to check on something."

As they approached the mouth of the cave, Taylor noted the fresh ashes in the stone circle that served as fireplace. A new pile of driftwood sat on the ledge just inside the mouth of the cave, keeping it out of the reach of the incoming tide should the water reach high enough. From the line of seaweed on the beach, the tide hadn't reached the cave in quite a while. Casually, Taylor explained that it was only really winter tides that flooded it. The ledge at the back of the cave was stocked with more wood plus a polystyrene cooler. Curiosity getting the better of him, Taylor opened it and wasn't surprised to find a selection of beers and cider plus a half empty bottle of vodka. On the opposite ledge, the surfboard still sat and, as he ran his hand over it, he could tell it had been freshly waxed. Reaching into the dark recess behind the old well-used board, his hand found the guitar. Carefully, he slid it out and carried it over to the mouth of the cave.

"This is the first guitar I ever attempted to play," he revealed as he took a seat on a rock. "No idea how old it is. No idea how long it's been hidden back there. No idea who originally bought it."

Gently, he strummed a few chords.

"And it's out of tune," he proclaimed with a grin. "Soon sort that."

Taking a seat on a nearby rock, Ellen watched as he teased the instrument back into tune. Satisfied with the tuning, he smiled over at her and began to play Lou Lou At 3am. He played a verse and the chorus then paused before playing a melody line that she hadn't heard before. After a minute or two, Taylor stopped.

"I guess someone is still playing this. Strings are new," he commented. "I checked it out before I left for London the last time. Put it back in tune then too. Guess the local kids still party here."

"And drink," added Ellen, pointing to an empty vodka bottle lying half buried in the sand.

"Not much else for them to do," he conceded. "It's about a four or five mile walk into Newquay. The village here is kind of sleepy. Not really a teenage paradise. Never has been."

"So, did you learn to drink here as well as play guitar?" she teased.

Blushing, Taylor nodded, "Not some of my prouder moments. I've woken up in the cave and on the sand with a few hangovers in my time."

"I'll bet," laughed Ellen.

Smiling at the memories, Taylor started to play the guitar again, picking out a Southern rock melody. Unable to resist the temptation, Ellen began to whistle then to sing along, improvising lyrics of beach bonfires and sunsets. With no pressure on them, the two members of After Life relaxed and just enjoyed the sounds of the beach mixed with the melodies.

"I knew singer Ellen couldn't stay hidden," mused Taylor as he finally laid the guitar down. "We should work on that bonfire sunset one. Think we're onto something there."

"We should," she replied then paused, "You were right. This place is inspirational. Atmospheric."

"Ah, the creative juices are beginning to flow!"

Giggling like a teenager, Ellen eventually managed to say, "I'm not even going to try to deny it."

"Jen will no doubt want us to play for her," admitted Taylor standing up. "She always does. Anyways, we better head back. We're going to be late for dinner."

Both of them were still giggling like two teenagers when they stumbled in the back door of the cottage.

"Ah, the wandering minstrels finally return," declared Jen, looking and sounding a little harassed. "Dinner's been ready for twenty minutes."

"My fault," apologised Ellen quietly. "That cliff path was a bit of a struggle for me."

"No harm done," assured Jen. "It's easy to keep lasagne warm."

"Your homemade lasagne?" quizzed her twin hopefully.

"Yes, and with bread from Artisan's in the village.

"Ah, I've died and gone to heaven!" he sighed theatrically. "My favourite homecoming meal!"

A discrete cough from the doorway stopped him. Flushing scarlet, he added, "Nana, your homemade pasties are also my favourite meal. My favourite meal ever."

"And a good thing too, son," replied the old woman. "That's the plan for tomorrow's dinner."

"Speaking of plans," began Jen as she dished up their meal. "I met Russ in Artisan's. He wants us to meet him and a few of the others on Thursday night. Said you've to bring a guitar or two along."

"Where to?" quizzed Taylor, taking his usual seat at the table and indicating to Ellen to sit to his right.

"To the bar at the hotel. He's trying to get a live music night off the ground. Says he needs all the help he can get. Even yours!" explained his sister, setting their meal before them.

"Could be fun," he agreed. "I'll speak to him before Thursday. See what he has planned."

Biting her lower lip, Jen confessed, "I kind of already promised you would be there and that you'd play."

"Oh, you did, did you, Jennifer!"

Sheepishly, his twin nodded. Trying to feign anger, Taylor looked over at Ellen, winked, then said, "Well, I guess we'll have to go then and you'll be buying the first round, sister dearest."

Shortly after dinner, Ellen excused herself, confessing that she was exhausted and said she was going for an early night. As she climbed the stairs, she could hear Taylor explaining about her collapse the night before in more detail than they'd revealed earlier. Once in the bedroom, she sat down on the bed, removed her tinted glasses and let out a long sigh. Every inch of her ached. It had been a long time since she had felt so tired.

Taking her time, Ellen slowly and methodically went through her night time ritual of creams and ointments. Some of the scars on her ribs were inflamed so she spent extra time on them. As she had been advised, she sat cross legged on the bed and focused on her breathing for a few minutes. Eventually, she was satisfied that all was well. With a yawn, she climbed into bed and, listening to the murmur of conversation from below, drifted off to sleep.

Downstairs in the kitchen, the twins were washing the dishes. Like a well-oiled machine, they worked efficiently together, their years of practice evident in the fluidity of movements. They chatted quietly about the band and about Taylor's song writing progress but, eventually, Jen steered the conversation on to Ellen. With the dishes all done and the kitchen tidy, she poured them both a drink then, as they sat together at the table, commented, "She's not what I expected."

"What did you expect?" asked Tailz curiously.

"She's so fragile. So shy," replied his twin. "You could see she was really struggling through dinner. Is she ok?"

"I'll check on her in a bit but she's fine," reassured Taylor warmly. "Off stage, she's shy. I guess she is a bit fragile. Being among strangers and having to eat in front of folk makes her uncomfortable at first. Ellen's very self-conscious about her arm. The last couple of weeks have been a huge challenge for her. Mentally and physically she's drained. I've never met anyone like her before. She's determined and driven beyond belief."

"Nana loves her," confessed Jen with a knowing smile. "Says she's your soulmate and then said you should be friends not lovers!"

"God, I love Nana," laughed Taylor before adding. "And I love Ellen too."

"She's the first girl you've ever brought home," commented his sister with a wink. "So, I guess she must be special."

"She is."

"It must be hard for her," Jen said quietly. "I can't imagine how you pick up the pieces after an accident like hers."

"She's tougher than she looks," replied Taylor. "There's a steely determination there. And she pushes herself to the limits. She hates it if we even suggest making allowances for her."

"I saw you help her with her meal," began his sister awkwardly.

He nodded, "We have an understanding about things like that. Things that are still awkward for her in front of strangers."

"Did she play any instruments before or was she always a singer?"

"She always sang but she was an accomplished pianist and could play a bit of guitar too," revealed Taylor. "Luke has helped her out a couple of times with the piano. Jokes he's her right-hand man."

"That's sick!"

"I know but sometimes you need a bit of sick humour to lighten things. Give her a few days and you'll understand. If she asks you for help with anything then you know you've earned her trust."

A strong salty, sea aroma wakened Ellen next morning. Opening her eyes, she saw Taylor was sitting on the edge of the bed, his hair still damp and his face flushed. He ran his fingers through the lengths of her hair as he said, "Good morning, sleeping beauty."

"Morning."

"Sleep well?"

"Like a baby. Best sleep I've had for a very long time. Must've been all that good, clean sea air yesterday."

"And nothing to do with the tour?" he teased. "You realise you've slept for over twelve hours straight?"

"I have?"

Taylor nodded, "It's almost eleven. Jen was wanting to take us out for lunch."

"Give me an hour. I'll be ready," promised Ellen, wriggling into a sitting position with a yawn.

"Let me jump in the shower before you," said Taylor. "I brought you a mug of tea. It's on the chest of drawers."

"Thanks. I take it you went surfing?"

"Sure did. Waves were awesome. I've been up since four thirty. Was on the beach waxed and ready to go before six."

"The beach we were at yesterday?"

Taylor shook his head, "No. I drove round to Newquay. With the wind, the waves were bigger round there. Met up with a few old mates. Was good to catch up. Good for my soul."

"I wanted to see you surf."

"There's always tomorrow. Same time and maybe the same place. Depends on the wind," he said, getting to his feet. "OK. Give me fifteen minutes then the bathroom's all yours. I'll be in my room so yell if you need me."

"Will do."

Artisan's was busy when the three of them entered but Jen spied one free table over at the back corner. Expertly, she weaved her way through the maze of tables to snag it before anyone else reached it. Both Taylor and Ellen followed her at a more sedate pace. They had just sat down when Taylor felt a hand on his shoulder.

"Tailz!" exclaimed a familiar voice.

"Davie!" said Taylor, turning round.

"Long time no see, mate. How's London? You still playing with the same band?"

"Sure am. Just finished a UK tour with Bodimead. Heading into the studio in a couple of weeks. Debut album in the making."

"Ah, dream finally coming true," sighed Davie. "You coming to the hotel on Thursday?"

"That's the plan," replied Taylor grinning. "I'll bring Ellen here with me. See if we can convince her to sing."

"Ellen, hi," said Davie, introducing himself before Taylor could make the introductions. "I'm Davie. Played drums for Tailz here a while back."

"Long while back," laughed Taylor. "What were we? Fifteen? Sixteen? Happy days."

"Well we can re-enact it all on Thursday. Russ has talked me into playing too. Iggy is in town and has said he'll play bass. Not seen him for over five years."

"I bumped into him in London last year. He's a banker now. Some high-flying city job. Couldn't believe it," replied Taylor. "Is there a rehearsal or are we just jamming on Thursday?"

"Just jamming. Russ and I will be there about five. Come by any time after that."

"Will do," promised Taylor.

"And you'll be there, Ellen? Do you sing or play?" quizzed Davie.

"I could be persuaded to sing perhaps," she replied coyly.

"Great. See you guys there. You too, Jen."

Once Davie had moved out of ear shot, Ellen asked how formal this music session was, slightly anxious to know what she was letting herself in for.

"It's just a big jam session in the local hotel bar. Blame my sister. She volunteered us for it."

"You'll love it. Just like old times," said Jen as she surveyed the lunch menu.

"Ancient times!" laughed her twin. "I've not played with all of those guys together for at least eight years."

"Could be fun, I suppose," agreed Ellen softly.

"No pressure on you to join us," promised Taylor warmly. "But I think you'll find it hard to resist."

"We'll see," giggled Ellen. "Now, what's good to eat in here?"

Over the next couple of days both Jen and Taylor spent their time showing Ellen around the area. On Wednesday, Nana asked Taylor to help her in the garden, saying she needed some digging done and help to fix one of the sheds' roof. Realising that her brother would be busy all day, Jen suggested to Ellen that they go shopping together and proposed a day trip to Plymouth. A little nervously, Ellen agreed, much to Taylor's silent delight.

It took the girls a little over an hour to drive to Plymouth. Expertly, Jen parked the car in the multi-storey carpark at the Drake Circus shopping centre. With a wink to Ellen, she declared, "Shopping!"

It had been a long time since Ellen had had the opportunity for a girly shopping trip. Initially, she felt a little self-conscious in various shops but Jen's enthusiasm for fashion soon rubbed off on her and she soon found herself in a department store's fitting room trying on jeans and tops.

By the time they stopped for lunch, both of them were laden down with bags. Discovering a mutual love of sushi, they headed to Yo Sushi for their late lunch.

"Thanks for this," said Ellen between mouthfuls, her chopsticks expertly balanced in her hand.

"For what?" asked Jen.

"For today. It's been years since I've had a day's shopping like this. A long time since I had a girls' day out," confessed Ellen.

"Then we need to arrange to do it more often," declared Jen with a grin. "Don't you get fed up always being surrounded by the boys from the band?"

"Occasionally," admitted Ellen. "It depends. If Luke's in a mood or hungover, it's kind of tough."

"He's damaged goods," muttered Jen.

"Oh, and I'm not?" giggled Ellen. "If anyone in the band's damaged, it's me."

"Yeah but he's a bit unhinged," countered Jen. "You're just a bit….damaged."

"Understatement of the day!"

There was an awkward pause before Ellen continued, "If it hadn't been for Taylor, I don't think I'd have stayed with After Life. Those first couple of weeks were tough."

"He's got a good heart," agreed Jen. "I was worried about him going back to London so soon after we lost mum. You helped him as much as he's helped you. He was hurting so bad. Wouldn't talk to any of us. I was scared he'd do something stupid."

"Two broken souls," whispered Ellen half under her breath.

"He loves you," Jen commented. "You're the first girl he's ever brought home. His eyes light up when you're around. You're great together."

"The first?"

Jen nodded, "The one and only."

"I'm honoured," said Ellen with a smile. "I was so scared that you and Nana would hate me. Worried that the way I am would…. you know……"

"Nana adores you!" interrupted Jen. "We both do. And I'm really looking forward to hearing you and my brother play tomorrow night. Can't wait to hear you sing."

"Well perhaps you won't need to wait till tomorrow," hinted Ellen. "Before we left, I said to Tailz that we need to practice a bit. He said if it was warm enough, he'd light the chimnea tonight and bring Lou Lou out."

"He told you her name?"

Laughing, Ellen revealed, "We've even written a song for her. Lou Lou At 3am."

"This I have to hear!"

The cottage garden was sheltered from the breeze and, with the chimnea blazing, the patio felt cosy and intimate. Lit tealights in old jam jars were scattered around the boundary of the paved area, their flames flickering in the darkness. Plucking a gentle melody, Taylor watched as Nana and Jen brought out bowls of crisps and dips and some beers and cider. He smiled over at Ellen, who was sitting on a pile of cushions beside the fireplace.

"You ok?" asked Taylor, noting that she was staring intently at the flames.

"Never better," she replied with a relaxed smile. "I was just daydreaming."

"Ghosts in those flames?"

With a wistful smile, she nodded before confessing, "A year ago I couldn't have sat here. Couldn't stand to see flames. My dad helped me over those ghosts. Calmed my fears."

"Shit! I never thought!"

"It's fine, Tailz," assured Ellen warmly. "In fact, it's more than fine. This is perfect."

As Jen and Nana sat down at the table, Jen passed them both a drink.

"You need to earn those," she teased.

"Just a few songs, Jen," stated Taylor firmly. "We're both off duty."

"You're never off duty," retorted his twin. "You have music in your veins instead of blood!"

"Son," interrupted Nana calmly. "Play me that song your mother loved so much."

With a nod, Taylor turned to Ellen, "Do you know Everybody's Talkin'?"

"Sorry. I don't believe I do," she confessed, feeling her cheeks flush with embarrassment.

"No worries. It's an old song."

Smiling over at his grandmother, Taylor began to play the classic song from Midnight Cowboy, a film that had been one of his mother's favourites.

"Everybody's talking at me. I don't hear a word they're saying."

It was the first time that Ellen had heard her band mate sing. The warmth and emotion in his voice tore at her heart as she saw how hard it was for him to sing his mum's favourite song. One half of her wished she knew the song so she could help him out; the other half of her was captivated by his raw heartfelt performance.

As the song ended, Ellen saw that his eyes were filled with unshed tears.

"Beautiful, son," complimented Nana proudly. "Now, missy, what are you going to sing for this old woman?"

"Sing Broken Doll," suggested Taylor, hoping that Ellen

would realise he needed a minute to recompose himself.

"Your wish is my command," she answered softly.

In the quiet darkness that surrounded the garden, Ellen's voice rang out clear and pure. While she sang, she kept her eye on the flames. Singing about the raw pain of being "broken" was a challenge when she could feel the heat of the fire by her side. Ever the professional though, she maintained her composure and sang note perfect to the very end.

"Wow!" gasped Jen. "That was amazing!"

"Lovely voice, missy. Soulful," complimented Nana with a nod of approval towards Ellen.

"What was that song you mentioned at lunchtime?" quizzed Jen. "The one about Lou Lou."

"It's not really about Lou Lou," explained Taylor. "We wrote it at 3am and I was playing Lou Lou at the time. Neither of us had a title in mind. Ellen suggested Lou Lou At 3am and it stuck."

"So, what is it about?"

"Listen for yourself," suggested Ellen softly.

The two musicians exchanged glances, then Taylor began the delicate lullaby intro. When Ellen began to sing, she kept her voice soft and warm, adding to the soothing tone of the music. The gentle vocal subtly added a silent, dark edge to the tale of betrayal. In front of her, she could see tears forming in Jen's eyes as she was swallowed up by the emotions of the lyrics.

"Wow!" exclaimed Jen again when the song ended. "Powerful stuff."

"Like it?" quizzed Taylor hopefully.

"Loved it," declared his twin sister.

"Straight from a bruised heart," commented Nana with a knowing nod towards Ellen.

"Thanks," said Ellen before taking a chug on her beer bottle. "What's next?"

For more than two hours, the two members of After Life sang and played. They played rock classics, some Beatles for Nana and then returned to play a couple of After Life songs. Conversation turned to the music night at the hotel, with Jen nudging Taylor to reminisce about past nights playing with his old school friends.

Just after ten, he laid his guitar down and said he was done for the night.

"You surfing tomorrow?" asked Ellen curiously.

"That's the plan. Want to come? I'm leaving at five thirty."

"Sure."

"Good. We can grab breakfast on the way back," said Taylor as he got to his feet. "I'm calling it a night. I'll see you in the morning."

"Night, son," said his grandmother warmly.

"Night, Nana."

With Taylor gone and the music over, Ellen felt more than a little shy and awkward sitting with his family. Beside her, the chimnea was burning down and the flames were nothing more than glowing embers. She was aware of Nana saying something to Jen then heard the scrape of a chair on the paving slabs. When she looked round, she was alone with Taylor's grandmother.

"Penny for them, missy," said the old woman with a smile.

"They're not worth that," joked Ellen quietly.

"You're a fragile little thing, aren't you?" mused Nana wisely. "A little wounded songbird. A lot like my grandson in that regard."

"The flames stirred up a few old ghosts," confessed Ellen, keeping her gaze on the embers. "The heat from them scares me."

"That's understandable."

"I can still hear the flames, the screams. Feel the heat and the pain. Sitting here, I've felt the pain in my arm all night. I've been able to smell and taste the flesh burning."

"Yet you don't move," commented the old woman calmly.

"Ghosts can't hurt me," stated Ellen. "I can't go through life being afraid of every flame I see."

"But you don't need to be so hard on yourself, missy. Taylor told me about you pushing yourself to the limits in that field in Wales. Told me how scared he was when he saw you'd collapsed."

"I didn't mean to scare him," protested Ellen, a wave of guilt washing through her. "I'd never hurt him."

"He's another wounded bird," said Nana, keeping her eyes on the chimnea. "He feels guilty about his mother. Blames himself that she passed away. Curses himself that he couldn't save her."

"What could he have done?"

"Nothing," answered the old woman simply. "By the time she

was diagnosed it was already too late." She paused to collect her thoughts. "I'm going to say this once, missy. He needs you to need him. He needs you to need him so that he can cope with the loss of his mother. I've already cautioned him and I'll say the same to you. Don't either of you confuse need with love. Don't confuse these feelings and end up hurting each other. I can see that your souls are attracted to each other but you should be soulmates not lovers."

Ellen could feel her cheeks flush scarlet at the old woman's boldness.

"I don't want to hurt him," she said quietly. "I love him. I need him around. We watch out for each other."

Getting to her feet and coming over to stand beside her, Nana laid a hand on her shoulder and said, "Keep your eyes wide open. Be honest with each other."

"We will," promised Ellen.

The old woman's words were preying on her mind as she climbed the stairs to bed. A light shone out from under Taylor's door and Ellen paused in the hallway, unsure whether to disturb him or whether to wait till morning. Before she could decide what to do, the door opened and Taylor stepped out into the hallway.

"Hi," he said quietly. "You ok?"

"Fine," she replied with a weary smile.

"You look worried," pressed Taylor, reaching out to hug her.

"I'm just tired," she paused before adding, "Sitting next to the fireplace stirred up a few ghosts."

"And you had a heart to heart with Nana," finished Taylor succinctly.

Ellen nodded, "She's just watching out for you."

"Interfering more like," he muttered as he drew her close. "Want to tell me about these ghosts?"

Ellen shook her head, "Actually, I want to write about them."

"It's late," cautioned Taylor softly. "And you'll need to be up early if you are coming with me."

"I know but I need to jot this down. Waken me in the morning," she said, brushing a kiss on his cheek.

"I'll waken you at four thirty. That gives you plenty of time to get dressed."

"But not much time to sleep," she observed.

"Sleep's over rated. I'll sleep when I'm dead."

"Well, I'd rather sleep while I'm alive," giggled Ellen. "I'll see you in the morning."

"Night, my lovely."

As she sat wrapped in a blanket on the beach watching the sun rise, Ellen felt the ghosts of the night before slip away to be replaced by a feeling of peace. Pulling the blanket tighter, she shivered in the chill dawn light, watching Taylor and his three friends head down the beach with their boards under their arms. A stiff breeze was blowing much to the surfers delight and they had been like a group of excited children when they saw the size of the waves.

From her vantage point, Ellen smiled as she watched Taylor proficiently paddle his board out into the surf, bide his time until the perfect wave came along then, after a few hand strokes to gather speed, spring to his feet on the board with well-practiced ease. For almost two hours, she watched the four surfers riding the waves. Occasionally, one or other of them would make a mistake, over balance and disappear headlong into the surf. The only one not to fall victim to the waves was Taylor, a fact he was bragging about as the guys came back up the beach, tired and hungry.

"Oh, that felt good," sighed Taylor as he picked up his towel. "Good for the soul."

"Looked cold to me," observed Ellen, feeling the chill seeping into her bones.

"It's not warm, I'll grant you that," he conceded. "Give me five minutes to get changed then I'll buy you breakfast to heat your up."

"You heading to Holly Dolly's, mate?" called over one of his surfing buddies.

"That's the plan."

"Catch you there. We'll get changed in the van."

Holly Dolly's turned out to be a café that overlooked the harbour. Trade this early was brisk and almost all of the pastel coloured tables were occupied. The clientele was a mix of fishermen, surfers and the occasional office worker. Classic 1960's music was playing, helping to create the warm, friendly atmosphere that Holly was famous for. Much to her surprise, Ellen learned that Holly was an elderly lady who had run the popular café for almost forty years. Watching her greet her regulars and dash between the counter and waiting on the tables, Ellen marvelled at her energy.

"Usual fry up, Taylor?" she called out when she spotted their arrival.

"Two of them, Holly, please," he called back. "And two mugs of tea."

"Take a seat, son. I'll be right over with them."

Taking a seat at a pale blue circular table in the corner by the window, Ellen asked how often he ate there. Laughing, Taylor confessed, "Too often! I also worked here after school for a few years. Before school too. Holly taught me to cook."

"You can cook?"

"Sure can," he said with a wink. "In fact, I enjoy cooking a meal when I get the chance. Doesn't happen too often."

"You'll need to cook for me sometime" Ellen said. "Even before, I wasn't much of a cook. Dad says I can burn water!"

"I'll see if Nana and Jen will let me make dinner before we leave. If not then I'll have to sweet talk Lizzy into letting me use her kitchen."

Their full English breakfasts surpassed expectations. Just as Holly had set their plates down, Taylor's three friends arrived and quickly grabbed the adjacent table. After a detailed analysis of their morning's surfing, conversation turned to the jam session at the hotel. Although he had introduced Ellen to them, Taylor hadn't said she was a member of After Life.

"You coming to listen to our boy tonight?" asked Phil, an old schoolfriend of Taylor's.

"Of course," replied Ellen shyly. "Need to show support for your local rock star."

This caused a ripple of laughter as the guys poked fun at Taylor, the "rock star".

"Last laugh will be on you, boys," stated Taylor, feigning indignance. "Just you wait till tonight."

"Will you be signing autographs?" teased Phil with a wink to

Ellen.

"Only if you buy me a drink first!"

The public bar adjoining the village's only hotel was already half full when Taylor walked in closely followed by Jen and Ellen shortly before six thirty. It had been their intention to arrive earlier but Nana has insisted they eat dinner before they left. While she had prepared their evening meal, the two girls had disappeared upstairs to get ready, leaving Taylor sorting out his guitars for the evening. When the girls had returned, Taylor had smiled as he noted that Ellen had allowed Jen to help her get ready. Her long, thick, platinum blonde hair had been braided into two French plaits. Now, as she followed him across the bar to the small corner stage, there was nothing about her appearance that suggested "rock queen".

"Cider?" asked Jen, reaching for her purse.

"Please," replied Tailz as he set down his guitar cases.

"Ellen?"

"Red wine. Shiraz if they have it," replied After Life's songbird softly.

"Grab a table. I'll be right back," promised Jen as she headed towards the bar.

"Snag that one beside the stage," suggested Taylor, pointing to an empty round table. "We can drag a couple of extra chairs over."

"Tailz!" came a yell from the doorway.

"Iggy," said Taylor quietly to Ellen before calling back, "Hi, mate. Good to see you."

"Likewise, boy," said Iggy, giving him a bear hug. "Oh, who's this beautiful creature?"

"Cut the crap, Iggy," cautioned Taylor with a grin. "This is Ellen. Ellen Lloyd."

"Girlfriend?"

"Don't look so shocked! Yes. Soulmate," replied Taylor. "Ellen, ignore everything this man says. This is Iggy Haynes."

"Please to meet you," said Ellen with a shy smile.

"Not as pleased as I am to meet you," purred Iggy.

"Stop it, Iggy. She's more than capable of dealing with your silver tongue."

Laughing, Iggy nodded, "Ok, I'll behave. Is that your beautiful twin over at the bar?"

"It is indeed," sighed Taylor, shaking his head.

"I'll be right back," promised Iggy as he made a beeline straight towards Jen.

Once he was out of ear shot, Ellen began to giggle, "Is he for real?"

"Sadly, yes," laughed Taylor. "Larger than life is our Iggy. Hard to believe he's a high-flying city banker by day."

"Virtually impossible," agreed Ellen.

A few moments later, Davie appeared with a pint of beer in his hand and his drumsticks poking out of his back pocket.

"I hear Iggy's arrived," he commented with a nod towards the bar. "And still stalking your sister."

"He's no chance there," stated Taylor bluntly. "She can't stand him."

Davie laughed before turning to Ellen, "I've been doing some research, young lady. No one told me you were Ellen Lloyd of Good Times and now After Life fame. Will you be singing with us tonight?"

Blushing, Ellen said, "Maybe."

"You should. Good Times were awesome. Saw you play a few times."

"Thank you," she said quietly. "We had some fun back then. Miss those guys."

"Let's see how tonight goes," suggested Taylor, sensing that Ellen was apprehensive about committing to sing. "You got a set worked out?"

"No," confessed Davie. "Russ was writing some stuff down on the back of a fag packet earlier. Said he wants to start with The Boys Are Back In Town."

"That's naff!" exclaimed Taylor, trying not to laugh. "Tell me he's not serious?"

"He's serious."

"Shit," laughed Taylor.

"It's the only thing he can sing in tune," joked Davie. "We'd best humour him."

By eight, the bar was packed full and the musicians were

ready to play. A short while earlier, Taylor had introduced Ellen to the final member of the evening's line up, Russ. She had been surprised to discover he was at least ten years older than the others until Jen explained that he'd been a music tutor at their high school. When the boys had been teenagers, Russ had encouraged them to form a band and then helped to showcase them at the various jam sessions he organised along the Cornish coast.

"Ladies and gentlemen!" roared Russ as the musicians took their places. "For one night only, The Boys Are Back In Town!"

The bar was instantly filled with raucous cheering and whistling as the makeshift band began to play and Russ stepped up to the mic. Both Tailz and Iggy came in on backing vocals as Russ reached the chorus. Considering it was completely unrehearsed, it flowed pretty smoothly with Davie holding it all together with some expert drumming. When the song came to an end, the packed bar was yelling for more.

Swiftly, Russ whispered to Taylor, who nodded and changed guitar.

"Thank you!" called out Russ to the audience, looking as though he was addressing Wembley Arena instead of the hotel bar. "Un- rehearsed we give you House Of The Rising Sun!"

For almost an hour, the band played rock classic after rock classic much to the delight of the crowd. From her vantage point at the side of the low stage, Ellen could tell that Taylor was enjoying playing with his friends and smiled to see him so relaxed. After a bit of persuading, Russ convinced Taylor to sing, telling the crowd, "This boy's the real deal. Tailz here is the lead guitarist with rock band After Life. A real, live, rock god in your midst, folks!"

With a grin, Taylor sat down on a low stool with Lou Lou balanced on his knee.

"Alright, let's see how this works out," he began with a nervous smile. "Wanted Dead Or Alive by Bon Jovi."

"It's all the same. Only the name will change," he sang, keeping his eyes firmly on Ellen.

As he sang, Taylor saw Ellen mouthing the words along with him, saw her suppress a giggle as he got a line wrong. Having her there helped to calm his nerves. Singing solo was seldom something he enjoyed, preferring to hide behind his guitars. It was almost with relief that he played the song's guitar solo then re-grouped his focus for the last section of the lyrics.

His fellow musicians were the first to applaud his success as the song ended.

"I'm not the only member of After Life here tonight," revealed Taylor as the cheers died down. "Ellen, step up here, girl!"

Taking a deep breath, Ellen slid her chair back from the table and stepped up onto the low stage.

"Folks, give a warm welcome to Ellen Lloyd!" yelled Davie as he handed her their only spare microphone.

"Thank you," she said, her voice slightly husky with nerves. "Tailz, what did you have planned?"

"Lou Lou At 3am?" suggested Taylor quietly. When she nodded, he turned back to the audience and explained, "This is an After Life song. It was written by Ellen and I late one night not so long ago and will be on our debut album later this year. This is Lou Lou At 3am."

A hush fell over the room as Taylor began to play. When Ellen started to sing, her tone soft and husky, there was an audible gasp of delight from the local audience. They hung on her every word. Discretely, she sang softer to ensure they kept listening keenly but she was also conscious that she hadn't warmed up at all for the performance.

The applause from the small audience was deafening when the song ended and was interspersed with loud cries for "more".

Signalling the others back on stage, Taylor and Ellen exchanged a few whispered words then Ellen nodded. While Taylor filled the rest of the band in on the plan, she addressed the room, "Alright, not too sure how this is going to work out. Because The Night, ladies and gentlemen."

It was almost eleven and the barman had just called last orders when the group of musicians prepared to play their final song for the evening. Despite her best efforts to escape, Ellen had been kept on stage all night, pulling out rock anthems from the very depths of her memory.

"Folks, tonight wouldn't have been possible without each and every one of you," said Russ warmly. "I hope you've had as much fun as we've had this evening. We'll leave you with one last song. The lovely Ellen here will perform the vocal duties one last time. Unrehearsed, we give you "We Are The Champions"!"

Trying not to giggle at the slightly cheesy climax to the evening, Ellen composed herself to sing one last time for the night. Keeping her vocal low and controlled, "I've paid my dues. Time after time. I've done my sentence but committed no crime."

Getting caught up in the song, she allowed her vocals to increase in volume until she was singing as though it were a two-thousand seat venue not a hundred seat bar. The power behind her vocals caught her fellow musicians off guard and, as she reached the chorus, she spied Taylor grinning at her with pride. As predicted, the small audience joined in with the Queen anthem in full voice. No one in the room was left in any doubt that the evening was going to go down in the bar's history as one of the best.

Taking a theatrical bow, Ellen handed the microphone to Russ and jumped down from the low stage into a huge hug from Jen.

"That was amazing! You were incredible!" gushed Taylor's sister excitedly.

"Thanks," said Ellen, reaching for her glass of wine. "That was fun. No pressure. Just the music. Loved it!"

"Everyone loved it!"

Appearing behind them, Taylor put his arms around both girls, "Brilliant night. Most fun I've had on stage for a long time."

The barman arrived with a tray of drinks for them, saying, "Compliments of the house. When can you come back and do that again, folks?"

"No idea," said Taylor with a grin. "Next time the planets align for us."

"How about Christmas or New Year?" he persisted. "Properly organised party night."

"We'll see," replied Taylor, declining to commit to anything. "Link in with Russ and Davie."

"Oh, I will! I will!"

All things musical were more controlled a few short days later when After Life entered the studio for the first time. They had been booked into the newly completed Hades Music Hall, which was sited in the basement of JR Management's London offices. As they entered the small lounge area, accompanied by Rocky, all five of them were a curious mix of nerves and excitement. A welcoming aroma of freshly brewed coffee greeted them as well as Jason Russell himself.

"Good afternoon," he said rather formally. "Welcome to Hades."

With a laugh, Luke commented, "Rather ironic considering we're After Life."

"True, Mr Court. Very true," agreed Jason with a smile. "Hades has been open for just over a week. We only officially opened on 5th May."

"The Day of the Dead?" queried Rocky with a frown. "That's cheesy even for you, Jason!"

"I know. I know but it was too good a publicity gimmick to miss," conceded Jason. "You have the honour of being the first band to record in here. One of our solo acts was in recording her new single last week so we've ironed out any teething problems."

"Good to know," said Jack. "Do we get a tour of hell or do we need to find our own way about?"

"Allow me to show you round."

Hades proved to be an impressive place as Jason showed them the live room, vocal booth, control room, two small rehearsal rooms, the fully fitted kitchen and shower room. The external walls had been left as exposed stone adding a dungeon effect to the studio. Gothic décor in the lounge plus a chequerboard floor throughout added to the effect.

"Impressive, Mr Russell," agreed Rocky when they returned to the lounge area. "Now, where have you hidden our production team?"

"Late lunch," explained Jason, checking the time. "They should be here any moment. I, on the other hand, need to dash. I've a meeting upstairs. Relax. Have a play. Get set up. Make yourselves at home until the others get back."

"Will do," said Rocky with a nod to Cal and Jack. "Better bring his kit in and start assembling it. If I know Cushy, he'll want drums and bass ready to go tonight."

After Life had just brought the last of Cal and Taylor's guitar cases in when they were joined by the two members of the production team. Swiftly, Rocky introduced the band to Stuart Cushnaghan, "Cushy" for short, who would be their producer and to sound engineer, Lee Michaels, explaining that he'd worked with them both before and that they would be in safe hands.

"No pressure on us then," joked Cushy in a broad Glasgow accent. "Right, kiddie winkles, let's get a plan thrashed out and get to work. Lee, get the kettle on!"

"I'll leave you to it," said Rocky. "I've some paperwork to sort out upstairs. Tailz, are you and Ellen alright to make your own way home tonight? I've an appointment out in Enfield at six."

"Sure," said Tailz. "We'll get ourselves home."

"Fine. I'll see you all tomorrow."

Once they were all seated in the lounge with a mug of coffee or tea, Cushy asked how many songs they had compiled for the record.

"Eleven at the last count," replied Ellen with a glance over towards Taylor. "Maybe a couple of others part written."

"Ideally, we need a few more. Jason indicated to us that he expects twelve on the album with the option to extend that to fifteen if he opts to do a deluxe edition release later. To get fifteen to the right standard, I'd prefer we started with about eighteen or twenty. Gives us wiggle room," explained the producer directly.

"Tall order," commented Luke calmly.

"This isn't nursery school, son," stated Cushy.

"We can pull the missing songs together," promised Ellen, hoping she sounded more confident than she felt. "I've a few ideas I've not had time to focus on. I might need some help to get the music written though."

"We're a team," added Jack. "We can pull our collective creative juices here."

"Ok," nodded the producer. "Let's get the eleven you've got on the board as a starting point then I'd like to hear you play. I missed your London shows. Usually, I prefer to see a band live first before I agree to work with them. Get a feel for them. You lot are an unknown entity right now." He paused then turned to face Ellen, "Apart from you, little miss. I heard you sing a long time ago. Worked with you too. Good Times. I'm expecting great things from you."

Blushing, Ellen promised to deliver and exceed his expectations.

"Right, get your arses into the room and get those songs on my nice, new, shiny whiteboard. Who's got the neatest writing?"

"Ellen!" said all the boys at once.

"Fine. Ellen, write up that board for me."

It was after five before After Life were ready to play. Setting up had taken longer than anticipated then they'd had to wait while Ellen warmed up before finally coming together in the live room.

"Right. Three songs. Any three that will tell me what After Life are all about. Any order. Heavy. Slow. Acoustic. Your choice."

A quick debate ensued before they chose to start with Swirling Mists then City Of Bones And Heartache and to finish with Lou Lou At 3am.

"Any time tonight," suggested Cushy sharply from the control room.

Taking a deep breath, Ellen stepped up to the mic and began the Latin chant, her clear, crisp vocals filling the confined space. Taking their lead from her confident start, the rest of the band poured all their energy and focus into the song while Ellen flooded the vocal with her passion for the song.

They raised the energy levels for City Of Bones And Heartache then brought everything to an acoustically perfect, mellow conclusion with Lou Lou At 3am. As the last notes faded away, the band looked to the control room for a reaction.

Through the window, they could see Cushy bent over the keyboard of his pc. To his left, Lee was focussed on a monitor but was nodding appreciatively.

"Well?" asked Luke, impatient to hear what the producer thought of them.

"A wee tad sloppy in parts. Need to slow some of those sectors down to retain the definition," began Cushy critically. "Ellen, you wouldn't happen to know the set up you had when we did the Good Times demo back then?"

"Sorry. I've no idea," she apologised. "That was nearly six years ago."

"No worries. We'll figure it out. I want that voice sounding pure. Pure perfection and, when needed, pure fucking evil!"

Ellen threw back her head and laughed before promising, "I'll be as sweet or as evil as you want me to be."

"Oh, you'll be beyond evil by the time I'm done, little miss," he assured her sincerely. "Right, I need Jack and Luke for a couple of hours. The rest of you can fuck off until tomorrow. Be here no later than two and be prepared to be here till the wee small hours. If the plan changes, I'll tell Rocky. Now, go home and write some more fucking songs for that half naked board."

"Yes, sir," said Taylor, resisting the temptation to salute the producer.

As the three members of After Life stood on the pavement outside Hades, Cal glanced up and down the street.

"Now what?" he asked.

"We do as the man said and go home," said Tailz. "You coming? Lizzy'll feed you."

"Nah," said Cal, shaking his head. "It's Monday. She doesn't do curry on a Monday. Maybe later in the week."

"Your loss," joked Taylor.

"I'll head back to the flat. See if I can get my creative juices flowing," he replied with a wink.

"Cal McDermid, you're incorrigible!" laughed Tailz. "And you'll go blind doing that!"

"Catch you tomorrow, guys!"

The warm welcoming aroma of Bolognese greeted Ellen and Taylor as they entered the kitchen.

"Only the two of you?" checked Lizzy, turning round from the cooker. "Where's Cal?"

"He headed home. Said something about releasing his creative juices," said Taylor with a mischievous grin.

"That boy!" sighed the older woman. "Beyond hope! Now, sit yourselves down. This is ready."

Over dinner, the two musicians told Lizzy about their first day in the studio, explaining about being dismissed with instructions to write more songs.

"Does that man think you can just push a button and pop out a song?" muttered Lizzy. "He's always been the same. Demanding!"

"You know him?" asked Ellen, smiling at their landlady's motherly reaction.

"Oh, I know him!" she declared. "He lived here for a few months a long time ago. One of few people I've asked to leave. Why Rocky and Jason still work with him I'll never know!"

"Because he's bloody good at what he does," stated Rocky bluntly as he entered the kitchen. "Sorry I'm late. Got caught up with Jason."

"There's plenty left," said his wife, getting up to fetch her husband a plate.

Taking a seat opposite the two members of After Life, Rocky said, "Cushy's bark is worse than his bite…..well most of the time. You'll always know where you stand with him. If you do what he says, he'll draw the best out of you all and we'll have one hell of a debut album to show for it."

"He was a hard task master when I met him before," replied Ellen. "Hard but fair."

"Do you two have any more songs to add to that board?" asked Rocky as Lizzy set his meal down in front of him.

"I have some half-finished lyrics for a few and can hear them in my head. If Tailz can work out the music, we might have a couple by tomorrow," said Ellen with a glance towards her band mate.

"Well, get upstairs and get to work, kids!"

As they climbed the stairs, Taylor asked, "Your room or mine?"

With a smile, Ellen answered, "Yours. Saves moving your amp over. I just need to grab my lyric book and a pen."

"I get the feeling this is going to be a long night," sighed Taylor.

"Me too. I hear sleep is over rated."

A few minutes later, Ellen entered Taylor's bedroom carrying her lyrics notebook, her pen tucked behind her ear. She had left her tinted glasses behind in her own room but had lifted her hoodie to ward off the evening chill.

"Right, what do you have?" asked Taylor as she settled herself cross legged in the middle of his unmade bed.

"Maybe enough," confessed Ellen softly. "In fact, between you and me, I have enough lyrics for a couple of albums. It's the music that's the challenge."

"A couple of albums?"

Ellen nodded then added, "If I can get my other lyrics book from my parents' house, we'd have loads to choose from. I brought one old one with me when I left but there's another one in my room back home. A lot of really dark stuff."

"Would you be able to fetch it?" asked Taylor hopefully. "Dark would work for After Life. The darker the better!"

"I've messaged my dad to see if he can bring it over. I didn't want to involve my mother. She'd read it then try to send me back to the shrink."

"Why?" The question was out before Taylor had thought it through.

"A lot of those songs were written just after the accident. There's a lot of morbid stuff in that book. Suicidal stuff. Evil lyrics. A lot of painful stuff."

"You sure you want to share it if your dad brings it?"

"No but I know there's at least two sets of lyrics that would be perfect for the band," she replied. "Now, want to hear what we've got to play with?"

"Sure do."

By midnight, they had pulled the bare bones of two new songs together. The first one, about a haunted beach, flowed almost perfectly from the off. Singing in the dim light of the bedroom added a sinister edge to it that Taylor prayed Ellen could recapture in the studio. As Ellen sang it through again, he could feel the chill sea air, almost tasting the salt on the air.

"Title?" he asked as they prepared to record a rough version to share with the others.

"Sands Of Death?"

"That'll do for now."

It took a couple of takes but they finally had a very bare version recorded and ready to share.

When he heard the second song for the first time, Taylor's heart skipped a beat. Immediately he recognised the setting that had inspired the lyrics. Ellen had written the song based around the graveyard where his mother was buried. The lyrics themselves spun a tale of a dying young girl falling into an open grave and being welcomed by her ancestors who dwelled beneath. There was a gothic feel to the song's story, coupled with an air of tragedy as the girl was returned to earth to die.

Methodically, he began to work out a melody that felt like it tied in with the way Ellen had sung it. After a moment or two, she stopped him.

"Too fast, Tailz. Slower. More ghostly."

He tried again but nothing seemed to flow right. For a moment, they sat in virtual silence then Ellen began to sing it softly to herself to a different tune. Impulsively, she changed a few of the lyrics, sang it to herself then declared she was ready to sing it properly. Mesmerised, Taylor listened as she morphed the song into a heavily blues influenced ballad.

"Can After Life do blues?" he quizzed when she was finished.

"Only one way to find out."

"I guess," he agreed as he lifted Lou Lou out of her case. "Ok, let's try this again."

By the time they were both satisfied with the song, it was almost two thirty. With a yawn, Taylor suggested they record it as it was and send it on to the others, guessing that Luke at least would still be up.

"Do we have a title for this one?" checked Taylor.

"Underworld Blues? Little Miss Lost?" suggested Ellen

"Evicted From Hell?" countered Tailz, settling Lou Lou back in her case.

"Not sure about that."

As he came to sit on the bed beside her, Taylor said, "How about Applegarth?"

"Pardon?"

"That's the name of the graveyard where my mum's buried," he explained quietly. "That was your inspiration, wasn't it?"

Ellen nodded. "Applegarth it is."

Lying back on the pillow, Tailz asked, "Any word from your dad?"

"Shit. Forgot about that," muttered Ellen, reaching for her phone. A green flashing light suggested she had a message. "He's found it and will get it couriered over tomorrow at some point."

"Another session tomorrow night then?" suggested Taylor with a yawn.

"As long as Cushy doesn't summon us," agreed Ellen as she lay down beside him. "I'll need an hour or so to read over the book to find the songs I have in mind."

"If they're too personal, you don't need to share them," said Taylor, pulling her towards him.

Resting her head on his chest, Ellen revealed, "I've not touched that book for years. Maybe three or four years. I wrote a lot of the emotions out of my system. Poured my pain into the pages. I'm not sure how much I'll be able to read never mind share."

"You don't need to," he assured her, kissing the top of her head. "There's no need to open old wounds here. We can write new songs. There's five of us. We can work together."

"I know," she replied, smiling up at him sleepily. "If I find the one I'm thinking on, I'll need Luke's help. It was written for piano accompaniment."

"You know he'll be your right hand anytime," joked Taylor, wincing inwardly at the warped humour.

"Tailz," began Ellen softly. "No more talking. No more work talk. Make love to me."

Tenderly, he removed her clothing, caressing her with feathery kisses as he stripped off each item. Touching her scarred skin no longer worried him and he even found himself tracing patterns in the swirling scars as they lay together. The touch of her hand on his inner thigh made him smile. Slowly, she ran her hand up the inside of his thigh before cupping his balls gently. With their eyes locked together, Ellen fondled him teasingly for a few moments then slid her hand up the length of his erect penis. A low moan of satisfaction escaped from Taylor's lips as he gently nudged her legs apart. He entered her with a hard thrust, feeling Ellen arch her pelvis up to meet him, encouraging him deeper.

"This isn't going to take long," he apologised as he nuzzled into her neck, kissing her tenderly.

"Make it hard and fast."

"You sure?" he checked. "I don't want to hurt you, my lovely."

"Hard and fast, Tailz," she commanded, their gaze locked once more.

The guitarist didn't need to be asked twice. His hunger for her was burning and he couldn't hold back much longer. With a few deep thrusts, he felt her come around him just before his release consumed him.

Underneath him, Ellen let out a small moan.

"Was that too rough?"

"No," she sighed. "That was perfect."

Carefully, he rolled over and lay beside her. Instead of resting her head on his chest as he expected her to do, Ellen rolled onto her side, curling into a ball. Instinctively, Taylor curled round her and was soon asleep.

When Ellen and Taylor arrived at Hades late the next morning, Lee called through to the small lounge to say there was a parcel waiting for her. Judging by the noise levels, the other members of the band were already in the live room. While Taylor went through to join them, Ellen went in search of the package. She found it lying on the coffee table, smiling when she saw the familiar scrawl of her dad's handwriting on the brown padded envelope. Her hand was trembling slightly as the vintage journal slid out and a note fell to the floor. Setting the book back down on the table, Ellen picked up the note. "Hope this is what you were looking for, angel. Smuggled it out past your mother. Love you. Dad x"

The mere sight of the familiar journal had her emotions in turmoil. Taking a seat on the leather couch, Ellen picked up the book and sat staring at it. Inside it, she knew all the pages were full; inside it, she knew were a lot of painful memories.

"Little miss," called Cushy from the control room doorway. "When you're ready!"

"Sorry," apologised Ellen, swallowing down a ball of emotion that had formed in her throat. "I'll just be a minute."

"We don't have all day!"

Without opening the journal, Ellen stuffed it and the note into her hobo bag then headed into the live room to join the rest of

After Life.

"Right," called through the producer. "Do we have any new material to go on that board?"

"Two," said Ellen. "I'll write them up."

"Not enough," cautioned Cushy bluntly. "We need another five, minimum, by next Monday."

"Five!" echoed Luke, glaring at the producer. "That's insane."

"No, it's fine," countered Ellen calmly. "We can come up with five for Monday." She paused then added, "Luke, I'll need your help with a couple of them. Need your right hand."

"You say the sweetest things," teased Luke, his mood instantly lightening. "Now, what did you two come up with last night?"

For the next few hours, After Life worked through the two new songs, adding in a bass line and drum track. When it came to Applegarth, they agreed the blues influences sounded great but both Jack and Luke expressed their concerns over it not sounding like After Life; Cal and Taylor both vehemently disagreed with them.

"Boys," called through the producer. "If you have an idea of how it should sound, let's fucking hear it!"

Neither Luke nor Jack said anything, but Cal spoke up, "I might have something of a compromise."

"Go for it," encouraged Jack, keen to hear what Cal had in mind.

"Ellen," began Cal, lifting his guitar from the stand. "Sing that first verse for me again."

"Boys," suggested Cushy, "Why don't the rest of you take a break. Someone go out and fetch dinner. Be back here in half an hour."

Once everyone had left the studio, the Scotsman called through from the control room, "Call it a hunch but you two need some space. I'll be back in fifteen minutes. Use the time wisely."

"Generous to a fault," muttered Cal as he settled down to play.

"He's hard but fair," acknowledged Ellen. "Now, what were you thinking of here?"

It was unusual for the Scottish guitarist to offer up an idea. It was even rarer for him to speak up against Luke and Jack. With a shy smile, he played a fuzz laden version of the song's melody that still maintained the blues elements but also captured the

After Life feel. Smiling, Ellen said, "You might be onto something here."

"You think?"

"I think," replied the band's songbird. "OK from the top. Verse and chorus."

Cal's interpretation of the song didn't quite fit the original phrasing but expertly Ellen tweaked the lyrics and, by the time Cushy re-entered the control room almost half an hour later, the two musicians were happy with the result. With the producer listening intently, they ran through the first verse and chorus for him.

"Works for me," he stated when they were done. "Needs work obviously but I think there's something there. Go eat. Be back in here in an hour ready to play it through." He paused then added, "Ellen, I also want to hear Broken Doll. Luke was talking about it before you got here."

"Sure," she agreed quickly. "Anything else?"

"Yeah. Let me get a rough recording of that Latin stuff at the start of Swirling Mists."

"Not a problem but I don't do "rough"," stated Ellen with an air of defiance.

Out in the lounge, the rest of the band were sorting out containers of Chinese food. With a slightly anxious look towards Taylor, Ellen sat down at the end of the couch, across from where he was sitting.

"I got you a special fried rice," he said with what he hoped was a reassuring smile. "Extra prawns."

"Thank you," she replied, relieved that it was something easy eat. Despite the countless meals they'd shared as a band, eating in front of them still made her feel self-conscious, especially in new surroundings.

Hunger killed conversation for a while as they devoured their meals. Gradually, they began to talk through the progress they were making. Both Luke and Jack had been in the studio till late laying down drum and bass tracks for the first three songs on the board.

"We stay back and do another three tonight when you guys leave," replied Jack. "Unless Cushy changes his mind."

"He wants some vocals to work with," explained Ellen, setting her half empty foil dish on the table.

"You really think we can pull another five songs together in less than a week?" asked Luke. "That's a huge ask of anyone."

"With your help we can," answered Ellen with a smile. "I already have the lyrics."

"Ah, the mystery parcel," teased Jack, flashing her a grin.

"No mystery," she declared. "I had my dad send over a lyrics journal I'd left at home. I brought one other one with me. Between them, we can pull five tracks together."

"How much stuff do you have up your sleeve?" asked Cal, immediately regretting his choice of words.

"More than enough," replied Ellen softly. "I'll warn you. There's some pretty dark stuff in there."

By the time a taxi dropped Ellen and Tailz off at the house, it was almost two o'clock in the morning. Both of them were exhausted after twelve hours in Hades.

"That place is aptly named," muttered Taylor as he staggered up the stairs.

"It's not so bad," said Ellen with a weary smile. "I'm going to grab a drink. Do you want anything?"

"Sleep."

"Get to bed then," she chided softly. "I'm going to make a start on the lyrics search. If I'm not up by ten, waken me, will you?"

Taylor nodded and stumbled the rest of the way up the stairs while Ellen stood at the bottom watching.

"Like a tired baby boy," she thought as she crept into the kitchen.

As quietly as she could, Ellen made herself some hot chocolate then tip toed up to her room, taking care not to spill any en route. Thoughtfully, Taylor had already opened her door and flicked on the bedside lamp. Her heart swelled at the simple, sweet gesture.

Carefully, she set the steaming mug down on the bedside table and dumped her blue bag on the bed. After singing for Cushy for almost two hours, her ribs were aching. He had been testing the extremes of her register but hitting the high notes repeatedly had put a strain on her. Slowly, she shed her clothes, then methodically went through her ritual of creams for her scars before finally climbing into bed. Having taken a mouthful of the sweet hot chocolate, she reached into her bag and pulled out the red leather-bound journal.

Her boyfriend, Tom, had given her the journal just before they had left for Thailand, suggesting she use it to keep a diary of the trip. It had lain in her suitcase unused for the duration of the trip until her dad had brought it to the hospital. She had stared at it for a few days then, prompted by one of the doctors, had started to write her thoughts down. They had poured out and filled the journal in less than two weeks. There were many times that she had been thankful for being naturally left-handed.

With a lump in her throat, Ellen opened the journal and began to read.

Next afternoon, when After Life arrived at Hades, Ellen asked to speak to Cushy. Leaving the others getting set up, the producer followed After Life's leading lady out into the lounge.

"Coffee?" he asked, pouring himself a mug.

"No, thanks," replied Ellen calmly.

"What can I do for you, little miss?"

"Allow me to borrow Luke for a day or so," she began. "I know you want him for bass tracking. I get that. However, if you want those five extra songs on that board, I need Luke to work on them with me. Well, on some of them. Tailz and I can work on some of them but I need Luke first."

The producer stared at her, his eyes boring into her. Trying not to let her nerves show, Ellen stared back.

"When I worked with you before, there was this spark about you," began Cushy without taking his eyes off her. "A fire burning in you. When you walked in here this week all shaded and mystique, I thought that spark was gone."

"No," replied Ellen icily, taking her tinted glasses off and staring him straight in the face. "The fire's still there. I was just burned by it."

She could see that she was making him uncomfortable. Her heart was pounding as she stared directly at the producer but she fought her inner demons to maintain the eye contact

"Ellen," he spluttered, realising his mistake.

"Mr Cushnaghan," interrupted Ellen sharply. "I lost my eye

and my arm, not my ambition. I can't play piano like I used to. Fact. I need Luke's skill to write the music. Fact. Do I like having to rely on others like this. No! Fact. Have I had to swallow my pride to keep that fire of ambition alive? Yes, I have. Fact."

"Ellen......"

"Yes?" she snapped.

"I'm sorry. I knew about your arm. Rocky told me. Jason also said. I didn't know about your sight."

"Save the sympathy," suggested Ellen coldly. "Now, can I take Luke or not?"

"I need him to finish something off tonight," replied the producer, secretly enjoying seeing her so riled. "Both of you are excused until Monday. I'll need Cal and Taylor for the next few days. There is one condition though, little miss. In fact, make it two."

"And they are?"

"One, you walk back in here with five songs ready to go on that board."

"Deal."

"And two," he said awkwardly, "Please don't take those glasses off in front of me again."

"No promises on that one but I respect the honesty."

"Fine," relented the producer reluctantly. "Let's get to work."

Things ran smoothly all afternoon in the live room as After Life worked on the songs they had on the board, under the producer's direction. He suggested tweaks and changes that they had never considered, drawing out the very best from each of them. It was an intense session and, after a few hours, there was an edge to the atmosphere. Just as it reached eruption point, Cushy called through, "Right, take a break for an hour. Lee's going out for curries. Give him your order. Taylor, Ellen, you both stay back here for half an hour."

While the others trooped out, Tailz glanced over at Ellen. He could see from the look on her face that she was starting to struggle.

"You ok, my lovely?" he asked as he passed her a bottle of water.

"A bit sore but I'm ok," she assured him with a smile, before taking a long drag on the bottle.

"People," called through the producer loudly. "I need a run through of Lou Lou At 3am."

"Yes sir," replied Taylor, his voice surprisingly loud and clear.

Suppressing a giggle, Ellen checked, "You ok?"

Keeping is voice low, Taylor confessed, "He's pissing me off with his demands."

"Relax," Ellen cautioned. "He knows his stuff."

"Less chatter!" came the booming Scottish voice of the producer. "Let's hear it!"

With a glance at each other, Taylor and Ellen composed themselves to perform. Singing Lou Lou in the bright studio felt alien, as both of them were more accustomed to performing it on stage. Both of them felt something was missing from the first couple of attempts.

"Cushy," called through Ellen. "Can you dim the lights for a few minutes please?"

"Certainly, Miss Lloyd," replied the producer, with more than a hint of sarcasm.

Lower lighting added an air of intimacy to the live room that made playing the acoustic song feel more familiar. After a couple more run throughs, Cushy asked Ellen to sing the vocal track without Taylor's assistance. Without complaint and with her band mate sitting watching, she poured her heart into the song.

"Thank you, Miss Lloyd," complimented the producer. "As agreed, you are now free until midday on Monday."

"Thanks," called back Ellen.

Setting Lou Lou back in her case, Taylor asked why Ellen had been excused for the next few days.

"I'm stealing Luke to work on those new songs," she revealed quietly. "I'll need some of your time too. Probably Saturday and or Sunday."

"Did you find the lyrics you were looking for?"

Ellen nodded, "And you were right. Some of them...most of them... are still too personal. Too raw. Between the two journals though, I've got eight we can try to work up. I've promised Cushy five for Monday."

"Still think it's a tall order," muttered the guitarist as they exited the live room.

"It is," agreed Ellen. "But, I can do it with your help and Luke's."

"I have every faith in you."

Ellen

Late on Thursday morning, Ellen made her way through Kensington in search of Luke's apartment. They had agreed to rehearse there instead of at the old church or the studio. He'd given her the address and promised to have lunch ready for her when she arrived. Finding the building proved to be trickier than she'd anticipated but, eventually, Ellen spotted it across the street. The building was almost hidden down a small, mews lane in between two imposing Victorian buildings.

"Come on up, princess," welcomed Luke as he answered the door entry buzzer. "Top floor. Door's open."

A few moments later, as she entered the luxurious apartment, Ellen felt as though she had stepped into a luxury hotel.

"In the kitchen," called out Luke. "Second door on your right."

"Hi," said Ellen as she entered the huge square kitchen.

"Good morning," replied the bass player warmly. "Tea?"

"Please. This place is fabulous!"

"One of the perks of a rock star uncle," laughed Luke as he switched on the kettle. "He's had this place for years. He's hardly ever here. Spends his time in his gothic palace in New York."

"Gothic palace?"

"Garrett runs a music store in Manhattan. His apartment is above the store. Three storeys of it. It's all decorated in a gothic theme. Lots of red and black. Gargoyles and sconces. The place is huge!" explained Luke, passing her a mug of tea. "I used to love staying there in the school holidays. Great house to watch horror movies in."

"I can imagine," laughed Ellen, visualising crucifixes and candelabra.

"So, princess, what have you brought for us to work on?"

"Lyrics. Lots of lyrics," she replied. "And some of the music."

"Lyrics are a good start. I assume you can sing them to give me a hint about the melody?"

"That's the plan. At least two of them need piano. Maybe three."

"Ah," mused Luke with a rare relaxed mischievous look. "So, all you really need is my right hand?"

"Something like that."

"Bring your tea. I'll show you the music room. It's upstairs."

A spiral staircase led them upstairs into a short hallway. There were only three doors opening off it. Heading for the middle of the three, Luke opened it and stepped aside to allow her to enter.

"Wow!" gasped Ellen, gazing round the vast room. "This is heaven!"

"Beats a day in Hades," quipped Luke with a wink. "Another perk of the rock star uncle."

A black Steinway grand piano dominated one end of the room. The pianist in Ellen naturally gravitated towards it.

"This is beautiful," she sighed as she gazed wistfully down at its keys.

Taking her tea from her, Luke told her to take a seat. Seconds later, he sat down on the stool beside her.

"Ladies choice."

"Your Song," said Ellen. "Guilty pleasure."

"Your secret is safe."

Together, they played the Elton John classic, both easily playing in sync with each other. Before Ellen could come in on vocals, Luke began to sing. The warmth and calibre of his voice took her by surprise.

"My guilty pleasure too," he confessed when the song was over. "Let's have lunch first then we can get to work on your songs."

When they returned to the music room an hour later, Ellen could feel her nerves fluttering in the pit of her stomach. While her working relationship with Luke had improved over the months, she was nervous about sharing these songs with him. The lyrics were so personal and she wasn't totally convinced she would be able to keep her emotions in check.

"Before we start," he said, taking a seat at the piano. "Can I play you something? Not sure if it's an After Life song but I think you'll like it."

Luke indicated that she should take a seat on one of the three couches scattered about the room while he composed himself at the piano. Keeping his head bowed, he began to play a slow but spinetingling intro. Without looking up, Luke started to sing, his voice low and raw. His lyrics told a tale of the grim reaper stealing children's parents and damning the orphans to a wretched life of purgatory. The light, delicate piano accompaniment added an extra edge of menace to it.

"That's brilliant," enthused Ellen when Luke was finished. "I love it!"

"Thanks," he said quietly. "I've never played that for anyone before."

"Why not? It's absolutely perfect for the band."

"I guess up until now we've not had a vocalist who could do it justice."

"Is that a compliment, Mr Court?" teased Ellen with a smile.

"I'll not lie, Ellen," said Luke, the old blunt direct Luke reappearing. "I was prepared to hate you. I thought you were all wrong for the band. Thought you'd fuck it all up. I was wrong. The others were right. You are just what After Life needed."

"Thank you," replied Ellen bashfully. "I'd be honoured to sing your song. Let's add it to the list for taking back to Hades on Monday."

Luke nodded then said, "Your turn, princess."

Before she lost her nerve, Ellen fetched her red leather lyrics journal from her bag and walked over to stand beside the piano. Laying the book down, open at the first song she'd selected, Ellen could feel her stomach doing somersaults.

"Here goes," she muttered almost to herself.

Keeping waltz time, Ellen sang the first song she had chosen. Deliberately, she had visualised an almost sweet, soft melody for it that starkly contrasted her dark lyrical content. Over three verses, she sang of the pain and smell of burning flesh; of the loss of a part of herself; of the lights going out in her soul. The song had a creepy but catchy chorus that by the third and final time Luke was singing along to.

"Powerful stuff, princess," he complimented. "Very graphic."

"Almost too graphic for me," admitted Ellen quietly.

"Does it have a title?"

"Danse De Mort En Flammes."

"Perfect," acknowledged Luke with a warm smile. "Now, let's tease out that melody. Love the waltz time signature. Adds a theatrical air."

Sitting side by side on the piano stool, they patiently worked their way through the song. At Luke's suggestion, they started with the chorus. He asked her to sing it over a few times then suggested tweaking the lyric slightly.

"No point in the French title if you don't add it into the song somewhere," he commented with his usual direct honesty.

"There's a fourth verse that I didn't sing for you," confessed Ellen. "The line's in it."

"Sing it, princess. All of it," commanded Luke calmly. "Bare that fragile soul."

Taking a deep breath, Ellen began the song again. When she reached the fourth and final verse, she faltered then swiftly re-composed herself to sing the verse about her soul doing a dance with death among the flames, begging them to devour it forever. She hit the final long, lingering note perfectly then turned her back on Luke in an attempt to shield her tears.

"Hey," he said softly as he approached her. "No tears. That was stunning and brave."

Tentatively, Luke placed his hand on her shoulder. With tears flooding down her pale cheeks, Ellen welcomed his embrace, allowing him to hold her while she sobbed.

"Sorry," she sniffed as she wiped roughly at her cheeks.

"No need to apologise," assured Luke, displaying a warmth she had never seen before. "That is one powerful, personal song. It takes balls of steel to share something like that."

"Perhaps," whispered Ellen as she stepped away from the bass player. "All the lyrics in that book bring everything to life. Writing them was my therapy after the fire."

"I get it," admitted Luke quietly. "After my parents were killed, I wrote endless poems. Garrett encouraged it. Said it was better than keeping all the emotions trapped inside. I've still got them all in a box downstairs," he paused. "I still read through them from time to time. Helps me to feel a connection to them."

"And I get that," replied Ellen with a sad smile. Taking a deep breath, she said, "Any chance of a cup of tea to steady my nerves?"

"Of course. Let's take a break for a few minutes then come back and work on Danse De Mort."

For the rest of the day and all of the next, Ellen and Luke

secreted themselves away in the apartment's music room. At Luke's suggestion, Ellen had brought an overnight bag with her on Thursday with enough clothes to see her through till Sunday. When she arrived shortly after breakfast, Luke had shown her into the bedroom next to the music room. It was a huge room with its own en suite and French doors that opened out onto a roof garden.

"This is Garrett's room but he won't mind a pretty girl in his bed for a few days. You may even be the first pretty girl to share his bed," joked Luke with a mischievous grin.

"Pardon?"

"Garrett's gay," explained Luke.

"Ah!"

"He's quite discrete," conceded Luke in a matter of fact tone. "As is his long term, live in vampire, Salazar."

"Salazar Mendes?" quizzed Ellen curiously.

Luke nodded, "They've lived together for years."

"As long as they are happy."

"True," agreed Luke. "Make yourself at home while I go make a start. I was thinking about that chorus from last night. I've an idea."

"I'll be through in a minute or two," Ellen promised.

As she entered the music room, Luke was finishing a phone call. Not wanting to intrude, Ellen made to leave but he signalled to her to wait. A few seconds later, he stuffed his phone back into his pocket.

"Garrett," he stated. "I was running something past him."

"One of the songs?"

Luke nodded.

"And?"

"Despite his love of blues, he says Flesh To Ashes needs to be heavier. Darker."

"And did he suggest how?"

"Not yet," replied Luke. "But, he said to give him a few hours and he'd come back to us. Think we've got his creative juices flowing."

With a giggle, Ellen commented, "Another one of the perks of having a rock star uncle?"

Joining in with her laughter, Luke nodded, "Has its advantages at times. Right, let's see how we get on with song number three. You ready to reveal it?"

"As I'll ever be," replied Ellen, laying the lyrics journal down on the piano. "This one is almost like a twisted nursery rhyme. Needs a very simple arrangement to start before we get right into it."

"Go for it."

Keeping her tone childlike and light, Ellen sang a poetic intro, "One, two, three, bouncing on Daddy's knee."

She counted in three's till she reached eighteen then let out a blood curdling wail. In that one scream, the song turned dark as the little girl morphed into an evil, nasty, twisted woman. The phrasing was swift, adding to the anger behind it all.

Almost four minutes later, she switched instantly back to the little girl voice to reprise the first section of the nursery rhyme intro.

"That one's fun," acknowledged Luke, getting up from the piano. "Let me run through something on my bass."

The song, promptly given the working title of Daddy's Little Princess, gradually took shape as the day wore on. Between them, they composed the bass and guitar tracking.

"Do we need to call Jack?" asked Ellen late in the afternoon.

"Maybe tomorrow," replied Luke. "Let's make a rough recording of the three songs and send them over to the others."

"Four songs," corrected Ellen. "We're including yours too."

"Fine. Four."

By late on Saturday night, they had amassed eight songs to take back to Hades on Monday. Both of them were creatively drained but more than satisfied with the potential album tracks. They had worked through dinner in order to get rough recordings made of the last three songs and now discovered they were ravenous.

"Indian?" suggested Luke as they headed downstairs.

"Suits me," agreed Ellen, her voice husky after singing for almost five hours straight.

"There's a restaurant a couple of streets away. They'll still be open and they deliver to local clients," explained Luke, reaching for his phone. "What do you fancy?"

"Nothing too hot and spicy," replied Ellen. "Something with chicken, please."

Luke nodded as he dialled the familiar number, "Sankar? Good evening, It's Luke Court. Am I too late to get some dinner sent round?"

Ellen watched as the bass player turned on the charm to persuade Sankar to deliver their late meal.

"You're a true gent. We'll have some paneer pakora, some vegetable samosas, a Murg korma with pilau rice, an Achari Gosht with lemon rice and two peshwari naans."

Laying the phone on the counter, Luke said, "He'll be here in twenty minutes with it."

"Regular customer, are we?" teased Ellen.

"Too regular," laughed Luke. Lifting a bottle of red wine from the rack, he confessed, "I love a good Indian. I also hate cooking."

Giggling, Ellen sat down at the breakfast bar and watched as he poured her a generous glass of Shiraz.

"To successful collaboration," toasted Luke.

"And a successful album," added Ellen, raising her glass.

"Amen to that," he sighed, sitting down opposite her. "Been a long time coming."

"So, what do you think is next for the band once the album's released?"

"Incessant touring until it's time to make a second one," he replied. "If I had to guess, Rocky will get us a UK headline tour then use that to try to get us either a European or US support slot. I overheard him talking to Jason about trying to match our sound with one of their more established acts. If I were you, I'd invest in a bigger, hardwearing suitcase, girl, as you're going to be living out of it."

"Dream lifestyle," laughed Ellen. "To quote you, "been a long time coming.""

Dinner, once it arrived, proved to be delicious and, over the aromatic Indian spices, Ellen and Luke fell into a discussion about films, both discovering a mutual love of vampire movies. When they'd eaten their fill, Luke replenished their glasses and suggested that they watch The Lost Boys before calling it a night.

He gave Ellen instructions about where to find the DVD and promised to be through to join her in a minute or two. The lounge room of the apartment was as luxurious as the rest with a huge intricately patterned Oriental rug dominating the room. Following Luke's directions, she found the DVD and managed to figure out the theatre sound system. By the time Luke returned with their glasses and a fresh bottle of wine, she had the film cued and ready to go.

Taking care not to spill any, he poured her another glass of Shiraz then went to fetch a bowl of popcorn for them to share. Sitting at opposite ends of the large Chesterfield, they both curled up to enjoy the film. The Lost Boys had always been one of Ellen's favourites and she had seen it countless times over the years. When they reached the scene where Michael was sharing a Chinese meal with "the Lost Boys", she still cringed at the maggots in lieu of rice scene.

Suddenly, Luke leapt off the couch, spilling wine everywhere and began stamping frantically all over the rug in front of the tv screen.

"Luke?"

"Maggots!" he screamed, still stamping his barefoot furiously into the rug. "Bastards are everywhere!"

A cold realisation hit her…he was tripping. Trying to remain calm, Ellen said, "They're harmless. The air dissolves them."

He spun round, his eyes blazing as they bored into her, "Don't talk shite! The air multiplies them. Look! They're wriggling all over the furniture. That settee will be infested in seconds. Move! Fucking move!"

The drug induced hallucination had instantly turned nasty. Before Ellen could get to her feet, Luke had overturned the large mahogany coffee table, still raving about maggots multiplying and growing.

As fast as she could, Ellen ran down the hall and upstairs to her room. Gasping for breath, she grabbed her phone from the bedside table where she had left it on to charge and called Taylor.

"Ellen?" came the sleepy response.

"Tailz, Luke's taken something! He's wrecking the place!"

"Where are you? Are you safe?" demanded Taylor instantly awake.

"I'm upstairs in my room," she replied, her heart pounding loud and hard in her chest.

"Where's Cal?"

"I think he's staying with Jack. He's not been here since Thursday night."

"Shit!" yelled Taylor. "Stay where you are. I'll waken Rocky. We'll be there as soon as we can. Lock your door."

"It doesn't lock."

"Then get into a room that does. Stay safe, Ellen, please. For me."

"I will," she promised, tears suddenly stinging at her eyes. "Hurry!"

Crouched down behind the locked en suite door, Ellen listened to Luke's drug induced tirade sweep through the house. She heard a loud smash of glass and assumed it was the tv screen. A few seconds later, she could hear him in the kitchen throwing things about. Silently, she prayed he would stay downstairs; prayed that he would steer clear of the music room.

After what felt like an eternity, she heard more glass smashing, heard Luke swear loudly, heard a strangled scream like noise followed by a thud then nothing.

An eerie silence fell over the apartment.

Anxiously, Ellen listened. She heard a few random thuds, a groan then nothing.

Instinct told her something was wrong.... very wrong.

A text message flashed up on her phone screen. "Five minutes away. Cal and Jack about ten minutes away. You ok? Tailz"

"Fine. Not sure about Luke. Going to check," she typed hurriedly.

Her fingers and hand were trembling as she unlocked the door. Quietly, Ellen tip toed from the en suite and across the bedroom out into the upper hallway. She paused at the top of the spiral staircase to listen for any sounds coming from the rooms below.

Deafening silence.

Stealthily, she crept down the stairs, half expecting Luke to jump out on her when she reached the bottom. The hallway was a scene of devastation. A huge, antique, gilt framed mirror lay shattered on the floor. The large vase of sunflowers that had sat on the console table lay smashed on the floor, water seeping into the rug. Beside it, the table had been upturned. Beyond that, Ellen saw a sight that made her blood run cold.

She could see Luke lying on the floor, half in the hall, half in the dining room. His bare feet were bleeding badly from treading on either the smashed mirror or glass elsewhere in the apartment. There was no movement from them. She watched the blood trickle down his soles, coursing towards his heels.

"Luke?" she called softly

No response.

With a total disregard for her own wellbeing, Ellen rushed over to her bandmate.

She found him lying face down in a pool of blood filled vomit, His right arm lay twisted at an awkward angle and, even to her uneducated eye, was obviously broken. Dropping to her knees beside him, she felt for a pulse. It was there but thready.

Without hesitation, Ellen dialled 999.

"I need an ambulance immediately," she gushed.

Moments later, safe in the knowledge that the ambulance was on its way, Ellen cleared the vomit away from Luke's mouth and nose. He was barely breathing. There was no way she could see to roll him over to try to resuscitate him as she had learned years before in her first aid class in school. All she could do was sit with him and wait.

"Ellen!"

With a start she looked up to see Taylor and Rocky coming down the hall.

"Help! It's Luke," she half shouted, half sobbed. "I've called an ambulance."

"Shit!" muttered Taylor, dropping to his knees beside her. "Rocky, help me turn him over. He's barely breathing."

"Watch his arm. Looks like its broken," cautioned Ellen.

Working together, Taylor and Rocky rolled After Life's bass player onto his back then Taylor began CPR. In the distance, they could hear a siren approaching.

"Ellen! Tailz!"

"Down here, Cal," called Rocky as the remaining members of

After Life charged into the apartment.

"There's an ambulance crew at our backs," said Cal, breathless after running up the stairs.

The next few minutes were chaotic as the paramedics arrived, swiftly assessed the situation and began to work on Luke.

"Anyone any idea what he's taken?" asked one of the paramedics.

"I don't know," replied Ellen. "We had wine with dinner then some more watching the film. He started hallucinating then began smashing the place up."

"Acid," stated Cal plainly. "I'd put my money on acid."

"How sure are you?"

"Let me check his room," said Cal, running down the hallway towards Luke's room.

He emerged a few seconds later with his friend's wallet in his hand.

"Strips of acid. No idea how many he's had but there's four missing from this."

Cal has a small folded strip of paper in his hand with four squares torn from it. Without hesitation, he handed it to the paramedic, who slipped it into a clear plastic bag.

"His ECG reading is all over the place," commented the other paramedic.

For almost an hour, they worked to stabilise Luke while the remaining members of After Life and Rocky looked on anxiously.

"Folks, we're ready to move him," announced one of the medics eventually. "We're taking him to Chelsea and Westminster if you want to follow us."

"Can I ride with you?" asked Cal, his face a mask of concern for his friend.

"Sure."

The familiar sterile smell hit Ellen as soon as they entered the hospital's accident and emergency department and she felt her stomach heave. Quashing the flashbacks that threatened to overwhelm her, she followed Taylor and the others over to the desk. The band stood back and let Rocky speak with the nurse behind the desk.

"Thanks," he said with a smile. "Straight through those doors and down to the right?"

"That's correct, sir."

"Thanks," said the band's manager before turning to the others. "This way. Cal's waiting down here. They're still working on Luke."

They found Cal sitting alone in a small waiting area. At the sound of their footsteps he looked up and forced a worried smile.

"Any news?" asked Ellen, before the others could find their voices.

"Not much. His heart stopped twice on the way here. They rushed him straight through. I've not see him since," replied Cal, his eyes filling up with unshed tears.

"Fuck," muttered Jack, flopping down onto a chair opposite Cal. "And they think the acid caused this?"

Cal nodded. "I've called Garrett. He's trying to grab a flight. Promised he'd be here tomorrow at some point."

"Was that necessary before we know what's going on?" asked Rocky.

"The hospital told me to call his family."

"He's young. He's strong," began Ellen softly as she sat down beside Cal. "He'll pull through. He has to."

"I hope so," sighed Cal wearily.

Together, After Life waited for news. At some point, Ellen must have dozed off as she rested her head against Tailz. She was wakened sharply when he moved in the seat. Through her sleep fog, she could hear voices. As she opened her eyes, Ellen saw they'd been joined by a doctor.

"And we've moved him to our Cardiology unit," she heard the doctor explain.

"Is he going to be alright?" Ellen heard Jack ask next.

"It's early days. We've placed Luke in a medically induced coma until we stabilise his heart rhythm. If it doesn't stabilise in the next eight to twenty-four hours, we'll operate. He's young though with no known history of cardiac problems so we hope, once the drugs are clear of his system, that it will settle back into a normal rhythm naturally."

"And his arm?" asked Cal anxiously.

"It was a clean break just above the elbow. We've realigned it and put it in a cast. Will take about six to eight weeks to heal," explained the doctor in a matter-of-fact tone. "We've also sutured several of the deeper lacerations to his feet."

"Can we see him?" asked Ellen sleepily.

"Only for a minute or two," replied the doctor firmly. "We've more tests to run shortly."

"Thanks, doctor," said Rocky as they all got slowly to their feet, each of them stiff from sitting on the uncomfortable plastic chairs.

They followed the doctor through the labyrinth of the hospital until they stopped outside the high dependency ward within the cardiology suite.

"Please take turns. No more than two or three of you at once. No more than five minutes each."

Rocky nodded, "Cal, come with me. You too, Ellen."

"No. Let Jack go," said Ellen. "I'll wait and go in with Taylor."

Five minutes later, when she entered the ward holding Taylor's hand tightly, Ellen felt herself begin to tremble. This whole horrible scene was bringing some of her deepest buried fears to life. A young nurse was sitting in the room keeping watch over the monitor output.

"You can talk to him," she said with a warm reassuring smile.

"Hi," said Taylor awkwardly. "You've given us all quite a fright this time, buddy. Some folk'll do anything to avoid having to put in the hours with the band."

"Don't listen to him, Luke," countered Ellen, trying to keep her voice steady. "We've worked twice as hard as these guys. You need to focus on getting well so we can finish these new songs off."

"Those rough recordings are on the money," acknowledged Taylor. "Even Cushy approved. Not sure what he'll say when he hears about this set back."

"It'll be fine," said Ellen, conscious that neither of them really knew if Luke could hear them or not. "We'll be able to work round all of this. Just focus on getting well."

Nervously, she stepped forward and kissed his clammy forehead.

"We'll see you later, Luke," she said hastily. "Behave till we get back."

"See you later, buddy," added Taylor quietly.

Once back out in the corridor, Ellen turned to Taylor and promptly burst into tears. Fear and exhaustion had finally caught up with her and Tailz held her close while she wept. Gently, he rubbed her back as he tried to assure her that Luke would be alright. Spotting them, Rocky came striding over and immediately took control.

"Come on. Let's get you home. Lizzy's cooking breakfast for us all," he said with fatherly warmth.

"Rocky's right," added Taylor. "And you need some rest."

"You all do," stated their manager. "I've called Cushy and Jason. Filled them in."

"What about Luke's apartment? And my stuff's still there," protested Ellen before a yawn almost consumed her.

"Get some food and some sleep then we can sort out a clean-up committee before Garrett gets here," said Rocky firmly.

Despite their protests about not being hungry, Lizzy set a cooked breakfast down in front of the members of After Life and ordered them all to eat. They were all too weary to argue with her. With their plates cleared, Lizzy sent them all to bed, promising to waken them in a few hours. A swift debate about who was sleeping where was immediately resolved by Lizzy.

"Taylor, take Ellen to her room. Stay with her. Cal take Taylor's bed. Jack, you can sleep in the other spare room. I've made up the bed. Now get upstairs all of you."

Ellen

Several hours later, Ellen awoke to find Taylor still sound asleep beside her. He had held her until she had fallen asleep then obviously rolled over to the other side of the bed. Taking care not to waken him, she crept out of bed and headed to the bathroom to shower. When she came out of the bathroom, Ellen could hear voices coming from downstairs. She recognised Rocky and Lizzy's but there was a third voice that was unfamiliar.

Half an hour later, with her damp hair pulled back into a loose ponytail, Ellen made her way downstairs. As she entered the kitchen, she spotted a visitor sitting at the table, a mug of tea in front of him.

"Hi," she said as both Rocky and Lizzy looked round. "Any news?"

"No change," replied Lizzy, as she got up to make Ellen some tea.

"Ellen, this is Garrett Court," introduced Rocky. "Luke's uncle."

Suddenly star truck, Ellen felt her cheeks redden as the iconic rock idol got to his feet to hug her.

"Thank you, darling, for taking care of him. If you hadn't found him when you did," Garrett paused.

"I wish I could've done more," apologised Ellen softly. "There was no way I could roll him over. I knew to do CPR but, well….. I can't."

"You did everything right from what I hear," said Garrett warmly.

"If you say so," replied Ellen awkwardly before taking a seat at the table.

As she set the mug of tea down in front of her, Lizzy said, "Cal and Jack are away to make a start on the clean-up. I said to Cal to fetch your bags. Saves you going back there too soon."

"I want to help," protested Ellen. "Besides, I've stuff in the music room as well as the bedroom. Cal won't know what's mine."

"We can both head over when you're ready," suggested Garrett with a smile. "I need to pick up some things for Luke before going back to the hospital."

"Thanks," she replied then added. "And thanks for letting me use your room."

"You're more than welcome," answered Garrett. "Any time you need somewhere to stay, let me know."

Accompanied by Taylor, Ellen and Garrett took a taxi back across London to the apartment. When they entered, the hallway was more or less restored to normal. There was an obvious gap on the wall where the mirror had hung.

"Never did like that mirror," commented Garrett casually as he stared the space on the wall. "It was my paternal grandmother's. Always reminded me of her."

Without pausing, he walked purposefully down the hall to the lounge. Both Taylor and Ellen hurried after him, dreading to see how bad the room was. Over the course of the afternoon, Cal and Jack had worked hard. While nowhere near its former glory, the lounge was more or less presentable. As they entered, the two After Life musicians were unmounting the remnants of the television from the wall.

"Afternoon, boys," called out Garrett. "Doesn't look too horrendous in here. Thanks."

"Should've seen it three hours ago," muttered Cal sourly.

"Have you kept an inventory for the insurance firm?"

"Yes, sir," replied Jack. "There's a list in the kitchen. You might want to add the dining room rug to it. Not sure the blood stains are going to come out of it. It's a mess."

"Add it on," advised Garrett calmly. "Have you much more to clean up?"

"Nah," replied Cal. "Just a few bits and pieces in the kitchen. We've put the crap in the back of Jack's van. We'll take it to the dump tomorrow."

"Thanks, Cal. Another one I owe you," sighed the older musician wearily. "That boy'll be the death of us all."

"I'll go and make a start on the kitchen," volunteered Taylor.

"Can I help?" asked Ellen.

"Leave the boys to it, angel," suggested Garrett softly. "You go and gather up whatever you need to pack. I'll grab a few things for Luke then we can head over to the hospital."

Her stomach lurched at the thought of returning to the hospital but Ellen forced a weak smile and said, "Give me fifteen minutes."

"No rush," replied Garrett. "I need to phone home first. Check up on things there."

It was almost an hour later before Ellen and Garrett entered the ICU ward. The only thing that had changed from earlier was that a different nurse sat in the corner watching the monitor activity. She offered a soft "hello" as they took a seat beside the bed.

"He looks so peaceful," mused Garrett sadly. "So many demons wrestling inside."

"He seemed so relaxed yesterday," commented Ellen, gently lifting Luke's hand and giving it a squeeze. "We'd worked all day then had a really late dinner. The movie was Luke's idea. I set the DVD up while he fetched some wine and popcorn. He must have taken the acid then. I wish I knew why."

"So do I, angel," said Garrett. "He's always messed about with alcohol and drugs. I've put him through countless hours of therapy and counselling but he always slips back. He might have gone too far this time."

"I hope not," replied Ellen, giving Luke's hand another squeeze. "He's an album to record. Plus, we've still a few songs to work on together."

There was a flurry of bleeps from the monitors and Ellen felt Luke's fingers twitch.

"I think he heard you, miss," said the nurse. "Keep talking calmly, please. I'm going to call the doctor in to check on these readings."

Feeling self-conscious, Ellen talked about the songs they had worked on, talked about the songs they still had to finish off. Around them, the monitors began to bleep erratically. An alarm went off and, before either Ellen or Garrett had time to react, a team of nurses, closely followed by the doctor, came running in.

"Outside!" barked the doctor sharply. "Now, please."

From the far side of the window in the corridor, Garrett and Ellen watched on helplessly as the medical team worked frantically on Luke. After a few minutes, the ward doors flew open and the team wheeled Luke's bed down the corridor at high speed.

All Ellen and Garrett could do was look on in shocked dismay. Instinctively, the older man put his arm around Ellen, drawing her close.

"Mr Court?" quizzed one of the doctors calmly.

"Yes," said Garrett quickly. "What's going on? Is he ok?"

"We've made the decision to take him to theatre. His heart isn't settling into a normal rhythm. In fact, if anything, it's deteriorated over the past two hours. We need to prevent any further episodes of ventricular fibrillation."

"What are you going to do to him?" demanded Garrett bluntly. "And in plain English, please."

"We're going to fit a pacemaker to regulate the heart's rhythm. His heart is beating too fast. If we don't get it under control, he's at high risk of cardiac arrest."

"Shit," muttered Garrett, pulling Ellen closer to him. "Thanks, doctor."

"He'll be in surgery for about three hours," explained the doctor. "You might want to go home for a while or go for something to eat. If there's any change, we'll call you straight away."

"Can we wait here?" asked Ellen quietly.

"Of course. I'll have someone update you as soon as there is any news."

"Thanks."

Together, they watched the doctor stride off down the corridor.

"There's a waiting room just along the hall," began Ellen. "Let's wait there."

"You go on ahead," replied Garrett, his voice thick with emotion. "I'm going to call Cal and Rocky. Let them know what's happening. Does Luke have a girlfriend in tow just now?"

Ellen shook her head. "He split up with Emily before the tour. He's not seeing anyone as far as I know. Check with Cal though."

"Thanks. I'll not be long," promised Garrett, forcing a smile. "Will I bring you back a coffee?"

"Tea, please," answered Ellen. "Black with sugar."

Almost half an hour had passed before Garrett reappeared

with two waxed paper cups. He apologised profusely for leaving her on her own for so long then explained that the rest of After Life would be with them in an hour or so. They sat in silence for a few minutes then Garrett said, "I was really impressed with the demos Luke sent through. You're a very talented young lady."

"Thanks," replied Ellen as her cheeks flushed scarlet at the compliment.

"From what I'm hearing, you've brought a whole new energy to After Life. A new vibe. Some balance."

"I don't know about balance," disputed Ellen with a smile. "My balance is awful!"

"Luke told me your story. Told me he acted like an asshole the night he met you," began Garrett then, with a wink, added, "And that you wiped the floor with him the next day playing Kashmir."

Ellen laughed, "That seems like a lifetime ago. I'm surprised he told you about that. I don't think he's even told the rest of the band. I was the only one who noticed he'd screwed up."

"Kashmir was the first song I taught him to play on guitar and bass," Garrett reminisced wistfully. "He's a natural musician. Music helped him to cope after his parents died. It was the only thing I could share with him that seemed to connect. I'm no good with kids or teenagers."

"Music is a good healer," agreed Ellen, staring down into her half empty cup. "It's helped me through some dark days."

"Of course," gasped Garrett, suddenly realising what he was saying. "Luke tells me you are an accomplished pianist."

"I was, I guess," she replied. "It's become a bit of a sick joke that he's my right-hand man."

"That is sick," agreed Garrett, grinning in spite of himself.

"Sometimes you need to just laugh at yourself. It's taken me a long time. After Life have really helped me see that."

"Well, I think we're all going to have to pull together to help him through this."

They were joined by the rest of After Life, who had the foresight to bring in some burgers and chips, shortly before eight. Neither Ellen nor Garrett had appreciated that they were hungry until they smelled the vinegar on the chips. As they ate, they filled the others in on what had happened then they all settled down to wait.

Three hours came and went… as did four….. and then five.

Garrett began to pace anxiously up and down the small waiting area.

Eventually, around midnight, there was a flurry of activity out in the corridor as Luke was brought back to the ward. Before any of them could get to their feet, the same doctor who had spoken to them earlier, entered the small waiting room.

"Apologies," he said warmly. "Things took a little longer than expected but surgery has been successful."

"Thank God," sighed Garrett. "Is he going to be ok?"

"One step at a time, Mr Court," cautioned the doctor. "We've stabilised his heart rhythm. We've monitored it for the last hour or two. There are indications that he may have had an underlying heart condition. We want to bring him round slowly. Once we've brought him round, we'll be able to do more tests to confirm that. Treatment and recovery would be the same either way."

"Can we see him?" asked Garrett anxiously.

"You can sit with him, Mr Court, but I'd like to restrict visitors for the first twenty-four hours."

The members of the band nodded and assured Garrett that they would wait at the hospital for as long as it took.

"No," protested Luke's uncle. "Go home, kids. Get some rest. You've an album to record. If I know Cushy, he'll expect at least some of you in tomorrow."

"You're not wrong," muttered Cal. "I've already been summoned."

"Likewise," confessed Taylor.

"Go home. I'll call if there's any news," promised Garrett firmly. "Ellen, do you want to see him before you go?"

"Mr Court, please," began the doctor, a hint of exasperation in his tone.

"Just for a minute then I'll go in," stated Garrett. "If Ellen wants to, that is."

"I'll just say a quick good night," said Ellen quietly. "And thank you, Garrett. I'll come back tomorrow afternoon. Do you need me to bring you anything?"

"I've no idea, angel," admitted the older man. "I'll message you in the morning."

It was a sombre After Life who gathered at Hades next day. As Taylor and Ellen arrived together, Cal was coming up the street towards them.

"Any news?" he called as soon as he was within earshot.

"Garrett said there was no change," replied Ellen. "He was going home for some sleep for a few hours. Poor man's not slept since he arrived here."

"He must be utterly fucked," observed Cal with his usual inimitable style.

Together, the three of them entered the building, descending the steep stairs down to the studio. In the lounge, they found Jack sprawled out, fast asleep on the couch. Hearing their arrival, Lee, the sound engineer, stuck his head out from the control room.

"Shh," he cautioned softly, indicating that they shouldn't disturb the sleeping drummer. He waved them into the room beside him.

The small control room was cramped with four people in it.

"Jack's been here all night," explained the sound engineer. "As have I. He's worked out drum tracks for those new songs you sent over and finished off recording the tracks from the white board."

"Impressive," said Taylor. "I'm not surprised though. He's a workaholic. When he's stressed, he works even harder."

"Guess we're all a bit stressed out," agreed Ellen quietly. "It's been a tough couple of days."

"Any update on Luke?" asked Lee.

"No change," replied Ellen.

"I'll warn you folks now," began the sound engineer cautiously. "Cushy wants a band meeting to agree a revised schedule here and he needs those bass tracks laid down somehow. Do any of you play bass by any chance?"

All of them shook their heads.

"Thought as much. We need to work out a Plan B here, folks, and fast."

"We're not replacing Luke and that's a fact," stated Taylor bluntly.

"And if he's out of action for more time than we have at our disposal?" challenged Lee calmly. "You guys need a Plan B to save this record."

"Lee's right," acknowledged Ellen. "I might have a Plan B but we'd need a day or so to give me time to get agreement."

"What are you thinking, my lovely?" quizzed Taylor, staring at her.

"There's only one person that Luke might agree to play in his place," she stated. "And that's Garrett."

"Can he play bass though?" asked Taylor.

Both Cal and Ellen nodded before Cal said, "Garrett taught him how to play."

"Once we know Luke's out of danger, we could ask Garrett to fill in," added Ellen. "We'd need to be careful here though. I'm not sure how he'd feel about being asked."

"He'll do anything for Luke," stated Cal emphatically. "Absolutely anything."

"We stand a better chance of getting him on board if Ellen or even Rocky ask him," commented Taylor.

"Sounds like you've got your Plan B," said Lee with a grin. "Now, can we get some work done today perhaps?"

After Life had worked through the new songs that Ellen and Luke had written over the weekend by the time Cushy thundered into Hades. He took up his usual seat in the control room and ordered them to start again and to focus on finalising the guitar parts. Feeling surplus to requirements, Ellen wandered back out to the lounge where Jack was still sound asleep. The drummer had rolled over and was now curled up on his side facing into the back of the couch. Trying to be as quiet as possible, Ellen made herself a mug of tea then curled up on the other couch with her lyrics journal.

She had just revised the lyrics for two of the songs when she felt her phone vibrate in her pocket. A message was displayed on the screen from Garrett, "Luke's waking up."

Abandoning all creative thoughts, Ellen rushed back into the live room.

"Luke's waking up!" she called out as she charged in. "Garrett just messaged me."

"That's nice, Miss Lloyd," snapped Cushy from the control room. "But you've just ruined that run through."

"Apologies, Cushy," she replied in a tone that made it crystal clear that she wasn't sorry in the slightest. "Guys, I'm going to the hospital, then I'm heading home."

"Message us if he wakes up while you're there," said Cal, anxious for news of his friend.

"Don't worry, I will," promised Ellen. "Cushy, do you want me here tomorrow?"

"Yes!" snapped the producer. "Be here for five. Vocals for the first three songs on that fucking board."

"Fine," agreed Ellen sweetly.

When Ellen arrived at the hospital, she found Garrett pacing up and down the corridor outside Luke's room. He hugged her tightly as he explained that the medical team were working on Luke to make him more comfortable.

"Has he come round yet?"

"Not totally. He's been kind of in and out for the last half hour but he was getting agitated," explained Garrett. "I think they were going to give him something to calm him a little but still allow him to wake up."

Before Ellen could respond, one of the nurses said they could go back in.

"Luke should be fully awake within the hour," said the doctor as he hung the chart back on the end of the bed. "He may be a little disorientated at first. Possibly confused. That's all perfectly normal and will pass."

Once the medical team left the room, Garrett and Ellen each took a seat on either side of the bed. Between them, Luke looked more peaceful than he had before. Most of the tubes were gone, leaving only a nasal oxygen cannula discretely increasing his oxygen supply, His arm was also in a fresh cast Ellen noted that extended from hand to shoulder.

"How are things in Hades?" asked Garrett casually.

"A bit fraught," admitted Ellen honestly. "I left Jack sound asleep in the lounge. He'd been there all-night tracking drums. Cal and Tailz are working on the guitar parts for the songs Luke and I worked on."

"And Cushy is growling at everyone," added Garrett with a knowing grin.

"Something like that," laughed Ellen softly. "He's hard on everyone but he's getting results. I've never heard the boys play like that. It's amazing what he draws out of people."

"When is he expecting you back?"

"Tomorrow at five," revealed Ellen. "Wants the first three vocal tracks."

"Sounds like a late night for you tomorrow then, angel."

"More than likely," she agreed, gently massaging Luke's hand. "We've bass tracks for six songs so we can focus on finishing those off first."

"What's the plan for the other bass tracks?"

"Good question," said Ellen with a smile.

She felt a movement at her hand as Luke's fingers tightened round hers. The movement didn't go unnoticed by Garrett, who smiled then winked at her.

"You could hire someone," he mused.

"Over my dead body," came the weak but clear reply from Luke.

"Welcome back," said Garrett warmly as his nephew's eyelids flickered.

"Garrett?"

"Yes," replied Luke's uncle. "Ellen's here too."

"Hi," she said softly, squeezing his hand.

"What happened?" mumbled Luke as he struggled open his eyes.

"You scared the crap out of Ellen here," began Garrett. "And took ten years off my life."

"We were watching The Lost Boys ......"

"And someone decided to do some acid," finished off Garrett bluntly.

"I did?"

"You did," replied Ellen, seeing the anger brewing on the older man's face. "You had a bad trip. You had a seizure and your heart suffered a cardiac arrest."

"Heart attack?" quizzed Luke, turning to stare at her as he struggled to get his eyes to focus.

"No. The doctor said it was a cardiac arrest. I believe there's a medical difference. You're lucky to be alive," explained Ellen calmly, keeping her explanation simple and trying not to scare her band mate. "The doctor will explain it all to you better than I can."

"My arm?" muttered Luke, feeling the weight of the cast for the first time.

"Somehow you broke it," said Garrett. "When Ellen found you, it was already broken."

"How?"

"No idea," replied Ellen. "It's a clean break. It'll heal soon."

"I'd better tell someone he's awake," commented Garrett, getting to his feet. "Keep him calm till I come back."

The weak bass player turned to watch his uncle leave the room then turned his head back to look at Ellen.

"Sorry," he said, his voice barely above a whisper. "You ok?"

"I'm fine. You scared the hell out of me. There was only so much I could do. You were barely breathing when I found you."

"What day is it? Sunday?"

"No," said Ellen, shaking her head. "It's Monday."

"Monday?" echoed Luke, a confused look flashing across his face.

"Yes. You've been here since late Saturday night. Garrett arrived yesterday morning. He's barely left your side."

A memory flashed into Luke's mind and he groaned, "His flat? Did I do any damage?"

Ellen nodded.

"Bad?"

"Pretty bad," she admitted. "Cal and Jack cleared it up yesterday. Tailz helped. It's ok. Garrett's seen it."

Luke groaned again. "I've pretty much fucked it all up this time, haven't I?"

"Pretty much," agreed Ellen with a smile. "But we'll work it out. You just need to focus on getting better."

At that moment Garrett returned, closely followed by a nurse and the doctor. Once again Ellen and Garrett were asked to step outside. After a few minutes, they were allowed back in but both were cautioned that Luke needed to rest.

"We'll stay for a bit then head off," promised Garrett, with a nod to Ellen for agreement.

"No more than half an hour," stated the nurse firmly.

With all the medical staff gone, Luke quizzed Ellen and his

uncle about what had happened. Keeping their answers suitably vague for fear of distressing him, they both did their best to reassure him. When he learned that he had been fitted with a pacemaker, his eyes filled up with tears.

"Hey," said Ellen softly. "Look at me. It's going to be ok. It's just a gizmo to keep your heartbeat regular. You'll be back in the studio in no time. You just need to give yourself time to heal, Luke."

"What would you know?" he growled half under his breath.

"More than you'll ever understand, Luke Court!" snapped Ellen sharply. "No self-pity allowed here, mister."

She paused, then decided to continue, "When I wakened up in that hospital in Thailand, I was thousands of miles away from home. Half my sight was gone. My arm was gone. I had extensive third-degree burns. I was a mess! You've wakened up a few miles from home, a bit battered, a little broken and with a few lifestyle choices to make. You'll walk out of here in a few days' time the same person though and pick up where you left off."

Her outburst had surprised Garrett but he sat and watched to see how his nephew would react.

"But I won't be able to play," whined Luke, staring at the white cast on his arm.

"Oh, poor Lukie," commiserated Ellen sarcastically. "You'll be playing again in a few weeks. Try facing up to never playing again!"

The two members of After Life stared intently at each other, eyes locked. It was Luke who glanced away first.

"I'm being an arsehole, aren't I?"

"Yes, you are," said Garrett bluntly. "Ellen's right. Keep this in perspective. It's a setback. You certainly have lifestyle choices, as Ellen succinctly put it, to reflect on but you'll be fine, son. And I second Ellen's thoughts here. No self-pity."

"Sorry," he said contritely. "Sorry, princess. Am I still your right-hand man?"

Stifling a giggle, Ellen pointed to the cast on his arm and suggested, "Maybe not for the next few weeks."

It was enough to lighten the mood once more.

"Folks," interrupted a nurse. "Luke needs to rest. Time to go. I'll give you a couple of minutes to say goodnight."

"What time is visiting tomorrow?" asked Garrett.

"Call in the morning and we'll confirm. If Luke has a good night, you'll probably be allowed in around lunchtime."

As they walked out of the hospital, Ellen heard her stomach grumble. Much to her acute embarrassment, Garrett heard it too.

"Hungry?" he asked with a mischievous grin.

"Apparently," confessed Ellen, her cheeks going scarlet as she spoke.

"Allow me to buy you dinner," suggested the older man. "Can't have you starving to death on me."

"You don't need to," protested Ellen awkwardly. "Lizzy'll have something I'm sure."

"Nonsense," stated Garrett firmly. "There's a good Italian restaurant near here. My treat."

"Thank you."

They fell into step with each other as Garrett led them along Kings Road towards the small family run restaurant. Not surprisingly, Luke was the topic of their conversation, with both of them expressing their relief at how well he seemed all things considered. Once seated in the restaurant, Ellen felt more than a little self-conscious. As she perused the menu, she felt her usual flutters of panic about what she could eat without assistance. Almost as if sensing her unease, Garrett said, "I really fancy some pizza. How do you feel about splitting a pepperoni with me?"

"Sounds perfect," replied Ellen.

"Red wine or beer to wash it down?"

"Red wine would be nice."

When the waiter approached to take their order, Garrett asked for an extra-large pepperoni, sliced, and a bottle of Sangiovese. Discretely, he slid the cutlery to one side then said with a wink, "Who needs a knife and fork for pizza?"

With a smile Ellen said, "Thank you."

"What for?"

"Your discretion," she answered softly. "Cutlery can be a challenge."

"I figured."

Taking a sip of his wine a short while later, Garrett said, "Can I ask you something?"

"Of course."

"What happened that night in Thailand? Luke just told me you'd had an accident there."

Ellen stared down into her glass for a moment or two. Talking about that night was never easy but she felt she owed Garrett an answer.

"I went to Thailand with my boyfriend and two members of the band I was in at the time, Good Times. Don't think you'd have heard of them," she began quietly. "We went there to celebrate my eighteenth birthday. A couple of days after it, we decided to go to a club. Thought it was a good idea to treat ourselves to a big night out. We had a great night then it all went wrong. Really wrong. My friend, Alex, was at the bar. He was clear of the worst of it and escaped more or less unscathed. The two guys and I were on the dancefloor when the petrol bomb was thrown into the middle of the club. It was thrown through a window. It landed not far from us. Within seconds it exploded. I don't really remember much other than trying to get to the side and being surrounded by screaming and dance music. A section of the roof collapsed. That's what killed most of the people, including my friends. A separate section fell and landed on me. All I remember was intense heat then pain then nothing till I woke up in hospital."

A tear slid down her cheek and her voice wavered a little as she continued, "My arm was too badly crushed and burned to save it. I have burn scars all the way up to my shoulder and all down my right side to just below my waist. My ribs were broken. My lungs were scorched. I lost the sight in my right eye. I see shadows through it and its very sensitive to light. The doctors thought the damage was caused by a bright flash of flame."

"No wonder you were so tough on my nephew back there," commented Garrett, his emotions numbed by her tale. "How long ago was this?"

"Almost six years ago now."

"How do you even begin to pick up the pieces after an ordeal like that?"

"Slowly," said Ellen with a wistful smile as the waiter arrived with their pizza. When the waiter left, she continued, "Tom gave me a journal before we left for Thailand. Tom was my boyfriend at the time. He said it was to record my memories of the trip. My dad brought it to me in the hospital. Encouraged me to write all the pain and anger and frustration and grief into the pages. Writing those lyrics was good therapy for me. Fortunately, I've always been a lefty."

"Did you ever record these songs?" asked Garrett between mouthfuls of pizza.

"Not yet. Some of them were the songs Luke and I were working on in your music room. Seven of mine and one of his."

"One of Luke's?" repeated Garrett, looking surprised.

Ellen nodded, "About the grim reaper stealing children's parents from them. "Children of Purgatory" he called it."

"It's very rare for him to share his songs," commented Garrett. "Luke doesn't even share them with me. Never did. I would occasionally stand outside his room and listen to him practice. You're honoured, angel. Shows he trusts you."

"I think we've worked out a mutual trust of each other," she said with a giggle. "It took us a while."

"You've given me food for thought," began Garrett. "Maybe I need to buy a leather-bound journal for my nephew to work this through his system."

"He might struggle to write things down till his arm heals," pointed out Ellen.

"True," conceded Garrett smiling. "And he's going to struggle to fulfil these recording commitments, isn't he?"

Ellen nodded, scared to voice the thought forming on her lips.

"I'll need to speak to Luke first, but I think I need to help my nephew out here," began Garrett cautiously. "If the band can keep it under the radar and Luke agrees to it, do you think it would help if I finished his bass tracks?"

"Yes," she replied without hesitation. "This album means so much to him. Means so much to all of us. If there's anything you can do."

"Leave that thought with me."

Life for the band slid into a new routine over the next week. With the drum tracking more or less complete, Jack was free to spend much of his time at the hospital. In the studio, Cushy pushed Cal and Taylor hard, drawing out a level of skill that neither musician knew they possessed. The producer preferred to work with them individually so, when one was locked away in Hades, the other was free to visit Luke. Ellen's schedule was more or less free as the producer declared he would leave the remaining vocals till last. With most of her time her own, Ellen split it between visiting Luke and discretely rehearsing with Garrett. As expected, Luke was more than happy for his uncle to step into his shoes and help out. The producer too had been surprisingly amicable to the compromise. His only words of caution were "make yourself sound like the boy, Garrett. He's going to have to sound like you sounding like him when they play this shit live."

Two weeks to the day after Luke's collapse, Garrett stepped into Hades for the first time with the rest of After Life. He'd agreed to come in and just play for an afternoon before starting his bass tracking next day. After a bit of a debate, Cushy had given him a deadline of 7th June to finish it. That gave him seven full days in Hades.

Time was slipping away from them rapidly. If they waited until Garrett was finished to start the vocals, it only gave Ellen seven days to record the remaining fourteen songs on the board. She voiced her concerns over this and a revised schedule was worked out, meaning Garrett would do his tracks during the day then she'd come in and put in a night shift.

"So, people," said Garrett as he lifted Luke's bass from its stand. "Where do you want to start?"

The four members of After Life exchanged nervous glances before Ellen threw back her head and laughed.

"I think there's only one place to start, don't you?" she giggled with a wink to Taylor. "Kashmir!"

"Touché, princess," commented Garrett, getting the joke. "Kashmir it is."

After Life and Garrett jammed for a couple of hours, enjoying just playing in the company of the older man. Eventually though, Cushy pulled rank, growling through the glass, "How about rehearsing some of the fucking songs on that fucking board before I grow old and die!"

"Chill, Cushy," called through Garrett calmly. He glanced at the partially completed board, noting the songs that still needed bass tracks. "How about we start with Flesh To Ashes?"

"Fine!" stated the producer sourly.

Only Ellen knew that Garrett had helped them develop the song. Her face a mask of calm, she took up her position and waited for her cue. The song had evolved into one of the darker songs on the board with a heavy, thunderous bass line. Keeping a husky menacing edge to her vocal, Ellen began to sing. Beside her, she saw Taylor smile and give her an approving nod. They had worked on the song's chorus, altering the lyrics to make it more fan friendly, more anthemic. As she reached the final chorus almost four minutes later, Ellen sang with a power that none of them had heard before. Her anger and passion flowed freely into the vocal.

"Now that's more like it," commented Cushy when the song was over. "Again, from the top. Jack, stick to the drums that you tracked. No improvisation. Cal, keep that rhythm tight. Taylor, let it flow. Don't hold back."

By the time they had run through the song another half a dozen times, the producer finally said, "Garrett, I think you've got it. That one will be first when you come in tomorrow."

Glancing at his watch, the older musician said, "Fine by me. Now, I need to step out for a couple of hours."

"If you have to," muttered Cushy. "Kids, break for dinner. Ellen, I need you back here at nine."

"What's the plan?" she asked.

"Vocals for this one," stated Cushy. "Then, if time allows, Lou Lou At 3am. Taylor, you'd better come back too just in case."

"Yes, sir," called back the guitarist.

With the studio in partial darkness, Taylor was struggling to stay awake as he watched Ellen work. They had barely had any time alone since Luke's collapse and part of him was glad to have her to himself for a few hours. Her steely determination never ceased to amaze him. Out of all of them, Ellen was the one who was least afraid of the intimidating producer. Seeing her stand her ground and, on occasion, defy Cushy, had impressed him. For the first time, Taylor found himself wondering who she would have evolved into if the accident hadn't derailed her career.

Over in the vocal booth, Taylor could see she was tiring. He could hear it in her voice too.

"Stop!" yelled Cushy, disturbing his train of thought. "Take ten then be ready to do Lou Lou."

"It's two in the morning," began Ellen as she reached for her bottle of water.

"I can tell the time, Miss Lloyd. Ten minutes then we record Lou Lou. I want to be clear of here by three thirty."

As she came to sit on the couch beside Taylor, Ellen commented, "It really will be Lou Lou At 3am."

"Very funny," replied Tailz as he slipped his arm around her shoulder. "Any word from Garrett on Luke?"

"I haven't checked my messages," said Ellen. "I'll check when we're done here. My phone's out in the lounge."

"Wonder when they'll let him out?"

"The doctor hinted that he'd only be there a few more days. Garrett had suggested a rehab programme to him. I'm not so sure he'll go for that plan," she replied.

"I think he's itching to get in here," admitted Taylor.

"I know but he can't play for another four weeks at least."

"It won't stop him trying. Determined little bugger at times."

"That he is," conceded Ellen with a yawn. "Do you think we can do this in a single take?"

"Not impossible but I'd guess the best we can hope for is three. Cushy might take pity on you after that."

"Maybe," mused Ellen wearily. "I can live in hope."

Wanting to keep the vocal fresh and natural, Ellen declined to record in the booth, insisting that Lee rig up a microphone for her in the live room. Seated on a high stool beside Taylor, Ellen took a deep breath then paused to regroup her thoughts. After working so long on Flesh To Ashes, her ribcage was throbbing. Pushing the physical discomfort to the back of her mind, Ellen gave Taylor the nod to start the song.

An air of calm descended on the studio, both of them transported back to the bedroom in Rocky and Lizzy's house where they wrote the song. Maybe it was Ellen's imagination but there seemed to be an extra delicacy to Taylor's playing as he focussed on the intro. Feeding from his energy, she kept the vocal warm and husky, pouring every last ounce of emotion that she possessed into the song. Taking a gamble, she allowed her mind to rest on the thoughts of betrayal that lay behind the song; allowed her anger and frustration at her mother's attitude to filter into her voice.

By the time she reached the final verse, Ellen was totally emotionally and physically drained. With the final note still ringing in the air, she fixed her gaze on the control room window, waiting anxiously for a reaction from the producer.

"Perfect," he said, a rare hint of emotion present in his own voice. "Time to call it a night."

It was as close to praise that the two members of After Life were going to get and they knew it.

They were surprised to find lights on in the house when they stepped out of the taxi and even more surprised to hear voices coming from the kitchen when they entered the hallway.

"That sounds like Garrett," commented Taylor, closing and locking the front door.

When they entered the kitchen, they found Garrett and Lizzy sitting at the table drinking hot chocolate.

"Didn't expect to see you here this late," said Ellen. "Everything ok?"

"Yes and no," replied Garrett with a smile. "I need to go back to New York for a couple of days. I'll be back on Wednesday. Thursday at the latest."

"Does that leave you enough time to finish up at Hades?" quizzed Taylor, hating to sound selfish.

"Plenty. I've spoken to Cushy. Agreed to send him some files if I can," explained the older musician. "Worst case scenario, I need to pull two all night shifts. I just need to fly back to sort out a few things at home."

"Does Luke know you're leaving?" asked Ellen softly, sensing something was wrong.

Garrett nodded, "I told him earlier. He understands."

"When's your flight?"

"I need to be at Gatwick for six thirty," he replied. "Straight flight into Newark."

"Would you two like a drink?" offered Lizzy warmly. "Kettle's hot."

"No, thanks," declined Ellen with a yawn. "I just need sleep. It's been a long night."

"Everything go ok with Cushy?" quizzed Garrett, concerned by how exhausted the two young musicians looked.

"Yes," said Taylor. "Ellen was incredible. We got Lou Lou done in a single take."

"Now that doesn't happen too often!" stated Garrett, a proud smile spreading across his weary face. "He's a hard man to please at times."

"Well, Ellen charmed him tonight," added Taylor, putting his arm around the band's exhausted vocalist.

"I'm just relieved he was happy with it," she sighed. "I don't think I had a second shot in me tonight. Flesh To Ashes took its toll. Didn't leave me much left for Lou Lou."

"Get to bed, kids," suggested Garrett, his tone oozing with fatherly concern. "I'll see you both later in the week. If anything changes, I'll let you know."

"Safe travels," said Ellen with another yawn.

"Night."

With a few hours to spare before she was due in Hades, Ellen decided to spend a couple of hours with Luke next day. As his condition had improved, he had been moved to a small private ward with open visiting. When Ellen walked into the room, she was pleased to see the band's bass player out of bed and sitting in the chair by the window.

"Hi," she called out brightly. "It's a beautiful day out there."

"Hi, yourself," greeted Luke, smiling and looking relaxed. "Was just thinking it looked like an afternoon for a beer garden."

"No chance!" laughed Ellen, laying her bag down on the bed.

"You could smuggle me out," he suggested with a wink. "Or bring me in some beers."

"No to both ideas," stated Ellen, sitting down on the chair opposite him. "What's the doctor had to say today?"

"He's happy with me. They had me doing a treadmill test this morning and some other shit. Plan seems to be to set me free on Friday, if everything stays stable," explained Luke. "I need to come back in once or twice a week for the first few weeks just to be monitored."

"Sounds promising. Any update on your arm?"

"Cast's on until the end of June then I'll get physio for it," he admitted dejectedly. "Seems the break isn't healing as fast as they'd hoped. They checked it out yesterday. New cast. Different angle. Oh, I don't know. Hurt like fuck yesterday while the cast was off."

"It'll just take time," soothed Ellen softly. "Be patient with yourself."

"Yeah, I guess," sighed Luke. "That's what the counsellor said too."

"Counsellor?"

Luke nodded, "Just between you and me, I've been seeing someone over the last few days. She's helping with the drug thing and a bit of anger management. Just putting it all into perspective." He paused. "I really don't know how you coped. How you cope. This has really screwed my head up."

"At first, I didn't," admitted Ellen. "But time is a great healer."

"And that iron streak of determination that you have, Miss Lloyd," he added.

"Maybe," giggled Ellen. "Any word from Garrett?"

"He messaged to say his flight has landed. Said he'd call me later. You know he's dashed off to attend to his pet vampire, don't you?" The air of sarcasm wasn't lost on Ellen.

"No. I didn't."

"Seems Salazar's gone off the rails a bit. He's dashed back to New York to sort him out. Guy's a bit unstable to say the least. Been in and out of rehab for as long as I've known him. He creeps me out," revealed Luke.

"I'm sure Garrett will be back in a few days," assured Ellen, feeling at a loss as to what to say. "Besides, he's still got some under cover bass tracks to finish off."

That was enough to divert Luke's attention away from his

uncle and back onto the album. They chatted about the progress made so far, the bass tracks still to be done and the vocals to be laid down.

"What's on the agenda for this evening? You got another long night ahead of you?"

"Yeah," sighed Ellen, checking the time on her phone. "Three tracks tonight, I think. Rats, Pyramid and City Of Bones And Heartache."

"Tough night ahead of you then."

"It'll be fine. They're all along the same range. Mid-range songs. Makes vocal sense to group them. Easier run tomorrow. Applegarth, Danse De Mort En Flammes and Swirling Mists."

"Take care of that voice, princess," cautioned Luke with a wink. "We need you in fine voice for the tour to launch this record."

"Tour?"

"Rocky and Jason dropped by last night. Jason's talking about a UK headline tour in October. Nothing's confirmed but he seemed pretty confident about it all."

"Now that's music to my ears!" Ellen declared with a broad smile. "I'd better make a move. I need to pick up something to eat before I head into Hades for my night shift."

"I'll walk you out to the lift," offered Luke, getting to his feet. "Doctor was nagging me to start walking about more. Legs are stiff after that treadmill too."

As the week wound on, the whiteboard in the corner of the live room began to fill up. A couple of times, Ellen noted that bass tracks were mysteriously updated overnight. Garrett was obviously keeping up his end of the bargain from across the pond. There had been little contact with him other than a message to say he was flying back overnight on Thursday and would be in Hades on Friday afternoon. After playing back some of the guitar tracking, Cushy had ordered Cal and Tailz into the studio on Friday to re-record a few parts. Ellen too was summoned earlier than planned. Much to the producer's annoyance, there was no sign of Jack.

"Where the fuck is he?" growled the Scotsman. "Jason has press coming in at four. That bastard needs to be here."

"I'll call him," offered Cal, reaching for his phone.

"Not so fast. I need you plugged in and playing shit," snapped Cushy. "Miss Lloyd, you call him. Tell him to get his scrawny arse in here."

"Will do," promised Ellen calmly as she headed back out to the lounge to make the call.

She found Lee in the kitchen making tea when she wandered through.

"Want a cup?" he called out. "Kettle's just boiled."

"Please. Black. Just a little sugar," she replied as she dialled Jack's number. The call went straight to voicemail. "Hi, Jack. It's Ellen. You're needed here at Hades as soon as. Call me when you pick this up."

"There you go," said Lee, offering her a steaming mug of tea.

"Can you sit it on the table, please?" requested Ellen. "I just need to put my phone away."

"Sorry," apologised Lee, looking a little awkward. "I forgot about the lack of hands."

"No worries," she said, flashing him a smile. She liked the gentle sound engineer. He was the polar opposite to the producer and, at times, seemed too soft compared to the domineering Scot. "What's the big deal with Jason visiting later? Cushy seems in a foul mood over it."

"He is," stated Lee, sitting down on the couch beside her. "Jason's bringing in a few guests to listen to you. He hates visitors interrupting the schedule and he's anxious about Garrett showing up while they are here. Doesn't want the media getting wind of his cameo appearance on the record."

"What kind of guests?"

"A couple of promoters, journalists and a photographer. He's lining up a photo shoot for early next week for the album promo," revealed Lee calmly. "No big deal really."

"Photo shoot?" quizzed Ellen, an anxious ring to her voice.

The sound engineer nodded, "Necessary evil of the job, sweetheart."

"Shit," muttered Ellen. "Don't tell me. Rocky knows all about this and has conveniently forgotten to tell us?"

"Rocky set it up."

"Where? Here?"

"No," said Lee, shaking his head. "Some old church, I think."

"I hate getting my photo taken," confessed Ellen, her voice no more than a whisper.

"It'll be fine. I'm sure Rocky will take care of you. I can see how much he cares about you and the rest of the band."

A voice from the control room shattered their conversation, "Miss Lloyd, get your arse in here!"

Raising an eyebrow, Lee watched as Ellen sat where she was, calmly sipping her tea.

"Miss Lloyd!" boomed the voice a second time.

Still, Ellen sat where she was.

Stifling a laugh, Lee asked," Are you going to go in?"

"When I'm ready," she replied. "This is a good cup of tea. Our esteemed producer can wait a couple of minutes till I'm done."

"You've got balls, sweetheart, I'll give you that," said Lee, getting to his feet. "I'm going out for a smoke. Don't keep him waiting too long."

When Ellen casually wandered into the live room a few minutes later, the producer's anger was written all over his face.

"Where the fuck is Jack?" he demanded. "Did you speak to him?"

"It went straight to voicemail. I left a message," answered Ellen. "He'll be here."

"But not on time!" yelled the producer. "Jason will be here in fifteen minutes. He's pulled the visit forward. I need you guys ready to play at least three songs for him."

Exchanging glances with the two guitarists, Ellen proposed, "Acoustic set. Lou Lou, Rats and Broken Doll."

"Jason wants to hear what After Life can deliver."

"And he will," countered Ellen, sounding calmer than she felt. "Without a bass player, acoustic is your best bet, is it not?"

"She's right," added Taylor, following Ellen's logic. "And they are all songs we play live acoustically on occasion."

"Fine!" spat Cushy in frustration. "Just don't let yourselves down here."

"We won't," promised Ellen. "Let's start running through those though. Get ourselves settled."

The three members of After Life were on their second run through of Rats when the studio door opened and Jason waltzed in followed by five guests. With his usual flamboyance, he waxed lyrical about After Life's potential and apologised for the unplanned absence of their drummer and bass player. Politely, he asked Ellen if they would start again and play a few songs for his guests.

"Of course," she replied shyly. "We're rehearsing some ideas for bonus acoustic tracks. Hope that's ok."

"It's perfect, Ellen. Thank you."

With an almost defiant smile towards Cushy, Ellen suggested that they start with Rats.

On her count, the two guitarists began the alternative intro, keeping their playing light. Ellen's whispery, ghost-like vocal added the right level of dark menace to the song. All through the track she was conscious of one of Jason's guests watching her every move. He looked too young to be one of the promoters and she deduced he had to be the photographer. Unable to resist a playful moment at the end of the song, Ellen ended with an angry hiss then burst out laughing.

"Gentlemen, this is Lou Lou At 3am," she announced.

The emotion of Lou Lou was not lost on Jason and his guests. All three members of After Life spotted the approving nods and smiles. Again, the photographer never took his eyes off Ellen as she poured her heart into the song. When the track ended, she gave him a brief smile then paused to take a drink of water.

"Broken Doll," she said simply, setting the water bottle down.

Behind her, she was aware of Cal and Tailz laying their guitars down. Lifting the microphone from its stand, Ellen moved slightly to one side, closer to Jason and his assembled guests. She bowed her head for a few seconds then began to sing. The crystal clarity of her tone caught even her bandmates off guard. Keeping her voice even and the tone clean and pure, Ellen poured her soul and all of her emotion into the acapella vocal. The pain of loss and agony of being broken reverberated around the room before the despair at the heartache of being discarded like a Broken Doll tugged at the heartstrings of the studio guests.

As they stood rooted to the spot in stunned silence, Ellen replaced the microphone on its stand and softly said, "Thank you."

"Thank you she says!" exclaimed Jason theatrically. "Gentlemen, the incredibly talented and humble, Miss Ellen Lloyd."

Ellen felt herself flush at the compliment.

"Ellen," began Jason. "Allow me to introduce Scott. He's going to be doing the photography for the record. I believe there's a session arranged for this weekend."

"Hi," said the young photographer brightly. "Looking forward to working with you and the rest of the band."

"Hi," she replied. "I'll warn you now, I'm not a fan of having my photo taken."

"I'll be gentle. Promise."

"I'll hold you to that," said Ellen with a smile, then remembering her band mates, added, "Allow me to introduce you to Cal and Taylor."

While Jason and his other guests moved into the control room to talk to the band's producer, Scott stayed back to talk to the band. He expressed a genuine interest in their music then asked if they had any ideas for the photographs needed to promote their record and for the CD booklet.

A sharp shout of "Scott, this way!" from Jason halted their conversation and, as quickly as they'd arrived, the guests departed.

"Back to work," stated Cush bluntly. "Ellen, if you sing Broken Doll like that later tonight, I'll die a happy man. That was fucking incredible!"

"Was that a compliment, Mr Cushnaghan?" she quizzed mischievously.

"Aye," he grunted. "Now, back to work. Guys, guitar track for Phoenix if you please."

"I'll leave you to it," said Ellen, giving Tailz a hug. "I'll be out in the lounge till I'm needed."

Curled up on the couch with a mug of tea, Ellen was completely focussed on the lyrics journal on her knee. In between sessions at Hades and hospital visits, she had been writing some new material. These new songs weren't necessarily potential After Life tracks but were more blues and piano based in her head. So engrossed was she in her work that she never heard the door opening.

"Kind of quiet around here," came a familiar voice.

"Luke!" gasped Ellen, dropping her journal. "What are you doing here?"

"Heard there was a good party happening," he joked with an impish grin.

"There will be no parties for you for a while yet, young man," cautioned Garrett from behind him.

"Chill. I'm kidding," promised Luke calmly. "Now, seriously, where is everyone?"

"Cal and Tailz are in the studio. There's no sign of Jack. He's been MIA all day," replied Ellen.

"He's parking the car," revealed Garrett. "He came to collect me at Gatwick then we both collected Luke from the hospital."

"Ah, so that's where he's been!" exclaimed Ellen. "I was trying to get hold of him. You missed Jason Russell. He was here an hour or so ago with some VIP guests and a photographer."

"Sorry we missed his royal highness," joked Garrett with a hint of sarcasm. "He really doesn't need to know of my involvement here."

"Speaking of which," began Ellen smiling. "I see from the board that you've been busy all week."

"When time allowed. I've still four tracks to complete by my count. Two tonight then two tomorrow night."

"Guess we're both here late," mused Ellen warmly. "I've two vocals to do later. We still need to work out the keyboards for Daddy's Little Princess. We've played about with it but piano worked best for the intro and outro sections."

"Missing your right-hand man, angel?" quipped Luke as he lowered himself onto the sofa beside her.

"Sure am," she replied. "I even tried playing the right-hand part with my left when the place was quiet. Total disaster!"

The band's bass player laughed then looked up at his uncle, "Fancy tickling the ivories for us too?"

"Perhaps. No Promises," replied Garrett softly.

Behind them, the door opened and Jack sauntered in, apologising for being so late. He lifted a bottle of water from the fridge and wandered through to the live room.

"Feel up to coming in for a few minutes?" Ellen asked Luke as they heard Cushy swearing loudly about the interruption.

"Just for five minutes," agreed Luke. "Then I need to go. I'm running out of juice here."

"And I need to get him home before I come back here," added Garrett, his voice filled with concern for his frail nephew.

"I told you, Jack'll drop me off and stay with me," muttered Luke petulantly. "I'm not a child."

"We'll see."

Luke's return to the studio was greeted with whoops of joy and much whistling from Cal and Taylor. The grin on his face was enough to let them all know how their bass player felt at being back where he felt he belonged.

"How long till you get that stookie off?" asked Cal, causing Tailz to snigger at the Scottish terminology for the cast on Luke's arm.

"Three weeks," replied Luke. "Then I start physio on it."

"And how long till you are fit to play?" asked Taylor, realising there was a lot more than the bass player's arm to heal.

"A while. I don't really know," admitted Luke. "Couple of months maybe."

"Just take it one step at a time," cautioned Garrett quietly.

"I've not got much choice!"

"Will you be ok for the photo shoot?" asked Ellen. "I'm sure that guy can angle your shots to hide your arm."

"You going to loan me your cloak?" teased Luke playfully.

"You planning on playing warlock to my witch?" retaliated Ellen promptly.

"Maybe."

After a few minutes more, they could all see Luke was tiring. Despite his protests, Garrett insisted on accompanying him back to the apartment. He promised to be no more than two hours and, together with Jack, they left the rest of After Life to resume recording.

By eight o'clock, Cushy was finished with Cal and Tailz for the day and summarily dismissed them, stating firmly that they were expected back at ten thirty next morning. Not keen to leave Ellen alone to put in another long vocal session, Tailz suggest he stay and keep her company.

"No, you don't," growled Cushy. "I need this songbird focussed on singing not shagging. Out!"

Stifling a giggle, Ellen hugged Taylor, promising him that she would be fine. Reluctantly, the guitarist left, just as Garrett returned carrying a large pizza box.

"Sorry I'm later than planned," he apologised. "Got caught up with a call."

"Did you get Luke settled ok?" asked Ellen, the smell of the pizza making her realise just how hungry she was.

Garrett nodded, "Left him with Jack. They were watching tv."

"I'm glad he's finally home," said Ellen as Garrett offered her a slice of pizza.

"Me too," agreed the older man as he bit into his slice of pepperoni. "I just wish I could stay longer. I need to fly home on Tuesday."

"He'll be fine. We'll keep a close eye on him," promised Ellen. "I'm not sure what the plan is but I think I heard Rocky say that we have a few weeks free after we're done here. Taylor was talking about going home for a while. Maybe Luke could go too for a few days."

"That's not a bad idea," observed Garrett softly. "Now, tell me about this song that needs keyboards. Luke was trying very hard to persuade me to play for you on it."

Ellen giggled before revealing, "He has a soft spot for it. We had fun working it out in your music room. It's a bit of a twisted nursery rhyme."

"Sounds intriguing."

Their conversation was interrupted by Cushy wanting to know if Garrett was ready to do some work.

"Give me fifteen minutes, Stuart," stated Luke's uncle firmly. "Dinner first then I'll be ready. I also want to hear this song that needs piano."

"You willing to play on it?" quizzed the producer bluntly.

"If I like what I hear," replied Garrett with a swift wink towards Ellen. "I've not played piano for a very long time."

"Any particular reason why?" asked Ellen curiously as she helped herself to a second slice of pizza.

"Long story. A personal one," he replied evasively. "However, if this song is as special as my nephew says it is, I could be persuaded."

"Technically," began Ellen. "I only need you to play half. You could be my stand in right hand man."

With a throaty laugh, Garrett countered, "Right hand sugar daddy is it?"

"Well," laughed Ellen. "You do have a tendency to call me angel."

"That I do."

"Bass tracks first!" growled the producer.

Curled up on a spare chair in the small control room, Ellen sat quietly watching Garrett work on the two tracks he was scheduled to record. He had insisted on being in the live room on his own, saying he needed space to focus. Watching the experienced musician work was a rare treat. Conscious that he was trying to replicate the rough recording that they had of Luke playing, Ellen was fascinated by his performance. He was a fast worker but seemed to be wrestling with the bassline for Sands of Death.

"Stuart, I'll record it Luke's way but then can we try something?" he called through after half an hour. "I want to change it."

"You need to sound like the boy!"

"Well, maybe for once the boy can try sounding like the uncle!"

"Aye, maybe," conceded the producer. "Fuck it! You're going to do it your way regardless, aren't you?"

Garrett nodded.

"Play!"

Half an hour later, both Cushy and Ellen had to agree that Garrett's tracking was sharper than the original version. With a satisfied smile forming at his lips, the bass player played it through flawlessly while the production team captured it.

"Miss Lloyd, you're up next," stated Cushy drily. "Start just with the song that needs the piano intro. See if it meets with Mr Court's favour."

Without a murmur, Ellen uncurled herself from the chair and

slipped into the live room. At her heel, Lee stepped in to finish setting up her mic in the small vocal booth.

"Lee," called Ellen. "Can we move it back out into the room, please? Be ready to set up a mic at the piano too."

"Confident are we, angel?" teased Garrett as he returned his bass to its case.

"I am," she replied calmly.

Taking her position behind the mic a few moments later, Ellen closed her eyes and took a few long, slow breaths. With a surprisingly wistful, childlike tone, she sang the gentle poetic intro, "One, two, three, bouncing on Daddy's knee. Four five six, his love sticks. Seven, eight, nine, yes princess, you are mine."

When the count reached eighteen, Ellen's tone instantly morphed into a blood curdling wail, instantly darkening the already sinister mood. Ignoring her initial instruction to stop after the intro, Ellen sang the full vocal then hissed defiantly as she began the backwards count to end the evil nursery rhyme. With each three, her tone became gradually lighter, returning to its childlike purity for the final line, "One, two, three, bouncing on Daddy's knee."

Silence filled the studio as Ellen waited for a reaction from Garrett. His facial expression initially gave nothing away as he watched the band's singer reach for her water bottle. A grin slowly spread across his face as Ellen watched him.

"That, angel, was incredible."

"So, is that a yes?"

"It's a yes."

"Thank you," said Ellen softly.

"Let's see if we can work this out," suggested Garrett. "You're playing your part here too though. Minimal involvement from me."

Sitting so close to Garrett at the studio's piano made Ellen feel a little uncomfortable. For the first time in his presence, she felt completely star truck and extremely self-conscious. Tentatively, he fingered the keys, smiling almost to himself, then delicately he played the melody line from the song.

"Something like this?" he said quietly.

"Almost," replied Ellen. "Let me sing that bit again."

Garrett nodded then called over, "Cushy, leave us alone for an hour, please. No arguments."

"Garrett, clock's ticking," replied the producer bluntly.

"One hour," stated Garrett firmly. "We need a little space here. I need a little space here."

"Fine," growled the producer.

Once they were both alone in Hades, Garrett let out a long sigh. He looked round at Ellen and smiled.

"It's been a long time since I've played piano," he confessed wistfully. "Not since my Royal Court days."

"If you want to back out, that's fine," began Ellen, at a loss as to what to say.

"And incur the wrath of my nephew?" he joked with a small smile. "No, I said I'd play and I will."

"Do you want to play something else first?" suggested Ellen warmly. "We could play just for fun till you're comfortable playing together."

"Ladies choice then," replied Garett chivalrously.

"Well, if Luke was here, I know what he'd play," teased Ellen.

"Your Song?"

Ellen nodded.

"Only if you sing."

"Deal."

Together, they played for most of the hour that they had claimed as their own. Gradually, they both relaxed and Garrett became more familiar with Ellen's technique and style of playing.

"Is this not torture for you, angel?" asked the older musician softly.

"It's not easy," Ellen admitted. "But, it's an opportunity to at least play something."

"I don't think I'd view it as positively, if the roles were reversed."

"It took time to come to terms with it. If I have actually come to terms with it," she replied quietly. "But, this is a thousand times better than playing nothing at all. It doesn't work for guitar so this is all I get every now and again."

"Let's make it count then."

By the time the producer returned, the two musicians were ready to record the piano sections. Fewer bass notes in the first section helped to keep it light and more childlike but a subtle change of tone to add an edge of darkness to it completed the outro.

They played the sections through on their own for the producer and waited for his reaction.

"Miss Lloyd, I need to hear it with the vocals. Care to oblige?"

"Sure," she agreed.

Again, they played the two sections. Hearing the vocals accompanying it added another dimension that met with the producer's approval.

"Play it like that again. Don't change a thing," commanded Cushy.

"What he says," laughed Garrett with a mischievous grin.

"But of course," agreed Ellen theatrically.

"You two taking the proverbial?"

"Never," declared Garrett as Ellen struggled to suppress a giggle.

It took them three attempts but, finally, the producer was satisfied with the piano section.

"Garrett, you're done till tomorrow night," said Cushy by way of dismissal.

"Thought I'd hang about and listen to Ellen's vocals," countered the senior musician.

With a gruff harrumph, Cushy snapped, "What is it with you attracting an audience, Miss Lloyd?"

"Caring friends?" suggested Ellen with a smile. "Cushy, can we dim the lights in here please?"

"Aye but why?"

"I want to take my glasses off. The light is too bright for me," commented Ellen calmly. "And don't panic, I won't stare at you."

"Whatever," muttered the producer, nodding to Lee to dim the lights in the live room.

"Do you want me to go?" asked Garrett softly. "I don't want to distract you."

"I'd be honoured if you stayed but...." Ellen paused suddenly feeling awkward in Garrett's presence.

"But, if I'm going to run screaming at the sight of you without those tinted spectacles, you'd rather I left?"

Ellen laughed, "Something like that."

"I'm not about to run off, angel," replied Garrett. "I just want to sit back and relax after a long day and listen to a talented lady sing."

Blushing, Ellen suggested that he take a seat on the sofa in the corner. Obediently, the older man crossed the room and settled himself on the couch while she prepared to deliver the vocals for Daddy's Little Princess.

The soft lighting of the studio added an extra air of darkness to the warped nursery rhyme. After a couple of false starts, Ellen adjusted her stance and nodded to the control room that she was ready.

As she began the haunting childlike count, the air in the room was reverberating at the purity of her tone. The blood curdling scream before the start of the first verse sent chills through the sound engineer, the producer and Garrett. The older man watched, totally mesmerised by her powerful delivery of the twisted tale. Alone in the dimly lit room and apparently oblivious to Garrett's presence, Ellen gave the song her all, pouring her very soul into the delivery. The gradual return from the evil dark depths to the light childlike voice was inspired.

The song was in the bag in one take.

"Absolutely fucking perfect!" declared Cushy. "Broken Doll in your own good time."

"Give me a minute," said Ellen, reaching for her water bottle. "That was tough."

"You ok?" asked Garrett from his seat in the corner.

Ellen nodded as she subconsciously ran her hand over her tender ribcage. The scars were on fire again and she could feel a sharp pain in her side as she breathed.

"You sure?" challenged the older musician with concern.

"I'm a little sore," confessed Ellen quietly. "Singing like that puts a strain on the scar tissue. I've scars on my lungs and they protest if I use my full range. I'll be fine in a few minutes."

"Is there nothing that can be done to loosen them off?"

"I've already had extensive laser treatment on them. There's nothing else that they can do. I'll look into more treatment if this gets worse. I guess I just need to retrain my body. Let it adjust to doing this again after five years."

"Take care of that voice, Ellen," cautioned Garrett. "Don't take too many risks with it."

"I won't," promised Ellen as she took a long chug on the water bottle.

"You ready, Miss Lloyd?" called out Cushy. "Clock's ticking back here."

"I'm ready."

Calmly, Ellen took a few slow deep breaths then keeping her tone clean, she began the acapella Broken Doll. The subtle lightness to the vocal added an element of fragility to the tragic tale being spun. There was an undercurrent of anger about being discarded that added new depth to the song. It was an emotionally charged performance but, for the second time, Ellen delivered a flawless vocal track for the producer.

"Miss Lloyd," began Cushy with more than a hint of emotion in his voice. "You are truly an inspiration. Go home. Get some sleep."

After so long away from their church basement rehearsal space, it felt weird being back without their instruments. When they'd quizzed him, Rocky said he'd chosen the church and small neighbouring graveyard as the setting to intentionally keep the band close to their roots. Cal had laughed and asked if there was a second shoot at The Anchor, stating that the pub was just as important a tie to their roots.

When they arrived, Taylor and Ellen were surprised to find Luke already there chatting casually with the photographer. He looked stronger than he had when he'd visited Hades but there was still a lingering frailty to him.

"Where's Cal and Jack?" asked Taylor, glancing round.

"On their way," replied Luke. "Van wouldn't start."

"That van needs a decent burial," muttered Taylor half under his breath.

"Don't let Jack hear you say that," said Ellen with a small smile. "He loves that van."

"True, but it's a wreck," stated Tailz. "So, what's the plan here?"

"Rocky got me the keys to the church so I've set my gear up in there," explained Scott, the photographer. "Need a few group shots then individual shots. After that, I've picked out a few spots in the graveyard we can use. I've a few ideas in mind to be sympathetic here."

"Do you need me in my stage clothes?" asked Ellen.

"Both," replied Scott, smiling at her. "Do you have your cloak with you?"

"Yes," answered Ellen. "But I left my eye patch at home."

"Shades are cool. Don't stress about it," he said. "Steampunk look works for me."

By eleven o'clock, the young photographer had After Life upstairs in the church and was working on the group shots. He was a quick worker and had soon captured all the indoor group shots he required.

"Individuals next," he declared. "Luke, do you want to go first?"

Using the ornately carved pew ends to hide the cast on the bass player's arm, Scott fired off a few shots. Handing Luke his own leather jacket, he suggested draping it over his shoulder to hide the cast as he posed him in various areas around the church.

"Thanks, buddy," said Scott when he was satisfied with the shots. "Jack, you're next."

It was almost one before it was Ellen's turn. Feeling bored and hungry, the rest of After Life had headed back to the basement to sort out some lunch. Alone in the church with the photographer, Ellen felt more than a little anxious.

"Relax," said Scott warmly when he noticed her nerves. "This will be painless. Promise."

"I'm not so sure," confessed Ellen timidly. "I'm beyond self-conscious about getting my photo taken."

"I hear you," said the photographer. "How about we start with some shots of you with your cloak on?"

Ellen nodded, quietly relieved at being able to hide in her hood for a while. Once she was cloaked, Scott suggested various poses, including one rather dramatic shot up in the pulpit. After half an hour, he declared he had more than enough stage clothes shots and asked Ellen to slip her cloak off again.

"Shit," he muttered half to himself. "I need to change cameras. Grab a seat for a few minutes till I fix this."

"No worries," she agreed as she unfastened her voluminous cloak.

Casually, she draped it over one of the pews then took a seat in the choir stall while she waited for Scott to switch cameras. With a few minutes to herself, she gazed around the neglected church, admiring the large stained-glass window that dominated the area behind the alter. The spring sun shining through was casting coloured shadows on the church floor. She smiled to herself as she admired the myriad of shimmering rainbows.

"Ellen," called out Scott from the far side of the church. "Do me a favour and climb back up into the pulpit, will you? I'll just be another couple of minutes."

"Sure," she said, getting to her feet and heading across to the narrow, intricately carved, wooden staircase.

Once up in the pulpit, her attention was drawn to the huge bible that lay open on the lectern within the actual pulpit. Gently, she fingered the fading, purple satin bookmark, allowing her fingers to run through the silky threads of its tassels. A smaller stained-glass frieze high up at the back of the church caught her eye and she stood drinking in its splendour while she waited on the photographer to say he was ready.

"Thanks, Ellen," he called out, breaking her concentration. "We're done."

"Pardon?"

With a laugh, Scott said, "Stealth tactics. I've got all the shots I need."

"But....," spluttered Ellen, more than a little confused as to what was going on.

"Come down and I'll show you."

Carefully, Ellen made her way back down the narrow, spiral stairs and was met at the bottom by Scott.

"I kind of lied," he confessed with a wink. "Camera was fine. I just needed you to be distracted for a few minutes. It gave me just enough time to fire off a few candid shots while you weren't so self-conscious about the whole thing."

"That was sneaky!" giggled Ellen as he showed her a few of the shots. "But thank you. You made that easy for me."

"All part of the service," declared Scott with a grin. "Let's grab some lunch and then we'll do the graveyard shift."

It was late afternoon before they were finally finished with Scott. Mid-afternoon, Luke had apologised and said he needed to head home. Seeing how exhausted he was, Jack insisted on driving him back to Garrett's place. While the band's drummer was away, the others worked with Scott on their individual outdoor shots. Just as they were finishing up, Jack returned.

"Right," called out Cal, "It's beer o'clock. We'll wait for you guys in The Anchor."

"Mine's a pint," called back Jack. "And it's Taylor's round!"

"Isn't it always," muttered Tailz with a weary sigh.

Much to their collective surprise, The Anchor was virtually empty when the three members of After Life entered. As usual, Maggie was behind the bar and, spotting her three regulars, called over "Beer, cider and a red wine?"

"Three beers, a cider and a red wine, Maggie," replied Taylor, heading towards the bar while Cal and Ellen made a beeline for their usual booth.

"Three?"

"Yeah. Jack'll be over in a bit. He's likely to bring a photographer guy with him."

"Your round again?" observed the barmaid as she set the first beer on the bar.

"Seems that way."

"No Luke today?" quizzed Maggie, noting the bass player's absence.

"Not today," replied Taylor, deciding against mentioning his friend's health.

"So, when do I get my signed copy of your record?" she teased as she poured Ellen's Shiraz into a glass.

"October probably," answered Taylor. "We're just finishing off the recording this week."

"Hand a few copies in when you get them. The other regulars keep asking me about you boys. We can sell a few for you."

"Thanks, Maggie. We'll sort you out with some as soon as we can."

"You should play in here too some night," suggested Maggie. "Locals would love it. Might be good publicity for you too."

"I like that idea," nodded Taylor, seeing the attraction of a small pub gig. "Let me run that past Rocky."

"What are we drinking to?" asked Cal as Tailz set the tray down on the table.

"Health, wealth and happiness?" proposed Ellen, lifting her glass from the circular tray.

"To a musical future?" suggested Tailz, taking his usual seat beside Ellen. "To the successful conclusion of recording the album?"

"A headline tour!" added Cal, grabbing his pint.

They had just bought a second round when Jack and Scott sauntered into pub.

"Hey, you're two pints behind," called out Cal as they approached.

"Difficult subject matter," quipped Scott as he slid into the seat opposite Ellen.

"Hey, who are you calling difficult?" laughed Jack as he took up his preferred position next to Cal. "I can only stay for one. I'm driving plus I need to get home to walk the dog."

"Well, in that case," commented Cal, reaching across the table. "I'll put this out of its misery for you."

"Is this your local?" asked Scott, scanning the bar and the mantelpiece filled with photos. "Neat place."

"We've been known to frequent the place from time to time," mused Taylor with a mischievous grin. "Where do you call home?"

"Nowhere really," revealed Scott. "Just now, I'm mainly based in America. I go where JJR Management tell me to."

"You worked with any big names?" asked Call curiously.

"A few. Most of the bands are on JJR Management's books," he explained. "But I've shot a few festivals and had passes for some of the bigger names."

"So, who are you working with next?" quizzed Ellen, sharing her bandmate's curiosity.

"I've a photo pass for Download then I fly back to America," replied Scott. "I'm commissioned to work with Silver Lake. Studio shots."

"Are they recording again?" asked Ellen excitedly. "I loved their debut. Love, love, love Dragon Song!"

"Yeah," nodded Scott. "They go into the studio today. Actually, Jake's sort of my landlord."

"You live with him?" quizzed Taylor.

Shaking his head, Scott continued, "No. Gary, the band's manager rents Jake's apartment. I crash there when I'm in town. He's cool about it."

"There's nothing cool about him," giggled Ellen, the effects of the wine catching up with her. "Jake Power's hot as hell!"

"Ah," teased Jack. "We've uncovered our songbird's rock star crush!"

Ellen flushed scarlet and giggled but didn't deny anything.

"Jake's a good guy," said Scott. "But he's loved up with Mz Hyde. Lori."

"Ah, the artist," exclaimed Ellen. "I love her covers. Her Weigh Station stuff is stunning. Oh, how cool would it be if she designed our cover?"

"Dream on!" laughed Taylor. "I'm sure Jason's already picked a lower budget option for us. I heard Rocky mention a name but it certainly wasn't Mz Hyde."

"Pity," sighed Ellen wistfully.

"Well, if you're ever in Delaware, I'll introduce you to them both," offered Scott with a wink. "They're good people."

"Anyone else you've worked with?" asked Cal, draining his pint.

"I did the Weigh Station tour over here last year. That's where I first met the guys from Silver Lake. Working with Weigh Station was good. Dan's fun to be around."

"He guested with us at Open Air in Wales," commented Taylor. "Seems like a genuine bloke."

"He is. They all are," agreed the photographer. "There was this one night….."

To celebrate the completion of the recording of After Life's debut album, Rocky invited the band plus Cushy and Lee to dinner at the house. An invite had been extended to Scott too but he had declined due to his Download commitments.

From up in her room, Ellen could smell the tantalising aroma of Lizzy's curry. It was making her stomach rumble, reminding her that she had skipped lunch. At the last minute, Cushy had asked her to re-record some of the vocals for Danse De Mort En Flammes meaning she had missed the band trip to Pizza Express. Part of her was sad that their time in Hades was over; part of her was excited to hear what the record sounded like and to hear what Rocky had planned for them. The band's manager had promised to outline their schedule for the rest of the year over dinner.

With a sigh, Ellen brought her thoughts back to the present and to the text message her dad had sent a few hours earlier.

"It's your mum's birthday on Friday. Will you come home for her party? Please. Dad x"

The last few telephone calls she had attempted with her mother had ended disastrously. No matter how hard she tried, Ellen felt that nothing she ever said or did was good enough for the woman. Each of the calls had culminated in Ellen ending it abruptly and cursing her mother under her breath.

A knock at the door startled her.

"Hey, my lovely," said Tailz softly. "You ready to come down? I hear Luke's voice downstairs."

"Almost. I'm trying to send a text to my dad."

"Everything ok?"

Ellen nodded, "Dad's asked me to go home next weekend for my mum's birthday. They're having a big party at her favourite restaurant for her fiftieth."

"Does she want you there?" asked Taylor, coming to sit on the bed beside her.

Without replying, she showed him the message.

"Maybe your dad needs the moral support?" he suggested. "I could come with you. Moral support for you."

"I don't know," sighed Ellen then she laughed. "I can stand up in front of thousands of people but I'm scared to show up at my own mother's birthday party. Don't want to risk causing a scene."

"Surely things would be ok in public?"

"Who knows," said Ellen sadly. "I'll stall him. Tell him I'll think about it."

"Well, if you decide to go, the offer's there," promised Taylor, giving her a hug. "I like your dad. He's cool."

"Thanks. Appreciate it but I don't really want to inflict my mother on you."

"Well, see what your dad replies and take it from there."

Ellen nodded, "Deal. You go on down. I'll be down in a minute."

When Ellen finally entered the kitchen, she discovered she was the last to arrive.

"Sorry," she said softly as she slipped into the empty seat between Taylor and Luke.

"Sorted?" asked Tailz quietly.

"I hope so," whispered Ellen with a smile.

"Right, boys and girl, time to celebrate and to talk about the future," proclaimed Rocky as he prepared to open a large bottle of champagne. "We did it. You did it. The record is in the bag!"

A cheer went up as Jack and Cal beat a drum roll on the kitchen table.

The cork exploded out of the bottle, bouncing off the ceiling before landing in the sink. Expertly, Rocky filled the row of crystal flutes in front of him then began to pass them round. When everyone had a glass, the band's manager said, "A toast to the album and to the success of After Life."

"To us," acknowledged Luke, before taking a tiny sip from his glass.

"And to Garrett, our invisible sixth member," added Ellen, raising her glass.

"To Garrett, the life saver," declared Cal theatrically.

"And to Ellen," added Luke warmly. "Who literally helped to save mine."

"Aye," began Cushy with a nod. "This is an album I'll not forget in a hurry."

"A dramatic debut," joked Lee.

"So, how do we follow that?" asked Rocky with a mischievous grin.

"A headline tour across Europe?" suggested Luke optimistically.

"Exactly!"

"Pardon?" said the bass player his eyes wide.

"Well, not across all of Europe," conceded Rocky. "And they're not all headline shows."

"Rocky," interrupted Taylor impatiently. "Just tell us the plan!"

"Ok," nodded their manager. "From 1st to the 10th October you'll be supporting Heritage in Holland, Germany, Sweden and Denmark. Hour long set each night. We get back on the 11th then start an eleven date UK headline tour ending in London on 25th October."

"Seriously?" exclaimed Ellen, scarcely daring to believe what she was hearing.

"Seriously. There is also a slim chance of a US tour early next year. Jason is working on that so I don't know any more than that for now."

"America?" quizzed Luke. "Really?"

"Really."

"And when will the record be out?" asked Jack, running through the dates in his mind.

"Hopefully, October 14th," replied their manager with a glance towards the producer for confirmation.

"That's the date I'm working to," confirmed Cushy. "And it needs a title, folks."

A short, boisterous debate followed as the members of After Life all pitched in their thoughts on an appropriate title for their debut. Gradually, one song title began to be mentioned more than the others.

"Alright," called out Jack firmly. "Are we agreed here?"

"Yes," replied the others.

"Ok. City Of Bones And Heartache it is!"

Another resounding cheer went up.

"Are you ready to eat yet?" asked Lizzy, looking at the clock. "Dinner's ready whenever you are."

Rocky nodded, "Cal, Tailz, help Lizzy to serve. Jack, fetch some wine and beer from out the back."

Dishing up dinner was little short of total chaos but, miraculously, nothing was spilled or broken and, within a few minutes, everyone was enjoying Lizzy's homemade chicken curry.

"What's the plan for over the summer?" asked Taylor, finally voicing the question they had all been dying to ask.

"I'm out on tour for July and August helping out an old friend," revealed Rocky. "Then Lizzy and I are taking a trip at the start of September for a couple of weeks. I guess school's out, kids."

"You mean we get to play and we get school holidays" giggled Ellen, feeling the effects of the champagne lightening her mood.

"Yes, Miss Lloyd, you do," said Rocky warmly. "Works out quite neatly. Gives Luke time to get back to full fitness."

"I saw the doctor on Friday before the photo shoot," began Luke almost shyly. "I should be back playing by the end of July if I do the physio. The heart issue's going to take a bit longer. Cardiologist suggested it would be September at the earliest before I was fit enough to tour."

"That does all tie in neatly," observed Ellen.

"I expect this to be a working holiday," commented Rocky. "You might want to consider writing stuff for your second record. Use this free time wisely."

"Well, I'm going home for a few weeks," announced Taylor.

"I might be heading down your way too," revealed Luke. "Garrett's wanting to rent a cottage for the summer on the coast somewhere. Wants me to get out of London for a bit."

"Cal, I might need a spare guitar tech for a few weeks," said Rocky. "You up for a few weeks' work?"

"Just tell me where and when."

"Jack, what about you? Any plans?" asked Tailz curiously.

"I'll see," replied the band's drummer vaguely. "Might go back to doing the courier bit. Could try offering drum lessons."

"If I need an extra pair of hands, would you be willing to be stage crew?" checked Rocky, keen to look after his boys.

"Sure. As long as it pays."

"And that just leaves you, princess," noted Luke with a tired smile. "What'll you do?"

"I'm not sure," replied Ellen softly. "I've some medical stuff to sort out. Nothing serious but I've a few appointments to arrange."

"For what?" asked Lizzy, concerned that the girl was hiding something.

"Laser treatment," explained Ellen. "I've spoken to my consultant about the scars on my ribs. He's prepared to try some laser treatment to loosen them off a little."

"When?" asked Taylor, a little shocked and hurt that Ellen hadn't mentioned this to him.

"There were a couple of options on offer. I'll likely try to take the first one which was the 26th June."

"Does this involve a hospital stay? Where will you go for this?"

"A couple of nights in the hospital in Guildford maybe," answered Ellen, feeling very self-conscious.

"And you've already arranged it all?" checked Rocky, slightly aggrieved that she hadn't informed him either.

"It's pencilled in," said Ellen. "I need to call tomorrow to confirm it all. If I go next week, it gives me plenty of time for a second or third round of treatment if it's needed before September."

"What's the recovery time?" asked Taylor, suddenly concerned about her.

"A few days till the redness and swelling dies down. It's fairly non-invasive," she explained. "If I need a second or third round that might be done as a day patient."

"Princess," said Luke calmly. "We trust you to do what's best for you. I think Tailz here is just worried about his girl."

"Oh!" she gasped sharply. "I never thought! Oh, I'm sorry!"

"It's fine," replied the guitarist. "We can talk later."

"Well, I'll be at Hades all summer," declared Cushy, in an effort to lighten the mood. "No rest for the wicked. We're booked solid through till mid-December. Only the odd day free."

"Healthy sign," commented Rocky. "And it'll keep you out of mischief, Mr Cushnaghan."

It was late before After Life decided to call it a night. Around ten o'clock, Luke had been the first to leave. He'd called a cab and left, promising to keep in touch and to let Taylor know if he was anywhere near Cornwall over the summer. Cal opted to leave with him, even offering to split the taxi fare. An hour later, Cushy and Lee apologised, saying they'd need to go. They let slip that they were returning to the studio for a few hours. Without being asked, Jack began to clear the table and, within a few seconds, Taylor had got up from his seat to help him.

"I'm going to call it a night," said Ellen around midnight with a yawn. "Thanks again for dinner, Lizzy. I love that curry."

"It's my pleasure," replied Lizzy with a smile. "It's easy to make. I could teach you."

"Maybe," said Ellen. "Cooking never was one of my strong points."

"Oh, it's easy when you know how."

Ellen giggled, "I doubt it! Night, folks."

A while later, just as she was drifting off to sleep, there was a knock at her door. Without waiting for an answer, Taylor slipped into the room.

"Want some company?"

"As long as it involves hugs," Ellen replied sleepily.

"Did you sort things out with your dad?" asked Taylor as he sat down on the bed.

"I think so," she replied, wriggling across to make room for him to join her.

"And?"

"I said we'd both be there for the party next Saturday," said Ellen almost reluctantly. "Dad insists we stay with them on Saturday night."

"You ok with that?"

"It's only one night," sighed Ellen. "Don't mention the laser stuff to them. Don't want to tell either of them just yet."

"Fine," agreed Taylor as he slipped into bed beside her. "I wish you'd mentioned it to me."

"Sorry," apologised Ellen. "I only got the call this afternoon proposing the dates. Up till then it was a just a vague plan."

"Will it help?"

"It should loosen up the scarring to my ribs. The doctor wasn't sure how much they can achieve in one full session."

"Will it hurt much?"

"Yes," replied Ellen quietly. "Last time it hurt like hell but the scars were fresher then."

"If they need to do more than one session, how long in between each of them?"

"Three or four weeks. Depends on how I heal."

"Will you come home with me?" asked Tailz, pulling her close. "Nana, Jen and I will look after you."

"I'd love to," whispered Ellen. "Lizzy had said I could stay here but I don't know…."

"I'll stay till you're able to come with me."

"Thanks."

During the train journey to Surrey the following Saturday, Taylor became more and more concerned about Ellen. As the day of her mother's party had grown closer, she had retreated further and further into herself. Midweek, they had gone shopping for a birthday present and for an outfit for Ellen to wear to the party. After a stressful couple of hours on Oxford Street, they had retreated to the sanctuary of a bar for a couple of drinks before heading back to the house.

"I feel over dressed," muttered Taylor as the train reached Guildford.

"You look great," complimented Ellen with an anxious smile. "You'll meet with my mother's approval for sure."

"As long as she likes flowers and champagne," said After Life's guitarist, glancing at the bouquet on the seat beside him.

"She does," stated Ellen. "Relax."

Taylor laughed, "How about taking your own advice, my lovely."

"Sorry," apologised Ellen, fingering the hem of her dress. She had forgone her usual rock chick look and bought a pretty, floral, summer dress. With Lizzy's help, she had curled her hair into long ringlet curls, transforming her look entirely.

"You look beautiful," complimented Taylor, reaching out to touch her knee.

"I feel like a stranger," confessed Ellen. "But, I know what she's like. If I'd turned up in my normal clothes, she'd pitch a fit."

"Where is your dad meeting us?"

"The pub along from the station," replied Ellen. "He'll take our bags and smuggle them into the house. We'll have time for a drink before we need to walk along to the restaurant."

"How many are coming to this party?"

"Dad said about a hundred guests."

"Just a small quiet celebration then?" Taylor laughed.

"My mother never celebrated anything quietly!"

They had just found a secluded table in the village pub when Ellen's dad arrived looking flushed and flustered. When he saw his daughter and Taylor, he smiled and quickly made his way over to them.

"Hi, guys," he said cheerfully. "Glad to see you made it. Ellen, you look stunning."

"Thanks, Dad."

"Can I buy you a drink. Mr Lloyd?" offered Taylor warmly.

"No, thanks. And it's Tim, son," replied Ellen's father. "Will you kids be ok here for an hour or so? She doesn't suspect a thing."

"We'll be fine, Dad," promised Ellen. "What's the plan?"

"Everyone's to be at the restaurant for seven. There will be champagne and canapes. Your mother wants to arrive at seven thirty and then there's a buffet arranged for eight. We've booked a band to play for the evening so, if folk want to dance, they can," explained Tim Lloyd hurriedly. "Your mother has this planned like a military operation!"

"Why am I not surprised!"

"Ellen," cautioned her father calmly. "Be nice. For me."

"I promised, didn't I?"

"Yes, you did," replied her dad. "I better run. I've a cake to drop off then I need to get back to the house to get changed."

"We'll see you in a bit then," said Tailz. "I'll buy you that drink later. Think you might need it by then."

Shortly after seven, Taylor held the door of the village's gastropub open for Ellen. Already they could hear the buzz of conversation from the assembled guests. Hand in hand, they made their way into the large dining area. Scanning the room, Ellen spotted several of her parents' friends, a group of her mother's fellow school board members and, over in the corner, a cluster of relatives.

"You ok?" asked Taylor, feeling her go tense beside him.

"I'll be fine," promised Ellen quietly. "Just spotted a few familiar faces. A few folk I've not seen for a while. My aunts and cousins are over in the corner beside the palm tree."

"Let me fetch you a drink," suggested Taylor, reaching out to pause a passing waitress. He carefully lifted two glasses of champagne from the tray and handed one to Ellen, "Let's start with you introducing me to your cousins. They've spotted you and are staring at us."

"I know. I can feel my aunt's eyes boring into me," giggled Ellen, taking a sip from her glass. "OK, let's do this."

Slowly, they made their way towards Ellen's relatives.

"Ellie!" shrieked her aunt. "I didn't know you were coming. Your mother never said. You look fantastic, sweetheart."

"Hi, Auntie Grace, Mum doesn't know I'm here. Dad suggested I keep it as a surprise," replied Ellen, forcing herself to smile. "Auntie Grace, this is my friend, my boyfriend, Taylor."

"Pleased to meet you," said Tailz politely, stepping forward to brush a kiss on Ellen's aunt's cheek.

"Oh, aren't you a charmer," she declared with a girlish giggle. "Lovely to meet you, son. Are you a musician too?"

"For my sins, yes," replied Taylor. "I'm in the same band as Ellen."

"Your mother never said you were in a new band!"

"I'm not surprised," muttered Ellen half under her breath. "Auntie Grace, Mum doesn't approve of the music we play. Dad loves us but Mum was pretty disgusted by it. She's only been to see us play once."

"Oh, sweetie, I'm sorry," said her aunt, giving her a hug. "She should be so proud of you, especially after everything that happened."

"Her loss," commented Ellen dismissively. "I'd invite you along to a show but I think we'd be a bit loud for you."

"Most likely," laughed her aunt. "Come and introduce your young man to the others. Young Michael will be thrilled to meet a rock star. He got a guitar for his last birthday. He's driving his poor mother insane with the noise."

Taylor laughed, "I remember doing the same thing to mine

and my Nana."

"To be fair," added Auntie Grace. "He's only had the thing for a couple of months but he's been taking lessons."

Within a few minutes, Taylor had been introduced to the rest of Ellen's family, including half a dozen cousins of varying ages. As predicted, Ellen's young cousin was excited to meet a real-life rock star and he soon had Taylor cornered between the palm tree and the window while he plied him with questions. With a smile, Ellen watched as After Life's guitarist patiently answered the teenager's endless stream of questions. Her aunts and uncles were soon quizzing her about life in London, all obviously delighted to hear she was doing so well. A couple of her cousins promised to come to see After Life the next time they played in the area.

On the stroke of seven thirty, there a was a "chinking" of glasses to alert everyone to the arrival of the guest of honour herself. As the assembled family and friends sang "Happy Birthday", Ellen watched her dad walk in with his arm around her mother's waist. Her mother was smiling and lapping up the attention.

Soon everyone was circled round Ellen's mother, congratulating her and presenting her with their gifts.

"Our turn," prompted Taylor, spotting a gap in the throng.

"If you insist," muttered Ellen, lifting the gift bag she'd brought containing a black freshwater pearl choker.

Spotting them approaching through the crowd of guests, Ellen's dad tapped his wife on the shoulder.

"Happy birthday, Mum," said Ellen, mustering as much warmth as she could.

"Ellen!" gasped her mother. "I never knew you were coming!"

"Dad thought it would be a nice surprise."

"Oh, and you brought your friend too!"

"Happy birthday, Mrs Lloyd," said Taylor, stepping forwards to kiss her on the cheek. "These are for you."

"Oh, they're gorgeous!" enthused Ellen's mother. "Thank you.... Taylor?"

"Taylor," repeated Tailz with a smile.

Silently, Ellen passed her gift to her mother.

"Darling, you didn't have to!"

"I wanted to."

"Thank you," said Olivia Lloyd, opening the gift bag. As she opened the box, she gasped, "These are very pretty. My favourite colour of pearls."

"Glad you like them," replied Ellen, inwardly relieved that her gift had met with approval.

"I'd better mingle with my guests," stated her mother bluntly.

"Of course," said Ellen, stepping aside.

Taylor put his arm around Ellen's shoulder as they watched her mother glide off towards the assembled guests.

"You ok?" he whispered.

Ellen nodded.

"Angel," interrupted Tim Lloyd, "Are you ok?"

"Dad, I'm fine," assured Ellen with what she hoped sounded like indifference. "She's not exactly thrilled to see me."

"I'm sorry," apologised her father. "I'm thrilled to see you both."

"Thanks."

"Let's grab a table. You can tell me all about this album you've made," suggested her dad with genuine interest. "When do I get to hear it?"

"Soon," promised Ellen as they followed him across the restaurant to an empty table beside where the band were setting up.

While Ellen spent a few minutes catching up with her dad, Taylor gravitated towards the musicians. He chatted to them about their planned set before returning to the table. In his absence, Ellen's dad had bought him a pint of cider.

"Thank you," said Tailz, raising his glass towards the older man.

"Beats that fizzy wine," commented Tim Lloyd, nodding towards his own pint of beer.

"Sure does," agreed Taylor with a grin. "Ellen, fancy playing with these guys later on? They've said we're more than welcome to play a couple of songs. Their guitarist has offered to lend me his acoustic if we want to play for a bit."

"I don't know," said Ellen falteringly.

"Great idea!" enthused her father. "You could play something from the album."

"Dad, this is Mum's party. She'll be furious if we steal her limelight."

"Leave your mother to me, angel," said her dad calmly. "All of our friends and family would love to hear you sing."

"I'm not so sure."

"Sing for me then," suggested her dad softly. "I'll deal with your mother."

With a sigh, Ellen smiled, "I'll think about it."

A short while later, her dad got to his feet saying he'd better circulate. The buffet was open and the guests had descended on the food like a plague of locusts. Without waiting to ask what Ellen wanted, Taylor got to his feet, declaring he was starving and disappeared off to fetch them some food. Alone at the table, Ellen glanced over at the band, who were playing some classic 1960's songs, gently introducing music to the evening.

"Ellie," interrupted her Auntie Grace. "Can we sit with you and your young man? I can't eat balancing this plate in one hand."

"Of course."

"Where is your young man?" asked her aunt as she sat down.

"He's gone to fetch us both something to eat," replied Ellen, watching her uncle squeeze his way into the seat next to her aunt.

"Have you seen your mother?" enquired her aunt.

Ellen nodded, "Not convinced she was pleased to see me though."

"I'm sure she was," assured her Uncle Philip in between bites of quiche. "My sister never was very good at sharing the limelight with anyone."

"I've no intentions of stealing the limelight from her tonight," replied Ellen honestly. "I'll be happy to just get out of here without any argument."

"Your dad told me you and your young man are going to sing for us later," commented her aunt.

"Oh, did he?" laughed Ellen. "He's desperate for us to get up there but I'm not so sure my mother will appreciate it."

"You could sing her Happy Birthday then dedicate a song to her," suggested Uncle Philip.

"Now that's an idea I like," stated Taylor, arriving back at the table with two plates of finger food.

"That could work," conceded Ellen somewhat reluctantly.

"Now, that's not a Surrey or a London accent," commented

Uncle Philip. "Where do you hail from, son?"

"Mawgan Porth," replied Taylor grinning.

"Where?"

"Cornwall," explained Taylor. "Just a few miles from Newquay."

"Never heard of it," replied the old man. "Never been west of Poole myself."

"You've not been in Poole since 1953!" laughed his wife before explaining that his parents had taken him there for a week when he was eight.

Giggling, Ellen said, "Uncle Philip, you should visit Cornwall. You'd love it."

"Oh, have you been, dear?" enquired her aunt.

"Yes. I stayed with Taylor's Nana for a few days in May. We're going back down soon, I hope. It's beautiful down there."

"First week in July," added Taylor, pleased to hear her enthusing about the trip.

"We'll see," said her uncle evasively. "More of a city man, myself."

Having eaten and also chewed over her uncle's suggestion, Ellen had excused herself from the table and gone in search of her dad. She found him talking to their next-door-neighbour at the bar. Quickly, she explained their idea, gaining his instant approval. Enthusiastically, he had elaborated on the schedule for the evening, revealing that the cake was due to be brought in at ten o'clock. It made sense for Ellen and Taylor to perform Happy Birthday then.

"And will you play a few more songs, angel?" asked her dad, almost pleading with her.

"One," relented Ellen then seeing the look of disappointment on his face, "Maybe two."

"Three?"

"Let's see how the birthday diva reacts," suggested Ellen, a hint of sarcasm to her tone.

On cue, at ten o'clock, Ellen and Taylor stepped up onto the low stage to join the band. Over to one side, Ellen could see the staff were ready to bring the birthday cake through. Beside her,

Taylor stood tweaking the tuning on the borrowed acoustic guitar. He gave her a reassuring smile as she stepped forward towards the microphone.

"Friends and family," began Ellen, her voice ringing out across the crowded restaurant. "I'd like to wish my mother a very happy birthday and to sing Happy Birthday to her."

A loud cheer went up that helped to settle her nerves somewhat. She spotted her dad ushering her mother across the room towards the front of the stage.

With a nod to Taylor, Ellen began to sing. She played it safe and sang clearly and confidently without embellishments.

"Rock it up, Ellen!" called out one of her dad's friends as she reached the last line.

With her mother now standing directly in front of her, Ellen couldn't resist. She heard Tailz whisper to the band to join in, then, on a quick count of three, Ellen reverted to "rock queen" and powered her way through a hard rock rendition, encouraging the guests to join in.

"Everyone, please give a huge fiftieth birthday cheer for my mother, Olivia Lloyd!" roared Ellen as the staff brought the large square cake forward.

With one big breath, Ellen's mother blew out all of the candles, earning another round of applause.

"Folks, while the staff cut up the cake and pass it round, we've been asked to relieve the band," explained Ellen warmly. "Taylor and I would like to play a couple of songs from After Life's new album. Is that ok with everyone?"

A huge cheer went up along with several cries of "Go, Ellen!"

"We'll take that as a yes," said Taylor, noting that Ellen's mother had vanished from sight. "This one's called Lou Lou At 3am."

As Taylor began the gentle acoustic intro, their small audience fell silent. The delicate lullaby melody filtered out across the room as Ellen began to sing. She kept her voice soft with a husky edge, focussing on the words and ignoring the emotions flying round in her head. Scanning the room, she searched for her mother but failed to spot her. She did spot her dad standing off to one side smiling at her. Keeping her dad in her line of sight, Ellen poured her mixed emotions into the song before allowing the acoustic outro to wash over her. Silently, she wondered if her mother had been listening and if she recognised that the betrayal reflected in the song was hers.

The guests' enthusiastic applause brought Ellen back to the present.

"Thank you," she said humbly as the applause died away. "This next one sounds a little different when we play it with the rest of the band. Sounds a whole lot louder! This is a song called Swirling Mists."

Around them the room fell silent as Ellen began the Gregorian chant to open the song. The air was electric as the assembled guests waited expectantly to hear what was about to follow. Instead of her usual rock queen vocal, Ellen kept things softer and more bluesy as she sang the three verses. Beside the stage, she could see her young cousin, Michael, hanging on her every note. With a wink to Tailz, she moved over and crouched down in front of the teenager to deliver the reprise of the Latin chant. Her simple gesture had obviously made the boy's night.

"Thank you," said Ellen softly as the cheers began to die away. On a whim, she changed her mind about which song to finish with. Swiftly, she whispered the change of plan to Taylor who nodded and said he needed to adjust the tuning. "Folks, tonight isn't about me or Taylor here. Tonight's my mother's big night and I think we've stolen more than enough of her limelight."

She paused as she saw her mother reappear beside her dad over by the bar.

"When I first sang solo at a school show about ten years ago, my mother helped me to choose the song. I was so nervous that night standing on the stage in the school assembly hall. It was that night and that song that set me on my musical journey," revealed Ellen. "I'd like to sing that song again tonight for my mother. Totally unrehearsed. I haven't attempted this one for a very long time. This is Hallelujah."

Praying that he didn't mess up, Tailz played the delicate intro to the popular Leonard Cohen song. Right on cue, Ellen began to sing, "Now I've heard there was a secret chord….."

Silence filled the restaurant as her clear voice rang out. Over at the bar, her mother looked to be crying. As the last lingering note of her final "Hallelujah" faded to nothing, Ellen bowed her head, allowing Tailz to finish the song with a delicate flourish.

"Thank you," said Ellen with a smile. "Thank you for indulging us. We'll hand you back to the band to get this party moving."

"More! More! More!" called out someone from the far corner.

"Not tonight," called back Ellen. "If you want to hear more, come to an After Life show."

Singing the three songs had taken its toll on her emotionally and Ellen was trembling by the time she returned to their table. Her aunt and uncle showered her with reassuring plaudits while Taylor darted off to fetch them both a well-earned drink from the bar.

"Ellen."

At the mention of her name, she turned in her seat and found herself face to face with her mother.

"Mum."

"Thank you," said her mother awkwardly. "Meant a lot to hear you sing Hallelujah. I can still see you standing on that stage in the school assembly hall. I was so proud of you that night." Her mother paused then added, "And I'm every bit as proud of you tonight."

"Thanks, Mum," replied Ellen, all too aware of the lump forming in her throat.

"Your dad's gone to speak to the band," explained her mother. "We both want you and Taylor up there with them. Will you sing some more for us?"

"Why not let them play for a bit then we can join them for two or three numbers at the end?" suggested Ellen, conscious that she didn't want to railroad the band who had been booked to play.

"If you think that will work better."

Ellen nodded, "Gives Taylor and I time to decide what we want to play and to check if the band know it."

It was almost twelve thirty before the last of the guests left the restaurant. While Ellen went to the bar to fetch some water, Taylor helped the band to pack up their gear. He felt it was the least he could do after they'd hijacked their set at the end of the evening.

"You ready to head back to the house?" asked Ellen as she watched him coil the last of the band's leads and toss it into a small plastic bucket. "Dad's called a taxi."

"Five minutes," promised Taylor. "I just need to help these guys out to their van."

"Ok. We'll meet you out front," said Ellen softly. "My parents are arguing about our sleeping arrangements."

"I don't mind taking the couch," offered Taylor. "Especially if it keeps your mother on side."

Giggling, Ellen said, "Actually it's my dad who wants you on the couch. My mother's all for us sharing my old room. I think she's drunk!"

"As long as she's happy."

Dead on their feet, Taylor and Ellen finally crawled into bed around 3am. When they'd returned to the house, her dad had insisted that they all have a night cap and then another, keeping Taylor talking about recording the album. With a smile, Ellen had watched her mother begin to fall asleep in her chair before she mumbled her apologies and staggered off to bed.

As she curled up beside the warmth of Taylor's naked body, Ellen let out a sigh. The party had gone smoother than she could ever have anticipated. Her dad had whispered to her that singing Hallelujah had been an inspired choice, revealing that that was what had brought her mother back on side.

"Penny for them?" whispered Taylor, sensing she was still awake.

"Was thinking about singing Hallelujah," confessed Ellen with a yawn.

"You did a fine job of it."

"Thanks. It's been a long time since I sang that one. Good Times used to play it. I've not sung it since," she revealed, making a rare reference to her previous band. "Comes complete with its own ghosts."

"No ghosts in here," promised Taylor, sounding more asleep than awake. "Now get to sleep. We've an early start. Our train's at ten thirty."

When Ellen wandered down to the kitchen in search of breakfast, she found her mother sitting at the table, nursing a cup of coffee.

"Morning," greeted Ellen. "Am I ok to help myself to some juice?"

"Of course," replied her mother. "The kettle's just boiled. Do you want a cup of tea?"

"I'll make one," said Ellen, lifting the orange juice from the fridge. "I said I'd take one up to Tailz."

"Is it serious between you and him?"

The direct question caught Ellen off guard. Pausing for a second or two till she'd poured her juice, she finally replied, "Yes. I think so. It's good."

"And he doesn't mind……you know?" faltered her mother awkwardly.

"No, mother. He doesn't mind my scars," stated Ellen plainly. "I've hidden nothing from him."

"He seems like a nice boy."

"He is. All the boys in the band are."

"Are you happy?"

"Yes," replied Ellen without hesitation. "Life's good, mother. Really good."

"I'm glad. I was proud to see you on that stage last night. Thank you," said her mother quietly. "And thank you for my pearls."

Without another word, Olivia Lloyd got to her feet and left the room.

As she sat in the waiting room at the skin clinic, Ellen could feel her stomach churning. Beside her, Taylor sat holding her hand but she could sense that he was almost as anxious as she was. He had confessed the night before, as they both lay curled up together neither of them able to sleep, that hospitals freaked him out. For the first time, he opened up to her about accompanying his mum to some of her chemo sessions, confessing his fears and feelings of utter helplessness as he had watched the cancer slowly eat her away. Despite her own nerves, Ellen had done her best to reassure him that her appointment wouldn't be so traumatic.

"Ellen Lloyd!" called a nurse sharply. "Ellen Lloyd!"

"Here," called back Ellen as she got to her feet.

Taylor lifted her overnight bag and followed her across the waiting room.

"Third door on your left," instructed the nurse bluntly, pointing down the corridor.

"Thank you," said Ellen nervously.

In the office, they found a young male doctor sitting reading over Ellen's case history.

"Morning," he greeted brightly. "Ellen?"

"Yes," she replied, instantly warming to him. "And this is my boyfriend, Taylor."

"Pleasure," answered the doctor. "I'm Isaac Law. I'll be performing the laser treatment later this morning. Have you had laser treatment before?"

Ellen nodded, "On my arm not long after the accident and on my ribs a few months later."

"How is the scarring on your arm? Do you mind if I examine it?"

Obligingly, Ellen removed her denim jacket to reveal the scarred remains of her arm. Gently, the doctor examined the skin, pausing a couple of times to refer back to her medical notes.

"You're taking great care of it. How's your range of movement?"

"My shoulder's tight if that's what you mean," replied Ellen. "It's really tight under my arm. In my armpit area."

The doctor nodded. "And your prosthesis? Is it comfortable?"

Ellen shook her head. "I gave up trying to wear it almost three years ago. Life's easier without it."

"I can't imagine that life's been easy," observed Dr Law. "I'd like to examine the scarring to your ribcage. Perhaps Taylor could step outside and give us a moment?"

"Sure," agreed Tailz almost with relief. "I'll be just outside."

With Taylor out of earshot, the doctor asked Ellen about the levels of pain she experienced.

"Some days are better than others," she admitted evasively.

"On a scale of one to ten, what does a good day feel like?"

"A five or a six," replied Ellen. "If I've been on stage the night before it's nearer a nine or ten."

"On stage?" quizzed Dr Law.

"I'm a singer with a rock band."

"Wow!" exclaimed the doctor. "I didn't expect that answer."

"That's what made me pursue this. We've a tour coming up in October. I really struggled on our last run. The scars on my ribs got so tight. They were agony."

"Let's take a look at them then we can chat through the options here."

Half an hour later, Ellen emerged from the doctor's office to find Taylor pacing restlessly up and down the corridor. She beckoned to him, explaining that she needed to go upstairs to the day surgery ward.

"Do you need to stay in tonight?" quizzed Taylor anxiously as they walked toward the lifts.

"Hopefully not. Dr Law said to come upstairs and get changed. They need to do some pre-treatment stuff before the actual laser treatment. We should be done by mid-afternoon."

"Will you be ok to go home then?"

"Should be. I'll be tender but this is the first round of treatment. We discussed a more invasive option for round two but Dr Law wants to see how the scars respond to today's treatment first."

"More invasive? What do you mean by that?"

"Surgery," revealed Ellen softly. "It might be the only option left now on the thick keloid scars. You know the ugly white rope ones that restrict my ribs from moving?"

Taylor nodded as his face paled a little, "Will surgery make a big difference?"

"Big enough, I hope."

It was early evening before Ellen was allowed to leave the hospital. Dr Law was pleased with how the initial laser treatment had gone but cautioned Ellen to take things easy for a couple of weeks. With Taylor present, the doctor explained that he had treated the scarring to her upper ribcage and arm with a view to improving her range of shoulder movement. He handed Ellen an aftercare sheet and an appointment card for 22nd July.

"Come prepared to stay for three nights," he instructed. "I'll talk to you before the 22nd but you need to be ready for surgery. I want to confer with a colleague but I'm confident I can loosen those keloid scars for you. I'll not lie. It won't be pleasant. Recovery will be painful and it'll take time."

Ellen nodded, feeling tears stinging at her eyes.

"How much time?" asked Tailz, taking Ellen's hand and giving it a squeeze.

"Six to eight weeks," replied the doctor. "I also want to check if there's anything to be done for your lungs. Breathing on the right is quite significantly compromised by the internal and external scarring."

"Thanks," whispered Ellen. "Can we go now?"

"Of course. If you've any concerns, just call me."

"Thanks, doc," said Taylor as he helped Ellen to her feet. "Thanks for everything."

As soon as they arrived back at the house, Ellen excused herself, saying she didn't want any dinner and that she was going straight to bed.

Having Rocky and Lizzy's house to themselves still felt strange. The older couple had left a few days earlier and, gradually, Taylor and Ellen had spread themselves out in the house. Taylor was sitting in the kitchen playing his guitar when Ellen came downstairs the morning after her treatment.

"Mornin'," greeted Tailz with a smile. "How're you feeling?"

"A bit tender but I'm ok," replied Ellen sleepily. "A cup of tea would help."

"Your wish is my command," teased Taylor as he laid his guitar down on the table. Filling the kettle, he continued, "I called Nana last night after you went to bed. Do you think you'll feel up to travelling down there on Saturday?"

"I'll be fine," assured Ellen. "It'll be good to get out of London for a couple of weeks."

"And you won't be too sore to sit in the car for five hours?"

"Tailz, I'll be fine."

"Good. I'll sort out car hire then," he said with a wide grin. "Will be good to go home for a bit. Catch some waves."

"Homesick?" she quizzed softly.

"Just a bit," he confessed as he passed her a mug of tea.

Ellen had long since dozed off in the passenger seat by the time Tailz turned off the road and down the narrow hedge-lined lane. Their journey had taken longer than planned thanks to a tailback on the A30 due to roadworks. As he parked the car beside the cottage, he could smell BBQ. Before he had the engine stopped, his twin sister came running round the side of the cottage.

"You made it!" she squealed excitedly. "I was getting worried."

"Roadworks," stated Taylor wearily as he climbed out of the car. "We got stuck in a jam on the A30 for an hour."

"That road's a nightmare," agreed his sister, hugging him tight. "Oh, it's good to see you."

A rather sleepy looking Ellen stumbled out of the car in time to see the twins hug each other. He never said much but she knew Taylor missed his sister more than he admitted.

"Ellen!" shrieked Jen when she saw her. "How are you?"

"Tender but I'm ok," replied Ellen, forcing a weak smile. "No hugs, please. No offense, Jen."

"Come on round. The BBQ is ready. I got some fresh fish down at the harbour this morning. I thought we'd BBQ them."

"Got any cider?" checked Taylor as he lifted their bags out of the boot.

"Sure do. Do you want one, Ellen?" asked Jen. "Or would you rather a beer?"

"Beer would be good," agreed the shy songstress following her round the side of the cottage.

The cottage garden and patio were exactly as Ellen remembered, only with more flowers. The colours in the raised beds and planters were stunning. As she took a seat at the table, Nana came out of the house carrying a pile of plates and cutlery.

"I thought I heard voices," she declared with a twinkling smile. "Welcome home, missy."

"Thanks, Nana. It's great to be back," replied Ellen warmly. "Thanks for having me."

"You're welcome here any time, with or without this troublemaker."

"Hi, Nana," greeted Taylor, appearing beside the old woman. He wrapped her in his arms and held her tight. "I've missed you," he whispered in her ear.

"Well, you're home now," said his grandmother warmly. "Make yourself useful and get those fish on to cook. Jen's prepared them all."

"Sure," he replied then with a sigh added, "Oh, it's good to be back."

A couple of hours later, their cleared plates still piled on the table, all four of them were chatting idly as the sun set. As dusk had encroached, it brought a chill to the air. Taylor had lit the chimnea to spread a little warmth. While he'd been busy with the kindling, Jen had lit the various candles that were scattered around the patio and garden. With a sleepy smile, Ellen thought it looked like a fairy garden. Her imagination began to run away with her as she spun fresh fairy influenced lyrics in her mind.

"Penny for them, missy," said Nana, nudging her knee gently. "You've not said a word for over half an hour."

"Sorry," apologised Ellen. "I was daydreaming."

"Writing lyrics in your head more like," teased Taylor, recognising the look.

"Well, you daydream to your heart's content," said the twins' grandmother. "Let us take care of you while you're here."

"Thanks," replied Ellen, trying to stifle a yawn. "I'll be fine in a day or two."

"Taylor said you've more surgery lined up," began Jen, ignoring the dark look her brother was firing at her.

Ellen nodded, "Two more, I think. I need to go back in a couple of weeks. Depending on how I heal just now and how the surgery goes, I might need another round of laser treatment at the end of the summer."

"It all sounds a bit space age to me," commented Nana. "Like something Bones would do on Star Trek!"

"I guess it is a bit," giggled Ellen, amazed to discover that Nana was a Trekkie.

"Just make sure you get plenty of rest," cautioned Taylor.

"Don't push yourself too hard. I know what you're like."

"I won't. I'll be sensible," promised Ellen. "In fact, if you don't mind, I'm going to head off to bed. I'll see you all in the morning."

"Night," called out Jen. "Sleep well."

"I'm going surfing first thing so don't panic if I'm not here when you get up," said Taylor.

"Ok. Be careful," replied Ellen. "Good night, everyone."

As she lay in the dark in the soft bed, she could just make out the others' voices outside. Part of her felt guilty for going to bed so early; part of her was relieved to be comfortable. Her shoulder, stump and upper ribcage were still sore, the damaged skin even more delicate after the extensive laser session. She knew it would all settle down in a day or so but, for now, the cool, cotton sheets against her fiery skin felt heavenly. Slowly, she drifted off into a deep, dreamless sleep.

Next morning, when she first opened her eyes, Ellen wasn't sure where she was then she heard Taylor laughing downstairs. A quick glance at her phone informed her it was after ten o'clock. She had slept for over twelve hours but had to admit she felt the better for it.

Taking her time, she got up, showered and dressed then made her way down to the kitchen. She smiled when she saw Taylor sitting at the table in a ragged T-shirt and long cut-off shorts, his feet bare.

"Morning," she said cheerfully. "I leave you alone for five minutes and you turn into a beach bum!"

"Morning, beautiful," greeted Taylor, smiling at her. "Sleep well?"

"Like a baby. I feel the better for it too."

"Good stuff. Do you feel up to walking to Artisan's for lunch?"

"Yeah," agreed Ellen. "I could do with stretching my legs. Where's your Nana?"

"Church," replied Jen. "Religiously every Sunday then she meets her friends for lunch. She won't be home until late afternoon."

"Are you coming for lunch too?"

"No. I've plans," said Jen with a wink. "I'm meeting a friend in

Truro. I'll be back for dinner though."

"Male friend?" quizzed Taylor, raising his eyebrows and staring at his twin.

"Yes, it is," replied Jen, blushing a deep shade of red. "He comes into the gallery where I work. We're meeting in Truro so he can show me an exhibition his paintings are in. Wants me to stock some in the gallery."

"As long as that's all he's showing you."

"Taylor!" shrieked Jen. "We're only having lunch!"

"Ignore him," advised Ellen. "Go and have fun."

"Thanks, Ellen. At least someone understands!"

Artisan's was quiet for a summer Sunday when Ellen and Taylor walked in. The small specialist baker only had six tables indoors and three outside the shop. The pavement tables were occupied but only one of the indoor ones was.

"Hi, Taylor," greeted Anna, the owner, from behind the counter. "Jen said you were due home. How's London?"

"Busy!" he called back as they took their seats.

"Russ was hoping to catch up with you," commented Anna, coming over with two menus for them.

"Don't tell me. Thursday night music slot at the hotel?"

Anna nodded, "I think he's hoping you'll play."

"We'll see," said Taylor with a grin as he accepted the menu from her.

"I'll tell him that's a yes then," teased Anna.

"It's a "we'll see," Anna," countered Taylor warmly. "I know what I want. Cheese and your homemade chutney on the rustic brown seeded."

Quickly reading over the menu, Ellen said, "I'll have brie and black grape on the rustic brown seeded, please."

"Tea or coffee?"

"Tea for me," said Ellen without hesitation.

"Coffee, please," added Taylor, passing the menus back.

While Anna fetched their order, he explained that Russ was Anna's brother.

"So, are you going to play on Thursday?"

"What do you think?" laughed Taylor.

"I think you'll be talking me into it too," giggled Ellen. "Might be a good proving ground for some new songs. Not sure how I'll hold up singing next week though. Might be too soon. We'll play that one by ear."

"You got something new?"

"A couple of half-formed ideas. Not really After Life stuff. I've a more blues sound in mind. Just a couple of ideas I've been toying with."

"Let me hear them later," suggested Taylor. "I thought we could take a walk along the beach on the way back. Tide looks about right to show you a secret."

"What kind of secret?"

"You'll see. Might help with those lyrics too."

The main beach was crowded with holidaymakers as Taylor and Ellen walked along it hand in hand. It was low tide and, at the base of the cliffs, several rock pools had been exposed, attracting curious children with small nets and buckets searching for sea creatures.

"This way," said Taylor, pointing towards a cave down near the water's edge.

"Another party cave?"

"No. You'll see."

Just inside the cave, there were four roughly hewn stone steps leading down into a second cave. The sand on the floor of this lower cave was soft and wet, sucking at the soles of their flip flops as they crossed it. At the far side, almost hidden in the dark, were six more steps leading up.

"Watch your head at the top," cautioned Taylor. "There's not much room."

Crouching low, Ellen climbed the steps, sensing her bandmate right behind her. At the top she found herself in another small, narrow cave and, ahead of her, she could see waves lapping at its mouth.

"Looks like we timed it nicely," noted Taylor, squeezing into the cave beside her. "On you go. You'll recognise where you are."

As she stepped out of the cave through the small waves, Ellen smiled. They were now on the small beach cove not far from the cottage.

"This is where your party cave is!"

"Exactly," stated Taylor. "Nana told me this was an old smuggler's escape route. You can only use it when the tide's really low on the village side. It saves a long walk round by road though."

"A secret passage to paradise."

"Or freedom," he suggested as they walked slowly across the sand.

Without thinking, Taylor stopped every few steps to pick up stones to skim. Before he realised what he was doing, he had a handful of palm-sized flat stones.

"How are you at skimming stones?" he asked with a cheeky grin.

"I've not done that for years!" giggled Ellen. "Dad taught me how one time we went to the Lake District."

"Want to try?"

"Sure. Why not?"

There wasn't much of a breeze and the cliffs were sheltering the sandy bay, leaving the water close to shore flat calm. Passing her a stone, Taylor said, "Ladies first."

Accepting the small stone, Ellen composed herself then let it fly gently. Both of them watched as it bounced twice before sinking out of sight.

"Two to beat," declared Taylor as he set his first stone free. It too bounced twice before disappearing.

Ellen's second attempt was more successful and the stone skipped four times before sinking. On his next throw, Taylor teased out five bounces. Feeling more confident, Ellen threw for a third time then watched as the stone seemed to skip on forever.

"Seven!" she squealed with delight.

"Ok, if I match seven or above, we throw again," stated Taylor.

"And if you throw less than seven?"

"You win."

"Deal," agreed Ellen as Taylor prepared to take his shot.

The light-coloured stone skipped four times then sank to the bottom.

"I win!" shrieked Ellen excitedly.

"Yes, you do."

Laughing, Ellen teased, "Lost your crown to a one-armed girl."

Joining in with her laughter, he said, "That's sick, girl!"

"But true."

"Sad but true," he conceded, giving her a hug. "You won fair and square."

Kicking off their flip flops, they walked along the beach, paddling in the shallows. The water was cool on their bare feet. Voices from further up the beach disturbed their peace and quiet and Taylor turned to see where they were coming from. It was two young teenage boys and they were dragging the surfboard out from the cave.

"Wait here," instructed Taylor bluntly. "I don't like the look of this."

Barefoot, he sprinted up the beach towards the two boys, noting with concern how ineptly they were handling the board.

"Hey, guys, where you going with that?" he asked, his tone firm but non-threatening.

"Taking it out to catch a few waves," replied one, his tone a bit too cocky for Taylor's liking.

Glancing back at the calm water, Taylor took a deep breath then said, "Put it back. There's no waves out there."

"Told you," muttered the other boy sourly.

"But there's breakers further out!"

"Put it back," repeated Taylor. "You're not strong enough to handle that board so far out. Fact!"

"I suppose you're an expert," spat the boy bitterly.

"Not an expert but I've surfed these waters for a long time. Today's not a good day to head out from here. Wind's all wrong. Tide's wrong. Now, put that board back!"

The boy dropped it in the sand at his feet, "How are we ever meant to learn?"

"Pardon?"

"If you are stopping us going out when its calm, how are we meant to learn to surf?"

The hint of exasperation in his voice tugged at Taylor's conscience.

"How much time have you spent trying?"

"Weeks!"

"Can you stand up on the board?"

"No," muttered the boy, staring down at his suntanned bare feet.

"What about you?" quizzed Taylor, turning his attention to the other boy.

"A bit. My brother showed me some stuff but he's gone back to the army. Won't be back for six months."

"Tell you what. I'll teach you both how to balance on the board. How to stand up. That's a lesson best learned on a calm day," offered Taylor generously.

"You will?"

Taylor nodded, "Now, bring the board down to the water's edge."

He ran back down the beach to where he'd left Ellen waiting. Hurriedly, he explained what was going on and admitted that "surf school" was in session for the next couple of hours.

"That's fine," she said softly. "I'll sit on the beach. I've got my lyrics book. I'll be quite content to watch you play teacher."

"You're sure?"

"Sure," she assured him as the boys reached them. "Have fun."

Having made herself comfortable in the shade near the mouth of the cave, Ellen sat and watched Taylor coach the two teenagers for a while then turned her attention to her lyrics journal. She was seeing her bandmate in a whole different light and had an idea of how to spin it into some lyrics. She had noticed he was more relaxed back in his home surroundings. His rock guitarist demeanour was long gone, replaced by a more chilled version of himself. She'd noticed it during their previous visit but not to the same extent.

Soon, she was lost in her creative thoughts as words flowed from her pen. Being at the beach and away from the city had already had a profound effect on her too. Ellen was aware she felt more relaxed, less on her guard, and, as a result, her creative spirit was flying free.

The afternoon disappeared and, before she realised it, Taylor was beside her, dripping salty water on her bare toes.

"Sorry we were so long," he apologised.

"Ugh! You're dripping!"

"Yeah. We progressed to lesson two and I got a bit wet," laughed Taylor.

Behind him, the two boys arrived at the cave carrying the board between them.

"Put it back carefully," cautioned Taylor sternly before adding, "You both did well today."

"Thanks," said the boys in unison.

"You're welcome. Now, you both know the deal, right?" replied Taylor. "Same time here tomorrow but bring your own boards. Boards that are suitable for you. I'll spare you another couple of hours and we can see how it goes. Deal?"

"Deal!"

As the boys scampered up the steep stairs taking them to the top of the cliff, Taylor sat down on the sand beside Ellen and sighed.

"That was fun," he confessed as he ran his fingers through the sand. "Reminded me of the guys who taught me to surf back in the day."

"Teacher Tailz," teased Ellen, closing her journal over.

"Never thought I'd see the day," he laughed. "Now, my lovely, what have you been creating this afternoon?"

"A couple of things. One's more or less there. The other needs work."

"Want me to grab the guitar from back there?"

Ellen shook her head. "Can we head back to the house? We can work on these after dinner."

"You ok?" asked Taylor anxiously.

"Fine, just a bit uncomfortable."

"You should've said earlier," he scolded softly. "Let's get you home."

"Don't fuss," said Ellen, getting to her feet and dusting the sand off her bum. "I just need some painkillers and a soft seat for a bit."

The sun was setting and the chimnea had been lit by the time Ellen and Taylor settled down to work on her new songs. Having declined to join them, they could hear the TV in the background as Nana settled down to watch David Attenborough on BBC 1. There was still no sign of Jen arriving home. She had called earlier to say she'd be later home than planned.

Adjusting Lou Lou's tuning, Taylor said, "Well, what have

you come up with?"

"Two. Well, two and a half," replied Ellen quietly. "Nothing destined for After Life. These are just for the fun of it."

"Let's hear them," he coaxed softly.

Keeping her voice soft, Ellen began a simple melody about fairy tale creatures appearing at dusk to clear away the sadness and evil of the day. She spun a very pretty tale with her words but the lyrics had an undercurrent of menace to them.

"That could be an After Life song," commented Taylor when the song ended. "It's dark enough. Creepy."

"Maybe," she agreed with a smile.

"What was the other one?"

"It's just a bit of fun," said Ellen, turning the page over in her journal.

Taking a deep breath, she surprised her bandmate by singing a fast paced almost folk song, a tale of smuggling a lover through the caves under the cliffs.

"Love it!" exclaimed Taylor with a grin. "But, can I suggest something?"

"Sure."

"Add in a verse or a couple of lines about leaving the husband dead on the other beach. Something about the tide washing away the blood of their passionate crime."

"I had a verse along those lines," admitted Ellen, showing him her notebook.

Quickly, he read over the verse then said, "Let's try it again. Include the lot and I'll see what I can come up with. I've an idea."

When Jen arrived home shortly before midnight, she found her twin and Ellen still out on the patio engrossed in the songs. They barely looked up as she called "Good night," to them.

Life around the cottage slipped into an easy routine as the days wore on. Most mornings, Taylor slipped out of the house to go surfing at dawn. As she began to feel stronger, Ellen accompanied him, spending her time on the beach enjoying the tranquillity of sunrise. Their days were whiled away by taking long walks, sitting in the garden writing and playing. Several times a week, Tailz would return to the beach late in the afternoon to continue his surf lessons with the two boys. As the days wore on and they learned who he was, music lessons were tagged on at the end of "surf school" for one of them. Evenings were generally family time spent enjoying a leisurely al fresco meal.

Mid-July, Taylor and Ellen returned to London for two weeks while Ellen underwent surgery on her scarred body. The delicate procedure took longer than anticipated, proving to be more extensive than she had envisaged. However, Dr Law was delighted with the results he had achieved, promising her that once she was fully healed, she would notice a significant improvement. As the surgery had been deemed a success, the doctor advised against any further laser treatment. Before she left the hospital, with strict after care instructions, he promised he was still investigating how best to treat the damage to her lungs.

Recovery from the surgery was slow, leaving Ellen feeling frustrated. She hated being a burden to Taylor and his family. For the first few days after they returned to the cottage, she was reliant on Jen and Tailz to help her wash and dress. Moving was agony. She had three lengthy wounds running from her spine round her ribcage plus several smaller wounds. Gradually though, the wounds healed and her strength began to return.

Watching Ellen putting herself through so much pain tore at Taylor's heart. It had taken most of his inner resolve to stay with her at the hospital, the visits bringing to life the ghosts of his mother's illness. He knew that Ellen's treatment was aimed at making things easier for her in the longer term but watching her suffer in silence was heart breaking. She insisted that he continue to surf and enjoy the summer while she recuperated back at the cottage. Filled with an urge to make things more bearable, he took to bringing her back small gifts every day. Sometimes, the gift was a shell from the beach or a cake from Artisan's. Occasionally, he brought her a bunch of wild flowers he'd picked on his way back from the beach.

On Bank Holiday Monday, the last Monday in August, Taylor left the house before sunrise as usual to head down to the beach. Along with the regular local early risers, he rode the waves for a couple of hours then agreed to join his surf buddies for breakfast at Holly Dolly's.

The harbourside café was packed when they arrived and the only free table was one of the outside tables. As ever, Holly was dashing from the kitchen to the counter to the tables. Resisting the urge to help his former employer with the breakfast rush, Taylor ordered his usual fry up and a mug of tea plus a round of toast, saying there was no urgency. When Holly finally brought his plate over, he smiled as he noted she'd added some extra bacon and an extra fried egg.

"Thanks, Holly," he said warmly.

"Sorry you had to wait for it," she apologised. "Breakfast girl called in sick."

"How about when I finish this I help you clear up?" he offered, unable to sit back and watch his old boss struggle any longer.

"That would be good, son," replied the old woman, looking relieved. "The lunchtime girl will be in at eleven but I'd like to get up straight before she gets here."

"Give me fifteen minutes then I'm all yours till she gets here," offered Taylor.

"You're a lifesaver, Taylor Rowe."

Working in the small kitchen brought back memories of his teenage years as Taylor washed the pile of dishes and scrubbed the place down. The breakfast rush was over and the café had quietened down, just a few regulars sitting enjoying a coffee over their morning newspaper.

"Taylor, I hate to ask," began Holly, popping her head round the kitchen door. "Could you watch the counter till I nip upstairs to get some change for the till?"

"Not a problem," he assured her. "Take your time."

"You know, I might sit down for a few minutes," sighed Holly wearily. "I'll be no more than half an hour."

"Take your time," he repeated softly.

A family of four were his first customers. They were looking for some sandwiches to take away, explaining that they were going out on a boat trip from the harbour. As he prepared their order, Taylor heard the shell windchimes that hung over the café's door tinkle.

"How does a guy get a coffee around here?" asked a familiar voice from behind him.

"Luke!" exclaimed Taylor, whirling round.

"Morning," greeted his bandmate with a grin. "Didn't expect to find you working here."

"Just helping out for a few minutes," explained Taylor.

Luke nodded, "No rush with that coffee. I'll grab a table outside."

"Ok. I'll join you when Holly gets back."

Carrying two mugs of coffee, Taylor stepped outside to join Luke. His bandmate was chatting on his phone as he sat down beside him.

"Sorry about that," apologised Luke, stuffing the phone back into his pocket. "Garrett checking up on me."

"So, what brings you down here?" asked Taylor curiously.

"R and R," replied the bass player with a wink.

"Music?"

"No. Rest and recuperation," joked Luke, stirring sugar into his coffee. "Garrett rented a cottage near Torquay for a few weeks. He brought his pet vampire over for a week. Didn't work out too well. They flew back to the States on Friday. I was bored so I hired a car and drove over here yesterday. Booked a room at the hotel for a couple of weeks."

"Can you unbook it?" asked Taylor. "There's room at the cottage. Nana would love to see you. Jen too."

With a laugh, Luke said, "That's a lie, Tailz! Your Nana is never glad to see me and has never approved of me."

"True," conceded Tailz. "But, she wouldn't want you in the hotel when there's a spare room with us."

"I'll think about it," promised the bass player. "How's my favourite songbird?"

"She's getting there," replied Taylor. "She's taken longer to heal than she'd like but she's stubborn. Keeps pushing herself. Never complains. How about you? You ok?"

"I'm ok," said Luke evasively. "Arm's still a bit stiff. I'm back playing though. Building it up."

"And your heart stuff?"

"Doc signed me off. Says I don't need to go back till December. Heart's still ticking."

"Glad to hear it. You scared the crap out of us," said Taylor.

"Fancy coming back to the cottage with me? Ellen would love to see you."

"Sure. So, what is there to do about here? Looks kind of quiet."

"Not a lot," admitted Taylor. "Surf's good. There's a weekly music night in the hotel. It's a quiet kind of place."

"Music night?"

"Yeah. Mate of mine hosts it every Thursday."

"You played recently?"

"I played a couple of songs last week," revealed Taylor. "Mainly, Ellen and I have been writing and playing at the house when she's felt up to it. Nothing too serious."

"Does your Nana still have a piano?"

"Yes."

"Good. I've a few things to run past my left-hand lady," said Luke with a wink.

The lyrics journal lay discarded beside the sun lounger, an empty coffee mug beside it. With a sigh, Ellen lay staring up at the sky, watching a white cotton wool cloud slip by. Boredom was setting in and she was anxious for Taylor to get back. He had called to say he would be later than planned. For a moment she had toyed with the idea of walking in to town to meet him but she changed her mind, worried in case he drove past her without seeing her. Instead, she decided to suggest a walk when he finally got back.

Half-heartedly, she picked up her lyrics journal and began to read through the most recent songs. Over the summer, she had written a few songs that would translate easily into After Life songs but most of her new lyrics were more blues based and even bordered on country. A couple of them were more piano based songs which only added to her frustrations. She could hear the songs in her mind but was unable to translate the thoughts into written music as she was.

Her inner songwriter seized control and she was soon lost in a new set of lyrics. So engrossed was she that she never heard the car pulling into the gravel driveway.

"Ellen!" called Tailz from the side of the house.

"Round the back," she called back without looking up from

the page in front of her.

"Well, that's a fine welcome, princess."

"Luke!" she exclaimed, dropping the book. "When did you get here?"

Before Taylor could caution her to move slowly, Ellen was on her feet and hugging Luke.

"You look fantastic," he complimented as he gently hugged her back. "How're the ribs?"

"Tender but almost healed," she replied warmly. "How're you? Ready to play again?"

"I'm good and, yes, I'm ready to play again," replied Luke then almost shyly added, "In fact, I need your help with something new."

"You need lyrics?"

"No. I need my left-hand lady," joked the bass player with a smile.

Hearing voices outside, Taylor's grandmother emerged from the cottage, drying her hands on a towel.

"Well, well, Luke Court," she commented, a slight edge to her tone. "What brings you all the way to Mawgan Porth?"

"I heard you were making those famous pasties of yours for dinner, Nana," he said sweetly, hoping that a little flattery would ease things with the old woman.

"Not tonight, I'm not," she retorted sharply, before adding, "Tomorrow maybe."

"Am I invited back tomorrow?"

"Maybe. Depends on how you behave today, doesn't it?" With that she turned on her heel and marched back indoors.

The three members of After Life burst out laughing. Between giggles, Ellen asked what Luke had done to upset her so much.

"More like what didn't I do," he admitted with a glance over at Tailz.

"We had a party here one night," began Taylor, picturing the scene clearly in his mind's eye. "It was about three years ago now maybe more. Nana was meant to be staying at my mum's but they had words and she arrived back here."

"Let's just say I was naked and high when she walked in," confessed Luke sheepishly. "We'll spare you the details but as she berated me in the kitchen, I pee-ed in her sink."

"Then she threw you out!" laughed Taylor.

"Yeah, she did," confessed Luke. "And she threw my clothes out that door after me."

"Poor Nana," giggled Ellen, visualising the scene. "You better behave or you've zero chance of that pasty."

"Well, he's guaranteed some lunch at least," revealed Taylor, setting a bag down on the table. "I picked up some sandwiches from Artisan's for lunch."

Over lunch, conversation centred around the band and the plans for the autumn tour. Both Ellen and Luke expressed their mild concerns over their personal fitness levels but were reassured by Taylor that they'd both be fine and that sets could be tweaked to accommodate them as need be. This prompted a change of topic as they each revealed what new music they had been working on over the summer. While Ellen showed Luke some of her new lyrics, Taylor darted indoors to fetch his guitar.

An hour or so later, Luke made a suggestion, "You mentioned a local music night, didn't you, Tailz?"

The guitarist nodded.

"Why not test some of these out there? Gives our little songbird here a chance to test her voice out too."

"We don't want to monopolise these sessions," countered Taylor. "But, you could be onto something. If we could get Jack and Cal down here, we could maybe swing an unofficial show."

"Let's walk before we run here, guys," interrupted Ellen anxiously. "I only got the ok to start light vocal work last week. I can't deliver a full After Life show within a couple of weeks."

"But, you could pull off an acoustic After Life show," countered Luke optimistically. "Say a sixty-minute set. Don't think I can manage much more right now."

"Perhaps," conceded Ellen, seeing where he was coming from. "Let's see how the next few days go. I agreed to sing three numbers this Thursday. If they go ok, we can talk to Russ about playing a short set next week. Say it's a farewell appearance."

"So, what are you planning to sing this week, little songbird?" quizzed Luke curiously. "Any of these new tunes?"

Ellen nodded, "I want to try some of the new bluesy ones. Something mid-range. Easier to sing."

"And Lou Lou," added Tailz with a grin. "If you don't sing it this week, Russ will be after your blood."

With a giggle, Ellen had to agree with him.

"Can I let you hear something?" asked Luke, sounding more than a little nervous.

"Sure."

"Tailz, will Nana let me play her piano?"

"She's gone out. Go for it. She's not due back till six. Jen's bringing her home after work," he replied. "But I'm going to have to leave you to it. I'm due down on the beach in a few minutes."

"The beach?" echoed Luke, raising his eyebrow at his bandmate. "Answering the call of the waves?"

"Something like that. I'm teaching two kids to surf. Long story," explained Taylor. "I'll be back before six. Luke, can you light the BBQ about half five?"

"Yup."

"Great. Play nice, children."

Nana's beloved piano sat in a corner of the living room. Feeling like they were breaking and entering, Luke and Ellen sat side by side on the stool then Luke carefully lifted the lid. Tentatively, he played a few notes then smiled.

"Perfectly in tune," he commented. "I didn't expect anything less."

"Nana loves this piano," said Ellen, running her hand gently over the keys. "Jen talked her into playing for us a couple of weeks ago. That old lady plays a mean honky tonk!"

"She sure does. Tailz's mum was a great pianist too. So is Jen."

"Well, what are we playing?" enquired Ellen, curious to hear what her bandmate had come up with.

"This," replied Luke, starting to play a blues influenced melody.

Keeping his head bowed and his eyes closed, After Life's bass player poured his soul into the music flowing from his fingertips. He paused mid-song to look at Ellen.

"This is where I need your magic, princess," he said slowly. "I need a solo, a bridge. A something."

"Does this have lyrics?"

Luke nodded.

"Start again," commanded Ellen calmly. "And let me hear the

lyric."

A lump formed in her throat as she listened to her friend sing about his brush with death, about losing heart, about abusing his soul, about destroying relationships through it. Upon hearing the song's story, Ellen understood what was missing and recognised his need to express personal pain at that point in the song.

"Christ, I wish I could still play," she said almost to herself.

"Sorry."

"Not your fault," Ellen muttered before taking a deep breath. "Compromise time. I can hear what I want you to play. Although maybe it'll work better as a vocal.... Let me sing it. Sound like a plan?"

"Go for it."

"Start at that second verse," instructed Ellen, getting up from the stool.

Standing with her back to him, she listened closely for the break in the song. As Luke played the last notes of the verse, Ellen began to sing. She kept her voice quiet at first, trying to create a slowing pulse effect then, as she had almost slowed to a stop, she hit a high C and, keeping things in her upper register, managed to vocalise a feeling of panic and despair, before dropping it back down to repeat the pulse. This time she quickened the pulsing rhythm until she was back to the beat of the song. She gave Luke the nod to resume.

Hitting the high notes had hurt and she took a few long, slow breaths before turning round to see her bandmate's reaction.

"Incredible," complimented Luke. "Fucking awesome in fact, princess."

"Was that what you had in mind?" she asked, placing her hand protectively over her ribs.

"No. That's better than I had in mind. So much raw emotion. I could never express that," he revealed then, noticing that she was clutching her ribs, asked, "You ok?"

"Those high notes hurt a bit," she confessed. "Pulled at the new scars. I'll be fine in a minute or two."

"You sure?"

"Sure. Just don't tell Tailz or Jen."

"Your secret's safe," promised Luke warmly. "Let's see if I can recreate that on piano?"

"Does it need to be on piano?" challenged Ellen, taking a seat on the couch. "Personally, I think the vocal worked well. Or it might work as a guitar solo if you added an ebow effect to give it that haunted edge. You could keep the original melody running underneath it all on piano. Add some depth to the emotions. To the pain."

"Not a bad idea."

"Let's get the music worked through on piano then record it on your phone," Ellen suggested. "If I feel ok in a bit, I'll try singing it again."

As the embers of the chimnea started to burn low, Luke suggested it was time he returned to the hotel. Despite Taylor's protests that he could stay at the cottage, the bass player politely declined, thanked Nana for her hospitality and got to his feet. He hugged and kissed both Jen and Ellen before Taylor walked him round to the front of the cottage to where he'd parked his hire car.

"You're very quiet, missy," commented Nana, watching Ellen as she stared after the two boys.

"Just tired," she replied evasively.

"Sore?"

Ellen nodded, "Don't tell Taylor. He'll only worry."

"I won't," promised the old woman, "But you will."

"I won't."

"No, you will," repeated Nana wisely. The old woman got stiffly to her feet, walked across the patio to where Ellen was sitting on a pile of cushions and added, "You both need to be honest with each other."

"Pardon?"

"Listen to your heart, missy," cautioned Nana, resting a hand on Ellen's shoulder. "You know I'm right."

Without another word, the old woman shuffled indoors leaving Ellen alone.

When Taylor came back round, he found Ellen staring into the glowing embers. The shadows from the chimnea and the candles that were scattered around the patio only accentuated her fragility.

"You ok?" he asked as he sat down at the picnic table to finish his cider.

"Just tired."

"I said we'd meet Luke tomorrow for lunch. Is that ok?"

"Of course. Artisan's?"

Taylor nodded, "Said we'd be there before one."

"Fine," said Ellen, distracted by the dying flames. "We'll need to find time to run through the songs for Thursday night. Do you think Russ would allow Luke in for a song or two?"

"Not sure Luke would do a solo."

"I think I can persuade him," said Ellen. "The song we worked on this afternoon has After Life potential. Think you'll like it."

"Yeah. Luke said. He also said you were singing. I hope you were careful."

"Don't fuss, Tailz," cautioned Ellen, her tone sharper than she'd intended. "I'm fine."

"Sorry," he said, reaching out to take her hand. "I worry. I just want to see you back to full health."

"Well don't worry. I'm fine," she assured him. "Yes, my scars nipped a bit….. a lot…after but I'm fine."

"I trust you to be careful," he said softly. "Come on. Time for bed. Forecast's good. I need to be up in less than five hours."

"You and your waves," laughed Ellen as she allowed him to help her to her feet.

Word had spread through the village by Thursday that there were three members of After Life due to play at the hotel's music night. When he'd heard that Luke was in town, Russ had jumped at the chance to slot him into the running order.

The three bandmates arrived shortly after six, planning to rehearse a bit before helping to set up for the evening. A few of the bar's regulars were already there but no one objected to the impromptu jam session. For an hour they played about with bits from After Life songs and the newer material that Ellen and Taylor had written over the summer.

Arriving with a tray of drinks, Russ declared, "Hope you weren't hoping for a drummer tonight, guys. Davie can't make it. He's got caught up."

"Not a problem," assured Taylor, lifting his cider from the

tray. "You singing tonight, mate?"

"Maybe one or two," replied Russ.

"Why don't we end the night with "With A Little Help From My Friends" or "We Are The Champions"?" suggested Ellen.

"Or both," countered Russ. "Two of my favourites right there."

"Yeah but do you know the tune?" teased Tailz mischievously.

"Of course, I do!"

"Who else is up tonight?" asked Ellen, diverting attention away from Russ' dubious vocal abilities.

"Well, there's you three," began Russ, pulling a crumpled sheet of paper out of the back pocket of his jeans. "Sam wants to sing a couple and Liz said she'd do a duet with Barry if we let her go on before nine. She's only got a babysitter until half past nine."

"Anyone else?" checked Taylor.

"Not unless anyone shows up on spec," replied Russ. "Think they all just want to hear the professionals."

"Who's that?" quipped Luke with a grin.

"You three!"

"Speaking of which," interjected Taylor, seizing the moment. "If we wanted to do an acoustic After Life show one night, would that be a problem?"

"No. When did you have in mind?"

"Next Friday night maybe?"

"Sounds good," nodded Russ. "Should liven the weekend up a bit."

"Keep this low key," cautioned Ellen quickly. "We don't want word getting out. This is a show just for local friends."

He nodded, "I hear you, girlie. Just testing that it all still works?"

"Something like that," muttered Luke, not entirely trusting the older local musician to keep it quiet.

By the time that they were ready to start the evening's entertainment, the bar was full. They had been joined by Jen, who was as eager to see them play as the rest of the small audience.

On the stroke of eight, Russ stepped up onto the small stage and welcomed everyone.

"First up tonight, folks, is our own Taylor Rowe," he

introduced enthusiastically. "Our own home-grown rock God!"

As Taylor took a seat on a tall wooden stool in the centre of the stage, Luke and Jen whistled loudly, much to his embarrassment.

"Thank you," he said, feeling his cheeks redden. "Eleanor Rigby."

"Who's she?" shouted one of the local fishermen from the bar.

"Friend of your Da's," called back Taylor with a grin.

Taking a sip from his beer, Luke leaned over and whispered to Ellen, "When did he start singing solo?"

"Shh," she cautioned. "Just listen."

The Beatles classic proved to be the ideal choice to start the evening. It kept the more mature clientele in the bar a little longer than usual. With barely a pause, Taylor continued his solo slot with another rock classic, Ralph McTell's "Streets Of London" then rounded things off with a rendition of The Kink's "Waterloo Sunset".

He took a bow then introduced Liz and Barry, two locals, before jumping down to join Jen and his band mates.

"Well I'll be damned," said Luke, slapping his friend on the back. "The boy can sing. You kept that quiet all those years."

"Guess I did," admitted Taylor sheepishly.

It was after nine thirty before Russ called Taylor back up on stage, inviting Ellen to step to up too.

"Evening," said Ellen softly. "We've a couple of new songs to try tonight but let's start with the first one we ever wrote together. This is Lou Lou At 3am."

Fidgeting nervously, Ellen listened to the familiar intro to the ballad and almost missed her cue to come in. Avoiding catching Luke's gaze, she focused on the first verse, gradually relaxing into the familiarity of the song. As she sang, she was aware of her freshly healed scars but, by keeping things in her mid-range, she felt confident that all was well.

Judging by the enthusiastic applause that filled the bar as the final notes faded away, the locals were happy with her performance.

"Thank you," acknowledged Ellen, pausing to take a sip of water. "We've not tried this one before so this could be interesting. This is Smugglin' Lovin' Blues."

Behind her, Tailz set the tempo by beating out the rhythm on the body of his guitar. The audience swiftly picked up on it and were quickly stamping their feet in time. With barely a second thought, Ellen began the fast-paced lyrical tale of smuggling a lover through a cave under the cliffs, leaving behind a murdered spouse to be washed out to sea on the next tide. Keeping her vocal crisp, she spun a compelling tale, leaving the audience baying for another verse.

"Sorry," she giggled breathlessly. "That's all there is but you've given me an idea. Maybe next time there will be a new final verse."

Behind her, Taylor was swapping guitars, giving her a much-needed moment or two to catch her breath.

"We've one more then it's time to welcome Sam up here," she revealed, noting that the older local folk musician was standing at the side ready to come up. "This is a new one. It tells the story of rising from defeat, of washing away those self-doubts. This is Cove Of Dreams."

For the final segment of the evening, the bar's piano, recently tuned, was moved out to the centre of the small stage. Once again, Russ stepped up to the mic.

"Don't panic. I'm not about to do a Chas'n'Dave act," he joked, indicating the piano. "I would like to welcome a very special guest up to entertain you. He's better known as the bass player from After Life but I'm assured he's an accomplished pianist. Ladies and gentlemen, please give a huge welcome to Luke Court."

Looking more than a little nervous, After Life's bass player stepped up on stage and took his seat at the modest piano. He gazed down at the keys, offering up a silent prayer to the muses, then said calmly, "This is Purgatory In The Mind."

Taking a deep breath, Luke bowed his head and began to play the delicate but almost evil intro to the song. Instantly, Ellen was transported back to her first visit to Luke's apartment and to the music room where he'd played her the song for the very first time. With bated breath she waited to hear his vocal.

Without looking at the small audience, Luke kept his gaze locked on a sign on the wall beyond the piano as he spun the tale of the grim reaper capturing children's parents and dragging them into hell. His low, at times almost hoarse vocal, added a degree of menace to the lyrics about the tortures endured by the orphans damned to a life of purgatory.

Initially, there was a moment of stunned silence as the song ended then a wave of applause swept on stage to overwhelm him. Swallowing down his emotions, Luke called out, "I need my left-hand lady up here. Ellen, get up here, girl!"

Quickly, Ellen made her way back on stage and took a seat beside her surprisingly nervous bandmate.

"That was brilliant," she whispered as she settled herself on the stool beside him.

"Thanks," replied Luke, a rare hint of shyness in his voice. He coughed then turned to face the room, "My guilty pleasure, folks. Your Song."

Leaving a trail of empty glasses along the bar, the last to leave closed the door behind them just after midnight. While Luke and Tailz were helping Russ to tidy up and dismantle the small temporary stage, the bar manager sent a round of drinks over to the table. It didn't escape Jen's attention when Ellen attempted to discretely swallow two painkillers.

"You alright?" she asked quietly.

Struggling to swallow the two pills, Ellen nodded. After a sip of her wine, Ellen added, "Yes. Just a bit tender."

"Be careful," cautioned Jen warmly. "Don't undo all the surgeon's good work."

"I won't," promised Ellen softly. "It did feel good to be back on stage tonight though. Reassuring."

"I don't know how you do it," commented Jen. "And you played beautifully with Luke, I wish I could've......."

She faltered over the end of her sentence.

"Heard me play with both hands?" finished Ellen with a sad smile.

"Sorry," apologised Taylor's twin. "Me and my big mouth."

"It's fine. I'll not lie. I miss playing," admitted Ellen, gazing down at where her hand should've been. "Playing with Luke is the closest I get these days."

"He's changed," observed Jen, watching the boys move the piano off the stage. "He's mellowed."

"I think his heart scare made him rethink a few things," agreed

Ellen, smiling as Tailz waved over to her.

"And what about you and my brother?" quizzed Jen. "Are you two in it for the long haul?"

"Ah, the million-dollar question. Have you been talking to your Nana?"

Jen laughed, "Maybe."

"Well, whatever she has been saying now, don't listen to her," interrupted Taylor as both he and Luke came back to join them.

"She's a wise woman your Nana," countered Ellen, putting her arm around him. "Very intuitive."

"Meddling more like," laughed Taylor.

As the sunrise began to light up the bedroom, Taylor rolled onto his side to watch Ellen sleep. He never tired of watching her, of marvelling at how peaceful and relaxed she looked and how beautiful. In slumber, there were no signs of the pain she was trying to hide from him. Gently, he fingered her long, blonde plait. Something his Nana had said echoed round in his head.

The old woman had cornered him in the shed where he kept his surfboards a few days before. She'd scolded him for taking some of her good bathroom towels down to the beach, lecturing him on which ones he was allowed to take in future and had then cautioned him about confusing his feelings for Ellen. He'd asked her what she'd meant and all she'd said was "soulmates don't have to be lovers, son. Remember that." Before he could ask what that was implying, she'd gathered up the bundle of damp, sour smelling towels and stomped off muttering about getting them washed.

Beside him, Ellen stirred in her sleep then opened her eyes. Over the months, he'd grown used to one clear blue eye and an opaque one watching him.

"Morning," he said, kissing her slowly. "I didn't expect you to waken for a while yet."

"Mornin'," she mumbled sleepily. "Was dreaming."

"Bad dream?"

Ellen nodded, "An old nightmare."

"You ok?"

"Tired," she answered with a yawn.

"I'm going down to the beach," said Tailz, kissing her again. "Try to get some more sleep. I'll see you for breakfast later."

"Which beach?"

"Just the cove. Waves should be ok today off there."

"Ok. Be careful," she mumbled as she closed her eyes and snuggled down further under the light duvet.

The early morning sun was glinting off the water making it difficult to spot Taylor as Ellen negotiated the steep, rocky staircase down to the cove. With Jen's help, she had packed a picnic breakfast which she had stowed in a rucksack along with a blanket. As her feet finally reached the sand, she saw Taylor surfing in to shore, perfectly balanced on his board. Over the summer, his dark hair had grown longer and the combination of sun and salt water had created auburn streaks through it. He had been transformed from rock star to beach bum and it suited him. Secretly, she hoped he would keep the longer hair but she understood there was a promise there to his mum to "keep it smart."

"Hey you!" he called as he ran up the beach towards her. "Didn't expect to see you down here."

"Thought I'd bring you breakfast," replied Ellen, wriggling the rucksack from her shoulders. "And watch you play."

"Thanks. I'm starving," said Taylor, taking the pack from her. "Waves are going off though. Wasn't planning to go back out."

Within a few minutes, Taylor had spread the rug and helped Ellen to lay out their breakfast of croissants, cheese and fruit. She'd brought a flask of coffee but confessed she had forgotten to bring any milk and sugar with her.

The small beach was deserted apart from seagulls loitering nearby, eyeing up their picnic. As they ate, they analysed their performances from the previous evening's music night. Both of them were hyper-critical of themselves; both of them were complimentary of Luke's performance. Between mouthfuls of croissant, Taylor announced that he'd heard from Cal.

"Can they get here for next week?"

"He thinks so. They got back from their trip with Rocky last week and have hired an old VW camper van. Jack wanted to tour Scotland in it. Cal's going to convince him to come here," explained Taylor. "Hopes they'll reach here about Wednesday."

"Where are they if it's going to take days to get here?"

"Somewhere north of Loch Lomond. One of those mad Scottish places I can't pronounce," laughed Taylor. "Cal said he'd promised to take Jack to see Loch Ness and Culloden and then they'd head south."

"I shudder to think what they'll get up to," giggled Ellen, visualising their bandmates travelling together in a beat-up VW van.

"I'm sure there will be plenty of tales to tell," agreed Tailz.

"It's funny to think that in a few days we need to leave here," mused Ellen, gazing down the beach and across the water. "London seems a lifetime away."

"It'll be hard leaving," admitted Taylor almost to himself.

"You'll be back again soon though."

"I guess," he sighed as he lay back on the rug to stare up at the cloudless blue sky. "It's been good being here. Great having you here. Quality family time, even if my darling brother has failed to show up."

"Precious time."

Tailz nodded, "Every time I need to leave, it gets harder."

"Well let's make the most of the time we have here," suggested Ellen softly.

The next few days slipped swiftly by. Realising that time was running short, Taylor finally starting doing all the odd jobs that Nana had been nagging him to complete all summer. While he was caught up with his DIY chores, Ellen and Jen treated themselves to a "retail therapy" day out in Plymouth. Over the summer, the two girls had grown close, forming a sisterly bond. Together, they shopped for clothes and shoes, trying to find suitable outfits that Ellen could wear under her cloak on the upcoming tour. During lunch, Jen worked hard to convince her that she should make life easier for herself and shed the cloak after the first few songs, adding that she could always put it back on for the encore and her "disappearing" act. She suggested they visit a Gothic boutique run by one of her school friends for inspiration. By the time they were heading back to the car, Ellen had a whole new stage wardrobe worked out and had placed an order with their designer for a few bespoke tops that would hopefully make her arm less obvious. For the first time in a long time, she felt confident about her new clothes.

It was after seven before the girls arrived back at the cottage. As Jen turned the car into the gravel driveway, her path was blocked by a bright red retro VW camper van with a large Scottish flag flying from its roof.

"Guess the boys have arrived," laughed Jen, switching off the engine.

"Looks like it," agreed Ellen. "Although I can't imagine driving the length of the country in that."

"Me neither."

They could hear voices and laughter coming from the rear of the cottage. Both girls exchanged glances and giggled. It was Nana's laugh that they were hearing.

"Lord knows what Cal is saying to her," laughed Ellen.

"How do you know it's Cal?"

"Trust me!"

As the two girls came round the side of the house, they saw Cal dancing with Nana. All the patio furniture had been moved to the side and he looked to be teaching her some ceilidh dancing.

"Jen!" called out Jack cheerfully. "Perfect timing. Do you know the Gay Gordons?"

"Pardon?"

"It's a dance. Come here, girl."

Dropping her shopping bags, Jen ran to join in. Taylor was sitting on top of the picnic bench playing his guitar to accompany the dance lesson.

"Princess, looks like it's you and me," said Luke, getting to his feet. "Will you do me the honour?"

Giggling, Ellen joined him on the patio, declaring, "I've no idea how to do this."

"Neither have I!" confessed Luke. "Follow Cal and Nana's lead. They're the experts."

Soon, the members of After Life were all dancing round the patio, taking the dance lessons all too seriously as Cal talked them through dance after dance.

"Enough!" declared Nana breathlessly after about half an hour. "You're making me dizzy, Callum."

"Sorry," apologised the band's guitarist. "You're a rare wee dancer, Nana."

"Flatterer," she teased as she flopped down into a seat. "I've not danced like that in years!"

"Well, I'll dance with you anytime," said Cal, lifting a beer from the table. "You're a better dancer than the girl I met at the ceilidh in Inverness. She had two left feet!"

"Jen," called over the old woman. "There are fish and chicken skewers in the fridge ready to go on the BBQ. Can you fetch them?

Luke, check if those coals are ready."

"They sure are," he called back, having taken a quick glance at the BBQ.

Dinner proved to be a hilarious affair as Jack and Cal entertained the others with tales of their adventures in the camper van and some of their experiences on tour with Rocky. They had spent six weeks on the road in America with a southern rock group called Dante from Kentucky. Conscious that Nana was listening closely, they kept their stories reasonably clean but a few of them earned the boys a stern stare from their hostess.

"Are you leaving that monstrosity in my driveway tonight, Callum?" quizzed Nana as she cleared the table.

"That was the plan."

"Hmph," muttered the old woman. "And just how long were you planning on leaving it there?"

"Till we leave on Sunday?"

"You'll need to move it before then, mate," said Taylor. "I need to get the car out tomorrow morning early."

"Tailz, take mine tomorrow," suggested Jen. "I don't need it back till ten. But don't leave my seats all wet and sandy."

"Thanks," nodded Taylor to his twin. "Want to catch some waves in the morning, Jack?"

"Could do. I'd need to borrow a wet suit and a board."

"Not a problem."

"I'm going in to watch that new murder drama on the BBC," said Nana. "Keep the noise down out here if you're going to play any more music. The family next door has visitors with young children. I don't want you disturbing them."

"Nana," began Jen with a warm smile. "Ellen and I will make sure the boys behave."

Once the old woman had retired for the night, Luke said, "Do you know what I fancy?"

"What?" asked Jack, raising an eyebrow.

"A beach bonfire night."

"We could do," agreed Taylor grinning. "Would mean we could play a bit too."

"I'm in," cried Cal without hesitation.

"Ok, beach it is," stated Taylor. "Gather up what we need."

Allowing Taylor to help her down the rough-hewn stone steps, Ellen confessed, "I've never done this before."

"Done what?"

"Late night beach party."

"Just relax. You'll enjoy it," promised Taylor. "I love the beach at night. It's got a special magic to it."

Over the years, After Life had partied in the beach cave many times and knew the routine. Before Taylor and Ellen joined them, Jack had the fire lit in the stone circle and Cal had the beers and cider open for everyone. There were small rugs spread out around the fireplace and blankets for each of them to ward off the chilly night air. Inside the mouth of the cave, Jen was busy filling large plastic bowls with crisps and she'd even found some marshmallows and skewers so that they could toast them.

Taking a seat beside Taylor, Ellen commented, "Anyone would think you guys have done this before. Slickly set up."

"We may have done this a few times," confessed Luke, bringing a bottle of Jack Daniels out of his bag. "It's been a while though."

"Couple of years," agreed Taylor, lifting Lou Lou carefully from her case.

"Ellen," called over Luke. "Let the guys hear Smugglin' Lovin' Blues."

"Pick an easy song to start with, Mr Court!"

"Ok, start with that folk ballad you sang the other night, princess."

Accepting a bottle of beer from Cal, Ellen nodded. Quietly, Taylor counted her in and, while he began to play a soft simple melody, Ellen began a wistful hum that she gradually wound up into a folk aria. Keeping her voice in her upper register, she sang a revised arrangement of Cove Of Dreams, creating a more haunting image of rising from defeat and banishing self-doubt. Her change of direction with the song almost caught Taylor off guard but he improvised as best he could.

"Like that," acknowledged Jack, who had begun to beat a slow steady rhythm on the plastic cool box by the final verse. "You could work that up into an After Life song."

"That was the plan," admitted Ellen as she took a mouthful of her beer. "OK. Smugglin' Lovin' Blues."

As she'd expected, Jack and Cal loved the quirky, fast-paced song, especially the new verse she added about the dead husband rising to haunt the lovers. Much to her surprise, they both felt it too had potential to be an After Life song, if she could add an edge of menace to the final verse. While Jen watched on, the band slipped into rehearsal mode and were soon animatedly discussing potential sets and running through the newer After Life material that was included in the debut album.

Gradually, the fire in the stone circle grew as did the pile of empty beer bottles. As the bottle of bourbon was passed round and, with a little prompting from Jen, the band were persuaded to play a few of her favourite songs.

The heat from the flames and the crackling of the burning driftwood began to stir feelings of fear in Ellen. Battling her inner demons, she gradually shuffled back a bit from the fire. She didn't want to put a dampener on the party but, sitting in such close proximity to a large, uncontained open fire, scared her. Eventually, as her nerve started to give, she got to her feet, wrapped the blanket round her shoulders and said she was going for a walk.

Slowly, she wandered down the familiar beach to the water's edge with only moonlight illuminating the way. Once down on the hard-packed wet sand, she stood just out of reach of the small waves and listened to the gentle lapping of the water. Slipping the blanket from her shoulders, Ellen allowed the cool night air to waft over her skin. In her mind, she could feel the searing pain as her skin had burned and blistered; in reality, she felt the cool wind caress her scarred skin. Focusing on the rhythm of the waves, she slowed her breathing and allowed an air of calm to descend on her.

"Where's Ellen?" asked Taylor, noticing that she was missing.

"I think she's gone for a walk," replied Jen, her words slightly slurred thanks to the mix of bourbon and beer.

"Shit," muttered Luke, staring into the flames. "Tailz, go after her."

"She'll be ok," said Taylor, taking another swig of Jack Daniels from the bottle.

"Go after her, you dick!" snapped Luke. "It's the fucking flames. We never thought."

"Fuck," muttered Taylor, scrambling to his feet. "Fuck. Fuck. Fuck."

The members of After Life looked on as he sprinted off down the beach into the darkness.

Within seconds, he had spotted her standing just out of reach of the water. In the moonlight, she looked more fragile than ever, her platinum blonde hair almost bleached white by the summer sun. She appeared to be daydreaming. Slowing his pace so as not to startle her, Taylor called out her name softly. No response.

"Ellen," he said as he reached her. "I'm sorry. I never...we never thought."

"Tailz," she almost yelped as he startled her back to reality.

Gently, he put his arms around her and drew her close. "I'm so, so sorry."

"For what?" she asked, resting her head on his shoulder.

"The bonfire. We never thought."

"Shh," she said softly. "My demons to deal with. No need for everyone to dance with them."

"You ok?"

Ellen nodded, "Now, I am."

"You should've said," chastised Tailz quietly. "Told us how you felt."

"And spoil the party? Don't be crazy. I can't go through the rest of my life avoiding bonfires, BBQs and chimneas. I need to learn how to cope. It was fine until I began to notice the heat and the noise."

"Noise?"

"The noise of the flames. Of the wood spitting and cracking. Wakened a few ghosts," explained Ellen calmly. "I'm fine though. I've got my head round it."

"How?"

"Tailz, the same way I live through every day. I put it into context in my head. I calmed myself down. I don't need a bonfire to trigger those demons. I just need to be awake. I live with this all day every day and, you know what, its ok. Shit happened. I'm alive. I'm living my dreams. I'm not about to consciously dwell on my nightmares."

"Ellen Lloyd, you are one incredible girl," he declared, hugging her tight.

She snuggled in closer to him then said, "We're missing the party. We should go back."

"In a few minutes," said Taylor as a rogue wave licked round their ankles.

Lowering his lips to meet hers, Taylor began to kiss her slowly and deeply. There had been very few opportunities for intimate moments over the summer and he wasn't about to waste this one. Her lips tasted of bourbon and her hair smelled of wood smoke.

"Good Smoke And Whisky," he murmured as he kissed the cool, pale skin of her throat, feeling her pulse throbbing against his lips.

"Pardon?"

"An old Molly Hatchet song that my mum loved," he revealed.

"Not exactly romantic," giggled Ellen as she ran her fingers through his hair. "I love this longer hair. When we get back, don't cut it. Please."

"We'll see," he said as he delivered feathery kisses along her exposed collarbone. "I want to make love to you, my lovely."

"Here?"

"Can you think of anywhere better?"

"Another first," she giggled.

Putting his arm around her, Taylor led her across the beach and out of the moonlight. He knew there was a niche in the cliff that would afford them some privacy. In the distance, they could hear the others singing along to a Beatles classic. As they reached the narrow, sheltered spot, Taylor lifted her up. The suddenness of his actions made her squeal then giggle.

"Wrap your legs around me," he instructed her. "And hold on."

Thankful that she had worn a short sundress. Ellen wound her long, slender legs around his narrow waist. Confidently, Taylor held her with one arm around her back while he fumbled with the button fly of his jeans, eventually freeing himself from the confines of his boxers too.

Playfully, Ellen bit his neck close to the hairline then began to nibble his earlobe, knowing that was one of his weak spots.

"This isn't going to take long," he whispered as he pulled the crotch of her skimpy panties to one side.

He allowed her body weight to help him lower her onto his erect manhood, penetrating deep inside her. From the ecstasy filled moan that she emitted, he judged that Ellen was as hungry for him as he was for her. Tilting his pelvis up slightly, Taylor thrust deep and hard up into her wet depths. Her fingers were still tangled in his hair and, with each powerful thrust, she tightened her grip. Moaning softly with pleasure, Ellen savoured each of the intimate strokes, feeling her orgasm building like a summer storm. The climax came equally hard and fast, Ellen's triggered spontaneously by Taylor firing his hot, creamy load deep inside her.

"Christ, I've missed you," he groaned as he thrust hard and deep one final time. "I love you."

"Love you too," she purred, suddenly feeling spent and sleepy.

Kissing her gently first, Taylor slid himself from her then carefully lowered her down until her bare feet were safely back on the icy cold, soft sand.

"We'd better head back," he said with reluctance.

"Pity," sighed Ellen as she adjusted her panties and her dress.

Picking up the discarded blanket, Taylor draped it over her bare shoulders. "Well, I guess there's no rush."

Reaching her hand inside the open fly of his jeans, Ellen said, "No, there isn't."

As they walked back up the moonlit beach, Ellen noted that the bonfire had burned down. They could still hear gentle music but the party scene looked to be winding down.

"What time is it?" she asked.

"After three," replied Taylor, checking the time on his phone. "You feel up to one more song?"

"Maybe."

Just as they reached the cave, but while they were still out of sight of the others, they watched Jack toss a large log onto the fire. A shower of sparks flew up in the air like fireworks on Guy

Fawkes night. Beside him, Taylor felt Ellen tense up and pause.

"It's ok," he whispered softly. "You're safe."

"I know," she replied, forcing a smile. "Ghosts."

Off to the side, half in and half out of the cave, Cal lay on a blanket sound asleep. The others all had blankets and beach towels wrapped round them to ward off the chills of the dead of night.

"You ready to sing for us, little songbird?" quizzed Luke, slurring his words.

"One song," replied Ellen as she sat down on a folder blanket.

"What'll it be?" asked Tailz as he reached over to lift Cal's abandoned guitar.

"Hallelujah."

"Oh, I love that song," sighed Jen as she snuggled closer to Jack.

With a smile, Tailz started to play the delicate intro.

Her voice soft and husky, Ellen sang, "Now I've heard there was a secret chord that David played and it pleased the Lord."

It was the first time the others had heard her sing the famous ballad. Only Taylor had heard it and he couldn't help but smile as he watched the various emotions cross the faces of his bandmates and sister.

When Ellen reached the chorus, Luke surprised them all by singing a harmony that matched her vocal tone to perfection. By the light of the bonfire, the three musicians from After Life played and sang, letting the final note linger into the night.

By eight o'clock on Friday night, the hotel bar was packed. Word had spread through Mawgan Porth and further afield that there was something special on the bill for the evening. From his view of the room from the table in front of the stage, Taylor spotted three of the band's diehard fans squeezing their way through the crowds.

"Looks like word has spread," he commented to the others. "The rail queens, well, three of them just came in."

"How the fuck did they find out about this?" asked Cal, spotting the three girls by the bar.

"My guess would be that someone has let slip about this on social media," proposed Ellen, staring straight into Luke's soul.

"Or someone's been posting photos on Instagram of the area."

"Shit," muttered Luke, a wave of guilt descending. "I might have accidentally given a clue now that I think of it."

"Doesn't matter," said Taylor, taking a mouthful from his pint of cider. "It beats playing to a half empty room. We play the acoustic set as planned. Let's just enjoy this one for ourselves."

"I agree," nodded Jack. "Let's just have some fun with this tonight."

"You ready, boys?" asked Ellen calmly. "And agreed, we open with an acoustic Swirling Mists as planned."

"Just like we rehearsed," said Luke, getting to his feet. "Nana, are you ready for some acoustic rock and fucking roll?"

Drawing her eyebrows down and giving him a stern stare, the old woman said, "I'm ready for some sweet music, young man."

"He's messing with you Nana," assured Taylor, giving her a hug. "I'm just glad to see you finally made it to an After Life show."

Before she could stop him, he kissed her on the cheek then bounded up onto the low stage. His three fellow musicians joined him, leaving Ellen sitting at the table with Nana and Jen.

"Good evening, folks," called out Taylor, once the four of them were in place.

A row of wooden bar stools, of varying heights, sat across the centre of the stage while Jack was perched on the end, seated on a Cajon wooden box drum. The centre stool stood empty.

"Nice to see so many of you here," continued Taylor sincerely. "And welcome to three of our regular rail queens of the After Life."

A huge cheer drowned out what he had been about to say, prompting a fit of nervous giggles from the guitarist.

"Thank you," he said when things quietened down enough for him to be heard. "I had been about to say, can we have a bit of hush, please, and we'll make a start."

An air of calm and quiet swiftly blanketed the crowd. Allowing the silence to build, Ellen bided her time then, after a couple of minutes, she lifted the microphone that lay in front of her on the table and began the Gregorian chanted intro to Swirling Mists. Her clear vocals soared through the bar. Beside her, Nana and Jen were in awe of the transformation in her. Gone was the shy girl who sang by their chimnea at dusk. She'd been replaced by After Life's queen of the night. As she reached the final words of the opening chant, Ellen got to her feet and walked towards the stage.

Up on the small platform, the boys began the acoustic version of their standard set opener, each of them focussed on keeping it slower, calmer and softer. Ellen, too, softened the vocal, keeping her voice warm and allowing a subtle hoarseness to add the edge to the song. The band's opening number was a far cry from the performances Taylor and Ellen had delivered at past music nights. Around them, the crowd were held spellbound by the acoustic magic being spun on stage. When the song returned to the Latin chant of the outro, Ellen walked round and off the stage, returning to her seat between Nana and Jen.

The crowd erupted into a cheering frenzy that echoed round the bar for several minutes before Taylor managed to make himself heard.

"Ladies and gentlemen, let's welcome our queen of the After Life back on stage. Ellen, get up here, girl!"

Amid a fresh round of appreciative cheers, Ellen returned to the stage, taking her seat between Taylor and Cal.

"Thank you," she said, looking immediately relaxed and at ease. "This next song is Rats."

Two songs later, as the three rail queens caught Taylor's eye, a thought struck him. He was mid-solo and almost lost his concentration. With a smile, he looked to his left at Ellen. The band's leading lady was totally relaxed and comfortable on the small stage. Even though she had her purple tinted, steampunk glasses on, Tailz could tell there was a twinkle in her eye. Silently, he wondered if his bandmates had shared the same thought as him. Had any of them realised that this was the first After Life show where Ellen had not hidden herself under her cloak; had any of them noticed that, although her arm was covered by the soft sleeve of her black top, that it was the first time she hadn't hidden it from their audience.

A couple of songs further into the set, Ellen said, "This next song we've only done once at an After Life show. It was kind of dropped into the set that night as an afterthought. Got us out of a hole. Folks, this is Broken Doll."

Much to the band's surprise, Ellen stepped down from her stool, crossed the stage and headed for the bar. With a little help from Russ, who was standing at the end of the bar, Ellen climbed up and sat down. She smiled out at all the expectant faces, took a deep breath and began to sing acapella. Gradually, she sang softer and softer, drawing her audience into the lyric and ensuring an almost eerie silence fell over the room.

From his vantage point on the stage, Taylor watched the crowd's reaction. Both his twin and Nana had tears in their eyes as they hung on Ellen's every word. The three rail queens were mesmerised and many of the bar's regulars' cheeks were wet with tears.

As Ellen brought the song to an end, she remained seated on the bar, stealing a moment or two to compose herself. Around her, the small audience were totally silent for a few seconds then their cheers erupted. Without being asked, Russ stepped forward and lifted her down from the wooden counter, whispering in her ear, "Beautiful song, gorgeous. Stunning."

"Thank you," she said softly as her feet touched the floor.

As Ellen made her way back on stage, the boys had moved the piano into position and Luke was standing there waiting for her.

"Folks," began Taylor. "Now, you're in for a rare treat. Luke's about to sing the next one."

Amid more applause, Luke and Ellen sat down at the piano and began the light, fragile intro to Depths Of The Pit. Rather nervously, Luke started to sing the twisted dark tale of the grim reaper collecting children's parents, rendering the innocent souls orphans condemned to a life of purgatory. When he reached the chorus, he flashed Ellen a look almost pleading for help. She smiled then joined in with an unrehearsed harmony part. Not wanting to steal his limelight, she let him perform the second verse solo then repeated her harmonies on the chorus. Together, they sang the third and final verse then Ellen left Luke to finish the last chorus on his own.

"Thank you, princess," he whispered at the end of the song.

"Let's hear it for Mr Luke Court!" yelled Taylor theatrically. "Ellen, what's next?"

"Danse De Mort En Flammes," replied Ellen as she stepped

away from the piano.

Over two hours after they had started, After life prepared to play their final song of the evening. Pausing for a drink of water, Ellen addressed their audience one last time, "Thank you to each and every one of you for coming out tonight. Thank you to all of you who have made me feel so welcome in your community all summer. It's been a privilege to play this first un-cloaked After Life show for you. We'll leave you with one last song. This isn't usually on our set but we feel it fits for this evening. Hallelujah!"

As ever, Ellen's performance of the Leonard Cohen ballad was perfect.

With the last notes ringing out over the room a few minutes later, Taylor called, "Thank you and good night!"

Handing her mic to Cal, Ellen jumped down from the stage straight into a huge hug from Jen.

"That was breath taking!" gushed Taylor's twin sister, tears glistening in her eyes. "I don't know how you do that. It's incredible to watch."

"Glad you enjoyed it," said Ellen, feeling her cheeks flush at the compliments. "I need a drink now!"

"There's a red wine waiting for you," said Jen, giving her a final hug. "You've most definitely earned it."

Re-taking her seat between Jen and Nana, Ellen took a mouthful from her glass then turned to Nana, "Did you enjoy that?"

"Yes, I did, missy," replied the old woman, her eyes bright with the excitement of the evening. "Every second of it."

"Wasn't too loud for you, Nana?" asked Luke as he jumped down to join them.

"No, young man. It was perfect," agreed the old woman. "And now I know who's been playing my piano when I've been out."

"We both were," defended Ellen, unsure whether Nana was about to berate him or not.

"And you play beautifully together."

"Thanks," said Ellen. Before she could continue the conversation, the rest of the band appeared at the table.

The bar manager sent Russ over with a tray of drinks and once they each had a full glass, Jack proposed a toast, "To the new album and a successful future for After Life!"

"To having a real tour bus someday!" joked Cal, thinking about their beat-up mini-bus.

"To us," added Ellen. "Uncloaked and proud."

Ellen

Rain was lashing down as Taylor and Ellen walked from the bus stop to the church hall for the first pre-tour rehearsal. They'd been back from Cornwall for a week and it had rained every day. Summer and surfing and the beach suddenly seemed a million miles away. Business meetings had filled the first few days and they had spent endless long hours with their accountant and the record label suits.

The album was in the final stages of being mixed but the label was keen to select a single from the twelve tracks. After much debate, Swirling Mists was chosen and a release date of 27th September agreed.

"Afternoon," called out Jack as Tailz and Ellen clattered into the rehearsal hall cursing the rain. "Wet out?"

"Just a tad," muttered Ellen, shaking her hair. "We stood for twenty minutes in it waiting for that damn bus."

"That kettle better be on," growled Taylor. "I'm soaked through."

"Kettle's on," called through Cal from the kitchen. "But there's no milk."

"Great," snarled Taylor. "Make it coffee, black, three sugars."

"No sugar either."

"Fuck it!" yelled Taylor. "I'll go and get milk and fucking sugar!"

As the usually mild-mannered guitarist slammed the door on the way out, Luke asked, "What's up with him?"

"No idea," sighed Ellen. "He's been like that all morning. Won't talk to me."

"He'll come out of it the way he went into it," prophesised Cal. "That's what my Granny used to say."

"Wise woman your Granny," noted Ellen, accepting a mug of coffee from the guitarist. "What's the plan here?"

"To rehearse?" suggested Cal with a wink.

"Very funny. What exactly are we planning to rehearse?" asked the band's singer. "Or should we try to work out a set for the support shows?"

"We need two sets," countered Luke. "First show's a support

slot but the second is a headline show."

"Ok, so a forty-minute set and a two-hour set," observed Ellen. "Any of you got a note of the set we played in Wales? We could build on it."

"I've got it here," said Jack, organised as ever. "But, I think we need a whole new set for both shows, especially for the UK shows."

"Agreed," added Luke. "Those After Life queens of the rail will be looking for new blood."

"Right, who's got pen and paper?" asked Cal. "Ellen, you can write this down then we've at least half a chance of being able to read it back."

The four of them had almost agreed a support slot set by the time Taylor stormed back in. He clattered around in the small kitchen making his coffee before finally joining them. There was still a thunderous look on his normally placid face and the others were all relieved when he agreed with the draft set list without complaint.

It took them longer to work out their revised full set but, eventually, after an inspirational lunch of pizza and chips, they had drafted three variations of the two-hour set that saw them include all the songs that had appeared on the white board in Hades.

It was mid-afternoon before they were ready to start rehearsing the short set. Just as Ellen had finished the opening chant to Swirling Mists, the door opened and Rocky marched in.

"People, I need a minute," he called out brusquely.

"What's up?" asked Cal, laying his guitar down.

"We have a problem. An artwork problem," stated Rocky as the band gathered round. "I've spent all day with Jason but we haven't come up with a solution as yet."

"I thought you had the artwork?" challenged Luke.

"So, did we," muttered their manager sourly. "Jason's rejected the proofs and I have to agree with him. They were shit. Didn't reflect the album's title or the music or the band. He gave the artist two weeks to revise it and they've walked. Without artwork, we've had to delay the release date."

"Delay it!" exclaimed Luke sharply. "For how long?"

"A couple of months. We're aiming for 16th December now,

assuming that is, that we get suitable new artwork commissioned."

"December?" echoed Jack calmly. "Still in time for Christmas. Not great but not the biggest disaster, is it?"

"Yes and no," conceded Rocky, sounding exasperated. "Current plan is to have a six track EP pressed to sell on tour. Plain cover. Logo only. Tour exclusive. Jason wants one extra new track for it. Trying to make it collectible. I hope you folks have one up your sleeve because you're back in Hades at the weekend to record it."

"We've a couple to choose from," said Ellen without hesitation.

"Good. Best news I've heard all day," sighed Rocky, looking weary. "Jason's putting out the feelers for a new artist to complete the cover art. Thinks he can call in a favour from somewhere. I'll not lie. It'll be a challenge to get someone new on board to work to such a tight deadline. And it'll be costly."

"These things happen for a reason," mused Ellen philosophically. "Let's just focus on making this tour a success. If the fans like what they hear, then they'll buy the EP and the full-length record in December. Win, win and we recoup some of the pennies to cover the additional costs."

"Best way to look at it," agreed Jack with a resigned smile. "Doesn't impact any of the shows, does it?"

"No. Well, not for this October's tour. It could impact the plans for next year a bit but I've got to trust Jason here. He's trying to pull a couple of US tours together. If he can get them back to back, it saves travel costs. I'll keep you all posted. When I know anything, you'll know too."

"All sounds too good to be true," muttered Luke, not daring to believe that the band could tour America. "Stuff dreams are made of."

"Dreams get you started. Discipline keeps you going," quoted Ellen succinctly. "Boys, we've work to do. We need to rehearse. Need to learn a new song in four days here, plus the sets we've worked out."

"Ellen's right," said Taylor. It was the first he had spoken since lunchtime. "Let's play."

The heavenly aroma of Lizzy's curry was wafting down the hallway when Ellen and Taylor arrived back at the house.

"I'm going upstairs," muttered Taylor. "Tell Lizzy I don't need dinner."

"Tailz, you ok?" asked Ellen caringly. "What's wrong?"

"I just need a bit of space."

With a heavy heart, Ellen watched him disappear up the stairs. Hearing voices, Lizzy called out, "Dinner's ready, kids!"

As she entered the kitchen, Ellen commented, "Sorry, Lizzy, it's only me for dinner. Taylor's gone upstairs. Said to tell you he didn't need dinner."

"Taylor's turning down a chicken curry?"

"Looks that way," sighed Ellen, taking her usual seat the kitchen table. "He's been in a foul mood all day. Won't say what's wrong."

"Leave him be," suggested the older woman wisely as she dished up their meal. "Rocky's been held up at the office. He'll be late in. Just us girls for dinner."

It was a rarity for the two women to share a meal and both of them agreed it made a pleasant change. As they chatted, Ellen found herself opening up to her landlady and revealing a little more about herself, her fears and her dreams for the future. Their conversation evolved into the kind of mother/daughter chat that Ellen would've loved to share with her own mother, if their relationship had been closer.

By ten o'clock, there was still no sign of Rocky and Lizzy declared she was going to watch the news. Carefully, Ellen reheated a bowl of curry for Taylor and some homemade naan bread. She stuffed the cutlery into the back pocket of her jeans then slowly made her way upstairs, carrying the bowl with the bread balanced on top. The delicate strains of Lou Lou echoed down the hallway and, as she'd hoped, Taylor's door was ajar.

"Hey," she said softly as she nudged the door open a little further. "Hungry?"

"I guess," replied the guitarist resignedly.

"Can I come in?"

"Sure," he said, coming round to take the bowl from her. "Thanks for this."

"No worries. Couldn't see you starve."

"Sorry about earlier," he apologised awkwardly. "Been a shit day."

"Want to talk about it?" suggested Ellen as she handed him the knife and fork from her pocket.

"Jen called early this morning" he began as he sat down on the end of the bed. "My arsehole young brother has stolen money from Nana and some of my mum's jewellery from Jen. He broke into the cottage while they were out."

"Oh!"

"Jen's called the police. She heard through a friend that he's developing an expensive drug habit."

"That's not good," sighed Ellen sadly

"No, it's not," agreed Tailz quietly. "If the police catch up with him, I may need to head home to help sort this mess out."

"I'll come with you if you want. If you think it'll help," offered Ellen, hating to see him so despondent.

"Thanks. I think I need to do this one on my own. Matt has a record for possession. He's no stranger to the local police."

"Sounds like he needs help."

"He's had help in the past," Taylor confessed. "Two years' worth of help."

Their heart to heart was interrupted by the ringing of his mobile phone.

"That's Jen," he said, reaching for the handset.

"I'll leave you to it," said Ellen, stepping back into the hallway. "You know where I am if you need me."

Dawn was just creeping across the sky when Ellen felt a hand on her shoulder, rousing her gently from a deep sleep. It was Taylor.

"Sorry to waken you. I'm heading home for a couple of days. The police picked Matt up late last night. I'll call you later when I know what's happening."

"You ok?" asked Ellen sleepily.

"Not really. I'll talk to you later."

Gently, he kissed her then disappeared back out into the dark hallway.

A strong aroma of coffee welcomed the four members of After

Life into Hades first thing on Saturday morning.

"Good morning," greeted Cushy. "Ready to work your wee arses off?"

"As we'll ever be," replied Luke curtly.

"Where's the cute one? Taylor?" quizzed the producer sharply.

"Family emergency," answered Ellen. "He's had to go home for a few days."

"Well, someone's going to have to pull double duty."

"That'd be me," acknowledged Cal. "It's cool."

"Fair enough. Get set up. I'll be in the office when you're ready."

During rehearsal, the band had agreed to try a different approach for this additional song to add a new dimension to the After Life sound. After some persuading, Luke had played his new song, Zielenleed for them. Allowing his vocals to dominate, Ellen had only come in on the bridge, reprising her pulsating vocal before stunning the others by hitting and holding that top C note. The decision that Zielenleed should be the new song for the EP was unanimous.

It was late afternoon before the band were ready to call Cushy through to join them.

"Took your bloody time," he muttered sourly. "You better have something fucking special for me to work with here."

"We do," stated Ellen, an air of defiance about her. "And Luke's going to sing this one."

"Mr Court?"

"Mr Court," echoed Ellen calmly.

"Let's hear it."

Keeping the arrangement simple, After Life performed the blues influenced song, all of them watching Luke's expression, worried that this was too personal for him to perform. During the solo, when Ellen hit her top note and held it, they all saw the producer smile. That was the only signal they needed to know that they were on to a winner.

"That'll do nicely," said Cushy as the song ended. "Give me five minutes to change a few settings next door then let's try this live. I want to capture that. The vulnerability of it. Miss Lloyd, how long can you hold that note for?"

"A bit longer if need be."

"This time, hold it until Cal's done."

"I'll try."

Over the next three hours, the producer put After Life through their paces. Every time they thought they'd delivered their optimum performance of Zielenleed, he challenged them to play better. Unused to singing for such an extended length of time, Luke's voice began to suffer, adding to the frailty of the song.

"Cushy, one more and I'm done," stated Ellen bluntly. "My ribs are in agony."

"Once more from the top. If you shower don't deliver this time, I want you back in here at nine o'clock tomorrow morning."

The four members of After Life exchanged glances, then, on Jack's count, started Zielenleed again. Right from the intro, Ellen could sense a change in their delivery and knew that this was "it."

Praying that she could hold it, she hit her top C and let it flow out across the room. Her breath held; the note held strong and soared beyond the end of Cal's solo into the repeat of the intro as Luke began the final verse. As Luke sang the last line of the last chorus, on a whim, Ellen hit the note again allowing it to diminish steadily as the band played the remainder of the song.

"And there we have it, people," called through Cushy. "Done. Dusted. In the bag. Good night."

Clutching her ribs, Ellen flopped down onto the nearest chair. Taking shallow breaths, she sat with her eyes closed, waiting for the waves of pain to pass.

"You alright, princess?" asked Luke, his own voice hoarse.

Without opening her eyes, Ellen nodded.

"What can I get you?" he asked.

"Nothing," she whispered. "Take me home."

"Come to mine. It's closer," suggested the bass player.

Ellen shook her head. "Thank you but I need to go home."

"Ok" he said with a nod over to Jack. "Bring your van round. We need to get our songbird home."

Supporting her between them, Cal and Luke half carried Ellen into the house while Jack waited outside. When she saw how much pain the girl was in, Lizzy began to panic.

"Lizzy, it's ok," whispered Ellen through gritted teeth. "Help me upstairs. What I need is in my room."

"Luke, help me with her," instructed the older woman sharply. "What on earth got her into this state?"

"Cushy," replied Luke. "He's a hard task master and this is one stubborn princess."

"Hmph," snorted Lizzy. "You don't sound much better than she does!"

Once upstairs in her room, Ellen asked Lizzy to fetch her a glass of water then directed Luke to where she kept her painkillers.

"Hey," he began, reading the label. "This is morphine!"

"I know," she said through gritted teeth. "And I need two of them right fucking now."

"Ok. Ok," he replied, opening the bottle.

Without waiting for Lizzy to return with the glass of water, Ellen swallowed down the two pills.

"You sure you're ok?" checked Luke tenderly. "You look like shit."

"If it's still like this tomorrow, I'll go to A&E," promised Ellen. "I think I've torn some of the newer lung scars."

"What does that mean?"

"Pain for a few days," she replied as Lizzy returned with the water.

"That man will never learn," muttered Lizzy. "Luke, there's hot water and honey for you downstairs. Go and drink it. Cal and Jack are having a cup of tea."

Without argument, the After Life bass player nodded and left the room. As soon as he was out of sight, Ellen asked Lizzy to help her undress and to apply the prescribed painkilling ointment to her ribs. When she raised the younger woman's top up, Lizzy gasped. She hadn't seen Ellen's scars since her surgery over the summer and wasn't prepared to see them so fresh and so raw.

"Lizzy, I'm fine," assured Ellen weakly as she noted the look of shock on her landlady's face. "It looks worse than it is."

"As long as you're sure. It looks so sore."

Ellen nodded, "Right now it is but it'll be ok in a day or so. Some sleep will help."

"Should I call the doctor?"

"No. Just help me with the cream then I'm going to bed. If it's still painful in the morning, I've promised Luke I'll go to A&E."

"What on earth were you both doing today?"

"Recording an extra song for the EP," explained Ellen, wincing as Lizzy touched a tender spot with the cold cream. "We must have sung it fifty times. Luke was doing most of the vocals. My sector was at the top of my range. Too many long high notes."

"Musicians," muttered Lizzy, continuing to massage the ointment into the younger woman's delicate skin. "You never learn."

"You try saying "no" to Cushy," stated Ellen, feeling the painkillers beginning to take effect. "Eventually, I did though. We're done. Track's recorded. Next stop is the tour."

"Well, I hope you're not singing that song every night!"

"Unlikely. Maybe at the headline shows. We'll see."

A week before the tour was due to start, After Life headed back to the church hall for some final rehearsals, still minus Taylor. The guitarist had kept in close contact with the band, promising to be back in time to rehearse for the tour. To Ellen, he'd confided his fears about returning to London and leaving Jen to cope with their young brother. Keeping an eye on him was proving to be a twenty-four-seven job but remaining clean was one of the conditions of Matt's bail. The twins had him under close observation while they searched for a facility for him. When they'd arrested him, the police had recovered the stolen jewellery but Nana's cash was long gone, invested in the drugs they had found in his possession. Listening to Tailz sounding so defeated tore at Ellen's heart. His family came first. She understood that but she also knew that the band needed him back.

As she stood on the low practice stage waiting for the others to decide where they were starting, Ellen allowed her mind to contemplate what changes they'd need to make to the set if Taylor didn't make it back to the fold in time. She hadn't spoken to him for a day or so and his text messages had been minimal the day before.

"Penny for them, princess?" called out Luke, jolting her back to reality.

"They're not worth it," she replied with a smile. "Are we ready to make a start here."

"Almost," he replied. "Jack's just changing one of his drum heads then we're good to go."

"Without me?" called out a voice from the doorway.

"Tailz!" exclaimed Ellen, her relief at seeing him plain for all to see. "When? How?"

"Just now. Car," he replied, coming over to hug her.

Resting her head on his shoulder, Ellen whispered, "Lord, I'm glad you're back. I was getting worried."

"Me too," he confessed as he held her tight. "I've missed you."

"Me too."

"Right, enough of the soppy lovey dovey shit," Cal yelled over. "You here to play, Taylor, or just to snog our lead singer?"

"Both," laughed Taylor as he kissed Ellen slowly and passionately for them all to see.

Blushing, Ellen said quietly, "You maybe better get ready to play. We can finish this later."

With a nod, Taylor stepped out of their embrace and reached for his guitar cases.

"Where are we starting?" he asked as he lifted his guitar from its velvet lined hard case.

"Swirling Mists?" suggested Cal with a glance at Ellen.

"We all agreed we'll still open with it?" she checked as she switched on her mic.

Around her, the boys nodded.

"Ok. Swirling Mists."

Methodically, the band worked their way through the draft support set, pausing occasionally to debate the running order based on the guitar tunings. It was late afternoon before they were happy with it and, as soon as they stopped playing, they all realised that they were starving.

"Pub?" suggested Cal, checking the time. "I think they do food up to six."

"Not for me," said Ellen. "Maybe later. I want a clear head when we run through our full set."

"Why don't I go over to the chip shop?" offered Taylor. "Usual order?"

"Sure, if you're paying," replied Jack.

"I'll come with you," said Ellen, seeing an opportunity to get Taylor to herself for a few minutes.

Outside, there was still some warmth to the autumn sun as they walked along the street towards the chip shop.

"Did you get things sorted out for Matt?" asked Ellen as they crossed the road.

"For the next three months anyway," sighed Taylor, his voice overflowing with sorrow.

"Three months?" echoed Ellen, not quite understanding.

"Matt was in court yesterday. He was sentenced to a minimum three months in prison. They took him to Dartmoor."

"Oh no!" gasped Ellen, genuinely shocked by the news.

"It's for the best," admitted Taylor sadly, "Gives Jen and Nana peace of mind about where he is, if nothing else. Hopefully, he'll get the help he needs while he's in there." He paused before adding, "He was lucky it wasn't a longer sentence. They were lenient in the circumstances. His lawyer put forward a strong case for him, focussing on his grief for mum. Oscar winning stuff."

Ellen was surprised to hear a bitterness to his words.

"Is he still grieving?"

"I doubt it," spat Taylor angrily. "His relationship with mum turned sour years ago. If he's feeling anything, it's guilt for the shit he put her through."

"Sorry," whispered Ellen. "I never knew."

"Families," he laughed sarcastically as they reached their destination. "Got to love them. You heard much from yours?"

"Not much," she admitted. "Dad's promised to come to the show in Holland and to a few of the UK shows. He said he'd bring my mother to the London show. I'll believe that when I see it."

"I was going to ask Rocky if Jen can tag along for a few shows. Nana is going away with her church for a week. She leaves on 18th October. I was hoping Jen could meet us in Manchester."

"Sounds good to me."

"She could earn her keep." continued Taylor. "She can help out. Run errands. That kind of thing."

"Talk to Rocky," suggested Ellen. "How are her camera skills? Didn't she do a photography course at college?"

"She did," replied Taylor, seeing where Ellen's mind was going. "Leave that thought with me, my lovely. It's genius."

Rehearsals for the remainder of the week ran smoothly. Knowing that their UK tour could make or break them, After Life pulled out all the stops to ensure their choices of headline set covered all eventualities. The way their schedule had been constructed, they played three shows then had a day off before repeating the cycle three times with a final two date slot. Zielenleed only featured on one out of the three draft two-hour sets and Ellen was quick to state that she was only prepared to try it live at the shows before the rest days. Remembering the toll that recording it took on her, they were all quick to agree with her.

As they wound up the final rehearsal on Sunday afternoon, Rocky arrived unexpectedly. Dangling a set of car keys, he strolled into the church hall with a mischievous look on his weathered face.

"Boys and girl, I have a surprise for you," he called out, rattling the keys.

"What you up to, old man?" quizzed Luke, reluctant to stop the rehearsal when they still had two songs to go.

"Come outside," suggested Rocky. "It's worth it."

Like obedient children, After Life followed their manager out of the church hall. Immediately outside, a large single decker tour bus was partially blocking the road.

"What the……?" gasped Cal, gazing wide eyed at the dark grey coach.

"Your home for the next three and a half weeks," stated Rocky. "And you've Garrett to thank for it when you see him."

"Garrett?" echoed Luke with frown. "He never said."

"He wanted it to be a surprise. Looks like he succeeded."

"Who's going to drive it?" asked Jack.

"You have a designated driver," explained Rocky. "Her name's Dana. Michael's also agreed to help out with the driving. Don't you want to take a look inside?"

Inside, the bus was more luxurious than the band could have ever hoped for. The couches in the lounge were dark grey leather and there was a lighter grey, kidney bean shaped table in the middle. A small kitchen area was kitted out with the basics – a coffee machine, a microwave and a fridge. As they toured the luxury coach, Ellen counted ten bunks, plenty of space for them all. A bright red carpet ran throughout the length of the bus.

"This is fabulous!" declared Ellen, taking a seat in the lounge when they'd finished their short tour. "Makes me feel like a rock star!"

"Garrett's surpassed himself with this," stated Luke. "Wish he could join us. It's been a while since he saw the inside of one of these."

"I think his days of tour buses are over," laughed Rocky. "This is a proverbial palace compared to some the vans we travelled in back in the day."

"Beats travelling in Jack's van," commented Taylor, gazing round. "This is going to make tour life very sweet. Very sweet indeed."

"That's the plan," agreed their manager. "Now, I need all of you back here, packed and ready to go at nine a.m. sharp. We need to be in Harwich by one."

Ellen

True to form, Luke was running late next morning. Both Ellen and Taylor had arrived with Rocky, packed and ready to go not long after eight thirty. A few minutes later, Cal and Jack came walking down the road, weighed down by their bags.

"Where is he?" growled Rocky as the clock reached nine fifteen. "That boy will be late for his own fucking funeral!"

"He's on his way," said Cal, checking his phone. "Taxi never turned up."

"Hmph," muttered the band's manager. "How far away is he?"

"Five minutes."

"The minute he gets here, we leave," stated Rocky bluntly. "If we miss this ferry...."

"Rocky," interrupted Ellen quietly. "He's here. Taxi just pulled up."

The band's bass player had barely sat his gear down on the floor when they heard the door slam and the engine start.

"You're late," spat Rocky as he stormed through the bus to go and sit with Michael and the driver.

"Charming welcome," laughed Luke as he gazed after their irate manager. "Which bunk is mine?"

"Middle bunk. Second left," directed Jack. "Cal's above you."

"Where are you?"

"Top. First left. Rocky's on the bottom."

"We're straight across. Both middle bunks," added Taylor. "Michael and Dana are at the far end."

"Beats piling into that minibus we took to Wales," Luke commented as he headed off to inspect his "bedroom" for the next three weeks.

It was a two-hour drive to the ferry terminal at Harwich. After Life whiled away the time chatting about the tour, each of them voicing their hopes and fears for the various shows. Not surprisingly, Luke was the most nervous of all of them. The thought of their support slot shows wasn't phasing him but he quietly voiced his fears about his stamina for the headline shows.

"We can pace it," promised Ellen reassuringly. "I'm not too

sure how I'll hold up for that first headline show either."

"You worried about those high notes?" asked Taylor, sensing her concern.

Ellen nodded.

"We're not doing Zielenleed in Utrecht, are we?" countered Luke, hoping to reassure her.

"I've been thinking about that," began their vocalist. "Our only song with a Dutch title. We really should do it."

"Let's wait and see how we feel on the day," suggested Taylor by way of a compromise.

Within half an hour of setting foot in the ferry, Cal began to turn various shades of green in front of them. Having explored the boat, they had piled into the restaurant area in search of lunch but, after two bites of his cheeseburger, the young Scotsman fled from the table.

"Go and find him," muttered Rocky to Jack. "Make sure he's ok."

"He'll be fine," said Jack. "I'll finish this then hunt him down. He'll be puking over the side."

"Someone might have warned me he gets seasick," said Rocky. "Anyone else suffering?"

The others shook their heads and continued with their meal. As they were finishing, Cal reappeared, his complexion paler than ever.

"You ok, son?" asked the band's manager, trying and failing to sound sympathetic.

"No," replied Cal. "I feel like shit. I'll be on deck near the back of the boat if you're looking for me. I just came back for some water."

"We'll be out in a few minutes," promised Ellen, passing him an unopened bottle of water from the selection of juices in the centre of the table. "Could do with some fresh air after being on the bus."

"We'll all be out in a bit," added Jack.

"Why didn't you say you get seasick?" quizzed Rocky.

Shrugging his narrow shoulders, Cal said, "Don't know. I always get sick on boats. Used to spew every time we went to visit my auntie in Rothesay. Spew my guts up even on the calmest day."

"Good job I booked flights back from Sweden to England," stated Rocky with a sigh. "I'll bear the "no boats" rule in mind for future tours."

Prior to arriving in Amsterdam, After Life hadn't met Heritage, the headliners for the five support shows. Only Ellen and Jack had actually listened to the band and only Ellen who had seen them play live a few years before. Shyly, she confessed that her previous band, Good Times, had opened for the heavy metal maestros when they had played The Underworld in Camden on their first UK tour.

"You're a bit of a dark horse still, Miss Lloyd," commented Jack with a wink. "Any other big names you've met or played with that you haven't shared?"

"Not that I can think of," replied Ellen with a smile that said otherwise.

"Will these guys remember you?" asked Cal curiously.

"I doubt it," said Ellen. "It was all a long time ago. We only played with them once."

Next afternoon, as the boys were loading their gear into the theatre, Ellen felt a hand on her shoulder.

"If it isn't the beautiful Miss Lloyd."

Turning round, she found herself face to face with Heritage's front man, Brad.

"Long time no see, Ellen," he said, giving her a hug. "How's life with After Life?"

"Hi," she replied warmly, totally amazed that Brad had remembered her. "Things are good. Great now that we're out with you guys this week."

"Glad to have you along. Thought we'd lost you and your voice forever when Good Times disappeared," he continued. "Was pleased to hear you were back. My sister saw you at that festival in Wales. You've her to thank."

"Your sister?"

Brad nodded, "She's a journalist. She interviewed you before your set. Sent me some video of your performance and said we needed to get you out on the road with us."

"I'll need to thank her next time I see her," laughed Ellen, still somewhat in shock that Heritage's front man even remembered her.

Checking his watch, he apologised that he needed to run. "If you guys need anything see Tom our manager. We'll catch up later."

"Thanks, Brad. Appreciate it."

As she stood watching him disappear into the backstage area, Jack came over to her.

"You must have made a hell of an impression on him back then."

"Guess I did," giggled Ellen, flushing scarlet at the thought.

As show time approached, each of the members of After Life grew quieter as they went through their pre-show rituals. Apart from the acoustic show in the hotel bar back in Mawgan Porth, they hadn't been on stage for five months. All of them were nervous. A knock on their dressing room door, fifteen minutes before they were due out on stage, shattered the silence. It was Tom, Heritage's manager, with a case of beer and a bottle of red wine as a gift for them from Brad and the boys.

"Looking forward to hearing your set," he said as he handed the gifts to Jack. "Your sound check was awesome."

"Thanks. We're looking forward to hearing Heritage," replied After Life's drummer.

"Have a great night," said Tom, turning to leave. "Venue's already more than half full. Should be a good lively crowd for you."

Standing at the side of the stage a few minutes later, Ellen could hear it was a loud crowd. They were singing along enthusiastically to the PA tape. Beside her, the boys were standing calmly waiting for their cue. Nervously, she fingered the edges of her cloak as she tried to focus on keeping her breathing calm. With seconds to go, Michael handed her a microphone with a silent nod.

The PA tape stopped and the cheers of the crowd echoed back stage.

"See you on the other side," joked Taylor with an impish grin.

Breathing slowly, Ellen watched out of sight as the boys took up their positions on the dark stage as she waited for the nod from Taylor. Wisps of smoke drifted off stage towards her.

Right on cue, she began the Gregorian chanted intro to Swirling Mists. The crowd fell silent as her vocals soared out into the hall, each of them hanging on her every Latin word. Four white spotlights flashed out from the back of the stage as the smoke began to clear and the boys of After Life surged forward into the thunderous main body of the song. With a green spot following her, Ellen glided across to her mark centre front then, on impulse, crouched down in the remaining whirls of smoke to sing the first verse. The passionate reaction of the Dutch fans dispersed any remaining nerves.

Three songs in, Ellen shook off her hood to reveal her long platinum mane, then declared, "This is Rats!"

As she prowled along the front of the stage, she spotted the "rail queens" and gave them a little nod. The song was a fan favourite in the UK but Ellen was amazed to hear the Dutch fans singing along almost word perfect.

There was no staircase down from the stage so the band had positioned three transport cases for Ellen to use to get down into the photography pit to allow her to roam along the rail during Taylor's guitar solo. Carefully, she jumped down from the lowest one and began her journey along the front row, pausing for the occasional fan photo.

Getting back up onto even the lowest of the black trunks proved challenging in her cloak but Ellen was rescued by two of the security staff who helped her up. She only just made it back to her spot in time to sing the final verse.

"Thank you!" she called out to the crowd. "Our debut album is due out in December. Just for this tour, we've produced a limited-edition EP that's available at our merch table. This next song is on that EP. This is Flesh To Ashes!"

The remainder of their set flew by in a flash and before any of them knew it, they were playing their standard set closer, Smoke On The Water.

As she stood in the wings with a bottle of water, Ellen watched the crowd as the boys finished off the classic song. Judging by the reaction of the by now capacity crowd, this tour was off to a great start.

Forty-eight hours later, Ellen stood at the side of another stage, a smaller stage, at the Tivoli Vredenburg in Utrecht. The music complex had multiple halls and, despite originally booking the four hundred capacity Cloud Nine room, they had been moved up to the Hertz room and had sold it out. Looking out at the room full of After Life fans was an incredible sight. She could see their "rail queens" in position centre front but noted that there was someone else in the middle of them. Straining to see in the dim light, Ellen burst out laughing when she discovered who it was.

"What's so funny?" asked Tailz, looking out from behind her. He paused then said, "Is that your dad in between the rail queens?"

"It sure is," giggled Ellen. "I can't wait to hear how he ended up in the middle of them!"

When she made her entrance on stage a short while later, Ellen walked out singing the final notes of the Gregorian chant. As the spotlights flashed around her, on a mischievous whim, she crouched down in the smoke and hissed menacingly at her dad and the die-hard fans surrounding him before powering her way into the first verse. The gesture wasn't lost on him as he blew her a kiss from behind the rail.

"Good evening, beautiful people of Utrecht!" screamed Ellen at the end of the opening trio. "Are you ready for a voyage into the After Life?"

A huge roar from the sell-out crowd drowned her out.

"I said, are you ready?" she roared once more.

Behind her Taylor and Cal approached and removed her cloak with a theatrical flourish. They had agreed that Ellen would perform uncloaked for most of the show. Underneath it, she wore skin tight, black, leather leggings and a black and purple bustier to with elbow length, lace sleeves, just long enough to cover her arm. "This next song is Cyclone!"

After Life had barely begun the hard and heavy number before they saw a mosh pit open in the centre of the room. Watching it morph into a circle pit, as the song progressed was mesmerising. Either side of her, Ellen sensed the band's guitarists keeping a close eye on it, ever mindful that these things could quickly flare up and out of control. Along the rail, the fans, including her dad, were headbanging in unison.

Immediately after City Of Bones And Heartache, mid-set, the lights dimmed momentarily to allow Michael to wheel out the transport case. Ellen seized the opportunity to swap her eye patch for her tinted steampunk glasses. Two white spotlights were trained onto the transport case as she and Taylor took their seats.

"Folks, this song is just a little bit special to us. This is the first song Taylor and I wrote together a few months back."

A knowledgeable cheer went up around them.

"This is Lou Lou At 3am."

Every voice in the room joined in as Ellen sang the ballad. With a smile to Taylor and a nod, she let the fans sing the final verse for her, joining them again for the last chorus. Both members of After Life could feel goosebumps tingling at the magic of the moment. From the side of the stage, the rest of the band were watching and much to his surprise Tailz spotted Garrett standing beside Luke.

"Thank you. That was beautiful," said Ellen, getting to her feet at the end of the song.

One of the spotlights went out and the other followed her to the edge of the stage. In the darkness behind her, the transport case was trundled off stage. Taking her time, Ellen sat down on one of the wedge speakers and gazed out across the sea of faces before her. Deliberately, she had walked to the side, not wanting to sing the next song in direct view of her father.

She took a deep breath then said simply, "Broken Doll."

Pouring her emotions into the acapella song, Ellen drew strength from the reaction of the fans in front of her. Singing that particular song was never easy for her but singing it knowing her dad was only a few feet away was harder than she'd anticipated. Her own emotions were threatening to overwhelm her as she saw some of the fans wiping tears from their eyes. She only just made it to the end of the song before tears flowed unbidden down her own cheeks. Allowing the applause from the fans to envelop her, Ellen sat with her head bowed as her bandmates returned to the stage.

"Folks, give it up for the incredibly talented Ellen Lloyd!" bellowed Taylor proudly.

In a move away from their norm, After Life had decided to do an encore for their headline shows. Choosing a song to round off the main set had caused a debate amongst them during pre-tour rehearsals but they had eventually all agreed on one song, Beyond The Edge Of Reality.

Taking a bow at the end of the song felt a little unnatural to Ellen, who was so accustomed to ending the show off stage, and, for those few moments, she allowed herself to enjoy the fans' adulation.

Once in the wings, Rocky thrust a bottle of juice towards her as Garrett stepped forward to embrace her.

"Breath taking performance, angel," he said, kissing her sweaty cheek. "Mind blowing."

Around them, they could hear the fans pleading for their return to the stage. Chugging down a few mouthfuls of the energy drink, Ellen tried to compose herself. To her left, she could see that Luke seemed suddenly anxious as he watched the piano being wheeled on stage.

"Ready, princess?" he asked, looking far from ready himself.

"As I'll ever be," she replied, handing the juice bottle back to Rocky. "Let's do this!"

Deafening cheers and whistles embraced After Life as they returned to the stage. While the boys sorted themselves out and Luke settled himself at the piano, Ellen addressed the crowd, "Thank you. This is a first for us, so be gentle with us. If you've bought our EP, this next song is on it and won't be on the album when it comes out in December. This is the first time we've attempted this one live. It could prove interesting."

The crowd cheered enthusiastically.

"I'd like to introduce the band to you. On guitar we have, Cal McDermid. On lead guitar, Taylor Rowe. Back there on drums, Jack Smart, and on bass and now on piano, Luke Court." She paused. "This is Zielenleed."

It didn't escape her sharp attention that the cheers for Tailz and Luke were just a little louder and a little longer than those for Jack and Cal.

As the applause died away, Luke started the blues based piano intro. One by one, the others came in on cue as Ellen stepped out of the spotlights towards the back of the stage. In the shadows, she smiled proudly as Luke sang about his close encounter with death, about how he almost destroyed himself and his relationships. There was a raw frailty to the chorus that focused on the agonies that his soul had endured.

The end of the second chorus was Ellen's cue to come in with her slow, pulsating vocal. A blue spotlight held her in its beam as she gradually slowed the pulse down then hit her top C and held it while Cal executed his short frantic, panic stricken solo. Cal's last note rang out as Ellen allowed her note to diminish then she began the pulse effect again, quickening the beats until Luke came back in on piano to perform the last verse.

This last verse was almost drowned out by the roar of appreciation from the capacity crowd.

"Give it up for Mr Luke Court!" roared Taylor over the cheers at the end of the song "And let's hear it for the awesome Miss Ellen Lloyd!"

"Now for a bit of fun," said Ellen. "This is a brand new one. This is Smugglin' Lovin' Blues!"

It was almost with relief, a few minutes later, that Ellen began to sing Smoke On The Water, their final song of the night. With a last lingering look out over the Dutch audience, she waited for her cue to "disappear", leaving the boys to finish off the show.

Standing in the wings with the remains of her energy drink, Garrett was the first to reach her to congratulate her on an incredible show. When the boys finally joined them, the older musician assumed the father figure role, hugging and congratulating each of them.

"Right, kids, get cleaned up," he said. "Get the gear packed up. I'm taking you all out for dinner."

"Too kind, Garrett," commented Rocky.

"Least I can do is feed these kids before you drive to Cologne."

"There's someone I need to fetch first," said Ellen.

"Who?" quizzed Garrett.

"My dad," she explained. "He was in the crowd. On the rail centre front."

"I was watching that guy. He's your dad?"

Ellen nodded, "Sure is."

"Then go fetch him and bring him to dinner, angel!"

Midnight had come and gone before the After Life contingent were finally seated in a local Asian-fusion restaurant. Using his powers of persuasion, Garrett had convinced them to stay open for an extra couple of hours just for them. The band had pushed two of the tables together to create one long table and were all talking at once about the show. Sitting between her father and Taylor, Ellen allowed the conversation to buzz around her. She could hear her dad chatting easily to Garrett as if they were old friends and smiled.

"You ok, my lovely?" asked Taylor quietly as the waiters delivered a selection of sushi platters to the table.

"Couldn't be better," she replied. "Look round."

Glancing around the table, Taylor drew her a puzzled look. "What am I looking at?"

"This," said Ellen. "We've just played a sell-out show. We've four support slots to play before a headline tour. Our record's due out in about ten weeks. And my dad's sitting chatting away to one of his idols as if they'd been friends forever. If this is as good as it gets then I'm happy."

"Guess you're right," agreed Taylor, following her logic with a grin. "Put it that way and it is pretty special."

There was a chill in the air when they left the restaurant in the small hours. Upon hearing that they were travelling through the night to Germany, the restaurant staff had boxed them up some sushi, spring rolls and tempura for the journey. The manager even threw in a couple of bottles of sake.

"You were awesome out there tonight," said Tim Lloyd, holding Ellen in his arms. "I am so proud of you."

"Thanks, Dad," she replied, resting her cheek on his chest. "I'm glad you were there."

"Me too," he said warmly. "I've booked a week off work so that I can see some of the UK shows too."

"Which ones?"

"I'll meet you in Manchester and follow you to the end, if that's ok?"

"Perfect," sighed Ellen, delighted to hear he'd be there. "We'll find you a bunk on the bus."

"Is there room?"

"Yes," she assured him. "Taylor's sister is joining us there too. You'll like Jen."

"Look forward to meeting her."

"Tim!" called out Garrett, interrupting their farewell. "Fancy a night cap?"

"Eh…. sure," replied Ellen's dad, still a little star struck. Softly he whispered to her, "Pinch me. Am I really going for a drink with Garrett Court?"

"Yes, Dad, you are," giggled Ellen. "Don't enjoy it too much. You've a flight to catch at lunchtime."

"I know. I'll behave," he promised. "Now, I'll see you in Manchester. Safe travels till then, honey."

As her dad stepped aside, Garrett stepped forward to say his goodbye.

"Incredible show, angel," he said, kissing her on the cheek. "I said to Luke I'd try to make it back for the London show. No promises though. It depends on how things are at home."

"Thanks for being here and for dinner," said Ellen, hugging him closely. "And thanks for taking my dad for a drink too."

"Pleasure," he replied warmly. "Nice guy. I'll see he gets safely back to his hotel too."

"Thanks," giggled Ellen, "Now, I'd best get on the bus before they leave without me."

"Travel safe."

Life for After Life over the next ten days was a whirlwind of travelling, press commitments, soundchecks and shows. In Germany, the audience had taken the band to their hearts, with Luke finding himself badged as the band's heart throb. His band mates teased him relentlessly until they reached their final stop in Stockholm. There, it was Cal who attracted the female attention. One group of local fans were fascinated by his long red hair. Much to the amusement of the others, he was exceedingly uncomfortable in the spotlight.

On stage over the four shows, After Life honed their set to perfection. They deviated from their original plan, seizing the opportunity to try one new song per night to gauge what the fans liked and perhaps didn't care for so much. For their final support slot in Sweden, they added Zielenleed into the set for the first time since the Utrecht show. All in all, the reaction from the crowd across the three countries was positive, fuelling After Life's motivation ahead of their UK tour.

Ellen

It was a mild sunny October Saturday morning when their bus pulled up outside The Globe in Cardiff for their first headline show. Having enjoyed a leisurely day off back in London the day before, they had hit the road before breakfast time to ensure they arrived at the venue for a midday load in. While the boys were hauling the gear into the venue, Ellen was despatched to a nearby juice bar to pick up some lunch.

As she was making her way back up the street, she saw someone entering the venue. The figure looked vaguely familiar but, from so far away, she couldn't decide who it could be. Logically, she fathomed that it had to be the local journalist who was scheduled to meet with them. Earlier in the week, they had received an email from a local university student asking to interview the band for the university's rock club newsletter. They were due to meet some local newspaper journalists after their sound check but the band had unanimously agreed to give the student some time around lunchtime.

"Lunch, guys!" she called out as she strolled back into The Globe.

"About time!" yelled back Cal. "I'm starving!"

Up on the stage, Taylor was deep in conversation with the stranger that Ellen had seen enter the building ahead of her.

"Is that the guy from the uni?" she asked Cal as he jumped down to take the bags from her.

"Aye," he replied. "He's a guitarist and was asking Tailz about his rig."

"What's the plan?" asked Ellen, following Cal back towards the stage.

"Eat and talk," he answered. "We're tight on time to get set up."

"Fair enough."

As Ellen climbed up onto the stage, Tailz and the student turned to face her.

"Ellen," began Taylor. "This is...."

"Alex!" shrieked Ellen.

"Ellen!" exclaimed the student, almost as shocked to see her as she was to see him.

"You two know each other?" guessed Taylor, looking confused.

"From way back," revealed Ellen with a warm smile. "Alex and I played together. He was the guitarist for Good Times."

"Guilty as charged," acknowledged Alex slightly sheepishly. "Although, I don't play much now. Too busy studying."

"I didn't realise you'd gone back to uni," said Ellen. "How long's it been since we caught up?"

"About four years, I think," replied her former bandmate. "I'm in third year. Studying Law."

"Law?"

Alex nodded, "Bit of a change of direction from Good Times."

"Just a bit," laughed Ellen. "So, you're here to interview us?"

"Yeah. I run the university's rock club and write a monthly newsletter. I didn't realise you were back out on stage though," he explained. "How are things with you? You ok? Healthwise I mean."

"Better than the last time we met, that's for sure," replied Ellen evasively. "So, what's your plan for this interview? Want to chat out here or are we heading back to the dressing room?"

"Need to be out here," said Jack firmly. "There's still a shit load to sort out up here."

A few minutes later, the five members of After Life were sitting on various transport cases, munching on their baguettes, as Alex prepared to start the interview. Shuffling through his sheaf of question sheets, he began by asking if this was the band's first headline show in Wales.

"I guess it is," replied Taylor. "We headlined in one of the tents at the Open Air festival back in May. This is the start of our first major UK headline tour. Until now, it's been bars and small clubs we've played up and down the country. We did a few shows in London not long after Ellen joined us but this is our first big tour."

"You've supported Heritage and Bodimead this year. How was it playing with those guys?"

"A bit daunting at first," confessed Ellen. "They were great with us though. Really supportive. We all learned a lot from watching them too."

"Ellen, has it been tough coming out as the new vocalist this year and the first female After Life vocalist, if my research is correct?"

"Yes and no," she replied, stalling for some thinking time. "It's never easy filling another vocalist's shoes. The boys have been great though. We had a few teething problems at the start till we got to know one another but they've got used to having a girl out front."

"After Life isn't the first band you've fronted though. How did it feel getting back out there in front of a crowd?"

"A bit overwhelming," confessed Ellen. "You know what happened with Good Times. You were there in Thailand so you saw the mess I was in after that. It took time to heal and recover. I hadn't been on stage in over five years when I got the job with After Life so there was an element of fear there. A bit of panic about whether I could still do it."

"I've not had the pleasure of seeing you guys live yet but my girlfriend keeps telling me how awesome you are in concert," revealed Alex. "Jilly follows you all over the place. She was in Holland and Germany a week or so ago. Christ, she even drove all the way to Cornwall to see you play in a bar."

"Rail queen," commented Luke with a wink.

"Has to be," agreed Tailz.

"Rail queen?" echoed Alex, looking confused.

With a laugh, Ellen explained that they'd nicknamed the core group of diehard fans the "rail queens".

"Wait till she hears that!" laughed Alex.

"We're very grateful to them," said Ellen quietly. "It's quite comforting to see a few familiar faces. They even had my dad among them in Holland. He loved it!"

Gradually, Alex steered his questions onto the band's music and forthcoming debut album. Using his charm, he teased some behind the scenes tails from them as Jack apologised that they'd need to get back to work. Alex asked Ellen if she'd spare him some more time to talk about her return after the accident in Thailand. With Rocky's blessing, she suggested that they continue the interview in the coffee shop across the street. Promising to be back before three, Ellen followed Alex out of the venue.

The small coffee shop was quiet when they entered and Ellen was grateful that her friend chose a discrete corner table to continue the interview at. Once the waitress had delivered their coffees plus a panini for Alex, he began by asking Ellen how she coped as the leading lady of After Life considering her disability.

"Subtle, Alex," she muttered. "I'll be honest, I don't appreciate being labelled as "disabled". No physically challenged person likes being labelled. However, I can't deny my limitations."

She paused, giving him a few seconds to apologise and rephrase the question.

"I'll break my answer down into three parts," began Ellen, staring down into the depths of her coffee cup. "If we start with my eyesight. I'm virtually blind in my right eye. I only see shadows with it but its hyper sensitive to light. That brings one set of challenges so I usually solve that one with an eye patch or occasionally my tinted glasses. Initially, the scars on my ribs caused a few issues with breathing and stamina. I've had treatment over the summer to loosen off some of the thicker scars so hopefully things with be easier. My cloak disguises my arm."

"Do you keep that cloak on for the full show?"

"Most of the time," replied Ellen. "It's a self-confidence thing. With my cloak draped round me, the fans don't see that I'm missing part of my arm. I have played a couple of shows where I've taken it off after a few numbers. Sometimes that decision is driven by the heat on stage. Sometimes it is down to self-confidence. Down to how I feel at that moment in time."

"How hard was it getting back out there after the tragedy in Thailand?"

Ellen paused for thought for a moment or two before answering, "It was tough. Very tough at times. There was so much to adjust to after Thailand. Not just the physical injuries but mentally too. The loss. The grief. Facing up to the fact I can't play any more wasn't easy. For the first two years, I couldn't sing. Wouldn't sing. Then, gradually, things began to improve. My confidence began to recover slowly. My self-belief. I worked with a vocal coach and my physio to get my breathing right and to retrain my body and my voice. About a year ago, I started to re-launch my career. There were a few rough knock backs then After Life placed their faith in me."

"How did it feel performing live with them for the first time? That first time back out on stage after everything?"

"Positively terrifying!"

"I'm coming to tonight's show. What can I expect?"

"Some damn good music!" laughed Ellen. "I'll let you judge for yourself."

"You used to write a lot of Good Times' material. Do you write much for After Life?"

Ellen nodded, "I've brought my fair share to the band. I've collaborated with Taylor and with Luke mainly. We all chip our tuppence worth in."

"Do you still keep your lyrics journal with you at all times?" asked Alex curiously.

Smiling, Ellen reached for her blue hobo bag and pulled out her leather-bound journal. "Always.".

The two friends chatted about the various songs Ellen had contributed to the band's set, discussed the album and what fans could expect from it. Just as they were finished their coffee, Ellen's phone vibrated on the table beside her. It was a message from Tailz saying they were waiting for her and were ready to start soundcheck.

"I need to go. Boys are waiting for me," apologised Ellen, slipping her phone back into her bag.

"Of course. It's been great talking to you. Great catching up," said Alex awkwardly. "Do you have any final words of wisdom for any budding rock stars in the uni?"

"Believe in yourself," said Ellen simply, as she got to her feet. "I hope you enjoy the show later. Hang about at the end. We can grab a drink or two."

"Thanks. I'd like that."

As she stood in the wings waiting for her cue to start Swirling Mists, Ellen could see Alex standing on the rail beside the "rail queens", wearing an After-Life t-shirt. It felt a bit surreal seeing her former bandmate in the audience. For a moment, she allowed herself to think back to playing with Good Times, lingering on the loss of her boyfriend and bandmate in the disaster. With a wistful sigh, she re-focussed her attention on the show ahead of her. The houselights were already out and the band were in position on the stage. Taking a calming breath, Ellen allowed her clear, strong vocals to soar over the crowd. This show was going to be special.

With the last Latin note hanging in the air at the end of the song, Ellen stepped back to Tailz and Cal to whisper, "Move Rats up to fourth on the list. City of Bones next. Change of plan."

Nodding, the two guitarists subtly moved off to spread the word to their rhythm power houses.

In a change to her usual routine, Ellen not only shook off her hood three songs in, she unfastened her cloak, allowing it to cascade from her shoulders onto the stage. Underneath, she was wearing a skin tight, black leather catsuit with an ornate jewelled belt slung low on her hips. The jewels were also studded across and down the heels of her stiletto boots.

"Cardiff, how the hell are you tonight?" she screamed.

The thunderous roar that came straight back at her suggested that they could do better.

"Cardiff!" she hissed menacingly. "Are you ready to enter the After Life?"

A louder roar surged back at her.

Crouching down and surveying the fans along the front rows, Ellen hissed again then screamed, "I said are you ready to enter the After Life?"

The wall of noise that hit her confirmed that the fans were ready. Gracefully, Ellen stood up, focused her gaze on the centre front row and in a cold, eerie voice said, "Rats!"

Filled with a new-found confidence, Ellen roamed the stage during the first two verses of Rats before signalling to Tailz that she was going down into the pit during his solo. As the guitarist stood in the spotlight for his solo, Ellen ran down the steps at the side of the stage ready to prowl along the rail. The fans waylaid her more than usual and she mis-judged her return to the stage. Thinking on her feet, Ellen stopped in front of the rail queens and Alex, climbed onto the step on her side of the rail and stood there to sing the final verse.

In front of her, the fans were in awe of her performance. Acutely aware of the mobile phones and cameras focused on her, Ellen dug deep to deliver the complex vocals. Between the verse and chorus, she seized the opportunity to run along the rest of the pit, making it back on stage just in time to deliver the final chorus.

At the end of the main set, as the band gathered in the wings, Ellen announced that she wanted to do Broken Doll to start the encore.

"You ready to go out there alone to do it?" challenged Luke calmly, concerned that it was too much for her.

Ellen nodded.

"Go for it, girl," encouraged Jack with a wink. "Then Tailz goes out for Lou Lou and we'll follow for Smoke On The Water. Drop Phoenix."

"How are we for time?" asked Cal with a glance at Rocky. "We got time to leave it in?"

Their manager nodded, "If Ellen gets out there right now."

"I'm gone," she said, taking a last chug on her water bottle.

A single blue spotlight was trained on Ellen as she stood alone in the centre of the stage. Around her, the crowd was murmuring, whispering, and there was an electrified air of anticipation.

"This is Broken Doll," introduced Ellen with a smile towards her friend in the front row. "Alex, this is for you."

Composing herself, Ellen elected to sing a softer, warmer version of the acapella song. Her emotions threatened to spill over into the lyrics as she sang the highly personal song for Alex. There may have been hundreds of pairs of eyes on her but she was focused on watching her former band mate throughout. The gesture wasn't lost on him and he blew her a kiss as the song came to an end.

"Thank you," said Ellen softly. "Now, I'd like to welcome Mr Taylor Rowe back out on stage."

Behind her, the transport case was wheeled into position as Tailz followed it out on stage.

"Cardiff, give it up for the incredible Queen of the After Life, Ellen Lloyd!" called out Taylor as she took a dramatic bow. "Folks, this is the first song we wrote together late one night. This is Lou Lou At 3am."

As she "vanished" from the stage and stood in the shadows of the wings, Ellen accepted the open bottle of Lucozade gratefully from Rocky.

"That was some show," commented the band's manager. "Deliver like that every night and I can die a happy man."

"You're not allowed to die, Rocky," giggled Ellen.

"How much of that was to impress your old boyfriend?" he quizzed with more than a hint of cynicism.

"None of it. I needed to do that for me," replied Ellen then conceded, "Maybe chatting to Alex reminded me of what else I still had in me to give out there."

"Whatever it was, it worked. You are one talented songbird."

"Thanks," she said, giving him a hug. "I'm an exhausted songbird right now."

Five shows, in six days, in five cities, spread across the remaining three countries of the UK, took their toll on all of the members of After Life. Each night they had mixed up the set a bit and, as agreed, added Zielenleed to the shows in Liverpool and Newcastle. The fans reaction to it on both nights prompted a late-night debate on the road to Manchester about whether to add it in for each of the remaining five shows. Eventually, they decided to add it to the growing set list. When they reviewed the list, the band discovered they were now at nineteen songs and would be pushing the curfew time for each show.

The bus had parked up at a truck stop a few miles outside of Manchester to allow the band to sleep. A mix up with dates and timings had left Rocky frantically phoning round to book hotel rooms for them for the next night, as he cursed himself for forgetting the band had a day off in the city. It was almost lunchtime before any of the band members stirred from their bunks. The first to rise, as usual, was Jack and the noise of him getting the coffee started soon wakened the rest of them. As the days of living in such close proximity to one another had passed, Ellen had become less self-conscious about the band seeing her without her glasses and about keeping her arm covered. Wearing only a vest top and shorts, she was next to stumble sleepily into the lounge.

"Coffee's hot!" called out Jack from his reclined position on the couch. "Cal's gone across to the café to get rolls or something for breakfast."

"Any orange juice left?"

"Think there's some in the fridge."

"Orange juice before coffee," muttered Ellen as she rummaged in the small fridge in search of the carton.

"Mornin'," mumbled a sleepy sounding Taylor from behind her. "Save some of that for me."

Shaking the carton, Ellen concluded there was enough for both of them.

"You pour the coffee. I'll pour the juice," she proposed, smiling at how much like a sleepy little boy he looked.

"Deal."

The last to appear, over an hour later, was the band's manager. He wandered through from the front of the bus looking triumphant.

"Hotel booked. Parking sorted. We're good to go," he declared.

"Go where though?" quizzed Luke cynically. "You better not have booked us into a flea pit, old man."

"Would I ever?" protested Rocky.

"We all remember that hotel in Sheffield two years ago!" stated Jack coldly.

"Yeah, ok," conceded Rocky, recalling the band competition to see who had sustained the most bug bites. "I've booked us into the Travel Lodge beside Manchester Arena. A mate of mine works at the arena. He's agreed that we can park the bus there today as long as we're clear of the yard by tomorrow at eleven."

"Did you book rooms for Jen and my dad?" asked Ellen. "They're arriving today."

"Yes, I did."

"When can we check in?" Taylor asked. "I really need a shower."

"Any time after two," replied Rocky. "Ten minutes and we pull out of here."

Late afternoon, Ellen and Taylor lay wrapped in each other's arms, watching cartoons on Taylor's laptop. When they'd finally checked into the hotel, they had shared a long, hot shower then lingered over their afternoon lovemaking, relishing having some privacy after several nights on the bus. On the table beside the bed, Ellen's phone buzzed.

"Shit!" she exclaimed. "What time is it?"

"Half four."

Glancing at the phone's screen, Ellen swore again, "My dad's downstairs."

Checking his own phone, Taylor muttered, "Fuck. Jen's been calling."

"Where is she?" asked Ellen as she wriggled free from the duvet.

"Eh.... downstairs with your dad," he confessed. "Says they're having a beer."

"Guess we'd better head down and face the music," said Ellen as she pulled on a hot pink lace thong.

"No rush," commented Taylor with a wink. "I haven't inspected those panties before. New, are they?"

"Taylor!" squealed Ellen as he reached out and pulled her back into bed.

Four empty beer bottles sat on the table in front of Jen and Tim Lloyd when Tailz and Ellen finally walked into the bar/bistro on the hotel's ground floor. They looked deep in conversation as the two members of After Life approached hand in hand.

"Sorry," apologised Taylor as they reached the table. "We fell asleep. Been a long week."

"And dressed in a hurry," commented his twin sister as she got to her feet to hug him. "Your T-shirt is on inside out."

Blushing, Taylor wrapped his arms around her and held her tight as he whispered, "Not much privacy on a tour bus."

Beside them, Ellen and her dad were greeting each other with hugs.

"You look tired," commented Tim Lloyd softly as he looked on his daughter with fatherly pride.

"Life's been busy," replied Ellen with a smile. "Good busy. Tour's been great."

"As long as you're not taking too much out of yourself."

"Dad, relax. I'm fine," she said warmly then, changing the subject, asked, "Now, what does a girl need to do to get a drink around here?"

"Allow me," offered Jen, reaching for her bag. "Shiraz?

Cider?"

"Please," said the two musicians in unison.

Over their drinks, Ellen and Taylor talked about the highs and the occasional low of the tour so far. Briefly, they laid out the itinerary for the next week and explained about the band rules as dictated by Jack for the "Do's and Don'ts" while on the bus.

"Did you remember your cameras?" Taylor asked his sister.

"Of course," she replied, feigning indignance. "I even bought a new lens for my Nikon."

"Well, consider yourself appointed official photographer for the rest of the tour," declared Ellen. "There have been a few guys in the pit each night but we've restricted them to the standard first three songs. Rocky's arranged a full all access pass for you. Hopefully, we'll be able to use some of your shots on our website and social media pages."

"No pressure on me then," giggled Jen a little nervously.

"Just have fun," advised Taylor, sensing her nerves. "Tim, how do you feel about being Mr Merchandise?"

"I'd be honoured."

Over the next six days, After Life were riding on a high as they performed to packed rooms across the country. The addition to their crew of Jen and Tim Lloyd had added to the camaraderie. On their day off in Birmingham, Cal disappeared for a few hours returning with two T-shirts each for Jen and Tim. He presented them to them over dinner amid much hilarity. Across the front of the black shirts, he'd had the band's logo applied and underneath, in childish script, the word "crew". On the backs, in the same childish scrawl, they read "Tailz's Twin" and "Ellen's Dad". The welcoming gesture wasn't lost on them and Rocky quipped, "Don't even think about getting Lizzy one!"

"It'd need to say Boss's Boss," teased Ellen as he glowered at her.

"Just don't even think about it, Miss Lloyd!" he cautioned with a twinkle in his eyes. "I'd never hear the end of it."

The good vibes continued as they left the stage in Birmingham, the following night, after another successful set.

"Boys and girl," declared Rocky when he entered the dressing room. "London's a sell out!"

"Pardon?" echoed Luke as he rubbed himself down with a towel. "Sold out? We've sold out in London?"

"Yes, we have," confirmed Rocky grinning. "Last night of the tour's going to be a big night."

"No pressure then," laughed Taylor, taking a long chug on his bottle of cider.

With their load in completed in record time, Rocky called the band together in the dressing room for a quick meeting. While the boys, along with Ellen's dad, had been carrying everything in, Jen had been sent on a mission to find them some lunch. She'd excelled herself by returning with the best pizzas they had ever tasted from a nearby Italian restaurant.

"Last show of the tour, boys and girl. Let's make this one count," began Rocky as he helped himself to another slice of pepperoni from the huge flat box on the table. "I have some possible good news on the artwork front at last."

"Halle-fucking-lujah!" exclaimed Luke loudly. "Thought we were going to have to do it ourselves."

"Don't joke, Mr Court," cautioned the band's manager. "If this final attempt fails then that is exactly what you'll be doing."

"So, what's the good news then, boss?" asked Taylor calmly.

"Jason has high hopes for this debut so he has decided to invest a little more capital in the venture. The success of the tour has helped sway this somewhat. He's approached Mz Hyde about designing your album cover."

"Mz Hyde?" echoed Ellen incredulously. "The same Mz Hyde that did the Weigh Station covers?"

"The very same."

"I love her work!" gushed After Life's vocalist. "She creates so much depth to her covers. Have you seen the Silver Lake Impossible Depths cover? I love that imp that she came up with. He's amazing."

"Good album that," added Jack casually. "I was listening to it last night."

"I love it," agreed Ellen with a nod. "Loved their first one too."

"That leads me onto my second bit of news," interrupted

Rocky. "My old mate, Jethro Steele, manages Silver Lake. He's in town just now with a couple of the members of the band and Mz Hyde. I've invited them along tonight."

"You've what?" shrieked Ellen shrilly.

"I spoke to him earlier. Suggested, if they've no plans for this evening, that they come down here."

"Fancy your chances of a duet with their front man, princess?" teased Luke, knowing full well how much she admired Jake Power, the American band's front man.

"I'd be too nervous. I couldn't."

"You could," said Rocky with confidence. "And you might just get the opportunity to."

"Oh shit," giggled Ellen nervously. "Well, if it helps to get Mz Hyde on side to design our cover, I'll do it."

"It's all only a big "if" right now," cautioned their manager, trying to keep their expectations realistic. "Let's just focus on the show tonight. We want to end this tour on a high note."

Buoyed by the excitement, After Life set up and sound checked without a hitch. Early afternoon, a courier dropped off a fresh pressing of the band's EP to sell at the show. Thinking on his feet, Ellen's dad had suggested that the band sign a couple of hundred and date them, adding to their collectability. Rocky loved the idea and Jen was sent shopping yet again, this time in search of permanent marker pens.

While the local support act set up and sound checked, After Life sat in the dressing room autographing two hundred and fifty CDs. The repetitive task helped to keep their growing nerves at bay. Seizing the chance to publicise things, Jen took a few candid photos and shared them online.

With the discs all signed and on display at the merchandise table, the band settled down in the dressing room to while away the remaining time. Quietly, Ellen slipped away with Jen to get ready for the show. The thought of the members of Silver Lake and Mz Hyde being in the audience had added to her growing nerves. She confided in Jen that she didn't want them seeing her arm and stated firmly that she'd keep her cloak on for the full set. Despite her best efforts, Taylor's twin failed to dissuade her from the plan.

Hearing American voices echoing down the narrow corridor

from the main dressing room, Ellen took one last glance in the cracked mirror then turned to Jen, "I think our guests have arrived."

"Sounds like it. You ready?"

"As I'll ever be."

When Ellen stepped into the room, it took her all her time not to let out a gasp. Both Jake Power and Rich Santiago from Silver Lake were standing there, deep in conversation with Taylor and Cal. To one side, Rocky was chatting to another man, with the longest white plait she had ever seen, and a young woman, who was leaning heavily on a walking stick.

"Darling!" called out Rocky in an overly theatrical voice. "We have rock royalty in our midst."

His booming voice, obviously aimed to impress their guests, caused the two Silver Lake musicians to turn around. Trying not to blush, Ellen observed that Jake Power was even hotter in the flesh than the photographs in the music magazines had alluded to.

"Ellen," continued Rocky, seemingly oblivious to her shyness. "Let me introduce you to Jake Power and Rich Santiago from Silver Lake, their manager and my old mate, Jethro Steele, and the beautiful Mz Hyde."

Taking a step towards her, Jake extended his hand and flashed her a dazzling, tanned smile.

"Nice to meet you," said Ellen, her voice quiet and nervous. "I was listening to your new album on the bus this morning. Love the vocals on Depths and adore Mysteries."

"Thank you," replied Jake, blushing at her kind words. "You have me at a disadvantage I'm afraid."

Ellen smiled then, before nerves got the better of her, turned to Lori Hyde and commented that she hoped she would be able to design their artwork for them.

"I hope so too," responded Mz Hyde, her American accent soft and warm. "If the numbers add up, we should have a deal. Are you playing anything from the new album tonight that would give me a clue to its theme?"

"Yes," revealed Ellen, rapidly trying to visualise the set list they'd agreed on at sound check. Her mind had dissolved into mush and she struggled to recall any of the song titles. "Three songs that might help are Pyramid, City Of Bones And Heartache then Cyclone near the end of the set."

"I'll listen out for them," promised Mz Hyde with a smile.

Before she could ask the artist anything else, Ellen heard Taylor asking, "How'd you guys feel about jammin' with us on stage tonight?" With a nod to Ellen, he added, "We could jam one of your songs?"

"I'm up for it," agreed Rich, a beer in his hand. "But, we'll need the loan of couple of guitars."

"Not a problem," assured Rocky. "We can sort you both out with something."

Taking a deep breath, Ellen asked Jake, "Will you duet Dragon Song with me?"

"Pick an easy one, why don't you?" he joked, flashing her one of his famous "Power" smiles. "It'd be my pleasure."

For the next hour or so, the band's guests settled themselves in the dressing room with After Life, relaxing over a few beers. Sitting quietly in a corner, Ellen watched Taylor and Cal as they fell into a serious discussion around amplifier preferences and pedal board requirements. Their almost child-like awe at being in the company of the two hugely successful musicians made her smile.

"Like little kids in a candy store," commented Lori Hyde with a giggle.

"They are, aren't they?" laughed Ellen, drawing her cloak around her. "Tailz'll be talking about this for weeks."

The American artist laughed, "Don't tell Jake I told you this but he was like that the first time he met Dan Crow from Weigh Station. Totally star struck."

"I know the feeling," said Ellen, immediately warming to Lori Hyde. "Dan guested with us in Wales in May. I was terrified I'd freeze and forget the words."

"Dan's a sweetheart. He gave me the first big break of my career. Helped me develop as an artist. He's part of the reason we're in London. We're here for the 25th anniversary show."

"Tailz and I have tickets for that. Luke too. Should be a great show."

"Should be."

Shortly before nine, Rocky rounded up After Life and, accompanied by the Silver Lake party, moved them out of the dressing room towards the stage. The support act had just finished their set and squeezed past them in the narrow corridor. As they passed Ellen, someone's hand caught her cloak, pulling it back over her shoulder. Cursing loudly, she swiftly drew the black velvet around her, fully aware that Jake and Rich had seen the withered stump of her right arm covered by its black satin sleeve. Neither of them said anything as they continued their way to the side of the stage.

Conscious of Jake Power watching her every move, Ellen took a few long, slow, breaths to compose herself, then from the shadowy darkness of the wings, began the Latin chanted intro to Swirling Mists. Focussing on the green lights and tendrils of smoke out on stage, she calmly allowed her voice to soar over the crowd before stepping out to join the band as the final pure note rang out.

Once she was into the familiar routine of the set, Ellen forgot about the American guests who were watching. Prowling the stage, she scanned the rail for familiar faces, noting that all the rail queens were present. She had been searching for one familiar face in particular and Ellen was disappointed not to have found it.

She had hoped her mother would've made the effort to attend at least one show.

Pushing her emotions aside, Ellen resolved to deliver the best performance of the tour. To accommodate their invited guests for the encore, After Life had made a few hurried amendments to the set. For the first time on the tour, Pyramid, with its thunderous riff, was moved up to second and was swiftly followed by fan favourite, Rats.

Taking care not to get tangled in the folds of her cloak, Ellen jumped down into the pit while Taylor executed his extended solo. Slowly, she made her way along the rail, pausing as usual with the fans to allow them a few seconds to take selfies. When she reached the rail queens, she stopped and signalled to Cal to come over to take a photo for the girls who had so loyally followed the tour. Keeping an ear out for where Tailz was at, Ellen realised she didn't have time to get back on stage for the final verse. Instead, she opted to stay where she was, centre front on the rail, and to climb up onto the narrow ledge behind the barrier to sing the final verse. As she moved into the chorus for the last time, Ellen finished her journey through the pit, running up the steps and back onto the stage in time to deliver the final line.

"London!" she screamed at the end of the song. "You're looking beautiful tonight!"

A huge wave of rapturous cheers swept over her.

"Are you ready to delve into the After Life with us, beautiful people of London?"

More deafening cheers surged towards the stage.

"I said are you ready to delve into the After Life, London?"

This time the roar from the sell-out crowd was apocalyptic, causing Ellen to laugh before she let rip one of her blood curdling screams.

"London, this is Danse De Mort En Flammes."

Mixing the set up as extensively was working like a charm. All of them were a little road weary but this new variation on the norm had raised the band's adrenaline levels and each of them was delivering just that little bit more.

Mid-set, Ellen stepped forward and sat on top of one of the wedge-shaped monitors, slightly left of centre stage. Behind her in the darkness, she could hear the piano being moved into position.

"Folks, we're going to slow it down a little. Turn the lights down. Add an edge of darkness to proceedings," began Ellen, keeping an evil tone to her voice. "This is Broken Doll."

The fans cheered enthusiastically. Ellen smiled at their obvious delight at the song making the set. She had intended to sing the acapella ballad with a more menacing vibe to it but, at the last moment, changed her mind. Instead, Ellen opted to sing it clearly, allowing her emotions to spill into the song. Around her, the venue lit up with flickering cigarette lighter flames and mobile phone candlelight creating a womb of warmth for her vocals. Her cheeks were wet with tears by the final lines of the very personal song, something that wasn't lost on the fans near the front. The rail queens too had tears in their eyes, feeling Ellen's pain through her raw performance.

Appearing beside her to help her to her feet, Luke called out, "Give it up for the incredible Queen of the After Life. The one and only Ellen Lloyd!"

Allowing him to hug her briefly, Ellen took a bow then followed Luke over to the piano that now sat centre stage in the spotlight.

"London, let me introduce you to the multi-talented Mr Luke Court, who is going to sing the vocal on this next one," introduced Ellen, aware that she could still detect her own emotional state in her voice. "Zielenleed. Translated, it means agony of the soul."

In the shadows, the remaining members of the band had assumed their positions. Silently, Ellen slipped into the darkness, glad of a few moments to regroup before she had to sing the challenging vocal arias. As she stood waiting for her cue, Ellen risked a glance into the wings to check if their guests were still watching. They were all still there, the two members of Silver Lake whispering animatedly to Jethro and Rocky. Only Mz Hyde had her eyes on the stage. She spotted Ellen looking over and smiled, giving her a thumb's up sign. With a sigh of relief, the After Life vocalist took the gesture as a good omen for their album cover's future.

As she started to sing the pulse effect at the end of the second verse, both Jake and Rich turned their attention to her. Focusing on the timing, Ellen slowed it right down then hit her top note as Cal began his solo. She could feel every inch of her straining but Ellen held the note till the guitarist played his corresponding final note. Gradually quickening the pulses, she guided Luke back in to finish with the final verse and chorus.

There was no doubting the fans appreciation for the song as the whistles and cheers rang out around the venue for several minutes after the last note had faded away. In the wings, the Silver Lake party's reaction was equally passionate.

"Oh, how to follow that?" declared Ellen as the cheers died away. "Let's try this. Kashmir!"

After Life rounded off the main body of their set with City Of Bones And Heartache, stepping off stage with the fans' thunderous appreciation booming around the venue.

While Ellen drank thirstily from her customary bottle of juice, Taylor turned to Jake and Rich, "You boys ready?"

As if by magic, Michael had appeared with two guitars for the guest musicians, having already added an additional mic and stand on stage.

"Watch for Ellen giving you the nod to come out," said Tailz with a grin as Ellen prepared to lead the band back out.

Both Jake and Rich nodded as After Life headed towards the stage. The crowd went wild at the sight of Ellen with her hood up and her cloak flowing around her. Tossing the hood back, she let out a long blood curdling wail.

"There's a special blend of magic in this room tonight," she purred into the microphone. "Silvery, watery magic."

She paused, scanning the audience, before continuing, "Time to make it a little more rich and powerful."

The crowd began to cheer loudly. A few fans down at the front had picked up on the cryptic clues and began to chant "Silver Lake, Silver Lake, Silver Lake Lake Lake."

"I'd like to welcome two new friends to the After Life," Ellen continued over the roar of the audience. "Rich Santiago and the heavenly Jake Power from Silver Lake, people!"

As the two members of Silver Lake walked out on stage the crowd screamed themselves into a frenzy. With confidence, After Life began the opening section of Dragon Song, Rich Santiago assuming a position on stage between Taylor and Cal. Centre stage, Jake stood beside Ellen, smiling out across the sea of faces before them. Despite having had no rehearsal, the two members of Silver Lake had comfortably slotted in with After Life. With a nod and a smile of encouragement, Jake indicated that Ellen should sing the first verse. Their voices came together for the chorus then Ellen insisted he sang the second verse and chorus. She was in awe of the guitar solo that Rich executed, so much so that she almost missed her cue to join Jake to sing the final verse and chorus together. Their voices had complimented each other well, with the duet passing all too quickly.

"Ladies and gentlemen, give it up for Rich and Jake!" screamed Taylor as the song ended. "Fucking awesome, guys!"

In the centre of the stage, Ellen stepped into Jake's embrace, asking if he'd stay out for one more song. The tall American shook his head, kissed her on the cheek then followed Rich off stage to the raucous cheers of the small London audience.

"Oh, how to follow that," repeated Ellen with a laugh as she gazed into the wings where their guests stood watching, guitars still in hand. "All good things have to come to an end. You guys have been an incredible crowd. Thank you. We'll leave you with Smoke On The Water."

Looking out over the crowd for the last time, Ellen felt her heart swell with pride. Seeing the rail queens smiling back at her; spying Jen beside the drum riser with her camera; knowing her dad was over in the corner at the merchandise table; hoping her mother was out there somewhere enjoying the show made the whole tour so much more personal and special. She was sad that it was coming to an end but she prayed that they'd done enough to pave the way to greater things.

Amid the usual flash of light and smoke, Ellen disappeared from the stage, leaving the boys to savour the dying seconds of the last show of the tour.

Ellen

Light flurries of snow swirled round Ellen's skirts as Taylor helped her out of the limousine that had driven them across London for After Life's debut album's launch party. The seven weeks since the end of the tour had flown by, their week long break a long-forgotten memory. Promotional activities had filled their diaries, culminating in a lavish launch party at the St Pancras Renaissance Hotel. Insisting that the venue be in keeping with the artwork designed by Mz Hyde and the dark themes of the music, Jason Russell had personally selected the location for its gothic opulence.

"Show time, boys and girl," declared Rocky, dressed in a black frock coat and top hat, as he led them into the magnificent building.

For the occasion, the band had hired gothic Victorian suits while Ellen opted for a Morticia Addams style dress with plunging neckline and long sleeves with draping, lacey cuffs that helped to disguise her arm. She had added a cloak over it but, instead of her trademark Eye of Horus eyepatch, she wore her round, purple tinted, steampunk glasses.

Several fans were gathered outside the hotel and, judging by how cold they appeared to be, had been there for some time. The band paused to pose for photographs and to sign autographs before Rocky ushered them inside.

The opulent function suite had been decorated in keeping with the album artwork and, thanks to the acquisition of some realistic panels, had been transformed into a gothic ossuary, not dissimilar to the Catacombs of Paris. Heavy red velvet curtains had been hung on the windows but the glass itself was covered with panels of fake skulls, humerus and femoral bones.

A low stage had been set up at the end of the room, backed by the room's feature brick, arched windows. Tall, free-standing candelabra stood at the edge of the stage. In the background, the band's album was playing.

When After Life arrived, their invited guests were already mingling with each other, enjoying champagne and canapes. The room was set out with ten round tables and some guests were already seated and deep in conversation. At the table in front of the stage, Lizzy sat chatting to Ellen's parents plus Nana and Jen. In the corner, a table had been reserved for the rail queens and their partners as thank you for their loyalty throughout the tour. The remaining guests were made up of some friends of the band, journalists, music promoters and various record label dignitaries. It was unfortunate that Mz Hyde, as the artist responsible for the cover and theme, was unable to attend but she had sent the band a personal message of congratulations along with a huge bouquet of flowers for Ellen.

Having made their way across the room. After Life greeted their families then took a seat at the table reserved for them just as Jason Russell took to the stage.

"Good afternoon, ladies and gentlemen," began Jason formally. "Welcome to the launch of After Life's long-awaited debut album City Of Bones And Heartache."

He paused to allow the polite applause to die down.

"It's been about eight months since I was invited into the After Life realm and this young band never cease to impress me. There have been challenges along the way for them but they've kept the end goal in sight, worked exceedingly hard and should be incredibly proud of the record we are here to launch today."

A movement to one side caught Ellen's attention and she turned to see who or what it was. Smiling, she noted that Garrett Court had just arrived but was waiting discretely at the back of the room. He spotted her watching him and smiled.

Moving her foot to her right to nudge Luke under the table, she whispered, "Garrett's here. Up at the back."

"Here?" echoed Luke quietly, looking shocked by the news.

Ellen nodded and he immediately turned round, scanning the crowded room for his uncle.

"I didn't think he'd make it," whispered Luke. "Glad he's here. It's his album too."

"Me too," agreed Ellen.

Reaching the end of his speech, Jason brought their focus back to the stage by declaring, "So, without further ado, I'd like to invite After Life up here to perform for you."

Smiling, amid a sea of camera flashes from around the room, the five members of the band climbed the stairs up to the small stage.

"Thank you," said Ellen warmly, aware of the others getting settled into position behind her. "It's been a long journey to get here as Jason said but now we'd like to welcome you to The City Of Bones And Heartache!"

Unable to resist the temptation, Ellen let out a blood curdling scream before commencing the vocals for the title track, the first of the three songs due to be performed for their guests. With a smile, she thought that perhaps they should have included earplugs in the gift bag that each guest had received on their arrival as she noticed several of the record label staff cover their ears as the volume levels rose.

The second song that they'd chosen to play was Rats. In the absence of a pit and a rail to prowl along during Tailz's guitar solo, Ellen wound her way through the tables, spending just a few extra seconds with the rail queens and pausing beside Garrett long enough to indicate that he should come down to the front to take the spare seat at their table. Ever the professional, Ellen made it back onto the stage in time to sing the final verse and chorus.

"Thank you," she said, breathing heavily. "We're going to leave you with something a little quieter. Picking just three tracks from the album to play for you today was difficult but choosing this one was the easy bit. This is the first song Taylor and I wrote together and it's been a firm favourite from day one. We'll leave you with Lou Lou At 3am."

Judging by the smiles around the room, the acoustic ballad was popular with their guests too. Instead of their usual transport case, a small gilt chaise longue had been brought on stage for her and Taylor. As they performed for the intimate audience, it seemed like a hundred years since they'd sat together in the bedroom of Rocky and Lizzy's house writing the music in the wee small hours. The moment wasn't lost on either of them as they both recognised that they were now on the cusp of achieving their dreams and ambitions.

With the applause still reverberating round the room, the band took a bow and left the stage.

A couple of hours later, as their guests were beginning to leave, Rocky called the band together. Having made sure that they each had a full glass, he proposed a toast, "Here's to each and every one of you. Thanks for all those long hours of rehearsal and recording, the endless hours of travelling and to the countless drumheads Jack has split along the way but it's all paid off. Not only do you have an incredible album on sale but you are also going to embark on your first US tour in January!"

"America?" gasped Luke, not daring to believe what he was hearing. "Seriously?"

"Seriously," confirmed Rocky grinning. "You hit the road on the west coast of America in January supporting Silver Lake."

"From The City Of Bones And Heartache to the City of Angels. I'll drink a toast to that," declared Ellen, raising her glass. "To us and the adventures yet to come!"

Coral McCallum
14 June 2018

Ellen

Book 4
(as yet untitled)
in the
Silver Lake series is
coming 2019

Running his hand through his long blonde hair, Jake sighed. It felt good to taste salt in the air. It felt good to feel sand under his feet. It felt good to be home. His fingers tangled in the strands of his hair, knotted after a sleepless night on the band's delayed flight out of LAX. Looking down, he realised that his hair was almost to his waist. Another indication that he'd been away from home too long. Mentally, he made a note to take a trip into town later to get his mane trimmed.

With his arms wrapped around his knees, Jake sat watching the sun make it way over the horizon, basking in its golden light. He was bone tired and couldn't remember when he had last slept for more than a couple of hours at a time. The band's flight had been scheduled to reach Philadelphia at ten o'clock the night before but a four-hour delay meant they hadn't landed until almost two o'clock in the morning. There had been the usual carnage in the baggage hall but, by some miracle, all of their suitcases and guitar cases had made it safely across the country. Tired and grumpy, the sleep deprived musicians had piled into the waiting SUVs for the long drive down the Coastal Highway. After so long in each other's company, each of them was keen to get back to JJL to collect their cars and trucks and say their "good nights". With little more than a grunt of farewell, Jake had loaded his gear into the back of his truck. Praying that it would start at the first time of asking, he had hauled himself into the cab for the final leg of the journey home.

He'd pulled into the driveway at the beach house just after five, reached to retrieve his house keys from his battered leather book bag and found them missing. Leaving his gear in the truck, he'd crept round to the back of the house to try the back door, hoping that Lori had left it unlocked. No luck. Both the screen door and the back door were locked. Knowing it was too early to waken his sleeping family, he'd headed across the sun deck to try the patio doors. They too were locked.

Muttering to himself, he'd hauled off his ripped Converse hi-tops and socks, leaving them scattered on the deck and wandered down to the beach to watch the sun rise.

As the sky lit up before him, Jake reflected on the last few months. When he'd left Rehoboth in January, the beach had been covered in eight inches of snow. Now, in the third week in June, it looked as though it was going to be a beautiful summer's day. This was the longest period of time that he'd spent away from home and, for the past ten weeks of the tour, his heart had been yearning for home.

To be continued………

ABOUT THE AUTHOR

Coral McCallum lives in Gourock, a small town on the West coast of Scotland with her husband, two student children and her beloved cats.

https://coralmccallum.wordpress.com

https://www.facebook.com/pages/Coral-McCallum

https://twitter.com/CoralMcCallum

Printed in Great Britain
by Amazon